# HOLD ME

## TWIST ME: BOOK 3

## ANNA ZAIRES

♠ MOZAIKA PUBLICATIONS ♠

Copyright © 2015 Anna Zaires and Dima Zales
http://annazaires.com/

Published by Mozaika Publications, an imprint of Mozaika LLC.
www.mozaikallc.com

Cover by Najla Qamber Designs
www.najlaqamberdesigns.com

e-ISBN: 978-1-63142-046-7
Print ISBN: 978-1-63142-066-5

# I

# THE RETURN

## JULIAN

*A* gasping cry wakes me up, dragging me out of restless sleep. My uninjured eye flies open on a rush of adrenaline, and I jackknife to a sitting position, the sudden movement causing my cracked ribs to scream in protest. The cast on my left arm bangs into the heart-rate monitor next to the bed, and the wave of agony is so intense that the room spins around me in a sickening swirl. My pulse is pounding, and it takes a moment to realize what woke me.

Nora.

She must be in the grip of another nightmare.

My body, coiled for combat, relaxes slightly. There's no danger, nobody coming after us right now. I'm lying next to Nora in my luxurious hospital bed, and we're both safe, the clinic in Switzerland as secure as Lucas can make it.

The pain in my ribs and arm is better now, more

tolerable. Moving more carefully, I place my right hand on Nora's shoulder and try to gently shake her awake. She's turned away from me, facing in the opposite direction, so I can't see her face to check if she's crying. Her skin, however, is cold and damp from sweat. She must've been having the nightmare for a while. She's also shivering.

"Wake up, baby," I murmur, stroking her slender arm. I can see the light filtering through the blinds on the window, and I know it must be morning. "It's just a dream. Wake up, my pet…"

She stiffens under my touch, and I know she's not fully awake, the nightmare still holding her captive. Her breathing is coming in audible, gasping bursts, and I can feel the tremors running through her body. Her distress claws at me, hurting me worse than any injury, and the knowledge that I'm again responsible for this—that I failed to keep her safe—makes my insides burn with acidic fury.

Fury at myself and at Peter Sokolov—the man who allowed Nora to risk her life to rescue me.

Before my cursed trip to Tajikistan, she had been slowly getting over Beth's death, her nightmares becoming less frequent as the months wore on. Now, however, the bad dreams are back—and Nora is worse off than before, judging by the panic attack she had during sex yesterday.

I want to kill Peter for this—and I might, if he ever crosses my path again. The Russian saved my life, but he endangered Nora's in the process, and that's not something I will ever forgive. And his fucking list of names? Forget it. There is no way I'm going to reward him for betraying me like this, no matter what Nora promised him.

"Come on, baby, wake up," I urge her again, using my right arm to lower myself back down on the bed. My ribs ache at the movement, but less fiercely this time. I carefully shift closer to Nora, pressing my body against hers from the back. "You're okay. It's all over, I promise."

She draws in a deep, hiccuping breath, and I feel the tension within her easing as she realizes where she is. "Julian?" she whispers, turning around to face me, and I see that she's been crying after all, her cheeks coated with moisture from her tears.

"Yes. You're safe now. Everything is fine." I reach over with my right hand and trail my fingers over her jaw, marveling at the fragile beauty of her facial structure. My hand looks huge and rough against her delicate face, my nails ragged and bruised from the needles Majid used on me. The contrast between us is glaring—though Nora is not entirely unscathed either. The purity of her golden skin is marred by a bruise on the left side of her face, where those Al-Quadar motherfuckers hit her to knock her out.

If they weren't already dead, I would've ripped them apart with my bare hands for hurting her.

"What did you dream about?" I ask softly. "Was it Beth?"

5

"No." She shakes her head, and I see that her breathing is beginning to return to normal. Her voice, however, still holds echoes of horror as she says hoarsely, "It was you this time. Majid was cutting out your eyes, and I couldn't stop him."

I try not to react, but it's impossible. Her words hurl me back to that cold, windowless room, to the nauseating sensations I've been trying to forget for the past several days. My head begins to throb with remembered agony, my half-healed eye socket burning with emptiness once again. I feel blood and other fluids dripping down my face, and my stomach heaves at the recollection. I'm no stranger to pain, or even to torture —my father believed that his son should be able to withstand anything—but losing my eye had been by far the most excruciating experience of my life.

Physically, at least.

Emotionally, Nora's appearance in that room probably holds that honor.

It takes all of my willpower to wrench my thoughts back to the present, away from the mind-numbing terror of seeing her dragged in by Majid's men.

"You did stop him, Nora." It kills me to admit this, but if it weren't for her bravery, I would probably be decomposing in some dumpster in Tajikistan. "You came for me, and you saved me."

I still have trouble believing that she did that—that she voluntarily placed herself in the hands of psychotic terrorists to save my life. She didn't do it out of some naïve conviction that they wouldn't harm her. No, my pet knew exactly what they were capable of, and she still had the courage to act.

I owe my life to the girl I abducted, and I don't quite know how to deal with that.

"Why did you do it?" I ask, stroking the edge of her lower lip with my thumb. Deep down, I know, but I want to hear her admit it.

She gazes at me, her eyes filled with shadows from her dream. "Because I can't survive without you," she says quietly. "You know that, Julian. You wanted me to love you, and I do. I love you so much I would walk through hell for you."

I take in her words with greedy, shameless pleasure. I can't get enough of her love. I can't get enough of her. I wanted her initially because of her resemblance to Maria, but my childhood friend had never evoked even a fraction of the emotions Nora makes me feel. My affection for Maria had been innocent and pure, just like Maria herself.

My obsession with Nora is anything but.

"Listen to me, my pet…" My hand leaves her face to rest on her shoulder. "I need you to promise me that you will never do something like that again. I'm obviously glad to be alive, but I would sooner have died than had you in that kind of danger. You are *never* to risk your life for me again. Do you understand me?"

The nod she gives me is faint, almost imperceptible, and I see a mutinous gleam in her eyes. She doesn't want to make me mad, so she's not disagreeing, but I have a strong suspicion she's going to do what she thinks is right regardless of what she says right now.

This obviously calls for more heavy-handed measures.

"Good," I say silkily. "Because next time—if there is ever a next time—I will kill anyone who helps you against my orders, and I will do it slowly and painfully. Do you understand me, Nora? If anyone so much as endangers a hair on your head, whether it's to save *me* or for any other reason, that person will die a very unpleasant death. Do I make myself clear?"

"Yes." She looks pale now, her lips pressed together as if to contain a protest. She's angry with me, but she's also scared. Not for herself—she's beyond that fear now—but for others. My pet knows I mean what I say.

She knows I'm a conscienceless killer with only one weakness.

Her.

Gripping her shoulder tighter, I lean forward and kiss her closed mouth. Her lips are stiff for a moment, resisting me, but as I slide my hand under her neck and cup her nape, she exhales and her lips soften, letting me in. The surge of heat in my body is strong and immediate, her taste causing my cock to harden uncontrollably.

"Um, excuse me, Mr. Esguerra..." The sound of a woman's voice is accompanied by a timid knock on the door, and I realize it's the nurses making their morning rounds.

*Fuck.* I'm tempted to ignore them, but I have a feeling they'll just come back again in a bit—possibly when I'm balls-deep inside Nora's tight pussy.

Reluctantly releasing Nora, I roll over onto my back, sucking in my breath at the jolt of pain, and watch as Nora jumps off the bed and hurriedly pulls on a robe.

"Do you want me to open the door for them?" she asks, and I nod, resigned. The nurses have to change my bandages and make sure I'm well enough to travel today, and I have every intention of cooperating with their plans.

The sooner they're done, the faster I can get out of this fucking hospital.

As soon as Nora opens the door, two female nurses come in, accompanied by David Goldberg—a short, balding man who's my personal doctor at the estate. He's an excellent trauma surgeon, so I had him oversee the repairs on my face, to make sure the plastic surgeons at the clinic didn't fuck anything up.

I don't want to repel Nora with my scars if I can help it.

"The plane is already waiting," Goldberg says as the nurses begin to unwrap the bandages on my head. "If there are no signs of infection, we should be able to head home."

"Excellent." I lie still, ignoring the pain resulting from the nurses' ministrations. In the meantime, Nora grabs some clothes from the closet and disappears into the bathroom that adjoins our room. I hear the water running and realize she must've decided to use this time to take a shower. It's probably her way of avoiding me for a bit, since she's still upset over my threat. My pet is sensitive to violence being doled out to those she views as innocent—like that stupid boy Jake she kissed the night I took her.

I still want to rip out his insides for touching her... and someday I probably will.

"No sign of infection," Goldberg tells me when the nurses are done removing the bandages. "You're healing well."

"Good." I take slow, deep breaths to control the pain as the two nurses clean the sutures and rebind my ribs. I've been taking half of my prescribed dose of painkillers for the past two days, and I'm definitely feeling it. In another couple of days, I'll go off the painkillers completely to avoid becoming dependent on them.

One addiction is plenty for anyone.

As the nurses are wrapping up, Nora comes out of the bathroom, freshly showered and dressed in a pair of jeans and a short-sleeved blouse. "All clear?" she asks, glancing at Goldberg.

"He's good to go," he replies, giving her a warm smile. I think he likes her—which is fine with me, given his homosexual orientation. "How are you feeling?"

"I'm fine, thanks." She lifts her arm to show a large

Band-Aid over the area where the terrorists cut out her birth control implant by mistake. "I'll be happy when the stitches are out, but it doesn't bother me much."

"Great, glad to hear it." Turning toward me, Goldberg asks, "When should we plan to head out?"

"Have Lucas get the car ready in twenty minutes," I tell him, carefully swinging my feet to the floor as the nurses exit the room. "I'll get dressed, and we'll go."

"Will do," Goldberg says, turning to leave the room.

"Wait, Dr. Goldberg, I'll walk out with you," Nora says quickly, and there's something in her voice that catches my attention. "I need something from downstairs," she explains.

Goldberg looks surprised. "Oh, sure."

"What is it, my pet?" I stand up, ignoring my nakedness. Goldberg politely averts his eyes as I catch Nora's arm, preventing her from walking out. "What do you need?"

She looks uncomfortable, her gaze shifting to the side.

"What is it, Nora?" I demand, my curiosity piqued. My grip on her arm tightens as I pull her closer.

She looks up at me. Her cheeks are tinged with color, and there is a defiant set to her jaw. "I need the morning-after pill, okay? I want to make sure I get it before we leave."

"Oh." My mind goes blank for a second. Somehow I hadn't thought about the fact that with her implant gone, Nora can get pregnant. I've had her in my bed for

11

almost two years, and during that entire time, she's been protected by the implant. I'm so used to that, it hadn't even occurred to me that we need to take precautions now.

But it had clearly occurred to Nora.

"You want the morning-after pill?" I repeat slowly, still trying to process the idea that Nora—my Nora—could be pregnant.

Pregnant with my child.

A child that she clearly doesn't want.

"Yes." Her dark eyes are huge in her face as she stares up at me. "It's unlikely from just one time, of course, but I don't want to risk it."

She doesn't want to risk being pregnant with my child. My chest feels oddly tight as I look at her, seeing the fear she's trying so hard to conceal. She's worried about my reaction to this, afraid I'll prevent her from taking this pill.

Afraid I'll force an unwanted child on her.

"I'll be right outside," Goldberg says, apparently sensing the rising tension in the room, and before I can say a word, he slips out the door, leaving us alone.

Nora lifts her chin, meeting my gaze head on. I can see the determination on her face as she says, "Julian, I know we never talked about this, but—"

"But you're not ready," I interrupt, the tightness in my chest intensifying. "You don't want a baby right now."

She nods, her eyes wide. "Right," she says warily. "I'm

not even done with school yet, and you've been injured—"

"And you're not sure if you want to have a child with a man like me."

She swallows nervously, but doesn't deny it or look away. Her silence is damning, and the tightness in my chest morphs into a strange aching pain.

Releasing her arm, I step back. "You can tell Goldberg to get you the pill and whatever birth control he thinks is best." My voice sounds unusually cold and distant. "I'll wash up and get dressed."

And before she can say anything else, I go into the bathroom and close the door.

I don't want to see the look of relief on her face.

I don't want to think about how that would feel.

## 2

### NORA

*S*tunned, I watch Julian's naked form disappear into the bathroom. He's hampered by his injuries, his movements stiffer than usual. Still, there is a certain grace to the way he walks. Even after his hellish ordeal, his muscular body is strong and athletic, the white bandage around his ribs emphasizing the width of his shoulders and the bronzed hue of his skin.

*He didn't object to the morning-after pill.*

As that fact sinks in, my knees go weak with relief, the adrenaline-induced tension draining out in a sudden whoosh. I had been almost certain he would deny me this; the expression on his face as we spoke had been shuttered, unreadable... dangerous in its opaqueness. He had seen right through my flimsy excuses about my school and his injuries, his undamaged eye gleaming with a cold blue light that made my stomach knot in dread.

But he didn't deny me the pill. On the contrary, he suggested I get a new method of birth control from Dr. Goldberg.

I feel almost light-headed with joy. Julian must be on board with the no-kids bit, his strange reaction notwithstanding.

Not wanting to question my good fortune, I hurry out of the room to grab Dr. Goldberg. I want to make sure I get what I need before we leave the clinic.

Birth control implants aren't easy to come by in our jungle compound.

"I took the pill," I tell Julian when we're comfortably ensconced on his private jet—the same plane that took us from Chicago to Colombia after Julian returned for me in December. "And I got this." I raise my right arm to show him a tiny bandage where the new implant went in. My arm aches dully, but I'm so happy to have the implant that I don't mind the discomfort.

Julian looks up from his laptop, his expression still closed off. "Good," he says curtly, and resumes working on the email to one of his engineers. He's outlining the exact specifications of a new drone he wants designed. I know this because I asked him about it a few minutes ago, and he explained what he's doing. He's been much more open with me in the past couple of months—

which is why I find it odd that he seems to want to avoid the topic of birth control.

I wonder if he doesn't want to discuss it because of Dr. Goldberg's presence. The short man is sitting at the front of the jet, more than a dozen feet from us, but we don't have total privacy. Either way, I decide to let it go for now and bring it up again at a more opportune moment.

As the plane ascends, I entertain myself by watching the Swiss Alps until we get above the clouds. Then I lean back and wait for the beautiful flight attendant—Isabella —to come around with our breakfast. We left the hospital so quickly this morning that I only managed to grab a cup of coffee.

Isabella comes into the cabin a few minutes later, her bombshell body squeezed into a tight red dress. She's holding a tray with coffee and a platter of pastries. Goldberg appears to have fallen asleep, so she heads toward us, her lips curved in a seductive smile.

The first time I saw her, when Julian came back for me in December, I was insanely jealous. Since then I've learned that Isabella has never had a relationship with Julian and is actually married to one of the guards at the estate—two facts that have gone a long way toward soothing the green-eyed monster within me. I've only seen the woman once or twice in the past couple of months; unlike most of Julian's employees, she spends the majority of her time outside the compound, working as his eyes and ears at several high-end private jet companies.

"You'd be surprised how loose-lipped people get after a couple of drinks at thirty thousand feet," Julian explained once. "Executives, politicians, cartel bosses... They all like having Isabella around, and they don't always watch what they say in her presence. Thanks to her, I've gotten everything from insider trading tips to intel about drug deals in the area."

So yeah, I'm no longer quite as jealous of Isabella, but I still can't help feeling that her manner with Julian is a little too flirtatious for a married woman. Then again, I'm probably not the best judge of appropriate married-woman behavior. If I were to stare at any man longer than a second, I would be signing his death warrant.

Julian takes possessiveness to a whole new level.

"Would you like some coffee?" Isabella asks, stopping next to his seat. She's more circumspect in her staring today, but I still feel the urge to slap her pretty face for the come-hither smile she gives my husband.

Okay, so Julian is not the only one with possessiveness issues. As messed up as it is, I feel proprietary about the man who abducted me. It makes no sense, but I gave up trying to make sense of my crazy relationship with Julian a long time ago.

It's easier to just accept it.

At Isabella's question, Julian looks up from his laptop. "Sure," he says before glancing in my direction. "Nora?"

"Yes, please," I say politely. "And a couple of those croissants."

Isabella pours us each a cup, sets the pastry platter on my table, and sashays back to the front of the plane, her lushly curved hips swaying from side to side. I experience a moment of envy before reminding myself that Julian wants *me*.

He wants me too much, in fact, but that's a whole other issue.

For the next half hour, I read quietly as I eat my croissants and sip my coffee. Julian appears to be concentrating on his drone design email, so I don't bother him; instead, I do my best to focus on my book, a sci-fi thriller I bought at the clinic. My attention, however, keeps wandering, my thoughts straying every couple of pages.

It feels odd to be sitting here reading. Surreal, in a way. It's as if nothing had happened. As if we hadn't just survived terror and torture.

As if I hadn't blown a man's brains out in cold blood.

As if I hadn't almost lost Julian again.

My heart starts beating faster, the images from this morning's nightmare invading my mind with startling clarity. *Blood... Julian's body cut and mangled... His beautiful face with vacant eye sockets...* The book slips out of my shaking hands, falling to the floor as I attempt to suck in air through a suddenly constricted throat.

"Nora?" Strong, warm fingers close around my wrist, and through the panicked haze veiling my vision, I see

Julian's bandaged face in front of me. He's gripping me tightly, his laptop forgotten on the table next to him. "Nora, can you hear me?"

I manage to nod, my tongue coming out to wet my lips. My mouth is dry with fear, and my blouse is sticking to my back from perspiration. My hands are clutching the edge of the seat, my nails digging into the soft leather. A part of me knows that my mind is playing tricks on me—that this extreme anxiety is unfounded— but my body is reacting as if the threat is real.

As if we're back at that construction site in Tajikistan, at the mercy of Majid and the other terrorists.

"Breathe, baby." Julian's voice is soothing as his hand comes up to gently cradle my jaw. "Breathe slowly, deeply... There's a good girl..."

I do as he says, keeping my eyes on his face as I take deep breaths to manage my panic. After a minute, my heartbeat slows, and my hands uncurl from the edge of my seat. I'm still shaking, but the suffocating fear is gone.

Feeling embarrassed, I wrap my fingers around Julian's palm and pull his hand away from my face. "I'm okay," I manage to say in a relatively steady voice. "I'm sorry. I don't know what came over me."

He stares at me, his eye glittering, and I see a mixture of rage and frustration in his gaze. His fingers are still gripping mine, as if reluctant to let go. "You're not okay, Nora," he says harshly. "You're anything but okay."

He's right. I don't want to admit it, but he's right. I haven't been okay since Julian left the estate to hunt down the terrorists. I've been a mess since his departure —and I seem to be even more of a mess now that he's back.

"I'm fine," I say, not wanting him to think me weak. Julian was tortured, and he seems to be handling it, whereas I'm falling apart for no good reason.

"Fine?" His eyebrows snap together. "In the past twenty-four hours, you've had two panic attacks and a nightmare. That's not fine, Nora."

I swallow and look down at my lap, where his hand is holding mine in a tight, possessive grip. I hate the fact that I can't just brush this stuff off, the way Julian seems to. Sure, he still has some nightmares about Maria, but this ordeal with the terrorists appears to have hardly fazed him. By all rights, he should be the one freaking out, not me. I was barely touched, whereas he'd undergone days of torment.

I'm weak, and I hate it.

"Nora, baby, listen to me."

I look up, drawn by the softer note in Julian's voice, and find myself captured by his gaze.

"This is not your fault," he says quietly. "Any of it. You've been through a lot, and you're traumatized. You don't need to pretend with me. If you start to panic, tell me, and I'll help you through it. Do you understand me?"

"Yes," I whisper, strangely relieved by his words. I

know it's ironic that the man who brought all the darkness into my life is helping me cope with it, but it's been that way from the beginning.

I've always found solace in my captor's arms.

"Good. Remember that." He leans over to kiss me, and I meet him halfway, cognizant of his injured ribs. His lips are unusually tender as they touch mine, and I close my eyes, my remaining anxiety fading as heated need warms my core. My hands find themselves on the back of his neck, and a moan vibrates low in my throat as his tongue invades my mouth, his taste familiar and darkly seductive at the same time.

He groans as I kiss him back, my tongue curling around his. His right arm wraps around my back, bringing me closer to him, and I feel the growing tension in his powerful body. His breathing speeds up, and his kiss turns hard, devouring, making my body throb in response.

"Bedroom. Now." His words are more of a growl as he tears his mouth away and rises to his feet, dragging me up off my seat. Before I can say anything, he wraps his fingers around my wrist and marches me toward the back of the plane. I give mental thanks that Dr. Goldberg is sound asleep and Isabella went back to the front of the plane; nobody's there to see Julian dragging me off to bed.

As we enter the small room, he kicks the door shut behind us and pulls me toward the bed. Even injured, he's incredibly strong. His strength both arouses and intimidates me. Not because I'm afraid he'll hurt me—I know he will, and I know I'll enjoy it—but because I've seen what he can do.

I've seen him kill a man with nothing more than a leg of a chair.

The memory should disgust me, but somehow it's exciting as well as scary. Then again, Julian is not the only one who's taken a life this week.

We're both killers now.

"Strip," he commands, stopping a couple of feet from the bed and releasing my wrist. The sleeves of his button-down shirt are ripped out to accommodate the cast on his left arm, and with the bandage across his face, he looks wounded and dangerous at the same time —like a modern-day pirate after a raid. His right arm is bulging with muscle, and his uncovered eye is startlingly blue in his tanned face.

I love him so much it hurts.

Taking a step back, I begin to undress. My blouse is first, followed by my jeans. When I'm wearing only a white thong and a matching bra, Julian says hoarsely, "Climb on the bed. I want you on all fours, with your ass toward me."

Heat slithers down my spine, intensifying the growing ache between my legs. Turning, I do as he says, my heart pounding with nervous anticipation. I remember the last time we had sex on this plane—and the bruises that decorated my thighs for days afterwards. I know Julian is not well enough for anything that strenuous, but that knowledge doesn't diminish my trepidation or my hunger.

With my husband, fear and desire go hand in hand.

When I'm positioned to Julian's satisfaction, with my ass at the height of his groin, he steps closer to me and hooks his fingers in the waistband of my underwear, pulling it down to my knees. I quiver at his touch, my sex clenching, and he groans, his hand trailing up my thigh to delve between my folds. "Your pussy is so fucking wet," he whispers roughly as he pushes two large fingers into me. "So wet for me, and so tight... You want this, don't you, baby? You want me to take you, to fuck you..."

I gasp as he curls those fingers, hitting a spot that makes my whole body go taut. "Yes..." I can barely speak as waves of heat wash over me, clouding my mind. "Yes, please..."

He chuckles, the sound low and filled with dark delight. His fingers withdraw, leaving me empty and pulsing with need. Before I can object, I hear the sound of a zipper being pulled down and feel the smooth, broad head of his cock brushing against my thighs.

"Oh, I will," he murmurs thickly, guiding himself toward my opening. "I will please you so fucking well"— the tip of his cock penetrates me, making my breath catch in my throat—"you'll scream for me. Won't you, baby?"

And not waiting for my response, he grips my right hip and pushes in all the way, startling a gasping cry out of my throat. As always, his entry batters my senses, his thickness stretching me nearly to the point of pain. If I hadn't been so turned on, he would've hurt me. As it is, his roughness only adds a delicious edge, intensifying my arousal and inundating my sex with more moisture. With my underwear down around my knees, I can't open my legs any wider, and he feels enormous inside me, every inch of him hard and burning hot.

I expect him to set a brutal pace to match that first thrust, but now that he's in, he moves slowly. Slowly and deliberately, his every movement calculated to maximize my pleasure. *In and out, in and out...* It feels like he's stroking me from the inside, teasing out every bit of sensation my body is capable of producing. *In and out, in and out...* I'm close to orgasm, but I can't get there, not with him moving at this snail's pace. *In and out...*

"Julian," I groan, and he slows his pace even more, causing me to whimper in frustration.

"Tell me what you want, baby," he murmurs, withdrawing almost all the way. "Tell me exactly what you want."

"Fuck me," I breathe out, my hands fisting in the sheets. "Please, just make me come."

He chuckles again, but the sound is strained, his breathing turning heavy and uneven. I feel his cock thickening further inside me, and I squeeze my inner muscles around it, willing him to move just a little faster, to give me that extra bit I need...

And he finally does.

Holding my hip, he picks up the pace, fucking me harder and faster. His thrusts reverberate through me, sending shockwaves of pleasure radiating out from my core. My hands clutch at the sheets, my cries growing in volume as the tension inside me becomes unbearable, intolerable... and then I splinter into a million pieces, my body pulsing helplessly around his massive shaft. He groans, his fingers digging into my flesh as his grip on my hip tightens, and I feel him grinding against my ass, his cock jerking inside me as he finds his release.

When it's all over, he withdraws from me and takes a step back. Shaking from the intensity of my orgasm, I collapse onto my side and turn my head to look at him.

He's standing there with his jeans unzipped, his chest rising and falling with heavy breaths. His gaze is filled with lingering desire as he stares at me, his eye glued to my thighs, where his seed is slowly leaking out of my opening.

I flush and glance around the room, searching for a tissue. Thankfully, there is a box on a shelf near the bed. I reach for it and use a tissue to wipe away the evidence of our joining.

Julian observes my actions silently. Then he steps back, his expression growing shuttered again as he tucks his softening cock back inside his jeans and pulls up the zipper.

Grabbing the blanket, I draw it up to cover my naked body. I feel cold and exposed all of a sudden, the heat inside me dissipating. Normally, Julian would hold me after sex, reinforcing our closeness and using tenderness to balance out the roughness. Today, however, he doesn't seem inclined to do that.

"Is everything okay?" I ask hesitantly. "Did I do something wrong?"

He gives me a cool smile and sits down on the bed next to me. "What could you have done wrong, my pet?" Looking at me, he lifts his hand and picks up a lock of my hair, rubbing it between his fingers. Despite the playfulness of his gesture, there is a hard gleam in his eye that deepens my unease.

I experience a sudden flash of intuition. "It's the morning-after pill, isn't it? Are you upset because I took it?"

"Upset? Because you don't want a child with me?" He laughs, but there is a harshness to the sound that twists my stomach into knots. "No, my pet, I'm not upset. I would make an awful father, and I know it."

I stare at him, trying to understand why his words are making me feel guilty. He's a killer and a sadist, a man who ruthlessly abducted me and kept me captive, and yet I feel bad—as if I inadvertently hurt him.

As if I truly did something wrong.

"Julian…" I don't know what to say. I can't lie that he would make a good father. He would see right through me. So instead I ask cautiously, "Do you *want* to have children?"

Then I hold my breath, waiting for his answer.

He looks at me, his expression unreadable once

more. "No, Nora," he says quietly. "The last thing you and I need are children. You can have all the birth control implants you want. I won't force you to get pregnant."

I exhale in sharp relief. "Okay, good. So then why—"

Before I can conclude the question, Julian rises to his feet, signaling an end to our discussion. "I'll be in the main cabin," he says evenly. "I have some work to do. Come join me when you get dressed."

And with that, he disappears from the room, leaving me lying in bed naked and confused.

## JULIAN

*I*'m in the middle of reviewing my portfolio manager's write-up on a potential investment when Nora quietly takes her seat next to me. Unable to resist the lure of her presence, I turn to look at her, watching as she begins reading her book.

Now that I've had a few minutes apart from her, the irrational need to lash out and hurt her is gone. In its place is an inexplicable sadness... an odd and unexpected sense of loss.

I don't understand this. I didn't lie to Nora when I said I don't want children. I've never given the subject much thought, but now that I'm considering it, I can't even imagine being a father. What would I do with a child? It would be just one more weakness for my enemies to exploit. I have no interest in babies, nor do I know how to raise them. My parents certainly weren't role models in that regard. I should've been glad that

Nora doesn't want kids, but instead, when she brought up the morning-after pill, it felt like a kick to the gut.

Like a rejection of the worst kind.

I had been trying not to think about it, but seeing her wipe my seed off her thighs brought back those unwelcome emotions, reminded me that she doesn't want this from me.

That she'll never want this from me.

I don't understand why that matters. I never planned to start a family with Nora. Marriage had been a way to cement our bond, nothing more. She's my pet... my obsession and my possession. She loves me because I've made her love me, and I want her because she's necessary to my existence. Children are not a part of this dynamic.

They can't be.

Catching me looking at her, Nora gives me a tentative smile. "What are you working on?" she asks, placing her book face down on her lap. "Still the drone design?"

"No, baby." I force myself to focus on the fact that she came for me in Tajikistan—that she loves me enough to do something so insane—and my mood begins to lift, the lingering tightness in my chest fading.

"What is it then?" she persists, and I smile involuntarily, amused by her inquisitiveness. Nora is no longer content to be on the fringes of my life; she wants to know everything, and she's growing bolder in her quest for answers.

If this were anyone else, I'd be annoyed. With Nora, however, I don't mind. I enjoy her curiosity. "I'm going over a prospective investment," I explain.

She looks intrigued, so I tell her that I'm reading about a biotech startup that specializes in brain chemistry drugs. If I decide to proceed, I would be a so-called angel investor—one of the first to fund the company. Venture capital is something that's always interested me; I like to stay on top of innovation in all kinds of fields and profit from it to the best of my ability.

She listens to my explanation with evident fascination, those dark eyes of hers focused on my face the entire time. I like it, the way she absorbs knowledge like a sponge. It makes it fun for me to teach her, to show her different parts of my world. The few questions she asks are insightful, showing me that she understands exactly what I'm talking about.

"If that drug can erase memories, couldn't it be used to treat PTSD and such?" she asks after I describe to her one of the startup's more promising products, and I agree, having arrived at the same conclusion just minutes earlier.

I hadn't anticipated this when I kidnapped her—the sheer enjoyment I would get out of spending time with her. When I first took her, I saw her solely as a sexual object, a beautiful girl who obsessed me so much I couldn't get her out of my thoughts. I didn't expect her to become my companion as well as my bedmate, didn't realize I would enjoy simply *being* with her.

I didn't know she would come to own me as much as I own her.

It really is for the best that she remembered to take the pill. Once we're both healed, our life can go back to normal.

*Our* normal, at least.

I will have Nora with me, and I won't let her out of my sight ever again.

It's dark when we land. I lead a sleepy Nora off the plane, and we get in the car to drive home.

*Home.* It's strange thinking of this place as home again. It was my home when I was a child, and I hated it. I hated everything about it, from the humid heat to the pungent smell of moist jungle vegetation. Yet when I got older, I found myself drawn to places just like this—to tropical locations that reminded me of the jungle where I grew up.

It took Nora's presence here to make me realize I didn't hate the estate after all. This place was never the object of my hatred—it was always the person it belonged to.

My father.

Nora nestles closer to me in the backseat, interrupting my musings, and yawns delicately into my shoulder. The sound is so kitten-like that I laugh and wrap my right arm around her waist, pulling her closer to me. "Sleepy?"

"Hmm-mm." She rubs her face against my neck. "You smell good," she mumbles.

And just like that, my cock turns rock-hard, reacting to the feel of her lips brushing against my skin.

*Fuck.* I blow out a frustrated breath as the car stops in front of the house. Ana and Rosa are standing on the front porch, ready to greet us, and my dick is bursting out of my pants. I shift to the side, trying to ease Nora away from me so my erection can subside. Her elbow brushes against my ribs, and I tense in pain, mentally cursing Majid to hell and back.

I can't fucking wait to heal. Even sex earlier today hurt, especially when I set a harder pace at the end. Not that it lessened the pleasure much—I'm pretty sure I could fuck Nora on my deathbed and enjoy it—but it still annoyed me. I like pain with sex, but only when I'm the one doling it out.

On the plus side, my erection is no longer quite as visible.

"We're there," I tell Nora as she rubs her eyes and yawns again. "I'd carry you over the threshold, but I'm afraid I might not make it this time."

She blinks, looking confused for a moment, but then a wide smile spreads across her face. She remembers too. "I'm no longer a new bride," she says, grinning. "So you're off the hook."

I grin back at her, unusual contentment filling my chest, and open the car door.

As soon as we climb out, we're attacked by two crying women. Or, more precisely, Nora is attacked. I just watch in bemusement as Ana and Rosa hug her, laughing and sobbing at the same time. After they're done with Nora, they turn toward me, and Ana sobs harder as she catches a glimpse of my bandaged face. "Oh, pobrecito..." She lapses into Spanish like she sometimes does when she's upset, and Nora and Rosa try to soothe her, saying that I'll recover, that the important thing is that I'm alive.

The housekeeper's concern is both touching and disconcerting. I've always been vaguely aware that the older woman cares about me, but I didn't realize her feelings are this strong. For as long as I can recall, Ana has been a warm, comforting presence at the estate— someone who fed me, cleaned after me, and bandaged my childhood scrapes and bruises. I've never let her get too close, though, and for the first time I feel a twinge of regret about that. Neither she nor Rosa, the maid who's Nora's friend, try to hug me like they did my wife. They think I wouldn't welcome it, and they're probably right.

The only person I want affection from—no, *crave* affection from—is Nora, and that's a recent development.

After the three women are done with their emotional reunion, we all head into the house. Despite the late hour, Nora and I are hungry, and we devour the meal Ana prepared for us with record speed. Then, replete and exhausted, we go upstairs to our bedroom.

A quick shower and an equally quick fuck later, I drift off to sleep with Nora's head pillowed on my uninjured shoulder.

I'm ready for our normal life to resume.

The scream that wakes me up is bloodcurdling. Full of desperation and terror, it bounces off the walls and floods my veins with adrenaline.

I'm on my feet and off the bed before I even realize what's happening. As the sound dies down, I grab the gun hidden in my nightstand and simultaneously hit the light switch with the back of my hand.

The nightstand lamp turns on, illuminating the room, and I see Nora huddled in the middle of the bed, shaking under the blanket.

There's no one else in the room, no visible threat.

My racing heartbeat begins to slow. We didn't get attacked. The scream must've come from Nora.

She's having yet another nightmare.

*Fuck.* The urge to do violence is almost too strong to be contained. It fills every cell of my body until I'm shaking with rage, with the need to kill and destroy every motherfucker responsible for this.

Starting potentially with myself.

Turning away, I draw in several deep breaths, trying

HOLD ME

to hold back the churning fury within me. There's no one I can lash out at here, no enemy I can crush to take the edge off my temper.

There's only Nora, who needs me to be calm and rational.

After a few seconds pass and I'm certain I won't hurt her, I turn back to face her and put the gun back into the nightstand drawer. Then I climb back on the bed. My ribs and shoulder ache dully, and my head throbs from my sudden movements, but that pain is nothing compared to the heaviness in my chest.

"Nora, baby…" Leaning over her, I pull the blanket off her naked body and place my right hand on her shoulder to shake her awake. "Wake up, my pet. It's just a dream." Her skin is clammy to the touch, and the whimpering noises she's making pain me more than any of Majid's torture. Fresh rage wells up, but I suppress it, keeping my voice low and even. "Wake up, baby. You're dreaming. It's not real."

She rolls over onto her back, still shaking, and I see that her eyes are open.

Open and unseeing as she gasps for air, her chest heaving and her hands clutching at the sheets in desperation.

She's not having a dream—she's in the middle of a full-blown panic attack, likely one caused by her nightmare.

I want to throw my head back and roar out my rage, but I don't. She needs me now, and I won't let her down.

Not ever again.

Rising to my knees, I straddle her hips and bend down to grasp her jaw in my right hand. "Nora, look at me." I make the words a command, my tone harsh and demanding. "Look at me, my pet. Now."

Despite her panic, she obeys, her conditioning too strong to be denied. Her eyes flick up to meet my gaze, and I see that her pupils are dilated, her irises nearly black. She's also hyperventilating, her mouth open as she tries to draw in enough air.

*Fuck and double fuck.* My first instinct is to hold her against me, to be gentle and calming, but I remember her panic attack during sex the night before and the way nothing seemed to help her then.

Nothing except violence.

So instead of murmuring useless endearments, I lean down, propping myself up on my right elbow, and take her mouth in a hard, brutal kiss, using my grip on her jaw to keep her still. My lips smash against hers, and my teeth sink into her lower lip as I roughly push my tongue inside, invading her, hurting her. The sadistic monster inside me thrills with delight at the metallic taste of her blood, while the rest of me aches at her mind's agony.

She gasps into my mouth, but the sound is different now, more startled than desperate. I can feel her chest expanding as she draws in a full breath, and I realize that my crude method of reaching her is working, that she's now focusing on the physical rather than the

HOLD ME

mental pain. Her fists uncurl, her hands no longer
grasping at the sheets, and she stills underneath me, her
body tensing with a different sort of fear.

A fear that arouses the darkest, most predatory part
of me—the part that wants to subjugate and devour her.

The rage that still simmers within me adds to this
hunger, mingling with it and feeding upon it until I
become this need, this mindless, terrible craving. My
focus narrows, sharpens, until all I'm aware of is the
silky feel of her lips, flavored with blood, and the curves
of her naked body, small and helpless underneath mine.
My cock stiffens to a painful hardness as she grabs my
right forearm with both of her hands and makes a soft,
agonized sound in the back of her throat.

Suddenly, the kiss is no longer enough. I have to
have all of her.

Letting go of her jaw, I push myself up with one arm,
rising onto my knees. She stares up at me, her lips
swollen and tinged with red. She's still panting, her
chest rising and falling in rapid tempo, but the unseeing
look in her eyes is gone. She's with me—she's fully
present—and that's all my inner demon requires at the
moment.

I climb off her in one swift motion, ignoring the
pang of pain in my ribs, and reach into the bedside
drawer again. Only this time, instead of a gun, I pull out
a braided leather flogger.

Nora's eyes widen. "Julian?" Her voice is breathless
with remnants of her panic.

"Turn over." The words come out rough, betraying the violent need raging inside me. "Now."

She hesitates for a moment, then rolls over onto her stomach.

"On your knees."

She gets on all fours and turns her head to look at me, awaiting further instructions.

*Such a well-trained pet.* Her obedience heightens my lust, my desperate hunger to possess her. The position showcases her ass and exposes her pussy, causing my dick to swell up even more. I want to swallow her whole, lay claim to every inch of her. My muscles tense, and almost without thinking, I swing the flogger, letting the leather threads bite into the smooth skin of her buttocks.

She cries out, her eyes closing as her body stiffens, and the darkness inside me takes over, obliterating all remnants of rational thought. I watch, almost as if from a distance, as the flogger kisses her skin again and again, leaving pink marks and reddening streaks on her back, ass, and thighs. She flinches at the first few strokes, crying out in pain, but as I find a rhythm, her body begins to relax into the strokes, anticipating rather than resisting the sting. Her cries soften, and her pussy folds begin to glisten with moisture.

She's responding to the flogging as if to a sensual caress.

My balls tighten as I drop the flogger and crawl up behind her, looping my right forearm under her hips to drag her toward me. My cock presses against her entrance, and I groan as I feel her slick heat rubbing against the tip, coating it with creamy moisture. She moans, arching her back, and I push into her, forcing her flesh to engulf me, to take me in.

Her pussy is unbelievably tight, her inner muscles squeezing me like a fist. It doesn't matter how often I fuck her; each time, it's new in some way, the sensations sharper and richer than in my memory. I could stay inside her forever, feeling her softness, her moist heat. Except I can't—the primitive urge to move, to thrust into her, is too strong to be denied. My heartbeat drums loudly in my ears, my body pulsing with savage need.

I hold still for as long as I can, and then I begin to move, each thrust causing my groin to press against her pink, freshly flogged ass. She moans with every stroke, her body tightening around my invading cock, and the sensations build upon each other, intensifying to an unbearable degree. My skin prickles from my impending orgasm, and I begin to drive into her faster, harder, until I feel her contractions begin, her pussy rippling around me as she screams out my name.

It's the last straw. The orgasm I've been holding off overtakes me with explosive force, and I erupt deep inside her with a hoarse groan, stunning pleasure rocketing through my body. It's a bliss unlike any other —an ecstasy that goes far beyond physical satisfaction. It's something I've experienced only with Nora.

Will ever experience only with Nora.

Breathing heavily, I withdraw from her body, letting her collapse on the bed. Then I lower myself onto my right side and gather her against me, knowing she needs tenderness after brutality.

And in a way, I need it too. I need to comfort her, to soothe her. To bind her to me when she's at her most vulnerable, so I can ensure her love.

It might be cold-blooded, but I don't leave important things like that to chance.

She turns around to face me and buries her face in the crook of my neck, her shoulders shaking with quiet sobs. "Hold me, Julian," she whispers, and I do.

I will always hold her, no matter what.

# II

# THE HEALING

## 4

## NORA

"Julian, do you have a minute?"

Entering my husband's office, I walk over to his desk. He looks up to greet me, and I marvel yet again at the tremendous progress he's made in his recovery over the past six weeks.

His arm cast is gone now, as are all the bandages. Julian tackled healing the same way as he approaches any goal: with single-minded ruthlessness and determination. As soon as Dr. Goldberg approved removal of the cast, Julian dove headfirst into physical therapy, spending hours each day on exercises designed to restore mobility and function to the left side of his body. With his scars beginning to fade, there are days when I almost forget that he was so badly injured—that he had gone through hell and emerged relatively unscathed.

Even his eye implant doesn't seem jarring to me

anymore. Our stay at the clinic in Switzerland and all the procedures cost Julian millions—I saw the bill in his inbox—but the doctors did a phenomenal job with his face. The implant matches Julian's real eye so perfectly that when he looks at me straight on, it's almost impossible to tell that it's fake. I have no idea how they managed to make it that exact shade of blue, but they did, right down to every striation and natural color variation. The fake pupil even shrinks in bright light and dilates when Julian is excited or aroused, thanks to a biofeedback device Julian wears as a watch. The watch measures his pulse and skin conductance and sends the information to the implant, allowing for the most natural-looking responses. The only thing the implant doesn't do is replicate normal eye motion... or allow Julian to see from it.

"That part—the connection to the brain—will take a few more years," Julian told me a couple of weeks ago. "They're working on it now in a lab in Israel."

So yeah, the implant is remarkably lifelike. And Julian is learning to minimize the weirdness of only one eye moving by turning his entire head to look at something straight on—like the way he's looking at me now.

"What is it, my pet?" he asks, smiling. His beautiful lips are fully healed now, and the fading scars on his left cheek add a dangerous, yet appealing edge to his looks. It's as if a bit of his inner darkness is visible on his face now, but instead of repelling me, it draws me to him even more.

Probably because I need that darkness now—it's the only thing keeping me sane these days.

"Monsieur Bernard just told me that he has a friend who'd be interested in displaying my paintings," I say, trying to sound like world-class art instructors give me those kinds of news all the time. "He apparently owns an art gallery in Paris."

Julian's eyebrows rise. "Is that right?"

I nod, barely able to contain my excitement. "Yes, can you believe it? Monsieur Bernard sent him photos of my latest works, and the gallery owner said they're exactly what he's been looking for."

"That's wonderful, baby." Julian's smile widens, and he reaches over to pull me down into his lap. "I'm so proud of you."

"Thank you." I want to jump up and down, but I settle for looping my arms around his neck and planting an excited kiss on his mouth. Of course, as soon as our lips touch, Julian takes over the kiss, turning my spontaneous expression of gratitude into a prolonged sensual assault that leaves me breathless and dazed.

When he finally lets me come up for air, it takes me a second to remember how I ended up on his lap.

"I'm so proud of you," Julian repeats, his voice soft as he looks at me. I can feel the bulge of his erection, but he doesn't take it further. Instead, he gives me a warm smile

ANNA ZAIRES

and says, "I will have to thank Monsieur Bernard for taking those photos. If the gallery owner does end up displaying your work, perhaps we'll take a little trip to Paris."

"Really?" I gape at him. This is the first time Julian's indicated that we might not be staying on the estate all the time. And to go to Paris? I can hardly believe my ears.

He nods, still smiling. "Sure. Al-Quadar is no longer a threat. It's as safe as it's ever likely to be, so with sufficient security, I don't see why we can't visit Paris in a bit—especially if there's a compelling reason to do so."

I grin at him, trying not to think about how Al-Quadar stopped being a threat. Julian hasn't told me much about that operation, but the little I do know is enough. When our rescuers raided the construction site in Tajikistan, they uncovered a tremendous amount of valuable information. After our return to the estate, every person even remotely connected to the terrorist organization was eliminated, some quickly and others slowly and painfully. I don't know how many deaths took place in recent weeks, but I wouldn't be surprised if the body count is well into the triple digits.

The man who's holding me right now is responsible for what amounts to a mass slaughter—and I still love him with all my heart.

"A trip to Paris would be amazing," I say, pushing aside all thoughts of Al-Quadar. Instead, I focus on the mind-boggling possibility that my paintings might be displayed in an actual art gallery. *My* paintings. It's so hard to believe that I ask Julian cautiously, "You didn't tell Monsieur Bernard to do this, right? Or somehow bribe this friend of his?" Since Julian used his financial clout to get me into the highly selective online program at Stanford University, I wouldn't put anything past him.

"No, baby." Julian's smile broadens. "I didn't have anything to do with this, I promise. You have a genuine talent, and your instructor knows it."

I believe him, if only because Monsieur Bernard has been raving about my paintings in recent weeks. The darkness and complexity that he saw in my art early on is even more visible now. Painting is one of the ways I've been dealing with my nightmares and panic attacks. Sexual pain is another—but that's a whole other matter.

Not wanting to dwell on my fucked-up mental state, I jump off Julian's lap. "I'm going to tell my parents," I say brightly as I head for the door. "They'll be very excited."

"I'm sure they will be." And giving me one last smile, he turns his attention back to his computer screen.

My video chat with my parents takes close to an hour. As always, I have to spend a solid twenty minutes assuring my mom that I'm safe, that I'm still at the estate in Colombia, and that no one is coming after us. After I disappeared from the Chicago Ridge Mall, my parents have become convinced that Julian's enemies are everywhere, ready to strike at a moment's notice. If I don't call or email my parents daily nowadays, they go into complete panic mode.

Not that they think I'm safe with Julian, of course. In their minds, he's no different than the terrorists who kidnapped me. In fact, I think my dad believes Julian is worse—given that my husband stole me away not once, but twice.

"A gallery in Paris? Why, that's wonderful, honey!" my mom exclaims when I finally get around to sharing my news with her. "We're so happy for you!"

"Are you still focusing on your classes?" my dad asks, frowning. He's less enthusiastic about my painting. I think he's afraid I will abandon all thoughts of college and become a starving artist—a fear that's beyond illogical, given the circumstances. If there's one thing I don't need to worry about these days, it's money. Julian recently told me that he set up a trust fund in my name and also named me as the sole beneficiary in his will. This way, if anything happens to him, I'll still be taken care of—by which he means I'll have enough money to run a small country.

"Yes, Dad," I say patiently. "Don't worry—I'm still focusing on school. I told you, I'm just taking a lighter load this quarter. I'll make up for it by taking a couple of classes in the summer."

The lighter load is something Julian insisted on when we returned, and despite my initial objections, I'm glad he did. For some reason, everything feels harder this quarter. My papers take me forever to write, and studying for exams is exhausting. Even with the lighter load, I've been feeling overwhelmed, but that's not something I want to tell my parents. It's bad enough that Julian is worried.

So worried, in fact, that he brought a shrink to the estate for me.

"Are you sure, honey?" my mom asks, peering at me with concern. "Maybe you should take the summer off, relax for a couple of months. You look really tired."

*Shit.* I was hoping the dark circles under my eyes wouldn't be as noticeable on video.

"I'm fine, Mom," I say. "I just stayed up late studying and painting, that's all."

I also woke up in the middle of the night screaming and couldn't fall back asleep until Julian whipped and fucked me, but my parents don't need to know that. They wouldn't understand that pain is therapeutic for me now, that I've grown to need something I once dreaded.

That the cruel side of Julian is something I've wholeheartedly embraced.

As we wrap up the conversation, I remember something Julian promised me once: that he'd take me to visit my family when the danger from Al-Quadar subsided. My heart jumps in excitement at the thought, but I decide to keep quiet until I have a chance to ask Julian about it at dinner. For now, I just tell my parents that we'll speak again soon, and log off from the secure connection.

There are now two things I need to discuss with Julian tonight... and both will be somewhat tricky.

"A trip to Chicago?" Julian looks vaguely surprised when I bring it up. "But you saw your parents less than two months ago."

"Right, for all of one evening before Al-Quadar kidnapped me." I blow on my cream-of-mushroom soup before dipping my spoon into the hot liquid. "I was also worried sick about you, so I'm not sure that evening counts as quality time with my family."

Julian studies me for a second before murmuring, "All right. You may have a point." Then he starts eating his own soup while I stare at him, hardly able to believe he would agree so easily.

"So we'll go?" I want to make sure there's no misunderstanding.

He shrugs. "If you want. After your exams are over, I'll take you there. We'll have to beef up the security around your parents, of course, and take a few extra precautions, but it should be possible."

I begin to smile, but then I remember something he told me once. "Do you think our going there would put my parents in danger?" I ask, my stomach twisting with sudden nausea. "Could they become a target if you're seen as being in close contact with them?"

Julian gives me an even look. "It's a possibility. A remote possibility, but it's not completely out of the question. There was obviously much greater danger when the terrorists were out for blood, but I do have other enemies. None so determined—at least as far as I know—but there are plenty of individuals and organizations who'd love to get their hands on me."

"Right." I swallow a spoonful of soup and immediately regret it, as the creamy liquid makes me feel even more nauseated. "And you think they might use my parents as leverage?"

"It's unlikely, but I can't completely rule it out. This is why I've had the security detail on your family from the start. It's a precaution, nothing more—but it's a necessary precaution, in my opinion."

I take a deep breath, doing my best to ignore the churning in my belly. "So would our going to Chicago increase the danger to them or not?"

"I don't know, my pet." Julian looks faintly regretful. "My best guess is no, but there are no guarantees."

I pick up a glass and take a sip of water, trying to get rid of the sickeningly fatty taste of soup on my tongue. "What if I go by myself?" I suggest without much thought. "Then nobody will think you're in any way close to your in-laws."

Julian's face darkens in an instant. "By yourself?"

I nod, instinctively tensing at the shift in his mood.

Even though I know Julian wouldn't harm me, I can't help being wary of his temper. I may be with him willingly now, but he still has absolute control over my life—just as he did when I was his captive on the island.

In all the ways that count, he's still my dangerous, amoral kidnapper.

"You're not going anywhere by yourself." Julian's voice is soft, but the look in his eyes is hard, like steel. "If you want me to take you to Chicago, I'll do it—but you're not stepping a foot off this estate without me. Do you understand me, Nora?"

"Yes." I take a few more sips of water, still feeling the aftertaste of soup in my throat. What the hell did Ana put in it this evening? Even the smell of it is unpleasant. "I understand." My words come out sounding calm rather than resentful—mostly because I'm feeling too sick to get angry at Julian's autocratic attitude. Downing the rest of my water, I say, "It was just a suggestion."

Julian stares at me for a few moments, then gives a minute nod. "All right."

Before he has a chance to say anything more, Ana walks into the room, carrying our next course—fish with rice and beans. Seeing my nearly untouched soup, she frowns. "You don't like the soup, Nora?"

"No, it's delicious," I lie. "I'm just not that hungry and wanted to save room for the main course."

Ana gives me a concerned look, but clears off our dishes without further comment. My appetite has been unpredictable since our return, so this is not the first time I've left a meal untouched. I haven't weighed myself, but I think I've lost at least a couple of pounds in recent weeks—which is not necessarily a good thing in my case.

Julian frowns also, but doesn't say anything as I start playing with the rice on my plate. I really, really don't want food right now, but I force myself to pick up a forkful and put it in my mouth. The rice also tastes too rich, but I determinedly chew and swallow, not wanting to have Julian focus on my lack of eating.

I have something more important to discuss with him.

As soon as Ana leaves the room, I put my fork down and look at my husband. "I got another message," I say quietly.

Julian's jaw tightens. "I know."

"You're monitoring my email now?" My stomach roils again, this time with a mix of nausea and anger. I guess I shouldn't be surprised, given the trackers still implanted in my body, but something about this casual invasion of privacy really upsets me.

"Of course." He doesn't look the least bit apologetic or remorseful. "I figured he might contact you again."

I inhale slowly, reminding myself that arguing about this is futile. "Then you know Peter won't leave us alone until you give him that list," I say, as calmly as I can manage. "Somehow he knows that you got it from Frank last week. His message said, 'It's time to remember your promise.' He won't go away, Julian."

"If he keeps harassing you via email, I'll make sure he goes away for good." Julian's tone hardens. "He knows better than to try to get to me through you."

"He saved your life and my life," I remind him for the dozenth time. "I know you're mad that he disobeyed your orders, but if he hadn't, you'd be dead."

"And you wouldn't be having these nightmares and panic attacks." Julian's sensuous lips flatten. "It's been six weeks, Nora, and you haven't gotten any better. You barely sleep, hardly eat, and I can't remember the last time you went for a run. He should've *never* put you in that kind of danger—"

"He did what was necessary!" Slapping my palms on the table, I rise to my feet, no longer able to sit still. "You think I'd be feeling better if you died? You think I wouldn't have nightmares if Majid mailed us your body in pieces? My fucked-up head is not Peter's fault, so stop blaming him for this mess! I promised him that list, and I want to give it to him!" By the time I get to the last sentence, I'm full-on yelling, too angry to care about Julian's temper.

He stares at me, his eyes narrowed. "Sit down, Nora." His voice is dangerously soft. "Now."

"Or what?" I challenge, feeling uncharacteristically reckless. "Or what, Julian?"

"Do you really want to go there, my pet?" he asks in that same soft tone. When I don't respond, he points at my chair. "Sit down and finish the meal Ana prepared for you."

I hold his gaze for a few more seconds, not wanting to give in, but then I lower myself back into my chair. The surge of defiant anger that came upon me so suddenly is gone, leaving me drained and wanting to cry. I hate the fact that Julian can win a fight so easily, that I'm still not fearless enough to test his limits.

Not over something as minor as finishing a meal, at least.

If I'm going to defy him, it will be over something that matters.

Dropping my gaze to my plate, I pick up my fork and spear a piece of fish, trying to ignore my growing queasiness. My stomach churns with every bite, but I persist until I finish nearly half of my portion. Julian, in the meantime, polishes off everything on his plate, his appetite obviously unaffected by our argument.

"Dessert? Tea? Coffee?" Ana asks when she comes back to clear off our plates, and I mutely shake my head, not wanting to prolong the ordeal of this tense meal.

"I'll pass too, thanks, Ana," Julian says politely. "Everything was wonderful, as usual."

Ana beams at him, clearly pleased. I've noticed that Julian has made it a point to praise her more often since our return—that in general, his manner toward her is slightly warmer these days. I don't know what caused the change, but I know Ana appreciates it. Rosa told me the housekeeper has been all but dancing on air in recent weeks.

As Ana begins clearing off the table, Julian gets up

and walks around to offer me his arm. I loop my hand through the crook of his elbow, and we head upstairs in silence. As we walk, my heart starts beating faster and my queasiness intensifies.

Tonight's argument only confirms what I have known for a while: Julian is never going to see reason on the issue of Peter's list. If I'm to keep my promise, I will have to take matters into my own hands and brave the consequences of my husband's displeasure.

Even if the thought of that literally makes me sick.

## 5

## JULIAN

*a*s soon we enter the bedroom, Nora excuses herself to freshen up.

She disappears into the bathroom, and I undress, enjoying the freedom of having both arms unencumbered by a cast. My left shoulder still aches during exercise, but I'm regaining my strength and range of motion. Even the loss of my eye doesn't bother me that much; the headaches and eye strain are lessening by the day, and I've learned to compensate for the blind spot to my left by turning my head more frequently.

All in all, I'm pretty much back to normal—but I can't say the same about Nora.

Every time I wake up to her screams, every time she starts hyperventilating out of nowhere, a toxic mixture of rage and guilt blankets my chest. I've never been prone to dwelling on the past, but I can't help wishing that I could somehow rewind the clock, undo the unintended consequences of my fucked-up choices.

That I could have Nora—my Nora—back.

She slips out of the bathroom a few minutes later, already showered and wearing a white fleece robe. Her smooth skin is glowing from the hot water, and her long, dark hair is piled haphazardly on top of her head, exposing her slender neck.

A neck that's beginning to look far too delicate, almost frail from her weight loss.

"Come here, baby," I murmur, patting the bed next to me. I had contemplated punishing her for her outburst at dinner, but all I want to do now is hold her. Well, fuck her and hold her, but the fucking can wait.

She walks toward me, and I reach for her as soon as she's within arm's length. She feels disturbingly light as I tug her down to my lap, the shadows under her eyes betraying her exhaustion.

She's completely worn out, and I don't know what to do. The therapist I brought to the estate three weeks ago appears to be useless, and Nora refuses to take the anti-anxiety meds the doctor prescribed for her. I could force her, of course, but I distrust those pills myself. The last thing I want is to get Nora hooked on them.

The only thing that seems to help her—temporarily, at least—is an emotional release achieved through sexual pain. It's something she requires now, something she begs for nearly every night.

My pet has become as addicted to receiving pain as I

am to giving it—and that development both pleases and devastates me.

"You barely ate again," I say softly, settling her more comfortably on my knees. Reaching up, I free her hair from the clip holding it up, and watch the dark mass spill down her back in a thick, glossy stream. "Why, baby? Is there something wrong with Ana's cooking?"

"What? No—" she begins saying, but then she corrects herself. "Well, maybe. I just didn't like the soup today. It was too rich."

"I'll ask Ana not to make it in the future, then." I distinctly remember Nora eating the soup and loving it before, but I decide against reminding her of that. I don't care what she eats, as long as she stays healthy.

"Just please don't tell her that I complained." Nora's gaze fills with worry. "I wouldn't want her to be offended."

"Of course." A smile tugs at my lips. "I'll take your secret to the grave, I promise."

An answering smile appears on her face, lighting up her features, and I feel much of the lingering tension between us dissipating. "Thank you," she whispers, staring at me. Then, placing one small hand on my shoulder and another on the back of my neck, she closes her eyes and presses her soft lips to mine.

I inhale sharply, my body tightening with instant lust. Her breath is sweet and minty, her slight weight warm in my arms. I can feel her slender fingers on my skin, smell her delicate scent, and my spine prickles with growing hunger, my cock hardening against the curve of her ass.

This time, though, the hunger doesn't come with the need to hurt her. Instead, it's tinged with tenderness. The darker impulses are there, but they're overshadowed by my stark awareness of her fragility. Tonight, more than ever, I want to protect her, heal her from the wounds she should've never sustained. I want to be her hero, her savior.

For just one night, I want to be the husband of her dreams.

Closing my eyes, I focus on her taste, on the way her breathing changes as I deepen the kiss. The way her head falls back and her body melts against mine, her fingernails gently scratching at my scalp as her hand slides into my hair. She's my world, my everything, and I want her so much I ache with it.

She's still bundled in her fleecy robe, the material soft on my bare thighs and cock. As good as it feels, however, I know her naked flesh will feel even better, so I grasp the tie at her waist, pulling on it. At the same time, I lift my head and open my eyes to look at her.

As the tie unravels, her robe parts, exposing a V of smooth, tan skin. I can see the inside curves of her breasts and the taut flatness of her belly, but her nipples and lower body are still covered, as if by design.

It's an erotic visual, made even more sensual by the way she's breathing, her ribcage moving up and down in a fast, panting rhythm. Her lips are reddened from the kiss, and her skin is softly flushed.

My little pet is turned on.

As if sensing my gaze on her, she opens her eyes, her long lashes sweeping up. We look at each other, and the aching need inside me grows. It's a feeling that's somehow different from the lust surging through my body, a complex want that's layered on top of my usual obsessive craving.

A yearning that terrifies me with its intensity.

"Tell me you love me." All of a sudden, I need this from her. "Tell me, Nora."

She doesn't blink. "I love you."

My arms tighten around her. "Again."

"I love you, Julian." She holds my gaze, her eyes soft and dark. "More than anything else in the world."

*Fuck.* My chest constricts, the ache intensifying rather than easing. It's too much, yet somehow not enough.

Bending my head, I claim her lips again, putting all the things I can't express in words into that kiss. I feel her breathing growing shallow, and I know I'm holding her too tightly, but I can't help it. Mixed with the overwhelming longing is a strange, irrational fear.

Fear that I might lose her. That she might slip away, like some beautiful, ephemeral dream.

*No.* I angle my head to delve deeper into her mouth, letting her taste, her scent, absorb me, chasing away the shadows. She won't slip away. I won't let her. She's real, and she's mine. I kiss her until we're both gasping for air, until the fear inside me abates, burned away by the scorching heat.

Then I make love to her, as tenderly as I can.

When I drift off to sleep some time later, it's with Nora cocooned safely in my embrace.

## 6

---

### NORA

$\mathcal{I}$t takes all of my willpower to remain awake as I hear Julian's breathing take on the even rhythm of sleep. My own eyelids feel heavy, my body lethargic from exhaustion and sexual satiation. All I want to do is close my eyes and let the comforting darkness swallow me, but I can't.

There's something I must do first.

I wait until I'm certain Julian is asleep, and then I carefully wriggle out of his hold. To my relief, he doesn't stir, so I get up and find the robe that had fallen on the floor during sex.

Quietly putting it on, I pad barefoot into the bathroom. My stomach, still unsettled from dinner, roils with nausea again, and I have to swallow several times to keep the food from coming back up.

It's probably not the best idea to do this when I'm feeling sick. I know that—but I also know that if I don't do this now, I may not have the courage to attempt it later. And I need to do this. I need to fulfill my promise, to repay the debt I owe Peter. It's important to me. I don't want to be the girl who can't take any action on her own, the wife who always lives in her husband's shadow.

I don't want to be Julian's helpless little pet for the rest of my life.

Splashing cold water on my face, I take several deep breaths to quell my nausea and walk back into the bedroom. The shades are open just a sliver, but the moon is full tonight, and there's enough light for me to see where I'm going.

My destination is the dresser, on top of which Julian's laptop is sitting. He doesn't always bring the computer into the bedroom, but he did tonight—which is another reason why I don't want to wait to implement my plan.

The plan itself is beyond simple. I'm going to take the laptop, access Julian's email, and send the list to Peter. If everything goes well, Julian won't find out about this for a while. And by the time he does, it will be too late. I will have repaid my debt to Julian's former security consultant, and my conscience will be clear.

Well, as clear as it can be knowing that Peter will likely kill the people on that list in horrifying ways.

*No, don't think about it.* I remind myself that those people are responsible for the deaths of Peter's wife and son. They're not innocent civilians, and I shouldn't think of them as such.

The only thing I should worry about at the moment is getting the list to Peter without waking up Julian.

I walk across the room as quietly as I can, my heart thumping heavily in my chest. When I reach the dresser, I stop and listen.

All is quiet. Julian must still be asleep.

Biting my lip, I reach for the laptop and pick it up. Then I pause to listen again.

The room is still silent.

Exhaling slowly, I walk back toward the bathroom, cradling the laptop against my chest. When I get there, I slip inside, lock the door behind me, and sit down on the edge of the Jacuzzi.

So far, so good. Ignoring the churning in my stomach, I open the laptop.

A password request box pops up.

I take another deep breath, fighting my worsening nausea. I expected this. Julian is paranoid about security and changes his password at least once a week. However, the last time he changed it was the day after Frank, Julian's CIA contact, emailed him the list.

Julian changed it when I was already hatching my plan—and I made sure I was nearby when he did so. I didn't stare at his laptop, of course. That would've been suspicious. Instead, I quietly filmed him with my smartphone while pretending to be checking my email.

Now if only I interpreted the recorded keystrokes correctly...

Holding my breath, I put in "NML_#042160" and hit "enter."

The computer screen blinks... and I'm in.

My breath whooshes out in relief. Now all I need to do is find the email from Frank, open the attachment, log into my own email, and send the list to the same email address that Peter has been contacting me from.

Should be easy enough, especially if I can keep my dinner down.

"Nora?" A knock startles me so much that I almost drop the computer. My lungs seize with panic, and I freeze, staring at the door.

Julian knocks again. "Nora, baby, are you all right?"

*He doesn't know I have his computer.* The realization causes me to start breathing again.

"Just using the bathroom," I call out, hoping Julian doesn't hear the adrenaline-induced shakiness in my voice. At the same time, I open Julian's email program and begin searching for Frank's name. "I'll be out soon."

"Of course, baby, take your time." The words are accompanied by the fading sound of footsteps.

I let out a relieved breath. I have a few more minutes.

I begin scanning through the emails containing the word "Frank." There are over a dozen from last week, but the one I want should have a little attachment icon next to it... Aha! There. Quickly, I open it.

It's a spreadsheet containing names and addresses.

Automatically, I glance through them. There are over a dozen rows, and the addresses run the gamut from cities in Europe to various towns in the United States. One in particular jumps out at me: Homer Glen, Illinois.

It's a place near Oak Lawn, my hometown. Less than a forty-minute drive from my parents' house.

Stunned, I read the name next to the address.

*George Cobakis.*

Thank God. It's nobody I know.

"Nora?" Julian's voice is back, and the tense note in it makes my heart jump into my throat. His next words confirm my fear. "Nora, do you have my computer?"

"What? Why?" I hope I don't sound as guilty as I feel. *Shit. Shit, shit, shit.* Frantically, I save the list to the desktop and open a new browser.

"Because my laptop is missing." His voice is tight with the beginnings of fury. "Are you in there with it?"

"What? No!" Even I can hear the lie in my voice. My hands are beginning to shake, but I get to the Gmail page and begin putting in my username and password.

The doorknob rattles. "Nora, open the door. Right now."

I don't respond. My hands are shaking so much that I mistype the password and have to put it in again.

"Nora!" Julian bangs on the door. "Open this fucking door before I break it down!"

I'm finally in my Gmail. My heart hammering in my chest, I search for the last email from Peter.

*Bang.* The door shakes from a hard kick.

My nausea intensifies, my pulse racing as I find the email.

*Bang. Bang.* More kicks against the door as I click "reply" and attach the list.

*Bang. Bang. Bang.*

I hit "Send"—and the door flies off the hinges, crashing to the floor in front of me.

Julian is standing there naked, his eyes like icy blue slits in his beautiful face. His powerful hands are clenched into fists, and his nostrils are flared, spots of color burning high on his cheekbones.

He's magnificent and terrifying, like an enraged archangel.

"Give me the laptop, Nora." His voice is frighteningly calm. "Now."

Bile rises in my throat, forcing me to swallow convulsively. Standing up, I walk over to him on trembling legs and hand over the computer.

He takes it from me with one hand and, before I can back away, wraps the other one around my right wrist, shackling me to him.

Then he looks at the screen.

I see the exact moment when he realizes what I did.

"You sent it to him?" Setting the computer down on the bathroom counter, he grabs my other arm and drags me closer to him. His eyes burn with fury. "You fucking sent it to him?" He gives me a hard shake, his fingers biting into my skin.

My stomach somersaults, nausea washing over me in sickening wave. "Julian, let go—"

And jerking out of his hold with desperation-fueled strength, I dive for the toilet bowl, just barely reaching it before I throw up.

"How long have you had this nausea?" Dr. Goldberg takes my pulse as I lie on the bed, with Julian pacing around the room like a caged jaguar.

"I don't know," I say, my eyes tracking Julian's movements. He's wearing a T-shirt and jeans now, but his feet are still bare. He's making circles in front of the bed, every muscle in his body taut and his jaw tightly clenched.

He's either still mad at me, or madly worried about me. I'm guessing it's a combination of the two. Within minutes of my throwing up, he had the doctor in our room and me bundled comfortably on the bed.

It reminds me of how quickly he acted when I got appendicitis on the island.

"I think I just ate something bad or maybe caught a virus," I say, turning my attention back to the doctor. "I started feeling sick at dinner."

"Uh-huh." Dr. Goldberg takes out a plastic-wrapped needle with a tube attached to a vial. "May I?"

"Okay." I don't particularly want him to take my

blood, but I have a feeling Julian won't let me refuse. "Go ahead."

The doctor finds a vein in my arm and slides the needle in while I look away. I'm still slightly nauseous and don't want to test my stomach's fortitude with the sight of blood.

"All done," he says after a moment, removing the needle and swabbing my skin with an alcohol-scented cotton ball. "I'll run the tests and let you know what I find."

"She's also constantly tired," Julian says in a low voice, stopping next to the bed. He's not looking at me, which annoys me a bit. "And she's sleeping poorly, with the nightmares and all."

"Right." The doctor rises to his feet, clutching the vial. "I need to run this to my lab. I'll be back within the hour."

He hurries out of the room, and Julian sits down on the bed, looking at me. His face is unusually pale, a frown etched into his forehead. "Why didn't you tell me you were feeling sick, Nora?" he asks quietly, reaching out to pick up my hand. His fingers are warm on my palm, his grip gentle despite the turmoil I sense within him.

I blink in surprise. I thought he would question me about Peter's list, not this. "It wasn't too bad at dinner," I say carefully. "I felt better after I took a shower and we... well, you know." I wave my free hand in a gesture meant to encompass the bed.

"We fucked?" Julian's tense expression eases slightly, unexpected amusement flickering in his eyes.

"Right." Heat crawls up my body at the mental images his words bring up. Apparently, I'm not too sick to be turned on. "That made me feel better."

"I see." Julian regards me speculatively, stroking the inside of my wrist with his thumb. "And you decided that since you were feeling so well, you were going to hack into my computer."

And there it is. The reckoning I anticipated. Except Julian doesn't seem as angry as before, his touch on me soothing rather than punishing.

It looks like food poisoning—or whatever I've got—has its perks.

I offer him a cautious smile. "Well, yeah. I figured it was as good of an opportunity as any." I don't bother apologizing or denying my actions. There's no point. It's done. I paid my debt to Peter.

"How did you know my password?" Julian's thumb continues moving over my wrist in a circular motion. "I never told you what it was."

"I filmed you when you were changing it a few days ago. After I found out that Frank came through on the list."

The corners of Julian's mouth twitch, almost imperceptibly. "That's what I thought. I was wondering why you were on your phone so much that day."

I lick my lips. "Are you going to punish me?" Julian

seems more amused than angry at the moment, but I can't imagine he'll let me off scot-free.

"Of course, my pet." There's no trace of hesitation in his voice.

My pulse jumps. "When?"

"When I choose." His eyes gleam as he releases my hand. "Now, would you like some water or anything?"

"Some crackers and chamomile tea would be nice," I say on autopilot, staring at him. I'd expected this, of course, but I still can't help feeling anxious.

"I'll get that for you." Julian gets up. "Be back in a few."

He disappears through the door, and I close my eyes, my earlier tiredness returning now that the adrenaline rush is over. Maybe I'll just catch a quick nap before Julian comes back...

A knock on the door startles me again, causing me to jerk to a sitting position. "Yes?"

"Nora, this is David Goldberg. May I come in?"

"Oh, sure." I lie back down, my heart still beating too fast. "Did you already run the tests?" I ask as the doctor enters the room.

"Yes." There is an odd expression on his face as he stops next to the bed. "Nora, you've been fatigued lately, right? And unusually stressed?"

"Yes." I frown, starting to feel uneasy. "Why?"

"Have you noticed anything else? Mood swings? Atypical food cravings or dislikes? Maybe some tenderness in your breasts?"

I stare at him, a cold fist seizing my chest. "What are you saying?" The symptoms he's listing—surely he can't mean...

"Nora, the blood tests I ran showed a strong presence of the hCG hormone," Dr. Goldberg says gently. "You're pregnant." He pauses, then adds quietly, "Given the timing of the implant removal, my best guess is you're about six weeks along."

7

JULIAN

Carrying the tray with tea and crackers, I walk up the stairs toward the bedroom. I should be furious with Nora, but instead, my worry for her is tinged with reluctant admiration.

She defied me. She locked herself in the bathroom and hacked into my computer to pay a debt that she believed was owed. She had to know that she would be caught, but she did it anyway—and I can't help respecting her for it.

I would've done the same thing in her shoes.

In hindsight, I should've expected this. She's been adamant about wanting to get the list to Peter, so it's not all that surprising that she decided to act on her own. From the very beginning, I've sensed a quiet, stubborn strength within her, a steel core that belies her delicate appearance.

My pet might be compliant much of the time, but

that's only because she's smart enough to choose her battles—and I should've known she'd choose to fight this one.

As I approach the bedroom, I hear voices and recognize Goldberg's slightly nasal pitch.

He's back with the test results, and Nora sounds upset.

*Fuck.* Fear, icy and sharp, bites at me. If it's something serious, if she's truly sick... Picking up my pace, I reach the door in two long steps. Tea sloshes over the rim of the cup, but I barely notice, all my focus on Nora.

Gripping the tray with one hand, I push open the door and step in.

She's sitting on the bed, her eyes huge in her colorless face as Goldberg says, "I'm afraid it *is* possible—"

My heart freezes. "What's possible?" I ask sharply. "What's wrong?"

Goldberg turns to look at me. "Oh, there you are." He sounds relieved. "I was just explaining to your wife that the morning-after pill is only ninety-five-percent effective when taken within twenty-four hours, and even though the likelihood of conception was low given the timing of the implant removal, there was still a small chance of pregnancy—"

"Pregnancy?" I feel like he's speaking a foreign language. "What are you talking about?"

Goldberg sighs, looking tired. "Nora is six weeks

pregnant, Julian. It looks like the morning-after pill didn't work."

I stare at him, stunned, and he says, "Listen, I know it's a lot to take in. Why don't I leave the two of you to discuss this, and I'll answer any questions you might have in the morning? For now, the best thing for Nora would be to get some rest. Stress is not good in her condition."

I nod, still mute with shock, and he swiftly departs, leaving me alone with Nora.

Nora, who's sitting there like a wax doll, her face nearly as white as the robe she's wearing.

Hot liquid spills over my hand, burning me, and I realize that I forgot about the tray I'm holding. The pain clears my mind, and I finally process the meaning of Goldberg's words.

Nora is pregnant.

Not sick. Pregnant.

The icy fear eases, replaced by a new, entirely foreign emotion.

Placing the tray with the half-full cup of tea on the nightstand, I sit down next to my wife and wrap my hands around her small palms. "Nora." I pull on her hands to get her to face me, and see that she's still shellshocked, her gaze blank and distant. "Nora, baby, talk to me."

She blinks, as if coming back to herself, and her hands jerk in my grasp. I release her and watch as she scoots back, drawing her knees up and wrapping her arms around herself. Her eyes lock with mine, and we stare at each other in silence as seconds tick by.

"Did you do this?" she finally asks, her voice a strained whisper. "Did you ask Dr. Goldberg to give me a placebo instead of the morning-after pill? Is the new implant in my arm a fake?"

"No." I don't bother being outraged at her accusation. If I'd wanted her pregnant, I might've considered doing something along those lines, and Nora is smart enough to know that. "No, my pet. This is as much of a shock to me as it is to you."

She nods, and I know she believes me. There is no reason for me to lie. She's mine to do with as I please. If I had impregnated her on purpose, I wouldn't deny it.

"Come here," I murmur, reaching for her. She's stiff as I pull her closer, but I ignore her resistance. I need to hold her, to feel her in my arms. Her hair tickles my chin as I pull her onto my lap and inhale deeply, closing my eyes.

Nora is not sick.

She's carrying my baby.

It seems surreal, unnatural. She's tiny in my embrace, barely bigger than a child herself. Yet she's going to be a mother—and I'm going to be a father.

A father, like the man who gave me life and molded me into what I am today.

Unbidden, an old memory comes to me.

*"Catch!" He throws the ball at me, laughing. I jump for it,*

*and my five-year-old hands close around it, snatching it from mid-air.*

*"I got it!" I feel so proud of myself, so full of joy. "Father, I caught it on the first try!"*

*"Good job, son." He grins at me, and in that moment, I love him. His approval matters to me more than anything else in the world. I forget about the frequent bite of his belt, about all the times he yelled at me and called me worthless.*

*He's my father, and in that moment, I love him.*

My eyes fly open, and I stare blankly at the wall, still holding Nora. I can't believe I ever loved that man. He's been the subject of my hatred for so long, I'd forgotten there were those kinds of moments.

I'd forgotten there were times he made me happy.

Would I make my child happy? Or would he or she hate me? I told Nora I would make an awful father, but I have no idea if that's the truth. For the first time, I try to imagine myself holding a newborn baby, playing with a chubby-cheeked toddler, teaching a five-year-old how to swim... The pictures come to me with surprising ease, filling me with an unsettling mixture of fear and longing.

With a desire for something I've never known.

A stifled sob startles me, and I realize that it's Nora.

She's crying, her slim body shaking in my arms. I can feel the wetness from her tears on my neck, and it burns me like acid.

For a moment, I had forgotten how much she doesn't want this child.

How much she doesn't want a child with *me*.

"Hush, my pet." The words come out harsher than I intended, but I can't help it. The unpleasant tightness in my chest is back, and with it, the irrational urge to hurt her. Fighting it, I say in a softer tone, "This is not the end of the world, believe me."

She stills, falling silent for a moment, but then another sob racks her body. And another.

I can't take it anymore. Her misery is like a hot knife plunging into my side—agonizing and maddening at the same time.

Thrusting my hand into her hair, I close my fist around the silky strands and pull her head back, forcing her to look up at me. Her eyes, wide and shocked, meet mine. I can see the tears sparkling on her lashes, and the sight enrages me further, awakening the beast inside.

Her lips tremble, parting as if she would speak, but I lower my head, swallowing her words with a deep, hard kiss. Lust, sharp and strong, kindles in my veins, hardening my cock and clouding my brain. I want her, and I want to punish her at the same time. I can feel her struggling against me, taste the salt from her tears, and it spurs me on, heightening the twisted hunger.

I'm not sure how we end up on the bed, with her stretched helplessly beneath me, but the clothes we're wearing seem like an intolerable barrier, so I tear them off, feeling more animal than man. My fingers close around her wrists, transferring both of them into my left hand, and my knees push between her thighs, parting them roughly.

I can hear Nora pleading, begging me to stop, but I can't. The need to possess her is like a fire under my skin, burning away all rational thought. Grasping my cock with my free hand, I guide it to her opening and penetrate her in one deep thrust, taking her body as I long to claim her heart and soul.

She's small and tight around me, her muscles clenching desperately to keep me out, but the squeezing pressure only intensifies my violent urge to fuck her. Her resistance maddens me, drives me to take her harder, to batter her with my cock as I hold her pinned under my body. Every thrust is a merciless claim, a brutal conquest of that which already belongs to me. I fuck her for what feels like hours, cognizant of nothing but the ferocious hunger seething under my skin.

It's not until I collapse on top of her, breathing heavily from an explosive orgasm, that the fog of lust clears from my mind, and I realize what I've done.

Releasing her wrists, I push up onto my elbows and gaze down at her, my cock still buried inside her body. She's lying underneath me, her eyes squeezed shut and her face pale. I can see a smear of blood on her lower lip. I either cut it with my teeth or she bit it in pain.

As I stare at her, she slowly opens her eyes, meeting my gaze... and for the first time in decades, I taste the bitter ashes of remorse.

## 8

## NORA

*M*y mind is blank, emptied of all thought as I look at Julian. I'm vaguely aware that he's still inside me, but that's all I can process at the moment. I feel broken, destroyed, the raw soreness of my body amplified by the deep, stabbing pain in my soul.

I don't know why this bout of rough sex felt so much like a violation. Why it reminded me of those early days on the island, when Julian was my cruel captor instead of the man I love. Only a couple of days ago, he tortured me with a flogger and nipple clamps, and I reveled in it, begging for more.

I begged today too, but it wasn't for more. Sex wasn't what I wanted—not with my heart breaking for the tiny life growing inside me.

For the innocent child conceived by two killers.

"Nora..." Julian's voice is an aching whisper. The

pain in it tugs at what remains of my heart. I want to hate him for hurting me, but I can't. It's part of his nature. It's who he is.

It's why any child of ours is doomed.

I hold his gaze, feeling like I'm crumbling into pieces. "Let me go, Julian. Please."

"I can't." His face twists, the scars around his eye standing out in stark relief. "I can't, Nora."

I swallow painfully, knowing he's not talking about our physical position. "I'm not asking that of you. Please, I just— I just need a moment."

He withdraws from me, rolling over onto his back, and I turn away onto my side, gathering my knees to my chest. The nausea that plagued me earlier is gone, but I feel weak. Exhausted. My body aches from Julian's hard use, and a sense of hopelessness engulfs me, adding to my growing despair.

I'm barely cognizant of Julian getting up. It's only when he presses a warm washcloth between my legs that I realize he must've gone to the bathroom and returned. I don't have the energy to move, so I lie still and let him clean the residue of sex off my thighs.

Afterwards, he pulls me into his embrace and covers us both with a blanket. As the familiar warmth of his body seeps into me, lulling me to sleep, I dream that I feel the brush of his lips against my temple and hear a whispered, "I'm sorry."

~

"As I began to explain last night, this pregnancy was improbable, but not impossible," Dr. Goldberg says as I sit down on the couch next to Julian. "The morning-after pill is ineffective about five percent of the time, and your probability of being able to conceive a few days after the removal of the old implant was also somewhere in the five-percent range, so if you do the math…" He shrugs, giving me a sheepish smile.

"What about the fact that Nora is still on birth control?" Julian asks, frowning. "She has a new implant in her arm—she's had it for weeks."

"Right." The doctor nods. "We'll have to remove that as soon as possible and have Nora start taking prenatal vitamins." He pauses, then adds delicately, "That is, if you want to keep the baby."

"We do," Julian responds before I can process the question. "And we want to make sure the child is healthy." He reaches for my hand and wraps his fingers around my palm, squeezing it possessively. "And Nora, of course."

Finally comprehending Dr. Goldberg's words, I glance at Julian. His jaw is set in hard, uncompromising lines. Abortion hadn't occurred to me as an option, but I'm surprised Julian is so vehemently against it. He claimed not to want children, and I can't imagine he'd be hypocritical enough to have moral or religious objections to the procedure.

"Of course," the doctor says. "Obstetrics is not my specialty, but I can examine Nora and remove the implant, and prescribe her the appropriate vitamins. I can also recommend an excellent obstetrician who might agree to oversee Nora's pregnancy here. I already emailed you her contact info."

"Good." Releasing my hand, Julian gets up, looking restless and tense. "I want the absolute best care for Nora."

"You'll have it," Dr. Goldberg promises, rising to his feet as well. Turning toward me, he says, "At least this explains something."

"Explains what?" I stand up too, uncomfortable being the only one sitting.

"Your persistent nightmares and panic attacks." The doctor gives me a sympathetic look. "It's not uncommon for pregnancy hormones to amplify anxiety, particularly in the wake of traumatic events."

"Oh." I stare at him. "So I'm not just overreacting to what happened?"

"You're not," Dr. Goldberg assures me. "Depression and anxiety can happen to pregnant women with much less provocation. You do need to take it easy and relax as much as possible, though, both for your sake and that of the baby. Acute stress during pregnancy can lead to all sorts of complications, including a miscarriage."

"I will make sure she rests and doesn't stress." Julian reaches for me again, intertwining his fingers with mine. It's as if he can't bear not to touch me today. "What about food, drinks?"

"I'll give you a list of what to avoid," Dr. Goldberg

says. "You probably know about alcohol and caffeine, but there are a few more things, like sushi and seafood high in mercury."

"All right." Julian turns his head to look at me. "Baby, would you be okay with the doctor examining you now and removing the implant?" His voice is unusually soft, his gaze filled with indefinable emotion.

"Um, sure." I see no reason to procrastinate, and I like that Julian asked, instead of just ordering the examination in his usual autocratic manner.

"Good." He lifts my hand—the one he's holding—and presses a kiss to the back of my wrist before letting it go. "I'll be back in a bit."

I nod, and Julian quietly exits the room, closing the door behind him.

"All right, Nora." Dr. Goldberg smiles at me, reaching for his bag and pulling out latex gloves. "Shall we begin?"

After the doctor leaves, I change into a swimsuit and go to the back porch, grabbing my Psychology textbook on the way. Pregnancy or not, I have an exam to study for, and I'm determined to do so—if for no other reason than to distract myself from the situation. My arm once again sports a tiny, Band-Aid-covered wound, and I try to ignore the faint ache there, not wanting to focus on the fact that my birth control implant is gone... and the reason why.

It's strange, but the broken feeling of last night is no longer there. It's been replaced by a kind of distant hurt. I should probably be traumatized and angry at Julian, but I'm not. Like the days right after my abduction, last night feels like it belongs to a different era, to a time before we became who we are. I know I'm playing that game with myself again—the one where I exist solely in the moment and push all the bad stuff into a separate corner of my brain—but I need that game to stay sane.

I need that game because I can't stop loving my captor, no matter what he does.

It doesn't help that the Julian of this morning is a far cry from the brutal savage of last night. From the moment I woke up, he's been treating me like I'm made of crystal. Breakfast in bed followed by a foot rub, constant little kisses and affectionate gestures—if I didn't know better, I'd think he's feeling guilty.

Of course, I do know better. Only a thin line separates the monster of last night from the tender lover of this morning. Guilt is an emotion that's as foreign to my husband as pity for his enemies.

When I get to the back porch, I grab a lounge chair under an umbrella and make myself comfortable. As always, the air outside is hot and humid, so thick it's almost smothering. I don't mind, though. I'm used to it. If it gets unbearable, I'll jump into the pool. For now, I open my textbook and begin re-reading the chapter on neurotransmitters.

I'm only halfway through when a moving shadow makes me look up.

It's Julian. Dressed in a pair of black swim trunks, he's standing next to my chair, his gaze traveling over me with unabashed hunger.

I lick my lips, staring up at him. In the bright sunlight, he's almost unbearably beautiful, the new scars somehow only adding to his stark masculinity. From his shoulders to his calves, every inch of his body is packed with lean, hard muscle. His powerful chest is dusted with dark hair, and his abs are clearly defined, with a line of hair trailing down from his navel into his shorts.

He's stunning, more gorgeous than any man I've known—and I want him.

I want him despite last night, despite everything.

"How are you feeling, baby?" he asks, his voice low and husky. "Any nausea? Tiredness?"

"No." I sit up, swinging my feet to the ground, and put down the textbook. "I'm okay today."

Julian sits down next to me and tucks a strand of my hair behind my ear. "Good," he says softly. "I'm glad."

"Did you come out for a swim?" I try to ignore the warmth pooling between my thighs at his touch. "I thought you would go to your office."

"I did, just for a few minutes, but I'm taking the rest of the day off."

"Really?" Julian's days off are so rare they're practically nonexistent. "Why?"

He gives me a wry smile. "I couldn't focus."

"Oh." I regard him cautiously. "Do you want to go for a swim then? I was thinking of diving in after I finished this chapter, but I can go now."

"Sure." Julian rises to his feet and offers me his hand. "Let's go."

I place my hand in his and let him lead me to the pool. As we approach the water, he suddenly bends down, slides his arm under my knees, and picks me up.

Startled, I laugh, wrapping my arms around his neck. "Julian! Don't throw me in! I like to walk in slowly—"

"I wouldn't throw you in, my pet," he murmurs, holding me as he descends into the pool. His eyes gleam with unexpected humor. "What kind of monster do you think I am?"

"Um, do I have to answer that?" I can't believe I'm in the mood to tease him, but I feel ridiculously lighthearted all of a sudden. Some weird hormonal fluctuation, no doubt, but I don't mind. I'll take lighthearted over depressed any day of the week.

"You do have to answer," he says, a wicked grin appearing on his face. The water is now up to his waist, and he stops, holding me against his chest. "Or else..."

"Or else what?"

"This." Julian lowers me a few inches, letting my dangling feet touch the water. He tries for a menacing scowl, but I can see the corners of his mouth twitching with a suppressed smile.

"Are you threatening me with a dunking, sir?" Wiggling my right foot in the water, I give him a look of mock reproof. "I thought we just established that you wouldn't throw me in?"

"Who said anything about throwing?" He steps further into the pool, letting the water creep higher up my calves. His fake scowl disappears, edged out by a darkly sensual smile. "There are other ways to deal with naughty girls."

"Oh, do tell..." My inner muscles clench at the images flooding my mind. "What kind of ways?"

"Well, for starters"—he bends his head, his lips nearly touching mine as I hold my breath in anticipation—"some cooling off is required."

And before I can react, he sinks down, lowering us both into the water—which immediately engulfs me up to my chin.

"Julian!" Laughing in outrage, I release my grip on his neck and push at his shoulders. The pool is heated, but the water is still cool compared to my sun-warmed skin. "You said you wouldn't!"

"I said I wouldn't throw you," he corrects, his wicked grin returning. "I didn't say anything about carrying you in."

"Okay, that's it." I succeed at slipping out of his hold and putting a couple of feet of distance between us. "You want war? You have it, mister!" Scooping up water with my palm, I throw it at him and watch, laughing, as it hits him square in the face.

He wipes the water away, blinking in stunned disbelief, and I back away, laughing even harder.

Recovering from his shock, he begins to advance toward me. "Did you just splash me?" His voice is low and threatening. "Did you just throw water in my face, my pet?"

"What? No!" I mockingly bat my eyelashes as I attempt to retreat to the deeper end of the pool. "I wouldn't dare—" My words end in a squeal as Julian lunges for me, closing the distance between us in a blink of an eye. At the last moment, I manage to jump out of his reach and start swimming away, still laughing hysterically.

I'm a good swimmer, but less than two seconds pass before Julian's steely fingers close around my ankle. "Gotcha," he says, dragging me toward him. When I'm close enough, he grabs my arm to bring me to a vertical position and wraps his muscular arms around my back, grinning at my ineffective attempts to push him away.

"Okay, you got me," I concede, laughing. "Now what?"

"Now this." Bending his head, he kisses me, the warmth from his large body counteracting the coolness of the water.

As his tongue invades my mouth, I tense involuntarily, memories of last night surfacing with sudden clarity. For a few dark moments, I relive the terrible feeling of helplessness, of painful betrayal, and I know I wasn't entirely successful at compartmentalizing the good and the bad. As much as I'd like to pretend that today is a day like any other, it's not, and no amount of playful laughter changes the fact that the evil in Julian's soul will never be completely eradicated.

That the monster will always lie in wait.

And yet, as he continues kissing me, the heat of desire grows within me, luring me under its spell. He's tender with me now, and my body softens, basking in that tenderness, in the insidious warmth of his embrace. I want to believe in the illusion of his caring, in the mirage of his twisted love, and so I let the dark memories fade, leaving me in the brighter present.

Leaving me with the man I love.

9

---

JULIAN

*N*ora and I end up swimming and playing in the pool until Ana comes looking for us, saying that lunch is ready. By then I'm starving, and I'm guessing Nora must be hungry as well. I'm also suffering from blue balls from all that making out, but that's something that will have to wait until later.

I want Nora to eat even more than I want to fuck her.

Seeing my pet like this—so happy, vibrant, and carefree—has gone a long way toward easing the heavy pressure in my chest, but it hasn't removed it completely. The look on her face after I took her... It haunts me, invading my thoughts despite my best efforts to put it out of my mind. I know I've done worse to her in the past, but something about last night *felt* worse.

It felt like I wronged her.

Perhaps it's because she's now completely mine. I no longer have to condition her, to mold her into what I need her to be. She loves me enough to risk her life for me, enough to want to be with me of her own free will. Everything I've done to her in the past was calculated to a certain extent, but last night I hurt her without meaning to.

I hurt her when all I wanted was to hold her, heal her.

I hurt the woman who's carrying my child—and even if Nora seems to have forgiven me for that, I can't forgive myself.

"What can I get for you, Nora?" Ana asks when we're seated at the dining room table. The older woman is beaming at my wife, as happy as I've ever seen her. "Some toast? Maybe a little plain rice?"

Nora's eyes widen at the housekeeper's words, but she manages to say calmly, "I'll have whatever you prepared, Ana. I'm better today, really."

Despite my earlier thoughts, I can't help smiling. Goldberg must've let something slip, or else Ana overheard us talking this morning. That's why Ana's smile is wide enough to swallow up her whole face: she knows about Nora's pregnancy and is overjoyed at the news.

At Nora's reassurance, Ana's expression brightens even more. "Oh, good. I realize now that you must've been baby-sick yesterday. It happens, you know," she says in a conspiratorial tone. "Right around six weeks is when they say it starts."

"Oh, great." Nora tries to keep the glumness out of her voice, but she's not entirely successful. "Looking forward to it."

"I'll make sure you have the best care, baby," I murmur, reaching across the table to cover Nora's delicate hand with mine. "I'll get you whatever you need to feel well."

I already contacted the obstetrician Goldberg recommended, emailing her while Nora was having her examination. I might not have planned to have this child, but now that it's here, the thought of something happening to it is unbearable. When Goldberg hinted at the possibility of abortion today, it was all I could do not to rip his throat out.

Planned or not, this child is my flesh and blood, and I'll kill anyone who tries to harm it.

Nora gives me a small smile. "I'm sure it will be fine. Women have children all the time." Despite her reassuring words, her voice sounds strained, and I know she's still uneasy with this development.

Uneasy with the fact that she's carrying my baby.

Taking a deep breath, I suppress the instinctive swell of anger. On a rational level, I understand her fear. Nora loves me, but she's not blind to my nature.

She can't be, especially after last night.

"Yes, it will be fine," I say evenly, giving her hand a gentle squeeze before releasing it. "I'll make sure of it."

And for the remainder of the meal, we avoid the topic, both of us more than happy to focus on something else.

I spend the rest of the day with Nora, completely ignoring the work that's waiting for me. For the first time in ages, I can't bring myself to care about manufacturing issues in Malaysia or the fact that the Mexican cartel is demanding lower prices on customized machine guns. The Ukrainians are trying to make amends and bribe me out of my alliance with the Russians, Interpol is up in arms about the CIA sending me Peter Sokolov's list, a new terrorist group in Iraq wants to get on the waiting list for the explosive, and I don't give a fuck about any of that.

All that matters to me today is Nora.

After lunch, we go for a walk around the estate, and I show her some of my favorite boyhood haunts, including a small lake on the edge of the property where I once encountered a jaguar.

"Really? A jaguar?" Nora's eyes are wide as we exit the forested area and emerge onto a small, grassy clearing in front of the lake. The tall trees surrounding it provide both shade and privacy from the guards—which is why I frequently spent time there as a child.

"They come out of the jungle sometimes," I say in response to Nora's question. "It's rare, but it happens."

"How did you get away from it?" She gives me a concerned look. "You said you were only nine."

"I had a gun with me."

"So you killed it?"

"No. I shot a tree next to it and scared it off." I could've killed it—my aim was excellent by then—but the thought of harming the fierce creature had been repellent for some reason. It wasn't the jaguar's fault it had been born a predator, and I didn't want to punish it for having the misfortune of wandering into human territory.

"What did your parents say when you told them about it?" Nora sits down on a broken tree trunk and looks up at me. Her smooth shoulders gleam with the light reflected off the lake. "Mine would've been terrified for me."

"I didn't tell them." I sit down next to her and, unable to resist, bend my head to press a kiss to her right shoulder. Her skin smells delicious, and the hunger ignited by our play at the pool returns, my body hardening at her proximity once more.

"Why not?" she asks huskily, turning to look at me as I lift my head. "Why didn't you tell them?"

"My mother was already frightened of the jungle, and my father would've been upset that I didn't bring him the jaguar's pelt. So there was no point in telling either of them," I explain. Reaching for her hair, I thread my fingers through the thick, silky mass, enjoying the sensuous feel of it sliding through my hands. My cock is stiff with need, but this is as far as I intend to take it for now.

There won't be sex until tonight, when she's comfortable in our bed and I can be sure I won't hurt her.

"Oh." Nora tilts her head, moving it closer to my hands, and regards me through half-closed eyelids. Her expression is reminiscent of a cat being petted. "What about your friends? Did you tell them what happened?"

"No," I murmur, my arousal growing despite my good intentions. "I didn't tell anyone."

"Why not?" Nora all but purrs as I slide my fingers through her hair again, lightly massaging her scalp in the process. "You didn't think they would believe you?"

"No, I knew they would believe me." I withdraw my hands from her hair as my need intensifies, threatening my self-control. "I just didn't have close friends, that's all."

Something uncomfortably close to pity flickers in her gaze, but she doesn't say anything or ask any follow-up questions. Instead, she leans closer and presses her lips to mine, her small hands coming up to rest on both sides of my face.

Her touch is strangely innocent and uncertain, as if she's kissing me for the first time. Her lips just barely graze mine, each touch a hint, a promise of more to come. I can almost taste her, almost feel her, and the urge to fuck her is so strong I shudder with it. It's only the memory of last night—of the wounded, betrayed look in her eyes—that enables me to stay still and accept her not-quite-kisses, my hands resting on her shoulders. I know I should stop her, push her away, but I can't.

Her hesitant kisses are the sweetest thing I've ever felt.

When I think I can't bear much more, her hot little mouth moves to my jaw and then trails down my neck, kissing and nibbling with the same torturous gentleness. Her hands release my face and slide down my body, her fingers closing around the bottom edge of my shirt. She begins to lift the shirt, and I groan as her knuckles brush against my naked sides, her touch leaving my skin burning in its wake.

"Nora…" I suck in my breath as she scoots down and kneels between my spread legs, her face at the level of my navel. "Nora, baby, you need to stop teasing me."

She ignores my directive, keeping my shirt bunched up. "Who's teasing?" she whispers, looking up at me. And before I can respond, she leans in and places a warm, damp kiss on my stomach.

*Fuck.* My entire body jerks, my balls tightening on a savage surge of lust. The sight of her kneeling there pushes my buttons in all the wrong ways, calling to my darkest desires. My hands knot into fists, and I take short, deep breaths, reminding myself that she's fragile right now.

That she's pregnant with my child, and I can't take her like an animal again.

Except she's licking my stomach now. *Fucking licking it.* Tracing each muscle indentation with her tongue, like she's trying to imprint it on her memory.

"Nora." My voice is hoarse. "Baby, that's enough."

She pulls back, looking up at me through those long, thick lashes of hers. "Are you sure?" she murmurs, still not letting go of my shirt. "Because I think I want more." And leaning in again, she scrapes her teeth over my lower abs, then sucks on the spot, her mouth hot and wet on my bare skin.

Skin that's right next to the throbbing cock still confined in my shorts.

*Fucking hell.*

"Nora..." I can barely form the words, my fingers digging into the bark of the tree in an effort not to grab her. "You don't want this, baby, stop it—"

"Who said that I don't want it?" Moving back, she looks up at me again, her gaze dark and heated. "I do want it, Julian... You made me want it."

I suck in a hard breath, my cock jerking as she releases my shirt and reaches for my belt buckle instead. "I don't want to hurt you."

Her lips curve up. "Yes, Julian, you do." She succeeds in undoing the belt, and her hand delves into my shorts, her slender fingers closing around my swollen length and squeezing lightly. "Don't you?"

I nearly explode, my hands reaching for her before

I even realize what I'm doing. "Yes…" My voice is closer to a growl as I drag her onto my lap, forcing her to straddle my legs. "I want to hurt you, fuck you, take you in every way possible and then some. I want to mark your pretty skin and hear you scream as I drive deep into your pussy and make you come all over my cock. Is that what you want to hear, my pet?" Gripping her arms tightly, I glare at her. "Is that what you want?"

She runs her tongue over her lips, her eyes gleaming with a peculiar darkness. "Yes." Her voice is whisper-soft. "Yes, Julian. That's exactly what I want."

*Fuck.* I close my eyes, literally shaking with lust. With the way she's straddling my lap in her dress, only a tiny thong separates her pussy from my dick. If I shift her up a few inches, I could be inside her, pounding her tight little body…

The temptation is unbearable.

*One, one thousand. Two, one thousand. Three, one thousand.* I force myself to do the mental count until I regain a modicum of control.

Then I open my eyes and meet her gaze again.

"No, Nora." My voice is almost steady as I let go of her arms and move my hands up to cup her face in my palms instead. "That's not how this is going to go."

She blinks, looking taken aback. "What—"

I bend my head, cutting her off with a kiss. Slowly and deeply, I invade her mouth, tasting her, stroking her with my tongue. Then I fist my hand in her hair and push her down between my legs, enjoying the look of shock on her small face.

"You're going to suck my cock," I say harshly. "And then, if you're a good girl, you'll get your reward. Understand?"

Nora's eyes widen, but she complies right away. Pulling my dick out of my shorts, she closes her lips around it and begins to stroke it rhythmically with her hand. The interior of her mouth is hot, silky, and wet, almost as delicious as her pussy, and the pressure of her hand is nothing short of perfect. I'm so near the edge all it takes is a couple of minutes, and the orgasm boils out of my balls, blasting ecstasy through my nerve endings. Groaning, I grip her hair and push deeper into her throat, forcing her to swallow every drop.

Then I pull out, kneel on the ground next to her, and make her lie down on the grass. "Spread open your legs," I order, tugging her dress up to expose her lower body.

She does as I instruct, her gaze filled with anticipation and a hint of wariness. I place my hands on her sleek, tan thighs and stroke them, enjoying the delicate texture of her skin. Then I bend down, hook my fingers into her pink thong, and pull it aside, exposing her glistening pussy lips.

"You have such a sexy pussy, baby." The words come out low and raspy as my hunger, just barely quelled, returns with a vengeance. Bending lower, I inhale her sweet, musky scent. "Such a beautiful, wet little pussy."

Her breathing hitches, a moan vibrating in her throat

as I press my lips to her folds, kissing them lightly. "Julian, please." She sounds tortured. "Please, I—I need you."

"Yes." I let my breath wash over her sensitive flesh. "I know you do." I give her slit a long, slow lick. "You'll always need me, won't you?"

"Yes." She pushes her hips up, begging. "Always."

"Then, my pet, here's your reward."

Pressing my tongue to her clit, I begin pleasuring her in earnest, drinking in her pleas and moans. When she finally shudders and cries out in release, I lap at her a few more times, drawing out her orgasm, and then I move up to lie beside her on the grass, folding my left arm under my head as a pillow and arranging her head on my right shoulder.

We lie like that for a while, gazing out at the shimmering water of the lake and listening to the quiet chirping of insects. I still want her, but the desire is more mellow now. More controlled. I didn't hurt her this time, but the heaviness in my chest is still there, still weighing on me.

Finally, I can no longer remain silent.

"Nora, last night... it wasn't because of Peter's list." I don't know why I feel compelled to tell her this, but I do. I want her to understand that I didn't intend to punish her at that moment, that the pain I inflicted was not part of some cruel design. I don't know why that would matter to her, coming from her kidnapper, or what the distinction really is, but I need her to know this. "It was a mistake. It shouldn't have happened."

She doesn't respond, doesn't acknowledge my words in any way, but after a few moments, she turns in my arms and rests her right hand on my chest, directly over my heart.

## 10

NORA

*O*ver the next two weeks, I do my best to manage the new reality of my situation. Or, more precisely, to go about my life and pretend that nothing's happening.

The nausea comes and goes. I've found that eating small, frequent meals helps, as does sticking to plainer foods. Under Ana's and Julian's watchful eyes, I dutifully take prenatal vitamins and avoid the foods on Dr. Goldberg's list, but I try not to dwell on those things. Until the baby bump shows up, I intend to act as if everything's normal.

Thankfully, my body is cooperating for now. My breasts have gotten a little bigger, and they're more sensitive, but that's the only change I've detected. My stomach is still flat, and I haven't gained any weight. If anything, because of my unsettled tummy, I lost a couple of pounds—a fact that worries Julian, who's doing his best to coddle me into madness.

"I don't need to rest," I protest in exasperation as he once again tries to make me nap in the middle of the day. "Really, I'm fine. I slept ten hours last night. How much sleep does a person need?"

And it's true. For the past couple of weeks, I've been sleeping much better. As strange as it is, knowing that my anxiety has a hormonal cause has alleviated it to a large extent, significantly reducing my nightmares and panic attacks.

My shrink tells me it's because I'm less worried about my head being messed up from everything that's happened. Apparently, stressing about being overly stressed is particularly bad for the psyche, whereas less convoluted stress factors—like having a child with a sadistic arms dealer—are less anxiety-provoking.

"The human brain is highly unpredictable," Dr. Wessex says, looking at me through her trendy Prada glasses. "What you *think* scares you might not be what weighs on your subconscious at all. You may worry about this baby, but it doesn't frighten you as much as the thought that you might never get a grip on your anxiety. If your panic attacks stem from pregnancy, then you know it's a temporary issue—and that helps you feel less anxious about it."

I nod and smile, as if that makes perfect sense. I do that a lot when I talk to her. If Julian didn't insist that I continue my twice-weekly therapy sessions, I would've already stopped them. It's not that I dislike Dr. Wessex—

a tall, stylish woman in her mid-forties, she's quite competent and seemingly nonjudgmental—but I find that talking to her just highlights the insanity that is my relationship with Julian.

*Why, yes, Doctor, my husband—you know, the man who hired you and insisted you come out to the middle of nowhere—kept me captive on his island for fifteen months, and now I'm so brainwashed I can't live without him and crave abusive sex. Oh, and we're having a baby. Nothing fucked up about that, of course. Just your regular, run-of-the-mill crime family.*

Yeah, sure.

In any case, trying to get me to take naps is the least egregious example of Julian's excessive coddling. He also monitors my diet, makes sure that the exercise routine I resumed is fully doctor-approved, and worst of all, treats me with kid gloves in bed. No matter how much I try to provoke him, he won't do more than hold me down in bed. It's as if he's afraid to unleash the brutality within himself, to lose control again.

"I told you, the obstetrician said rougher sex is okay as long as there's no spotting or leaking of amniotic fluid," I tell Julian after he takes me gently yet again. "I'm healthy, everything's normal, so there's really no harm."

"I'm not taking any chances," he replies, kissing the outer rim of my ear, and I know he has no intention of listening to me on the topic.

A part of me still can't believe that I want this from him, that I miss the dark edge to our lovemaking. It's not that I'm ever left unsatisfied—Julian makes sure I have at least a couple of orgasms every night—but something within me craves the intoxicating blend of pleasure-pain, the endorphin rush I get from truly intense sex. Even the fear he makes me feel is addictive in some way, whether I want to admit it or not.

It's sick, but the night we learned about my pregnancy—the night he forced me—has featured in my fantasies more than once in recent days.

What Dr. Wessex would say about that I don't know, and I don't care to find out. It's enough that the memory of that trauma, just like the recollections of my time on the island, have somehow taken on an erotic overtone in my mind.

It's enough to know that I'm completely twisted.

Of course, Julian's uncharacteristic gentleness in bed is not the only issue. Another casualty of his smothering concern for me is my self-defense training. It's particularly frustrating because for the first time in weeks, I have energy. Sleeping well has reduced my fatigue, and schoolwork no longer tires me as much. I've even been able to resume running—after first pre-clearing the activity with the doctor, of course—but Julian refuses to let me do anything that could possibly result in bruises. Shooting is also out of the question; apparently, firing a gun releases lead particles that could, in some unknown quantity, harm the unborn baby.

There are so many restrictions it makes me want to scream.

"You know this is only temporary, Nora," Ana says when I make the mistake of expressing my frustration to her at breakfast. "Just a few more months, and you'll have a baby in your arms—and then it will all be worth it."

I nod and paste a smile on my face, but the housekeeper's words don't cheer me up.

They fill me with dread.

In a little over seven months, I will be responsible for a child—and the idea terrifies me more than ever.

"You still haven't told your parents about the baby?" Rosa gives me an astonished look as we leave the house to go for our morning walk.

"No," I say, sipping a fruit smoothie with powdered vitamins. "I haven't gotten around to it yet."

"But I thought you talk to them every day."

"I do, but the subject hasn't come up." I probably sound defensive, but I can't help it. In terms of things I dread, telling my parents about my pregnancy is right up there with childbirth.

"Nora…" Rosa stops under a thick, vine-draped tree. "Are you worried they won't be happy for you?"

I picture my dad's probable reaction to learning that his not-quite-twenty-year-old daughter is pregnant with her kidnapper's child. "You could say that."

"But why wouldn't they be happy?" My friend looks genuinely confused. "You're married to a wealthy man who loves you and who'll take good care of you and the child. What more could they want?"

"Well, for one thing, for me not to be married to said man at all," I say drily. "Rosa, I told you our story. My parents aren't exactly Julian's biggest fans."

Rosa waves a dismissive hand. "All that is—how do you say it?—water under the bridge. Who cares how it all began? What matters is the present, not the past."

"Oh, sure. Seize the day and all that."

"There's no need to be sarcastic," Rosa says as we resume our walk. "You should talk to your parents, Nora. It's their grandchild. They deserve to know."

"Yeah, I'll probably tell them soon." I take another sip of my smoothie. "I'll have no choice."

We walk in silence for a couple of minutes. Then Rosa asks quietly, "You really don't want this child, do you, Nora?"

I stop and look at her. "Rosa . . ." How do I explain my concerns to a girl who grew up on the estate and who thinks that this kind of life is normal? That my relationship with Julian is romantic? "It's not that I don't want a baby. It's just that Julian's world—*our* world—is too fucked up to bring a child into it. How could somebody like Julian make a good father? How could I make a good mother?"

"What do you mean?" Rosa frowns at me. "Why wouldn't you make a good mother?"

"I'm in love with a crime lord who abducted me, and who kills and tortures people as part of his business," I say gently. "That hardly qualifies me to be a good parent. A case study for one of Dr. Wessex's papers, maybe, but not a good parent."

"Oh, please." Rosa rolls her eyes. "A lot of men do bad things. You Americans are so sensitive. Señor Esguerra is far from the worst there is, and you shouldn't blame yourself for caring about him. That doesn't make *you* bad in any way."

"Rosa, it's not just that." I hesitate, but then decide to just say it. "When we were in Tajikistan, I killed a man." I exhale slowly, reliving the dark thrill of pulling the trigger and watching Majid's brains splatter all over the wall. "I shot him in cold blood."

"So what?" She hardly blinks. "I've killed too."

I gape at her, stunned into silence, and she explains, "It was when the estate was attacked. I found a gun, hid in the bushes, and shot at the men attacking us. I wounded one and killed another. I later learned that the wounded one died too."

"But you were only a child." I can't get over my shock. "You're telling me you killed two people when you were what—ten, eleven?"

"Almost eleven," she says, shrugging. "And yes, I did."

"But… but you seem so—"

"Normal?" she supplies, looking at me with a

strange smile. "Nice? Of course, why wouldn't I be? I killed to protect those I care about. I killed men who came here to bring us death and destruction. It's no different from cutting off the head of the snake that wants to bite you. If I hadn't killed them, more of our people would've died. Maybe they would've killed my mother, as well as my father and brother."

I don't know what to say to that. I could never have imagined that Rosa—cheerful, round-cheeked Rosa— was capable of something like that. I've always thought that evil leaves a trace. I see it in Julian, etched so deeply into his soul that it's a part of him. I see it in myself now, too. But I don't see it in Rosa. Not at all.

"How do you not let it affect you?" I ask. *How do you retain your innocence?*

She looks at me, and for the first time, she appears older than her twenty-one years. "You can choose to let the black stuff tarnish you, Nora, or you can brush it off," she says quietly. "I chose the latter. I killed, but that's not who I am. I don't let that act define me. It happened, and it's done. It's in the past. I can't change the past, so I'm not going to dwell on it. And neither should you. Your present, your future—that's what matters."

I bite my lip, my eyes beginning to burn incipient tears. "But what kind of future can this child have with parents like us, Rosa? Look at what's happened to me and Julian over the past two years. How can I be sure my baby won't be kidnapped or tortured by Julian's enemies?"

"You can't be sure." Rosa's gaze is unflinching. "Nobody can be sure of anything. Bad things can happen to anyone, anywhere. There are soldiers who live to a ripe old age, and office workers who die young. There's no rhyme or reason to life, Nora. You can choose to live every moment in fear, or you can enjoy life. Enjoy what you have with Julian. Enjoy this baby you have growing inside you. It's a gift, not a curse, to bring forth life. You might not have chosen to bring a child into this world, but it's here now, and all you can do is love it. Treasure it. Don't let your fears spoil it for you." She pauses, and then adds softly, "Don't let your soul get tarnished by what you can't change."

## 11

### JULIAN

"So what's the damage?" I ask Lucas as we leave the training area. I'm breathing hard, my muscles are sore, and my left shoulder is aching, but I feel satisfied.

I'm nearly back to my former fighting shape—as the three guards limping away can testify.

"There was another hit in France, and two more in Germany." Lucas wipes the sweat off his face with a balled-up towel. "He's not wasting any time."

"I didn't think he would." Given Peter Sokolov's singular focus on revenge, I know it's only a matter of time before he eliminates the rest of the men on that list. "How did he do it this time?"

"The French guy was found floating in a river, with marks of torture and strangulation, so I'm guessing Sokolov must've kidnapped him first. For the Germans, one hit was a car bomb, and the other one a sniper rifle."

Lucas grins darkly. "They must not have pissed him off as much."

"Or he went for expediency."

"Or that," Lucas agrees. "He probably knows Interpol is on his tail."

"I'm sure he does." I try to imagine what I would do if someone hurt my family, and a shudder of fury ripples through me. I can't even imagine what Peter must be feeling—not that it excuses his endangering Nora to get this fucking list.

I still want to kill him for that.

"By the way," Lucas says casually, "I'm having Yulia Tzakova brought here from Moscow."

I stop dead in my tracks. "The interpreter who betrayed us to the Ukrainians? Why?"

"I want to personally interrogate her," Lucas says, draping the towel around his neck. "I don't trust the Russians to do a thorough job." His expression is as impassive as ever, but I see a hint of excitement in his pale gaze.

He's looking forward to this.

I narrow my eyes, studying him. "Is it because you fucked her that night in Moscow?" The Russian girl came on to me first, but I passed on her invitation—and then Lucas expressed an interest in her. "Is that what this is about?"

His mouth hardens. "She fucked me over. Literally. So yeah, I want to get my hands on the little bitch. But I also think she might have some useful info for us."

I consider that for a moment, then nod. "In that case, go for it." It would be hypocritical of me to deny Lucas some fun with the pretty blonde. If he wants to personally make her pay for the plane crash, I see no harm in that.

She would've been dead before long in Moscow anyway.

"Did you already negotiate this with the Russians?" I ask as we resume walking.

Lucas nods. "Initially, they tried to say they'd only deal with Sokolov, but I convinced them it wouldn't be wise to get on your bad side. Buschekov saw the light when I reminded him of the recent troubles at Al-Quadar."

"Good." If even the Russians are inclined to accommodate me, then my vendetta against the terrorist organization achieved its intended effect. Not only is Al-Quadar utterly decimated, but my reputation is substantially enhanced. Few of my clients are likely to double-cross me now—a development that promises to be good for business.

"Yes, it's helpful," Lucas echoes my thoughts. "She'll be arriving here tomorrow."

I raise my eyebrows, but decide against commenting on the speed of this development. If he wants to play with the Russian girl this badly, it's his business. "Where are you going to keep her?" I ask instead.

"In my quarters. I'll be interrogating her there."

I grin, picturing the interrogation in question. "All right. Enjoy."

"Oh, I will," he says grimly. "You can bet on it."

~

After I take a shower, I go looking for Nora. Or, rather, I check my computer for the location of her embedded trackers and go directly to the library, where she must be studying for her finals.

I find her sitting at a desk facing away from me, typing furiously on her laptop. Her hair is tied up in a loose ponytail, and she's wearing a huge T-shirt that falls down to her knees.

*My* T-shirt, from the looks of it.

She's started doing that lately when she has to study. Claims my T-shirts are more comfortable than her dresses. I don't mind in the least. Seeing her dressed in my clothes only emphasizes the fact that she's mine.

Both she and the baby she's carrying.

She doesn't react as I step into the room and walk up to her. When I reach her, I see why.

She's wearing headphones, her smooth forehead wrinkled in concentration as she pounds at the keyboard, her fingers flying over the keys with startling speed. For a second, I consider leaving her to it, but it's too late. Nora must've seen me out of the corner of her eye, because she looks up and gives me a dazzling smile, removing her headphones.

"Hi." Her voice is soft and a little husky. "Is it dinnertime already?"

"Not quite." I smile back and place my hands on the nape of her neck. Her muscles feel tight, so I begin kneading them with my thumbs. "I just did a few rounds with my men and came here to take a shower before I go back to my office. Figured I'd check on you on the way."

"Oh." She arches into my touch, closing her eyes. "Oh, yeah, right there... Oh, that's so good..."

She sounds like I'm fucking her, and my response is instantaneous.

I get hard. Very hard.

*Fuck.*

Drawing in a breath, I rein in my lust, like I've been doing for the past two weeks. When I take her tonight, it will again be in a careful and controlled manner. Regardless of the provocation, I will not risk damaging the baby.

"Is that your Psychology paper?" I keep my tone even as I continue to massage her neck. "You seem to be really into it."

"Oh, yeah." She opens her eyes and tilts her head to look at me. "It's on Stockholm Syndrome."

My hands still. "Is that right?"

She nods, a dark little smile curving her lips. "Yes. Interesting subject, don't you think?"

"Yes, fascinating," I say drily. My pet is definitely getting bolder. Taunting me—likely in the hopes that I'll punish her.

And I want to. My hands itch to bend her over my knee, hike up that giant T-shirt, and spank her perfectly shaped ass until it's pink and red. My cock throbs at the image, especially when I imagine spreading open her cheeks afterwards and penetrating her tight little asshole—

*Fucking stop thinking about it.* I see Nora's smile deepen as her eyes flick down to the bulge in my jeans. The little witch knows exactly what she's doing to me, what kind of effect she's having on my body.

"Yes, I'm loving it," she murmurs, her gaze returning to my face. "I'm learning so much about the topic."

I inhale slowly and resume rubbing her neck. "Then you'll have to educate me, my pet," I say calmly, as if my body isn't raging with the need to fuck her. "I'm afraid I skipped Psychology at Caltech."

Nora's smile turns sardonic. "You're just a natural then, aren't you?"

I hold her gaze silently, not bothering to reply. There's no need for words. I saw her, I wanted her, and I took her. It's as simple as that. If she wants to label our relationship, to make it fit some psychobabble definition, she's free to do so.

She'll just never be free of me.

After a few moments, she sighs and closes her eyes, leaning into my touch again. I can feel her muscles slowly relaxing as I massage her shoulders and neck. The challenging expression fades from her face, leaving her looking peculiarly young and defenseless. With her eyelashes fanning over her smooth cheeks, she seems as innocent as a newborn fawn, untouched by anything bad in life.

Untouched by me.

For a moment, I wonder what it would be like if things were different. If I were just a boy she met in school, like that Jake I took her from. Would she love me more? Would she love me at all? If I didn't take her the way I did, would she have been mine?

It's foolish to wonder about that, of course. I might as well speculate about time travel or what I'd do if the world came to an end. My reality doesn't allow for what-ifs. What if my parents didn't die and I finished Caltech? What if I'd refused to kill that man when I was eight? What if I'd been able to protect Maria? If I think about all that, I'll go insane, and I refuse to let that happen.

I am what I am, and I can't change.

Not even for her.

"I talked to my parents this afternoon," Nora says as we sit down to dinner that evening. "They asked me again about visiting them."

"Did they now?" I give her a sardonic look. "And is that all you talked to them about?"

Nora looks down at her salad plate. "I'm going to tell them soon."

"When?" It pisses me off that she keeps acting like the baby doesn't exist. "When you deliver?"

"No, of course not." She looks up and frowns at me. "How do you know I didn't tell them yet, anyway? Are you listening in on my conversations?"

"Of course." I don't listen in on everything, but I've eavesdropped a few times. Just enough to know that her parents remain in blissful ignorance of the latest development in their daughter's life. Still, it wouldn't hurt to have Nora think all her conversations are monitored. "Did you expect me not to?"

Her lips tighten. "Yes, perhaps. Privacy being a basic human right and all that."

"There's no such thing as a basic human right, my pet." I want to laugh at her naïveté. "That's a made-up construct. Nobody owes you anything. If you want something in life, you have to fight for it. You have to make it happen."

"Like you made my captivity happen?"

I give her a cool smile. "Precisely. I wanted you, so I took you. I didn't sit around pining and wishing."

"Or dwelling on the construct of human rights, apparently." Her voice holds just the faintest edge of sarcasm. "Is that how you will raise our child? Just take what you want and don't worry about hurting people?"

I inhale slowly, noting the tension in her features. "Is that what worries you, my pet?"

"A lot of things worry me," she says evenly. "And yes, raising a child with a man who lacks a conscience is fairly high on the list."

For some reason, her words sting. I want to reassure her, tell her that she's wrong to worry, but I can't lie to her any more than I can lie to myself.

I have no idea how I'm going to raise this child, what kind of lessons I'm going to impart. Men like me—men like my father—aren't meant to have children. She knows it, and I know it too.

As though sensing my thoughts, Nora asks quietly, "Why do you even want this baby, Julian? Why is it so important to you?"

I look at her silently, unsure how to answer the question. There's no good reason for this child to be as important to me as it is. No reason for me to want it as badly as I do. I should've been upset—or at the very least, annoyed—by Nora's pregnancy, but instead, when Goldberg gave us the news, the emotion I felt was so foreign that I didn't recognize it at first.

It was joy.

Pure, unadulterated joy.

For a brief, blissful moment, I was truly happy.

When I don't respond, Nora exhales and looks down at her plate again. I watch as she cuts a piece of tomato and begins to eat her salad. Her face is pale and strained, yet each of her movements is so graceful and feminine that I'm hypnotized, completely absorbed by the sight of her.

I can watch her for hours.

When I first brought her to the island, the mealtimes were my favorite part of the day. I loved interacting with her, seeing her battle her fear and try to maintain her composure. Her stoic, fragile bravery had delighted me almost as much as her delicious body. She'd been terrified, yet I could see the calculation behind her timid smiles and shy flirting.

In her own quiet way, my pet has always been a fighter.

"Nora..." I want to take away her stress, her understandable worry, but I can't lie to her. I can't pretend to be someone I'm not. So when she looks up, I say only, "This baby is part you, part me. That's reason enough for me to care." And when she continues to look at me, her expression unchanging, I add quietly, "I'm going to do the best I can for our child, my pet. That much I can promise you."

The corners of her lips lift in a fleeting smile. "Of course you will, Julian. And so will I. But will that be enough?"

"We'll just have to wait and see, won't we?" I respond, and as Ana brings out the next course, we focus on the food and let the topic rest.

## NORA

"*D*id you see the girl who was brought here this morning?" Rosa asks during our usual walk. "Ana said she was handcuffed and everything."

"What?" I give Rosa a startled look. "What girl? I went for a quick run before breakfast, and I didn't see anything."

"I didn't see anything either. Ana told me she spotted her, and she's really blond and beautiful. Apparently, Lucas Kent is keeping her in his quarters." Rosa is clearly relishing imparting this bit of gossip. "Ana thinks she might've betrayed Señor Esguerra in some way."

"Really?" I frown. "I don't know anything about any of this. Julian didn't mention it to me." In general, since I hacked into Julian's computer, he's been telling me less about his business. I don't know if that's because he now distrusts me or because he's trying to keep me as calm as possible in light of the pregnancy. I suspect it's the latter, given how overprotective he is these days.

"Do you want to walk by Kent's house to see?" Rosa's eyes glitter with excitement. "Maybe we can peek in his window."

I gape at her. "Rosa!" This is the last thing I would've expected from her. "We can't do that."

"Come on," my friend cajoles. "It'll be fun. Don't you want to see who this blond girl is and why Kent's got her?"

"I can just ask Julian about it. He'll tell me."

Rosa gives me a pleading look. "Yes, but I might die of curiosity before he does. I just want to see what Kent's doing with her, that's all."

"Why?" I have no desire to see Julian's right-hand man torture some unfortunate woman, and I have no idea why Rosa wants to witness something so disturbing. "If she betrayed Julian, it won't be pretty." My stomach lurches at the thought. Today is not one of my better days, nausea-wise.

Rosa flushes. "Just because. Come on, Nora." Grabbing my wrist, she begins to tug me in the direction of the guards' quarters. "Let's just go over there. You're pregnant, so no one will get mad at you for snooping."

I let myself get towed behind her, flabbergasted by her inexplicable desire to play spy. Normally, Rosa displays little interest in matters concerning my husband's criminal activities. I can't fathom what's behind her unusual behavior, unless…

"Are you interested in Lucas?" I blurt out, stopping and bringing us both to a halt. "Is that what this is all about?"

"What? No!" Rosa's voice takes on a higher pitch. "I'm just curious, that's all."

I stare at her, noting the brighter blush staining her cheeks. "Oh my God, you *are* interested."

Rosa huffs and lets go of my wrist, crossing her arms over her chest. "I'm not."

I hold up my palms in a conciliatory gesture. "Okay, okay. If you say so."

Rosa glares at me for a moment, but then her shoulders slump and her arms drop to her sides. "Okay, fine," she says glumly. "So maybe I do find him attractive. Just a little bit, okay?"

"Okay, of course," I say with a reassuring smile. With his blond hair and fierce, square-jawed face, Lucas Kent reminds me of a Viking warrior—or at least Hollywood's depiction of one. "He's a good-looking man."

Rosa nods. "He is. He doesn't know that I exist, of course, but that's to be expected."

"What do you mean?" I frown at her. "Have you ever tried talking to him?"

"Talking about what? I'm just the maid who cleans the main house and occasionally brings the guards some treats from Ana."

"You can ask him what his favorite food is," I suggest. "Or how his day went. It doesn't have to be anything complicated. Just a simple hello would probably put you on his radar." As I say this, I realize that being on the radar of a man like Lucas Kent may not be the best thing for Rosa—or any woman, really.

Before I can take back my suggestion, Rosa sighs and says, "I've said hello to him before. I just don't think he *sees* me, Nora. Not like that. And why would he? I mean, look at me." She gestures derisively toward herself.

"What are you talking about?" I still don't think getting Lucas's attention would be a positive development in Rosa's life, but I can't let that comment slide. "You're very attractive."

"Oh, please." Rosa gives me an incredulous look. "I'm average at best. Someone like Kent is used to supermodels—like that blond girl he's got with him now. I'm not his type."

"Well, if you're not his type, then he's a fool," I say firmly, and mean it. With her pleasantly round face, warm brown eyes, and bright smile, Rosa is quite pretty. She also has the kind of figure I've always envied: lush and curvy, with a nipped-in waist and full breasts. "You're a beautiful girl—a guy would have to be blind not to see that."

She snorts. "Right. That's why my love life is so great."

"Your love life is limited by the borders of this

estate," I remind her. "Besides, didn't you tell me you dated a couple of the guards?"

"Oh, sure." She waves her hand dismissively. "Eduardo and Nick—but that doesn't mean anything. Guards are limited in their selection too, and they're not that picky. They'll fuck anything that moves."

"Rosa." I give her a reproving look. "Now you're just exaggerating."

She grins. "Okay, maybe. I should probably say 'anything *female* that moves'—though I hear Dr. Goldberg gets some action, too. Rumor has it tattooed guys are his fave." She waggles her eyebrows suggestively.

I shake my head, involuntarily grinning back, and we both burst into laughter at the image of the staid doctor getting it on with one of the big, tatted-up guards.

"Okay, now that we've established you're crushing on Mr. Blond and Dangerous," I say a couple of minutes later when we stop laughing and resume walking toward the guards' housing, "can you please tell me again why you want to spy on him with this chick?"

"I don't know," Rosa admits. "I just do. It's sick, I know, but I just want to see what he's like with another woman."

"Rosa..." I still don't get it. "If she arrived here in handcuffs, they're not exactly having a romantic date. You know that, right?"

"Yes, of course." She sounds remarkably flippant. "He's probably doing something horrible to her."

"And you want to see that why?"

She shrugs. "I don't know. Maybe I'm hoping that seeing him like that will help me get over this silly crush. Or maybe I'm just morbidly curious. Does it really matter?"

"No, I guess not." I hurry to keep up with her fast stride. "But I can tell you right now that Dr. Wessex would have a lot of fun with you."

"Oh, I'm sure," she says and grins at me again. "It's a good thing you're the one in therapy then, isn't it?"

The guards' barracks are on the very edge of the compound, right next to the jungle. Mixed in with the cluster of small, boxy buildings are a few regular-sized houses. From my earlier explorations, I know that they're occupied by some of the higher-ranked employees in Julian's organization and guards who have families.

As we approach, Rosa makes a beeline for one of those larger homes, and I follow her, half-running to keep up. My stomach is beginning to feel unsettled, and I'm already regretting that I gave in to this insanity.

"This is it," she says in a hushed tone as we go around the side of the house. "His bedroom is here."

"And you know this how?"

She grins at me. "I might've been out here a time or two before."

"Rosa…" I'm discovering a whole new side to my friend. "You've spied on the poor man before?"

"Just once or twice," she whispers, crouching under a window as I hang back a few feet and observe. "Now, shhh." She presses her finger to her lips in a silencing gesture.

I lean against a tree trunk, cross my arms, and watch as she slowly rises and peeks into the window. I'm astounded that she's bold enough to do this in broad daylight. Even though this side of Lucas's house faces the forest, there are plenty of guards in the area, and they could theoretically spot us hanging around.

Before I can voice that concern to Rosa, she turns toward me with a disappointed look on her face. "They're not there," she says in a low voice. "I wonder where they could be."

"Maybe he took her elsewhere," I say, relieved by this development. "Let's go."

"Hold on, let me just check something." Still crouching, she moves toward a window further to the left.

I reluctantly trail after her, increasingly nauseous and uncomfortable with the situation. Another minute, I promise myself, and I'll head back.

Just as I'm about to tell her that I'm leaving, Rosa lets out a soft gasp and waves for me to come closer. "There," she says in an excited whisper, pointing at the window. "He's got her right there."

Now my own curiosity kicks in. Bending down, I

make my way to where Rosa is hiding and crouch next to her. "What is he doing?" I whisper, almost afraid to know.

"I don't know," she whispers back, turning to look at me. "He's not in the room. She's alone there."

"What is *she* doing then?"

"See for yourself. She's not looking this way."

I hesitate for a moment, but the temptation proves to be too much. Holding my breath, I rise just enough to see over the lower rim of the window, barely cognizant of Rosa peeking in next to me.

As I feared, the view inside makes my stomach flip.

The room I'm looking at is large and sparsely furnished. Judging by the black leather sofa near the wall and the TV on the opposite side, it must be Lucas's living room. The walls are painted white, and the carpet is gray. It's a starkly masculine room, functional and uncompromising, but it's not the decor that catches my attention.

It's the young woman in the middle.

Completely naked, she's tied to a sturdy wooden chair, her feet spread apart and her hands bound behind her back. Her head is lowered, her tangled blond hair concealing her face and much of her upper body. All I can see of her are narrow feet and long pale limbs covered with bruises.

Limbs that appear far too thin for a girl of her height.

As I stare in horrified fascination, she lifts her head

in a sudden jerky movement and looks directly at me, her blue eyes sharp and clear in her delicately featured face.

I instantly duck, my pulse racing from a burst of adrenaline. Rosa, however, is still looking in the window, her expression that of avid curiosity.

"Rosa," I hiss, grabbing her arm. "She saw us. Let's go."

"Okay, okay," my friend concedes, letting me tug her away. "Let's go."

We head back toward our usual path in silence. Rosa appears to be deep in thought, and I can't bring myself to speak, my nausea intensifying with every step. As we pass by a set of rose bushes, I kneel down and throw up while Rosa holds my hair and repeatedly apologizes for causing me distress in my condition.

I wave her apologies away, shakily getting back on my feet. What disturbs me the most is not the fact that I saw a woman bound and likely about to be tortured.

It's that the sight didn't shock me as it should have.

Julian doesn't join me for dinner that night. According to Ana, he has an emergency call with one of his Hong Kong associates. I consider going to his office to listen in, but decide to use the time to call my parents instead.

"Nora, honey, when are we going to see you again?" my mom asks for the dozenth time after I give her a quick update on my classes. My dad is traveling for business, so it's just the two of us on video chat today. "I miss you so much."

"I know, Mom. I miss you too." I bite the inside of my cheek, my eyes suddenly burning with tears. *Fucking pregnancy hormones.* "I told you, Julian said we'll be able to come at some point soon."

"When?" my mom asks in frustration. "Why can't you just give us a date?"

*Because I'm pregnant, and my overprotective kidnapper/husband refuses to even talk about going anywhere right now.* "Mom…" I take a breath, trying to gather my courage. "I think there's something you should know."

My mom leans closer to the camera, instant worry creasing her forehead. "What is it, honey?"

"I'm eight weeks pregnant. Julian and I are having a baby." As soon as the words are out, I feel like a slab of granite was lifted off my shoulders. I hadn't realized until this moment how heavily this secret weighed on me.

My mom blinks. "What? Already?"

"Um, yeah." This is not the reaction I was expecting. Frowning, I lean closer to the camera. "What do you mean, *already?*"

"Well, your dad and I figured that with the two of you being married and all…" She shrugs. "I mean, we were hoping it wouldn't happen for a while, and you'd get to finish school first—"

"You figured I'd have children with Julian?" I feel like

I'm in an alternate universe. "And you're okay with that?"

My mom sighs and leans back, regarding me with a weary expression. "Of course we're not okay with that. But we can't live our lives in denial, no matter how much your dad might want to try. Obviously, this is not what we wanted for you, but—" She stops and heaves another sigh before saying, "Look, honey, if this is what you want, if he really does make you as happy as you say, then it's not our place to interfere. We just want you happy and healthy. You know that, right?"

"I do, Mom." I blink rapidly, trying to contain a fresh influx of emotional tears. "I do."

"Good." She smiles, and I'm pretty sure I see her eyes glistening with tears of her own. "Now tell me all about it. Have you been sick? Have you been tired? How did you find out? Was it an accident?"

And for the next hour, my mom and I talk about babies and pregnancy. She tells me all about her own experience—I was an oops baby for her and Dad, conceived during their honeymoon—and I explain that I hurt my arm when I was abducted by the terrorists and had to have the implant out for a short time. It's the closest I can come to the truth: that Al-Quadar cut the implant out of my arm because they mistook it for a tracking device. My parents know about my abduction from the mall—I had to explain my disappearance to them somehow—but I didn't tell them the full story.

They have no idea that their daughter acted as bait to save her abductor's life and killed a man in cold blood.

By the time we finally wrap up our conversation, it's dark outside, and I'm beginning to feel tired. As soon as we disconnect, I shower, brush my teeth, and get in bed to wait for Julian.

After a while, my eyelids grow heavy, and I feel the lethargy of sleep stealing over me. As my mind begins to drift, an image appears in front of my eyes: that of a girl bound and helpless, tied to a chair in the middle of a large, white-walled room. Her hair, however, is not blond.

It's dark… and her belly is swollen with child.

## 13

## JULIAN

*I*t's nearly midnight by the time I finish work and get to our bedroom. Entering the room, I turn on the bedside lamp and see that Nora is already asleep, curled up under the blanket. I shower and join her there, pulling her naked body to me as soon as I get under the sheets. She fits me perfectly, her curvy little ass nestling against my groin and her neck pillowed on my outstretched arm. My other arm, bent, rests on her side, my hand cupping one small, firm breast.

A breast that feels a little plumper than before, reminding me that her body is changing.

It's bizarre how erotic I find that knowledge, how the thought of Nora growing round with child turns me on. I've never thought of pregnant women as being sexy, but with my wife, I find myself obsessed with her still-slim body, fascinated by its possibilities. My sex drive, always strong, is through the roof these days, and it's all I can do not to attack her constantly.

If not for my twice-daily jerk-off sessions, I wouldn't be able to restrain myself.

Even now, after I just masturbated in the shower, lying wrapped around her like this is torture. I'm not willing to move away, though. I need to feel her against me, even if all I'm going to do is cuddle her. She needs rest, and I have every intention of letting her sleep. However, as I settle more comfortably on the pillow, she stirs in my arms and says sleepily, "Julian?"

"Of course, baby." I give in to temptation and nuzzle the soft skin behind her ear as I slide my hand from her breast to the warm folds between her legs. "Who else could it be?"

"I—I don't know…" Her breathing catches as I find her clit and press on it. "What time is it?"

"It's late." I push one finger into her to test her readiness, and my dick throbs at the slickness I feel in her tight, hot channel. "I should let you go back to sleep."

"No." She gasps as I curve my finger inside her, hitting her G-spot. "I'm okay, really."

"Are you?" I can't resist tormenting her a little. I have to rein in my sadistic urges these days, but hearing her beg is not something I can pass up. Lowering my voice, I murmur, "I'm not so sure. I think I should stop."

"No, please don't." She moans as I circle her clit with

my thumb and simultaneously rub my hard-on on her ass. "Please don't stop."

"Tell me what you want me to do to you then." I continue circling her clit. She feels like live fire in my arms, her body warm and sleek. Her hair smells flowery from her shampoo, and her inner walls flex around my finger, as if trying to suck it deeper into her pussy. "Tell me exactly what you want, my pet."

"You know what I want." She's panting now, her hips shimmying as she tries to force my fingers into a steady rhythm. "I want you to fuck me. Hard."

"How hard?" My voice roughens as dark, depraved images invade my mind. There are so many dirty things I want to do to her, so many ways I want to take her. Even after all this time, there is an innocence to her that makes me want to corrupt her. Makes me want to push her to the limits. "Tell me, Nora. I want to hear every detail."

"Why?" she asks breathlessly, grinding her pelvis against my hand. Her pussy is dripping now, coating my fingers with her wetness. "You won't do what I want."

"You don't get to ask why." Stilling my hand, I let some of the darker craving seep into my voice. "Now tell me."

"I—" She sucks in her breath as I resume playing with her clit. "I want you to fuck me so hard it hurts." Her voice quavers as I push a second finger into her, stretching her small opening. "I want you to tie me up and make me do what you want."

"Do you want me to fuck your ass?"

Her pussy clenches around my fingers as a shudder ripples through her body. "I—" Her voice breaks. "I don't know."

If my balls didn't feel like they're about to explode, I'd find her evasiveness amusing. One of these days I'm going to make her admit that she's grown to like anal sex, that she enjoys being taken that way. In fact, I'm going to make her *beg* for my cock in her little asshole. For now, though, all this talk is just that: talk. As much as I'd love to fuck every one of her tight holes, I can't. I won't risk the baby for momentary pleasure.

This verbal interlude will have to be enough until Nora gives birth.

Withdrawing my fingers from her body, I grip my dick and guide it to her warm, wet pussy. She moans as I begin to push into her. With both of us lying on our sides and with her legs closed, the fit is even tighter than usual, and I go slowly, ignoring the savage lust pounding through my veins.

*Do not hurt her. Do not hurt her.* The words are like a mantra in my brain. She arches her back, curving her spine to better accommodate me, and I slide my hand to the front of her sex, seeking out the small bud peeking through her folds. As my fingers make contact with her clit, she gasps out my name, and I feel her spasming around me, her inner muscles contracting as she finds her release.

My heart thumping heavily in my chest, I take deep

breaths and hold still, trying to contain my own impending explosion. When the urge to come abates slightly, I begin to thrust into her, rubbing her engorged clit at the same time. She lets out an incoherent noise, something between a moan and a gasp, and her body tenses in my embrace. As I continue to fuck her in short, shallow strokes, she tenses even more, crying out, and I feel her swollen flesh clamping down on me as she reaches her second peak.

The sensation of her milking my cock is indescribable, the pleasure sharp and electric. It zings through me, hurling me into a sudden climax. Groaning harshly, I grind my pelvis against her, burrowing deep into her pussy as my seed bursts out with violent, orgasmic force.

Afterwards, we lie there trying to catch our breath, our bodies glued together with sweat. As my heart rate slowly returns to normal, a feeling of satiation, of relaxed contentment, spreads through me. I know I should get up and bring Nora to the shower for a quick rinse, but it feels too good to just lie there, holding her as my cock softens inside her body. Closing my eyes, I let myself luxuriate in the moment, my thoughts drifting as I start to sink into the heavy nothingness of sleep.

"Julian?" Nora's soft voice jolts me out of my near-slumber, sending my heartbeat spiking.

"What is it, baby?" My tone is sharp with sudden worry. "Are you okay?"

She lets out a heavy sigh and turns around in my

arms, moving back to look at me. "Of course I'm okay. Why wouldn't I be?"

I exhale slowly, too relieved—and sexually replete— to get annoyed at her exasperated tone. "What is it then?" I ask more calmly, bringing the blanket up to cover her. The room is cool from air conditioning, and I know Nora gets chilly when she's tired.

She sighs again as I tuck the blanket around her. "You know I'm not made of glass, right?"

I don't bother replying to that. Instead, I stare at her, eyes narrowed, until she blows out a breath and says, "I just wanted to let you know that I talked to my parents, that's all."

"About the baby?"

"Yes." A pleased smile curves her lips. "Mom reacted surprisingly well."

"She's a smart woman, your mother. What about your father?"

"He wasn't on the call, but Mom said she'll talk to him."

"Good." I find it strangely satisfying, knowing that Nora finally took this step. It means she's that much closer to acceptance, to finally admitting that the baby is a fact of our lives. "Now you can stop worrying about it."

"Right." Her eyes gleam black in the soft light of the bedside lamp. "The hard part is over. Now all I need to do is give birth and raise the child."

Her tone is light, but I can hear the fear underneath

the sarcasm. She's terrified about the future, and as much as I want to reassure her, I can't tell her that everything will be all right.

Because deep inside, I'm just as terrified as she is.

Given the late night in the office, I sleep longer than usual, and when I wake up, Nora is already stirring.

Hearing my movements, she rolls over in bed and gives me a sleepy smile. "You're still here."

"I am." Giving in to a momentary impulse, I pull her close, wrapping my arms tightly around her. Sometimes it feels like the time we have together is not enough. Even though I see her every day, I want more.

I constantly want more with her.

She drapes her leg over my thigh and burrows even closer, rubbing her nose against my chest. My body reacts predictably, my morning erection stiffening to a painful hardness. Before I can do anything, however, she distracts me by speaking. "Julian..." Her voice is muffled. "Who's the woman in Lucas's house?"

Surprised, I pull back to look at her. "How do you know about that?"

"Rosa and I saw her yesterday." Nora seems reluctant to meet my gaze. "We were, um... passing by." She glances up at me through her lashes.

"Were you now?" Propping myself up on my elbow, I

study her, noting the flush on her face. "And why were you passing by? You don't normally walk in that area."

"We did yesterday." Pulling the blanket around herself, Nora sits up and gives me a determined look. "So who is she? What did she do?"

I sigh. I didn't want Nora exposed to that drama, but it looks like I can't avoid it. "The girl is the Russian interpreter who sold us out to the Ukrainians," I explain, carefully watching Nora's reaction. My pet is just getting over her nightmares, and the last thing I want is to trigger a relapse.

As I speak, Nora's eyes grow wide. "She's responsible for the plane crash?"

"Not directly, but the information she gave to the Ukrainians led to it, yes." If Lucas hadn't decided to take charge of the situation, I would've sent someone to Moscow to take care of the traitor—if the Russians hadn't done it for me first, that is.

As Nora digests that information, I see her expression changing, darkening. It's fascinating to observe. Her soft lips stiffen, and her gaze fills with pure hatred. "She almost killed you," she says in a choked voice. "Julian, that bitch almost killed you."

"Yes, and she killed nearly fifty of my men." It's that loss that eats at me more than anything—and I know it eats at Lucas as well. Whatever punishment he decides to dole out to his prisoner will be no less than she deserves, and I see that Nora is reaching the same realization.

As I watch, she jumps off the bed, leaving the blanket there. Grabbing her robe, she pulls it on before starting to pace around the room, visibly agitated. The brief glimpse of her naked body arouses me again, but I keep my gaze focused on her face as I get up.

"Does it bother you, my pet?" I ask. Nora stops pacing, her eyes straying to my lower body before she looks up at me. "Is that why you want to know about her?"

"Of course it bothers me." Nora's voice is filled with a tension I can't quite define. "There's a woman tied up on our compound."

"A female traitor," I correct. "She's hardly an innocent victim."

"Why couldn't you let the Russian authorities take care of it?" Nora steps closer. "Why did you need to bring her here?"

"Lucas wanted this. He has a bit of a... personal... relationship with her."

Nora's eyes widen with comprehension. "He had an affair with her?"

"More of a one-night stand, but yes." I walk toward the bathroom, and Nora follows me there. When I turn on the shower and begin brushing my teeth, she picks up her own toothbrush and does the same. I can see that she still looks agitated, so after I rinse out the toothpaste, I say, "If this really bothers you, I can have him take her away somewhere."

Nora puts down her toothbrush and gives me a

sarcastic look. "So he could torture her with no one the wiser? How would that make it better?"

I shrug, walking over to the shower stall. "You wouldn't see it." I leave the stall door open, so I can talk to her. The shower is spacious enough that no water will get out.

"Right, of course." She stares at me as I begin to lather up. "So if I don't see it, it's not happening."

I let out another sigh. "Come here, baby." Ignoring the soap covering my hands, I reach for her and tug her into the stall with me. Then I take off her robe and throw it on the floor outside the stall.

She doesn't resist as I bring her under the hot spray with me. Instead, she closes her eyes and stands still as I pour shampoo into my palm and begin massaging it into her scalp. Even wet, her hair feels good to the touch, thick and silky around my fingers.

It's strange how much I enjoy taking care of her like this. How the simple act of washing her hair both soothes me and turns me on. At moments like these, it's easier to forget the violence within me, to quell the cravings I can't give in to for months to come.

"What difference does it make whether Lucas is the one to mete out punishment, or if it's the Russians?" I ask when I'm done lathering her hair. Nora's not saying anything, but I know she's still thinking about the interpreter, obsessing about her fate. "The outcome would be the same. You know that, my pet, right?"

She nods silently, then tilts her head back to rinse off the shampoo.

"So why are you dwelling on it?" I reach for the hair conditioner as she wipes the water off her face and opens her eyes to look at me. "Do you want her to walk free?"

"I should." She stares at me as I begin working the conditioner into her hair. "I shouldn't want her to suffer like this."

My lips curl with savage amusement. "But you do, don't you? You want revenge just as much as I do." Her agitation makes sense to me now. As with the man she killed, Nora's middle-class sensibilities are clashing with her instincts. She knows what society dictates she *should* feel, and it bothers her that the actual emotions she's experiencing are quite different.

It's not human nature to turn the other cheek, and my pet is starting to realize that.

Nora closes her eyes again and moves her head under the spray. The water cascades down her face, turning her lashes into long, dark spikes. "I wanted to die when I thought you were dead," she says, her voice barely audible through the running water. "It was even worse than when I lost you that first time. When I saw the girl, I figured she did *something* to harm your business, but I didn't realize she'd caused the crash."

I picture how Nora must've felt that day, and an acute ache spreads through my chest. I'd go insane if I ever thought I'd lost her. "Baby…" Stepping closer, I use my back to shield her from the spray and cup her face in my palms, staring down at her. "It's over. That episode in our lives is over, okay? It's in the past."

She doesn't reply, so I bend my head and take her mouth in a deep, slow kiss, comforting her the only way I know how.

## 14

NORA

*I*'m losing myself. Slowly and surely, I'm being drawn into Julian's dark orbit, sucked in by the twisted morass that is this estate.

I've known this for a while, of course. I've been observing my own transformation with a kind of distant horror and curiosity. Things that once seemed abhorrent to me are now part of my everyday life. Murder, torture, illegal arms dealing—intellectually, I still condemn it all, but it no longer bothers me as it once did. My moral compass has been gradually tilting off-course, and I've been letting it happen.

I've been letting Julian's world change me without so much as putting up a fight.

Even before I knew what the blond girl had done, her plight didn't affect me on any kind of deep emotional level. Like Rosa, I had been morbidly curious rather than appalled. And now that I know she's the interpreter who nearly killed Julian, the hatred surging through my veins leaves little room for pity. I understand that it's wrong to let Lucas punish her in this manner, but I don't *feel* the wrongness of it.

I want her to suffer, to pay for the agony she put us through.

The fact that I can think at all right now, much less analyze my disconcerting emotions, is bizarre. I'm in the shower, and Julian is kissing me, drugging my senses with his touch. His hands are cradling my face, and my body is responding to him as always, the warm water sluicing over my skin adding to the burning heat within me. My thoughts, however, are cold and clear. There's only one solution I can see, only one way I can attempt to salvage what remains of my soul.

I have to get away.

Not permanently. Not forever. But I have to leave, even if it's just for a couple of weeks. I need to regain my sense of perspective, re-immerse myself in the world outside our compound.

If not for my own sake, then for the tiny life I'm carrying.

"Julian..." My voice shakes when he finally releases my lips and slides one hand down my back, making my sex pulse with need. "Julian, I want to go home."

He stops abruptly and lifts his head, still holding me against him. His gaze hardens, the heat of desire morphing into something cold and menacing. "You *are* home."

"I want to see my parents," I insist, my heart beating rapidly in my chest. With Julian's powerful body surrounding me and the steam from the shower fogging up the stall, I feel like I'm trapped in a bubble of naked flesh and lust. My body clamors for his touch, but my mind screams that I can't give in. Not with so much at stake.

A muscle starts ticking in his jaw. "I told you I'll take you at some point. But not now. Not in your condition."

"Then when?" I force myself to hold his gaze. "When I have an infant to care for? Or a toddler? How about when the child is full-grown? Do you think it'll be safe for me to go then?"

Julian's lips thin into a hard, dangerous line. Backing me up against the shower wall, he grasps my wrists and pins them above my head. "Don't push me, my pet," he murmurs, his erection pressing into my stomach. "You won't like the consequences."

Despite my determination, a tendril of fear coils in my chest. I know Julian won't hurt me right now, but physical punishment is not the only weapon in my husband's arsenal. Images of Jake's brutal beating flash through my mind, bringing with them a sickening chill.

"Don't," I whisper as he leans down and brushes his lips against my ear, the tender gesture a stark contrast to the threat of his body looming over me. "Julian, don't do this."

He straightens, his eyes like hard blue gems. "Don't do what?" Transferring my wrists into one of his large palms, he trails his free hand over my breasts and down my belly, his fingers grazing over my burning skin.

"Don't—" My voice breaks, his touch making my core throb with need despite the lingering chill. "Don't let it be like this."

His hand comes up, his fingers catching my jaw in an inescapable grip. "Like what?" he asks, his tone deceptively even. "Like you're mine?"

My breath catches. "I'm your wife, not your slave—"

"You're whatever I wish you to be, my pet. I own you." The casual cruelty of his words hits me like a blow, knocking all air out of my lungs. Something of my reaction must've shown because his grip on me eases, his tone softening slightly as he says, "This is your home, Nora. Here. With me. Not out there."

"They're my parents, Julian. My family. Just like *you* are my family now. I can't spend my whole life locked in a cage for my safety. I'll go crazy." I can feel tears gathering behind my eyelids, and I blink rapidly, trying to hold them back. The last thing I want is to show what an emotional mess I am these days.

*Stupid pregnancy hormones.*

Julian stares at me, his eyes glittering with frustration, and then, with an abrupt movement, he releases me, stepping back. Turning off the water, he steps out of the stall, grabbing a towel with barely controlled violence. His cock is still hard, and the fact that he's not already on me is surprising, even considering his new, treat-Nora-like-glass approach.

Moving cautiously, I follow him out of the shower, my wet feet sinking into the plush softness of the bathroom mat. "Can you please—" I begin, but Julian is already stepping toward me with the towel. Wrapping it around me, he pats me dry before stepping back to grab another towel for himself.

"What does all this have to do with Yulia Tzakova?" His words stop me in my tracks as I'm about to leave the bathroom. When I turn toward him in confusion, he clarifies, "The Russian interpreter you saw yesterday. Does she have anything to do with your sudden desire to see your parents?"

I consider denying it for a second, but Julian can tell when I'm lying. "In a way," I say carefully. "I just need some time away from here, a change of scenery. I need a breather, Julian." I swallow, holding his gaze. "I need it badly."

He stares at me, and then, without saying another word, goes into the bedroom to get dressed.

At breakfast, Julian is silent, seemingly absorbed with emails on his iPad. I feel ignored—an unfamiliar sensation for me. Usually, when we have meals together,

I have Julian's undivided attention, and the fact that he's focusing on something else bothers me far more than is reasonable.

I debate trying to break the silence, but I don't want to make things worse. As it is, this morning's argument probably killed my chances of getting off the estate. I should've waited until a more appropriate time to bring up the visit to my parents; blurting it out in the middle of a make-out session hadn't been the smartest move.

Of course, there's no guarantee that a different approach would've altered the outcome. Once Julian makes a decision, I have little chance of changing his mind, especially if the matter concerns my safety. I fought him on the trackers, and they're still embedded in my body. Julian will never let me remove them, just as he might never let me off the compound. For all intents and purposes, he does own me, and there's nothing I can do about that fact.

Trying not to give in to the dull despair pressing down on me, I finish my eggs and get up, not wanting to linger in the tense atmosphere. Before I can step away from the table, however, Julian looks up from his iPad and gives me a sharp look. "Where are you going?"

"To study for my exams," I reply cautiously.

"Sit." He gestures imperiously toward my chair. "We're not done yet."

Suppressing a flare of anger, I return to my seat and cross my arms. "I really have to study, Julian."

"When is your last final?"

I stare at him, my pulse accelerating as a tiny bubble of hope forms in my chest. "It's flexible with the online program. If I finish all the lectures early, I can take the exams right away."

"So early June?" he presses.

"No, sooner." I place my sweaty palms on the table. "I can potentially be done in the next week and a half."

"Okay." He looks down at the iPad again and types something as I watch him, hardly daring to breathe. After a minute, he looks up again, pinning me with a hard blue gaze. "I'm only going to tell you this once, Nora," he says evenly. "If you disobey me, or do anything to endanger yourself while we're in Chicago, I *will* punish you. Do you understand me?"

Before he even finishes speaking, I'm halfway around the table, nearly knocking over his chair as I leap on him. "Yes!" I don't even know how I end up on his lap, but somehow I'm there, my arms wrapped around his neck as I rain kisses all over his face. "Thank you! Thank you! Thank you!"

He lets me kiss him until I run out of breath, and then he frames my face with his big hands, gazing at me intently. I can see the gleam of desire in his eyes, feel the hard bulge pressing into my thighs, and I know we're going to continue what we started this morning. My body begins to pulse in anticipation, my nipples tightening under the fabric of my dress.

As if sensing my growing arousal, Julian smiles darkly and rises to his feet, holding me against his chest.

"Don't make me regret this, my pet," he murmurs as he carries me toward the stairs. "You don't want to disappoint me, believe me."

"I won't," I vow fervently, winding my arms around his neck. "I promise you, Julian, I won't."

# III

---

# THE TRIP

## 15

NORA

*I'm going home. Oh my God, I'm going home.*

Even now, as I look out the window of the plane at the clouds below, I can hardly believe this is happening. Only two weeks have passed since our conversation at breakfast, and here we are, on our way to Oak Lawn.

"This plane is nothing like what I've seen on TV," Rosa says, gazing around the luxurious interior of the cabin. "I mean, I knew we wouldn't be flying on a regular airline, but this is *really* nice, Nora."

I grin at her. "Yes, I know. The first time I saw it, I had the same reaction." I sneak a quick glance at Julian, who's sitting on the couch with his laptop, seemingly ignoring our conversation. He told me he's planning to meet with his portfolio manager while we're in Chicago, so I'm guessing he's going over prospective investments in preparation. It's either that or the latest drone design modification from his engineers; that project has been taking up a lot of his time this week.

"My first time flying, and it's on a private jet. Can you believe it? The only way this could be better is if we were going to New York," Rosa says, bringing my attention back to her. Her brown eyes are bright with excitement, and she's practically bouncing in her plush leather seat. She's been like this for several days, ever since I got Julian to agree to have her come with us to America—something my friend has been dreaming about for years.

"Chicago is pretty nice too," I say, amused at her unintentional snobbery. "It's a cool city, you'll see."

"Oh, of course." Realizing she insulted my home, Rosa flushes. "I'm sure it's great, and I don't want you to think I'm ungrateful," she says quickly, looking distraught. "I know you're only bringing me along because you're nice, and I'm ecstatic to be going—"

"Rosa, you're coming along because I need you," I interrupt, not wanting her to go into this in front of Julian. "You're the only one Ana trusts to make my morning smoothies, and you know I need those vitamins."

Or at least that's what I told my obsessively protective husband when I asked to have Rosa come with us. I'm fairly certain I could've made the smoothies myself—or just swallowed the vitamin pills—but I wanted to make sure he'd allow my friend to join us. To this day, I'm not sure if he agreed because he believed me, or because he didn't have any objections to begin with. Either way, I don't want Rosa to inadvertently rock the boat… or the private jet, as the case may be.

It still doesn't feel entirely real, the fact that we're on our way to see my parents. The past two weeks have simply flown by. With all the exams and papers, I barely had time to think about the upcoming trip. It wasn't until three days ago that I was able to catch my breath and realize that the trip was, in fact, happening, and Julian had already made all the necessary preparations, beefing up the security around my parents to White House levels.

"Oh, yes, the smoothies," Rosa says, shooting a cautious look in Julian's direction. She finally caught on. "Of course, I forgot. And I'll be helping to unpack all the art supplies, so you don't overtire yourself."

"Right, exactly." I give her a conspiratorial grin. "Can't have me lifting heavy canvases and all that."

At that moment, the plane shakes, and Rosa's face turns white, her excitement evaporating. "What—what is that?"

"Just turbulence," I say, breathing slowly to combat an immediate swell of nausea. I'm still not entirely out of the morning-sickness phase, and the plane's jerky motion is not helpful.

"We won't crash, will we?" Rosa asks fearfully, and I shake my head to reassure her. When I glance over at Julian, however, I see that he's looking at me, his face unusually tense and his knuckles white as he grips the computer.

Without thinking, I unbuckle my seatbelt and get up, wanting to go over to him. If Rosa is afraid of crashing, I can only imagine how Julian must feel, having experienced a crash less than three months ago.

"What are you doing?" Julian's voice is sharp as he stands up, dropping the computer on the couch. "Sit down, Nora. It's not safe."

"I just—"

Before I finish speaking, he's already next to me, forcing me back into the seat and strapping me in. "Sit," he barks, glaring at me. "Did you not promise to behave?"

"Yes, but I just—" At the expression on Julian's face, I fall silent before muttering, "Never mind."

Still glaring at me, he steps back and takes a seat across from me and Rosa. She looks uncomfortable, her hands twisting in her lap as she gazes out the window. I feel bad for her; I'm sure it's awkward to see her friend being treated like a disobedient child.

"I don't want you to fall if the plane hits an air pocket," Julian says in a calmer tone when I show no further signs of trying to get up. "It's not safe to be walking around the cabin during turbulence."

I nod and focus on breathing slowly. It helps with both nausea and anger. Sometimes I forget the facts and start thinking that we have a normal marriage, a partnership of equals, instead of… well, whatever it is we have. On paper, I might be Julian's wife, but in reality, I'm far closer to his sex slave.

A sex slave who's desperately in love with her owner.

Closing my eyes, I find a comfortable position in the middle of the spacious leather seat and try to relax.

It's going to be a long flight.

"Wake up, baby." Warm lips brush against my forehead as my seatbelt is unbuckled. "We're here."

I open my eyes, blinking slowly. "What?"

Julian smiles at me, his blue gaze filled with amusement as he stands in front of me. "You slept the entire way. You must've been exhausted."

I had been a bit tired—the aftermath of all the studying and packing—but an eight-hour nap is a new record for me. Must be those pregnancy hormones again.

Covering a yawn with my hand, I get up and see Rosa already standing by the exit, holding her backpack. "We landed," she says brightly. "I barely felt the plane touch down. Lucas must be an amazing pilot."

"He is good," Julian agrees, wrapping a cashmere shawl around my shoulders. When I give him a questioning look, he explains, "It's only sixty-eight degrees outside. I don't want you to get cold."

I suppress the urge to snicker. Only someone from the tropics would consider sixty-eight degrees "cold"—

though, to be fair, it probably is a bit chilly for the short-sleeved dress I'm wearing. Chicago weather in late May is unpredictable, with cool spring days interspersed with summer-like heat. Julian himself is dressed in a pair of jeans and a long-sleeved, button-up shirt.

"Thank you," I say, looking at him. On some level, I do find his concern touching, even if he takes it too far these days. Of course, it doesn't hurt that the feel of his large hands on my shoulders makes me want to melt against him, even with Rosa standing only a few feet away.

"You're welcome, baby," he says huskily, holding my gaze, and I know he feels it too—this deep, inexplicable pull we have toward one another. I don't know if it's chemistry or something else, but it ties us together more securely than any rope.

The clanging of the plane door opening snaps me out of whatever spell I was under. Startled, I step back, grabbing the shawl so it doesn't fall. Julian gives me a look that promises a continuation of what we started, and a shiver of anticipation runs through me.

"Is it okay for me to go down?" Rosa asks, and I turn to see her waiting impatiently by the open door.

"Sure," Julian says. "Go ahead, Rosa. We'll be right there."

She disappears through the exit, and Julian steps closer to me, making my breath catch in my throat. "Are you ready?" he asks softly, and I nod, mesmerized by the warm look in his eyes.

"In that case, let's go," he murmurs, taking my hand. His big, masculine palm engulfs my fingers completely. "Your parents await."

The car that takes us from the airport to my parents' house is a long, modern-looking limo with unusually thick glass.

"Bulletproof?" I ask when we get in, and Julian nods, confirming my guess. He's sitting in the back with me and Rosa, while Lucas is driving, as usual.

I wonder if the blond man resents this trip for taking him away from his Russian toy. The last I heard, the interpreter was still alive—and still held prisoner in Lucas's quarters. Julian told me that Lucas assigned two guards to watch over her in his absence and make sure she's all right. Apparently, he doesn't want anyone else to have the privilege of torturing the girl.

That whole situation makes me sick, so I try not to think about it. The only reason I even know as much as I know is because Rosa refuses to leave it alone, constantly begging me to ask Julian for updates. Her strange obsession with Julian's right-hand man worries me, even though I'm coming to the conclusion that Rosa was right about Lucas having zero interest in her. Still, as much as I don't want her to get involved with him, I also don't want her to be heartbroken—and I'm afraid things are trending in that direction.

"Are you sure your parents don't mind us coming so late?" Rosa asks, interrupting my thoughts. "It's almost nine in the evening."

"No, they're really anxious to see me." I glance down at my phone, which pings with yet another text from Mom. Picking it up, I skim the message and tell Rosa, "My mom already has the table set."

"And they don't mind me tagging along?" She chews on her lower lip. "I mean, you're their daughter, so of course they want to see you, but I'm just the maid—"

"You're my friend." Impulsively, I reach across the limo aisle and squeeze Rosa's hand. "Please stop worrying about it. You're not imposing."

Rosa smiles, looking relieved, and I glance at Julian to see his reaction. His face is impassive, but I catch a glimmer of amusement in his gaze. My husband is clearly not worried about imposing on my parents so late in the evening. And that makes perfect sense. Why would something like that faze him when he unapologetically abducted their daughter?

This should be an interesting dinner indeed.

"Nora, honey!" As soon as my parents' door swings open, I'm enveloped in a soft, perfumed embrace. Laughing, I hug my mom and then my dad, who's standing right behind her. He holds me tightly for a few moments, and I feel his heart beating rapidly in his chest.

When he pulls back to look at me, there is a sheen of moisture in his eyes. "We are so glad to see you," he says in a low, deep voice, and I smile up at him through my own veil of tears.

"Me too, Dad. Me too. I really missed you and Mom."

As soon as I say that, I remember that I'm not alone. Turning, I see that my mom is looking at Rosa and Julian, her smile now stiff and unnatural.

I take a deep breath to prepare myself. "Mom, Dad, you already know Julian. And this is Rosa Martinez. She's my best friend on the estate." I invited Lucas to join us for dinner as well, but he refused, explaining that he's part of the security detail tonight and needs to remain outside.

My mom nods cautiously at Julian. Then her smile warms a fraction as she looks at my friend. "It's nice to meet you, Rosa. Nora told us all about you. Please, come in."

She steps back to welcome them, and Rosa walks in, smiling uncertainly. She's followed by Julian, who strolls in looking as cool and confident as ever.

"Gabriela. It's so good to see you." Giving my mom a dazzling smile, my former captor leans down to brush his lips against her cheek in a European gesture. When he straightens, she looks flushed, like a schoolgirl with her first crush. Leaving her to recover, Julian turns his attention to my dad. "It's a pleasure meeting you in person, Tony," he says, extending his hand.

"Likewise," my dad says, his jaw tight as he takes Julian's proffered hand in a white-knuckled handshake. "I'm glad you were finally able to make it out here."

"Yes, so am I," Julian says smoothly, releasing my dad's hand. I notice red finger marks on his hand where my dad purposefully squeezed too hard, and my heart skips a beat. However, when I sneak a glance at my dad's hand, I realize with relief that there's no corresponding damage there.

Julian must've forgiven my dad this small act of aggression—or at least I'm hoping that's the case.

As we walk toward the dining room, I steal covert looks at my husband's handsome profile. Having my former captor in my childhood home is beyond strange. I'm used to being with him in exotic, foreign locations, not Oak Lawn, Illinois. Seeing Julian in my parents' house is a bit like encountering a wild tiger in a suburban mall—it's bizarre in a scary way.

"Oh, honey, you're so thin," my mom exclaims, eyeing me critically as we enter the dining room. "I knew you wouldn't start rounding out with the baby yet, but you look like you've lost weight."

"I know," Julian says, placing a hand on my lower back. His touch both warms and discomfits me, coming as it does in front of my parents. "With the nausea, it's been tough getting her to eat well. At least she stopped losing weight. You should've seen her four weeks ago."

"Was it really bad, honey?" my mom asks sympathetically when we stop in front of the table. She's keeping her eyes on my face, clearly determined to ignore Julian's possessive gesture. My dad, however, grits his teeth so hard I can practically hear the grinding noise.

"It got better once we learned that I'm pregnant. I started eating plainer foods at regular intervals, and it seemed to help," I explain, flushing. It's odd to talk about my pregnancy in front of my dad. We had danced around the issue during our video chats, with Dad gruffly asking after my health and me brushing off his inquiries. I know he hates the fact that I'm pregnant at my age, and despises the whole situation with Julian. My mom probably feels the same, but she's much more diplomatic about it.

"I hope you can eat tonight," my mom says worriedly. "Your dad and I prepared a lot of food."

"I'm sure I'll manage, Mom." Smiling, I sit down in the chair Julian pulls out for me. "Everything looks delicious."

And it's true. My parents have outdone themselves. The table has everything from my dad's rosemary chicken—a recipe he only uses for special occasions—to my grandmother's tamales and my favorite dish of roasted lamb chops. It's a feast, and my stomach growls in appreciation at the delicious smells emanating from the glass-covered platters.

Julian takes a seat to the left of me, and Mom and Dad sit down across from us.

"Come, sit next to me on this side," I tell Rosa, patting the empty chair to my right. I can see my friend still doesn't feel comfortable, convinced she's somehow imposing. Her usual bright smile is uncertain and a bit shy as she sits down next to me, smoothing her palms over the front of her blue dress.

"This table is amazing, Mrs. Leston," she says in her softly accented voice.

"Oh, thank you, sweetheart." My mom beams at her. "Your English is so good. Where did you learn to speak like that? Nora told me you've never been to the US before."

"No, I haven't." Looking pleased at the compliment, Rosa explains how Julian's mother taught her American English when she was a child. My parents listen to her story with interest, asking a number of follow-up questions, and I use this opportunity to excuse myself to visit the restroom.

When I return a few minutes later, the atmosphere at the table is thick with tension. The only person who appears at ease is Julian, who's leaning back in his chair and regarding my parents with an inscrutable gaze. My dad is visibly bristling, and my mom has her hand on his elbow in a classic calming gesture. Poor Rosa looks like she'd rather be anywhere else.

I sit down and debate asking what happened, but I have a feeling it would stir up the hornet's nest even more. "How's the new job going, Dad?" I ask brightly instead.

My dad takes a deep breath, then another, and attempts something that's supposed to be a smile. It looks more like a grimace, but I give him credit for trying.

Before he can answer my question, Julian leans forward, placing his forearms on the table, and says, "Tony, you may not be aware of this, but your daughter is now one of the wealthiest women in the world. She will want for nothing, regardless of her choice of profession or lack thereof. I understand that having a child during college is not optimal, but I would hardly call it 'destroying her life,' particularly in this situation."

My dad's chest swells with fury. "You think the child is the only problem? You stole—"

"Tony." My mom's voice is soft, but the inflection in it makes Dad stop mid-sentence. She then turns toward Julian. "I apologize for my husband's bad manners," she says evenly. "Obviously, we're well aware of your ability to provide for Nora financially."

"Good." Julian gives her a cool smile. "And are you also aware that Nora is becoming a sought-after artist?"

I pause in the middle of reaching for a lamb chop and gape at Julian. A sought-after artist? Me?

"I know that a gallery in Paris expressed some interest in her paintings," my mom says cautiously. "Is that what you mean?"

"Yes." Julian's smile sharpens. "What you may not

know, however, is that the owner of that gallery is one of the leading art collectors in Europe. And he's very intrigued by Nora's work. So intrigued, in fact, that he just sent me an offer to purchase five of her paintings for his personal collection."

"Really?" I can't hide the eagerness in my voice. "He wants to buy them? For how much?"

"Fifty thousand euros—ten per painting. Though I'm sure we can negotiate for more."

I stop breathing for a moment. "Fifty *thousand*?" I would've been ecstatic to get five hundred dollars. Hell, I would've taken fifty bucks. Just the fact that someone wants my doodles is beyond belief. "Did you say *fifty thousand euros?*"

"Yes, baby." Julian's gaze warms as he looks at me. "Congratulations. You're about to make your first big sale."

"Oh my God," I breathe out. "Oh. My. God."

I can see the same shock reflected on my parents' faces. They, too, are stunned by this turn of events. Only Rosa seems to take this development in stride. "Congratulations, Nora," she exclaims, grinning. "I told you those paintings are amazing."

"When did you get this offer?" I ask Julian when I can speak again.

"Right before we got here." Julian reaches over to give my hand a gentle squeeze. "I was going to tell you later tonight, but I figured your parents might want to know too."

"Yes, we definitely do," my mom says, finally recovering from her shock. "That's... that's incredible, honey. We're so proud of you."

My dad nods, still mute, but I can see that he's just as impressed. And possibly beginning to change his mind about the potential of my hobby.

"Dad," I say softly, looking at him, "I don't intend to drop out of college. Even with the baby on the way, okay? Please, don't worry about me. Truly, I'm all right."

My dad stares at me, then at Julian, and then at me again. I wait for him to say something, but he doesn't. Instead, he reaches for the platter with the lamb chops and pushes them toward me. "Go ahead, honey," he says quietly. "You must be hungry after the long trip."

I gladly take the offering, and everyone else begins loading their plates.

The rest of the dinner goes about as well as could be expected. While there are a few tense silences, the majority of the meal is spent in relatively civil conversation. My mom asks about life on the estate, and Rosa and I show her some photos on Rosa's phone. In the meantime, my dad gets into a political discussion with Julian. To everyone's surprise, the two of them turn out to have the same cynical views on the situation in the Middle East, though Julian's knowledge of geopolitics far exceeds that of my dad's. Unlike my parents, who get their news from the media, Julian is part of the news.

He shapes the news, in fact, though few outside the

intelligence community know that.

I have to give my parents their due. For people who believe that Julian belongs behind bars, they are surprisingly gracious hosts. I suspect it's because they're afraid of losing me if they alienate Julian. My mom would dine with the devil himself if that would ensure continued contact with her only daughter, and my dad tends to follow her lead when it comes to difficult situations.

Still, they watch Julian during the meal, eying him as warily as they would observe a savage creature. He's smiling, his potent charm turned on full-blast, but I know they can sense his ever-present aura of danger, the shadow of violence that clings to him like a dark cloak.

When we get to coffee and dessert, Julian gets an urgent text from Lucas and excuses himself to step outside for a few minutes. "It's nothing serious," he tells me when I give him a worried look. "Just a small business matter that needs my attention."

He walks out of the house, and Rosa chooses that moment to visit the restroom, leaving me alone with my parents for the first time since our arrival.

"A business matter?" my dad asks incredulously as soon as Rosa is out of earshot. "At ten-thirty at night?"

I shrug. "Julian deals with people in different timezones. It's ten in the morning somewhere."

I can see that my dad wants to question me further, but thankfully, my mom jumps in. "Your friend is really nice," she says, nodding toward the hallway where Rosa went. "It's hard to believe she grew up like that." She lowers her voice. "With criminals, I mean."

"Yes, I know." I wonder what my parents would think if they knew that Rosa had killed two men. "She's wonderful."

"Nora, honey..." My mom casts a furtive glance around the empty room, then leans forward, lowering her voice further. "I know we don't have much time right now, but tell us one thing. Are you truly happy with him? Because now that you're both on US soil, the FBI might be able to—"

"Mom, I can't live without him. If anything happened to him, I'd want to die." The stark truth escapes my lips before I can think of a gentler way to say it. I soften my tone. "I don't expect you to understand, but he's everything to me now. I truly love him."

"And does he love you back?" my dad asks quietly. He looks older in this moment, aged by the sorrowful pity I see in his eyes. "Is someone like that even capable of loving you, honey?"

I open my mouth to reassure him, but for some reason, I can't bring myself to say the words. I want to believe that in his own way Julian does love me, but there is a tiny kernel of doubt that's always present with me.

My dad hit the nail on the head.

Is Julian capable of love?

Truthfully, I still don't know.

## 16

## JULIAN

*T*he black Lincoln is already waiting when I step outside.

"I told them you were busy, but they insisted on this meeting," Lucas says, melting out of the shadows near the house. "I figured it was best to let you know."

I nod and walk over to the car.

The window in the back rolls down. "Let's take a ride," Frank says, unlocking the door. "We need to talk."

I give him a hard look. "I don't think so. If you want to talk, we're going to do it right here."

Frank studies me, likely wondering how much he can push me, and I see the exact moment he decides not to annoy me further.

"All right." He climbs out of the car, his gray suit stretching across his round stomach. "If you don't mind the nosy neighbors, sure."

I scope out our surroundings with a practiced

glance. Unfortunately, he's right. There's already a curtain twitching across the street.

We're beginning to attract attention.

"There is a small park around the block," I say, reaching a decision. "Why don't we walk in that direction? You have exactly fifteen minutes."

Frank nods, and the black Lincoln pulls away, likely to circle the block. I have no doubt there is additional security staying out of sight, just like my men. There is no way the CIA would leave one of their own with me without protection.

"All right, talk," I say as we start in the direction of the park. I gesture for Lucas to follow at some distance. "Why are you here?"

"The better question is: why are you?" Frank's voice is edged with frustration. "Do you know how much trouble your presence is causing us? The FBI knows you're in their jurisdiction, and they're going apeshit—"

"I thought you took care of that."

"I did, but Wilson refuses to let it drop. He and Bosovsky are sniffing around, trying to dig up a cover-up. It's a fucking mess, and your visit isn't helping."

"How is this my problem?"

"We don't want you in this country, Esguerra," Frank says as we round the corner. "You have no reason to be here."

"No?" I quirk an eyebrow. "My wife's parents are here."

"Your wife?" Frank snorts. "You mean that eighteen-year-old you kidnapped?"

Nora is twenty now—or will be in a couple of days—but I don't correct him. Her age is hardly the main issue. "That's the one," I say coolly. "As you know full well, since you dragged me from dinner with her parents... my in-laws."

Frank gives me an incredulous stare. "Are you fucking serious? Where do you get the balls to look these people in the eye? You abducted their daughter—"

"Who is now my wife." My tone sharpens. "My relationship with her parents is none of your fucking business, so stay out of it."

"I will—if you stay out of this country." Frank stops, breathing heavily from keeping up with my longer stride. "I'm not kidding about this, Esguerra. We can delete files and records, but we can't erase people. Not in this matter."

"You're telling me the CIA can't silence two nosy FBI agents?" I give him a cold look. "Because if they're the only issue—"

"They're not," Frank interrupts, quickly realizing where I'm going with this. "It's not just the FBI, Esguerra." He reaches up to wipe the sweat off his forehead. "There are higher-ups who are nervous about your presence here. They don't know what to expect."

"Tell them to expect me to visit with my in-laws and leave." For once, I'm being entirely truthful with Frank.

"I'm not here to conduct business, so your higher-ups don't need to worry."

Frank doesn't look like he believes me, but I don't give a fuck. If the CIA knows what's good for them, they'll keep the FBI off my back.

I'm here for Nora, and anyone who doesn't like it can go straight to hell.

When I return to the house, I find Nora arguing with Rosa about cleaning up the table.

"Rosa, please, today you're the guest," Nora says, reaching for the platter with the remnants of the lamb. "Please, just sit, and I'll help my mom—"

"No, no, no," Rosa objects, walking around the table and picking up dirty dishes. "You have the baby to worry about. Please, this is my job. Let me help."

"I'm ten weeks along, not nine months—"

"She's right, baby," I say, stepping up to Nora and plucking the platter from her hands. "It's been a long day, and I don't want you overtiring yourself."

Nora starts to argue, but I'm already carrying the platter to the kitchen, where Nora's parents are packing away the leftovers. As I walk in, Gabriela's eyes widen, but she accepts the platter from me with a quiet "thank you."

I smile at her and walk back to the dining room for more dishes.

It takes a few more trips for Rosa and me to clear off the table and bring everything to the kitchen. Nora sits on the living room couch, watching us work with a mixture of exasperation and curiosity.

Finally, the table is clean, and the Lestons come out of the kitchen to join us. I take a seat next to Nora on the couch and pick up her hand, bringing it to my lap so I can play with her fingers.

"Gabriela, Tony, thank you for a wonderful dinner," I say when Nora's parents sit down next to Rosa on the second couch. "I apologize that I had to step out and missed dessert."

"I saved you a slice of cake," Nora says as I massage her palm. "Mom packed it for us to go."

I give her mother a warm smile. "Thank you for that, Gabriela. I appreciate it."

Gabriela inclines her head. "Of course. It's unfortunate that your business took you away so late in the evening."

"Yes, it is," I agree, pretending not to notice the inquiry implicit in her statement. "And you're right, it *is* getting late…" I glance down at Nora, who's covering a yawn with her free hand.

"Nora says you're staying at a house in Palos Park," Tony says, watching us with an unreadable expression. "Is that where you're sleeping tonight?"

"Yes, that's right." The house is on the far edge of the community, with enough empty acreage surrounding it that Lucas was able to implement the required security features. "That's where we'll be staying for the duration of our visit."

"The two of you are welcome to use Nora's room if you wish," Gabriela offers, sounding uncertain.

"Thank you, but we wouldn't want to impose. It would be better if we had our own space for these two weeks." Still holding Nora's hand, I get up and give the Lestons a polite smile. "Speaking of which, I believe it's time for us to go. Nora needs her rest."

"*Nora* is fine," the subject of my concern mutters as I usher her toward the exit. "I'm capable of staying up past ten, you know."

I stifle a grin at the grumpy note in her voice. My pet doesn't like to admit that she tires easily these days. "Yes, I'm aware. But your parents need their rest too. Tomorrow is Thursday, isn't it?"

"Oh, right, of course." Stopping before we reach the front door, Nora turns to her parents. "I forgot that the two of you have work tomorrow," she says contritely. "I'm sorry. We probably should've left earlier—"

"Oh, no, honey," her mother protests. "We're so happy to have you here, and we told you to come this evening. When are we seeing you next?"

Nora looks up at me, and I say, "Tomorrow evening, if that works for the two of you. This time dinner will be at our house."

"We'll be there," Tony says, and I watch both Lestons hug and kiss Nora as they say their goodbyes.

## 17

### NORA

When we get into the limo, I realize that I *am* tired, the tense excitement of the evening dissipating and leaving me drained. Rosa again takes a seat across the aisle from us, and Julian pulls me close to him, draping his arm over my shoulders. As his warm masculine scent surrounds me, I relax against his side, letting my thoughts drift.

My former captor and I just had dinner with my parents. Like a family. It's so absurd I still can't believe it happened. I'm not sure what I imagined when Julian agreed to take me for a visit, but this wasn't it.

I guess on some level, I had simply refused to think about how something like this might go—my kidnapper sitting down to a civilized meal with my family. It was like a wall I'd put up in my mind, so I wouldn't have to worry. When I had thought of going back home, I had pictured myself with my parents... just the three of us, as though Julian would stay in the background, remaining part of my other, darker life.

It was ridiculous to think that way, of course. Julian never stays in the background. He dominates whatever situation he's in, bends it to his will. And even in this— in my relationship with my parents—he's taken charge, inserting himself into our family on his own terms, perfectly comfortable where other men would cringe in shame.

Apparently, a conscience is a useful thing to lack.

"How are you feeling, my pet?"

At Julian's murmured question, I tilt my head to look up at him, realizing I've been silent for the past few minutes. "I'm okay," I say, cognizant of Rosa's presence a couple of feet away. "Just digesting everything."

"Oh?" Julian gives me an amused look, loosening his grip on me so I can sit more comfortably. "Food-wise or thought-wise?"

"Both, I guess." I smile, realizing my unintentional joke. "It was a good meal."

"Yes, it was." Even in the dim interior of the car, I can see the sensuous curve of his mouth. "Your parents did a good job."

I nod. "They definitely did." I wonder what it must've been like for them, having dinner with the man who abducted their daughter.

With the criminal who's now their son-in-law and father of their grandchild.

Sighing, I snuggle back against Julian's side and close my eyes.

The insanity of my life has reached a whole new level.

~

It takes less than twenty minutes to reach the wealthy community of Palos Park. Growing up, I've always known of its existence, driving past it on the way to the Tampier Lake preserve. The residents of Palos Park tend to be lawyers and doctors, and I've never heard of anyone renting a house there for a couple of weeks.

Of course, Julian isn't just anyone.

The house he chose is on the very edge of the community, isolated by a tall, wrought-iron fence. Once we get past the electronic gates, we drive down a winding driveway for another couple of hundred yards before reaching the house itself.

Inside, the house is luxuriously appointed, nearly as nice as our mansion at the estate. From gleaming parquet floors to modern art on the walls, everything about our vacation residence screams "extreme wealth."

"How much did you pay for this?" I ask as we walk through an enormous dining area. "I didn't realize a house like this could be for rent."

"It's not," Julian says casually. "I bought it."

My jaw falls open. "What? When? You said you rented it."

"I said I got a house for our visit," he corrects. "I never said how I got it."

"Oh." I feel foolish at my assumption. "So when did you have a chance to buy it?"

"I began making the arrangements right after we agreed on this trip. It took almost a week for the prior owner to move out, but the house is now ours."

*Ours.* The word rolls so easily off his tongue that it doesn't register for a second. Then I process what he said. "*We* own this house?" I ask carefully. "As in, both of us?"

"Technically, one of our shell corporations owns it, but I made you a fifty-percent shareholder in that corporation, so yes, *we* own it," Julian says as we enter a spacious bedroom with a four-poster bed.

"Julian..." Stopping in front of the bed, I look up at him. "Why did you do this? I mean, the trust fund was more than enough—"

"Because you belong to me." He steps closer, a familiar heat igniting in his gaze as he reaches for the buttons of my dress. His fingers brush against my naked skin, making my nipples pebble with need. "Because I want to take care of you, spoil you, make sure you'll never want for anything in your life..." Despite his tender words, his eyes gleam darker as he finishes unbuttoning the dress and lets it fall to the floor. "Any other questions, my pet?"

I shake my head, staring up at him. I'm now wearing only a blue thong and a matching bra, and the way he's looking at me reminds me of a hungry lion about to pounce on a gazelle. He may want to take care of me, but at this particular moment, he also wants to devour me.

"Good." His voice is a deep, menacing purr. "Now turn around."

My pulse quickening in nervous anticipation, I do as he says. Even though I crave the darkness now, there is a tiny, instinctual curl of fear in my belly. Julian has always been unpredictable. For all I know, the domesticity of this evening reawakened his sadistic desires, unleashing the demon he's kept in check these recent weeks.

A warm, treacherous throb begins between my thighs at the thought.

As I stand there, I hear a quiet rustling, and then a soft cloth covers my eyes.

A blindfold, I realize, holding my breath. Deprived of my vision, I feel infinitely more vulnerable. My right hand twitches with the sudden urge to lift my arm and tear off the piece of cloth.

"Oh, no, you don't." Julian catches my arm, his fingers like steel cuffs on my wrist. Leaning down, he whispers in my ear, "Who said you could do that, my pet?"

I shiver at the heat of his breath. "I just—"

"Quiet." His command vibrates through me, adding to the heated pulsing between my legs. "I will tell you when to speak." Releasing my wrist, he pushes me forward, causing me to stumble and land face down on the bed. "Don't move," he orders, stepping closer.

I obey, hardly breathing as he runs his hands over me, starting with my shoulders and ending with my thighs. His touch is gentle, yet somehow invasive, like that of a stranger. Or maybe it just feels that way because of the blindfold. I can sense him behind me, but I can't see anything, and he's touching me like he would an object... doing with me whatever he pleases. I can feel the calluses on his large, warm palms, and the memory of our first time together flashes through my mind, making my belly tighten with anxiety and dark need.

When he's done stroking me, he rolls me over onto my back and rearranges me on the bed, placing a pillow under my head. Then he grabs my arm, and I feel him looping a rough-textured rope around my wrist. He secures the other end of that rope to what I can only assume is one of the bed posts.

After that, he walks around the bed and does the same with my other arm.

I'm left lying there like some kind of a sexual sacrifice, my arms stretched out diagonally and the blindfold still covering my eyes. I'm even more helpless than usual, and that fact both alarms and thrills me, like most of my interactions with Julian. For other couples, this is only pretend. But for us, it's as real as it gets. I don't have the option to say no. Julian will take me whether I want it or not, and perversely, that knowledge deepens the needy ache in my sex.

"You're beautiful." His harsh whisper is accompanied by a feather-light brush of his fingers over the sensitive skin of my stomach. "And all mine. Aren't you, my pet?"

"Yes." My breathing turns uneven as his fingers approach the top of my thong. "Yes, all yours."

The mattress dips as he climbs onto the bed and straddles my legs. The material of his jeans feels rough on my naked thighs, reminding me that he's still fully clothed. "That's right. . ." He leans down, the buttons of his shirt pressing into my stomach as he covers me with his hard, broad chest. His teeth graze over my earlobe, causing gooseflesh to rise over my arms as he murmurs into my ear, "Nobody will ever have you but me."

I suppress a shudder even as my core floods with liquid heat. From a different man, this would be just possessive pillow talk, but from Julian, it's both a threat and a statement of fact. If I were ever so foolish as to allow another man to touch me, Julian would kill him without a second thought.

"I don't want anyone but you." It's true, yet my voice shakes as Julian kisses my neck, then sucks on the tender flesh under my ear. "You know that."

He chuckles softly, the deep, masculine sound reverberating through me. "Yes, my pet. I do."

He climbs off me, and I sense him moving to the foot of the bed. When he catches my right ankle, I know why.

He's going to tie my legs as well.

The rope is looped around my ankle as I lie there, my heart racing. Julian rarely restrains me so thoroughly. He doesn't have to. Even if I were inclined to fight, he's strong enough to control me without ropes and chains.

Of course, I'm not inclined to fight. Not when I know what he's capable of, what he's willing to do to possess me.

When my right leg is secured, he reaches for my left. His hands are strong and sure as he wraps the rope around my ankle and ties the other end to the remaining bedpost, leaving me lying there with my legs spread open. It's a disconcerting position, and as soon as Julian moves back, I instinctively try to bring my legs together. I can't close them more than an inch, of course. Like the ropes around my wrists, the ankle restraints hold me tightly in place without cutting off my circulation.

My kidnapper may not be into traditional BDSM, but he certainly knows how to tie someone up.

"Julian?" It occurs to me that I'm still wearing my underwear, both the bra and the thong. "What are you going to do to me?"

He doesn't respond. Instead, I feel the mattress dip again as he gets up, and then I hear his footsteps and the sound of the door closing.

He walked out of the room, leaving me tied to the bed.

My heart starts beating faster.

I flex my arms, testing the rope again even though I know it's futile. As expected, there's almost no give in the restraints; the rope bites painfully into my skin when I try to pull on it. I'm nearly naked and alone, blindfolded and tied up in this unfamiliar house. And even though I know Julian won't let anything bad happen to me, I can't help the tension that invades my body as seconds tick by with no sign of his return.

After a couple of minutes, I test the rope again. Still no give in it... and still no sign of Julian.

I force myself to take a breath and slowly let it out. Nothing terrible is going on; nobody is hurting me. I don't know what game Julian is playing, but it doesn't seem particularly brutal.

*But you want brutal*, a small, insidious voice inside my head reminds me. *You want pain and violence.*

I quiet that voice and focus on remaining calm. Julian's mercurial approach to lovemaking may excite me, but it also frightens me. The sane part of me, at least. I want pain, yet I dread it in equal measures. It's always that way nowadays. It's as if I've been split in two, the remnants of the person I used to be warring with who I am now.

Another few minutes crawl by.

"Julian?" I can no longer remain silent. "Julian, where are you?"

Nothing. No response of any kind.

I rub the back of my head against the sheets, trying to dislodge the blindfold, but it doesn't budge more than an inch. Frustrated, I yank at the restraints with all my strength, but all I succeed in doing is hurting myself. Finally, I give up and try to relax, ignoring the anxiety creeping through me.

A few more minutes pass. Just when I think I might go out of my mind, the door creaks open, and I hear the soft sound of footsteps.

"Julian, is that you?" I can't hide the relief in my voice. "What happened? Where did you go?"

"Shhh." The sound is followed by a tickling sensation across my lips. "Who told you that you could speak, my pet?"

My pulse jumps at the cold note in his voice. Is he punishing me for something? "What—"

"Hush." His fingers press on my lips, silencing me. "Not another word."

I swallow, my throat suddenly feeling dry. He's not touching me anywhere but my lips, yet my body ignites, my earlier arousal returning despite my growing nervousness.

Or maybe because of it. It's impossible to tell.

"Suck on my fingers." His whispered command is accompanied by increasing pressure on the seam of my lips. "Now."

Obediently, I open my mouth and suck two of his large fingers in. They taste clean and slightly salty, the edges of his short nails rough against the tender roof of my mouth. I swirl my tongue around his fingers as I would over his cock, and his hand jerks, as though the sensation is just as intense for him.

Just as I'm starting to get into it, Julian withdraws his fingers and runs them down the front of my body, leaving a cool, damp trail on my skin. I shiver in response, my inner muscles tensing as his fingers circle my navel, his nails scraping lightly over my belly. *Lower*, I will him silently, *please, just go a bit lower*, but he lifts his hand instead, depriving me of his touch.

I open my mouth to plead with him, but then I remember that he doesn't want me to speak. Swallowing, I suppress the words, not wanting to displease him when he's in this unpredictable mood.

If Julian is indeed punishing me for something, I don't want to provoke him further.

So instead of begging, I lie still, waiting, my breathing fast and shallow as I try to listen to his movements. I can't hear anything. Is he just standing there watching me? Staring at my semi-naked body stretched out and restrained on the bed?

Finally, I hear something. A scraping noise, as if he picked up something from the nightstand.

I wait, listening tensely, and then I feel it.

Something cold and hard sliding under the tight band of my bra, pressing between my breasts.

I almost flinch in shock, but manage to remain still, my heart beating frantically.

*Snip.* The noise is unmistakeable.

It's the sound of metal cutting through thick fabric. Julian just used scissors on the front of my bra.

I allow myself a small exhalation of relief, but then I tense again as I feel the cold scissors sliding down my body.

*Snip. Snip.* Both sides of my thong are cut, the dull edge of the scissors pressing into my hipbones. I feel the warmth of Julian's hand as he pulls the mangled scrap of fabric off my body, and then I hear him suck in a breath. He's looking at me. I know it. I picture what he's seeing as I lie there naked, with my legs wide open, and a flush heats up my skin at the pornographic image in my mind.

"You're already wet." His voice, low and thick with lust, makes me burn even more. "Your pussy is dripping for me." He accompanies the words with a butterfly-soft touch on my aching clit. His fingertips feel rough on my sensitive flesh, yet fire rockets through my veins, filling me with desperate need. Unbidden, a moan escapes my throat, and I lift my hips toward him, silently begging for more.

This time, he answers my plea.

I feel the mattress dip again as he climbs onto the bed, settling between my legs. His hands, large and strong, grip the top of my thighs, and then he lowers his head to my sex. I feel his hot breath wash over my open folds. I almost whimper in anticipation, but I hold back at the last second, not wanting to do anything to cause

Julian to change his mind. I want his touch. I need it. It's agonizing to be without it.

And then I feel it—the soft, wet pressure of his tongue between my folds, the pressure that both quenches and intensifies the ache. He doesn't lick me; he just holds his tongue against my clit, but it's enough. It's more than enough. I rock my hips in small, spasmodic movements, creating the exact rhythm I need, and the tension within me grows, the pleasure gathering in a hot, pulsing ball within my core. His tongue moves then, his lips closing around my clit in a strong sucking motion, and the ball bursts, shards of ecstasy blasting through my nerve endings as I cry out, no longer able to stay silent.

Before my orgasm is completely over, he starts licking me. Just soft, gentle licks that extend the pleasurable aftershocks coursing through my body. It feels good, even with my clit swollen and sensitized, so I lie there, enjoying it, limp and content from my release. It's not until a minute later that I realize that the pleasure is sharpening again, growing stronger, transforming into that aching tension.

I gasp, arching toward his mouth, needing more pressure to bring me over the edge, but he keeps touching me with those light licks, his tongue just barely grazing over my clit.

"Please, Julian…" The words escape before I can remember the restriction on speaking, but to my relief, he doesn't stop. Instead, he keeps licking me, his tongue moving in a rhythm that slowly and torturously winds me tighter, pushing me closer but not letting me get what I need. I try to push my hips higher, but I can't gain much leverage, stretched and spread as I am.

All I can do is endure, utterly at the mercy of whatever pleasure-torment Julian chooses to dole out.

Just when I think I can't bear much more, he shifts to the side, moving his right hand from my thigh to my throbbing sex. His large, blunt fingers probe my entrance, and I moan as he pushes two of them in, penetrating me with startling swiftness. I'm almost there, it's nearly what I need... and then his thumb presses hard on my clit.

I fly apart, acute pleasure rippling through my body as I convulse, gasping and crying out.

"Yes, that's it, baby," he murmurs. His hand leaves me, and I hear the sound of a zipper coming down. I register it only dimly. I feel drunk on orgasms, worn out by the brutal intensity of it all. My heart is pounding as if I ran a race, and my bones feel like they've turned to jelly.

There's no way I could possibly want more, yet when he covers me with his large body, a tiny twitch of renewed sensation makes my belly tighten. He's naked, having already removed his clothes, and I can feel his heat, his hardness. His raw male power. Even if I weren't restrained, I'd feel helpless and small, surrounded as I am by him, but with the rope on my ankles and wrists, that feeling is magnified. I can hardly breathe under his weight, but it doesn't matter. Even air feels optional at the moment.

All I need is Julian.

He shifts on top of me, propping himself up on his elbows. The hard, smooth tip of his erection brushes against my inner thigh as he lowers his head to kiss me, and I tense with anticipation as I feel him beginning to press in.

I'm wet and slick from the orgasms, my body primed for his possession, yet I still feel the stretch as his thick cock forces apart my inner walls, the sensation stopping just short of pain. His tongue invades my mouth at the same time, and I can't even moan as he begins to move, his thrusts deep and rhythmic. It's overwhelming, the feel of him, the taste of him, the way his body completely dominates and claims mine. I can't see, can't move. I'm drowning, and he's my only salvation.

I don't know how long it takes before the pulsing tension coils in my core once more. All I know is when Julian comes, I come with him, shuddering and crying out in his embrace.

Afterwards, he removes the blindfold and the ropes and carries me to the shower. I'm so exhausted I can barely stand, so Julian washes me, taking care of me as if I were a child. When he brings me back to bed, he pulls me into his arms, and as I fall asleep, I hear him say softly, "I will give you the world, my pet. The whole fucking world—just as long as you're mine."

## 1 8

### JULIAN

*I* wake up the next morning to the familiar feel of Nora sprawled on top of me. As usual, she's sleeping with her head pillowed on my chest and one of her slim legs draped across my thighs. I can feel the soft, plump weight of her breasts against my side, hear her even breathing, and my cock stiffens as recollections of last night invade my mind in graphic detail.

I don't know why I occasionally feel this urge to torment her, to hear her beg and plead. Why the sight of her bound to my bed gives me such satisfaction. When we were driving from her parents last night, I planned to take her gently and have her go to sleep, but when I saw her standing next to that four-poster bed, my good intentions went up in smoke. Something about the way she had been looking at me sharpened the dangerous hunger inside, bringing the darkness to the surface.

ANNA ZAIRES

What I wanted to do to her only began with ropes, and if I hadn't made myself walk out of the room after tying her up, I would've broken the vow I made to myself the night I hurt her.

The vow to keep violence out of our bedroom for the next few months.

Thankfully, leaving her for a bit and taking a cold shower in one of the guest rooms seemed to do the trick, taking the edge off the craving. When I came back, I was more in control, able to settle for torturing her with pleasure instead of pain.

A change in Nora's breathing brings my attention back to her. She shifts on top of me, making a soft noise, and rubs her cheek against my chest. "You didn't get up yet," she murmurs sleepily, and I smile, a peculiar sense of wellbeing spreading through me at the pleased note in her voice.

"No, not yet," I confirm, stroking her smooth, naked back. "I will in a few moments, though."

"Do you have to?" Her words are muffled. "You make a nice pillow."

"I'm glad I can be of use."

At my dry tone, she moves her head, looking up at me through her long, dark lashes. "Does it bother you? That I sleep on top of you like this?"

"No." I grin at her question. "Do you think I'd let you if it did?"

She blinks. "No. Of course you wouldn't." Moving off me, she sits up, pulling the blanket up around her. "We

196

should probably get up. I wanted to go for a run before breakfast."

I sit up too. "A run?"

"Yes. It's safe here, isn't it?"

"Not as safe as at the compound." The idea of her running out there makes me uneasy, even with all the security measures and no obvious threat in sight. If anything were to happen to her...

"Julian, please." Nora begins to look upset. "I'm just going to run here, in Palos Park. I won't go far, but I can't stay cooped up in this house for two weeks—"

"I'll go with you." I get up and walk over to the closet to find a pair of running shorts. "Get dressed. We should hurry. I'm guessing Rosa is already preparing breakfast."

We start the run with an easy jog to warm up. It's a brisk sixty degrees out, but moving keeps me from feeling the chill, even though I'm not wearing a shirt. I debate having Nora put on more layers, but she looks comfortable in her cropped leggings and a T-shirt, so I decide to let it slide.

As we exit our driveway and turn onto the street, I keep a careful eye on neighbors' cars pulling out of their garages and people stepping out for their own morning run. Being around so many strangers makes me uneasy. My men are strategically positioned all around the community, so I know we're safe, but I can't help watching for signs of danger.

"You know nobody's going to jump at us from the bushes, right?" Nora says, obviously noticing my preoccupation with our surroundings. "It's not that kind of neighborhood."

I glance at her. "I know. I vetted it."

She smiles and picks up speed. "Of course you did."

I match her pace, and we run at a fast clip for the next several blocks. A light sheen of perspiration appears on Nora's face, making her golden skin glow, and I find myself increasingly distracted by the sight of her. She always looks sexy when she runs, her petite body athletic and feminine at the same time. The tight, round muscles of her ass bunch and flex with every step she takes, and I can't help picturing my hands squeezing those globes as I slam my cock into her.

*Fuck.* At this rate, I'm going to need another cold shower.

"What are you doing after breakfast?" Nora asks breathlessly as we pass a jogging couple. "Do you have some work to do?"

"I have that meeting with my portfolio manager in the city," I reply, trying to control the urge to turn and glare at the male jogger. The fucker eyed Nora a bit too appreciatively when we ran past him. "I'll be back before dinner."

"Oh, that's good." She's beginning to pant as she

speaks. "I want to get a haircut today, and maybe meet with Leah and Jennie."

"What?" I turn my head to stare at her as we round the corner. "Where exactly are you planning to do these things?"

"At the Chicago Ridge Mall. I messaged Leah and Jennie last week, letting them know I'd be in town, and they said they were going to come in today and stay for the long Memorial Day weekend." She says it all in one long breath, then gulps in more air and gives me an imploring look. "You don't mind if I see them, right? I haven't seen Jennie in two years, and Leah—" She abruptly falls silent, and I know it's because she was going to say she saw Leah the last time she was in that cursed mall, when Peter let her act as bait for Al-Quadar. My pet doesn't realize I already know about that meeting—and about Jake's presence that day.

"You're not going to that mall." I know I sound harsh, but I can't help it. Just the thought of her wandering around that place by herself is enough to make me see red. "It's too crowded to be safe."

"But—"

"If you want to meet with your friends, you can do so here at the house or at some restaurant in Oak Lawn —*after* I make sure it's secure."

Nora's lips tighten, but she wisely doesn't voice any objections. She knows this is as far as she can push me. "Okay, I'll ask them to meet me at Fish-of-the-Sea," she says after a minute. "What about my haircut?"

I eye the long, thick ponytail hanging down her back. It looks beautiful to me, especially with the end swinging back and forth over her shapely ass. "Why do you need one?"

"Because"—she pants as we pick up the pace—"I haven't had so much as a trim in two years."

"So?" I still don't see the problem. "I like your hair long."

"You are such a *guy*." She can barely speak but somehow manages to roll her eyes. "I need to shape this mess. It's driving me crazy."

"I don't want you cutting it short." I don't know why I care all of a sudden, but I do. "If you trim it, don't take off more than a couple of inches."

Nora gives me an incredulous look as we stop to let a car pull out of the driveway in front of us. "Really? Why?"

"I told you. I like it long."

She rolls her eyes again as we resume running. "Yeah, okay. I wasn't going to shave it off or anything. I just want to get some layers put in."

"No more than a couple of inches," I repeat, giving her a hard look.

"Uh-huh, sure." I get the impression she's doing a third eye-roll in her head. "So I'll go for the haircut then?"

"Not at the Chicago Ridge Mall. Find a quiet place nearby, and I'll have my men secure it."

"Okay," she gasps as we begin a full-out sprint. "It's a deal."

Before I leave for the city, I make sure Nora is fully set with her plans for the day. I assign a dozen of my best men to be her security detail and give them orders to be as unobtrusive as possible. She probably won't even notice their presence, but they'll make sure nobody suspicious gets within three hundred feet of her.

"I'll be fine," she says when I hesitate in the hallway before leaving the house. "Really, Julian. It's just a haircut and lunch with the girls. I promise everything will be all right."

I take a deep breath and release it. She's right. I'm being paranoid at this point. The precautions I'm taking are the best way to keep her safe outside the compound. Of course, I could always keep her *inside* the compound for the rest of her life—that would be optimal for my peace of mind—but Nora wouldn't be happy that way, and her happiness matters to me.

It matters far more than I would've ever expected.

"How are you feeling?" I ask, still reluctant to go for some reason. "Any nausea? Tiredness?" I glance at her stomach—a stomach that's still flat in the tight jeans she's wearing.

"No, nothing." She gives me a reassuring smile when

I look up to meet her gaze. "Not even a hint of nausea. I'm as healthy as a horse."

"All right then." Stepping toward her, I lift my hand to lightly stroke her cheek. "Be careful, baby, okay?"

"Okay," she whispers, looking up at me. "You too, Julian. Stay safe, and I'll see you soon."

And before I can step away, she rises up on her tiptoes and plants a brief, burning kiss on my lips.

## 19

NORA

"Rosa, are you sure you don't want to go with me?"

"No, no, I told you—I have a lot to do before dinner. Señor Esguerra is trusting me to impress your family with this meal, and I don't want to disappoint him. You go ahead, have fun catching up with your friends." Rosa practically shoos me out of the enormous kitchen. "Go, or you'll be late for your hair appointment."

"All right, if you're sure." Shaking my head at Rosa's stubborn sense of duty, I head to the main entrance, where a car is already waiting for me. Thankfully, it's not the limo, but a regular-sized black Mercedes. I won't stand out too much, though this car, like the limo, also looks to be equipped with bulletproof glass.

The driver is a tall, thin man I've seen around the estate, but never spoken to. Julian told me this morning that his name is Thomas. Thomas doesn't introduce himself or say much this time either, all his attention focused on the road. As we leave the driveway, I see two black SUVs pull out behind us and follow us at some distance. It makes me feel like I'm the First Lady—or maybe a mafia princess.

The latter is probably a better comparison.

It takes less than a half hour to get to the hair salon. It's not an upscale place, but it has a good reputation in the area, and most importantly, Julian deemed its location easy to secure. I hadn't expected to get an appointment so easily, but they'd had a cancellation this morning and were thus able to fit me in at eleven.

"Just a little trim, please," I request after a tattooed, purple-haired lady shampoos my hair and leads me to one of the cutting stations. "No more than a couple of inches."

"Are you sure?" she asks. "Look at how thick it is. You should at least get some layers put in."

I frown, studying my reflection in the mirror. "Will it still be long?"

"Of course. You won't lose any of the length—it'll just be shaped nicely. The shortest layers, those around your face, will be well below your shoulders."

"In that case, go for it." I try to sound decisive, even though I feel nothing of the kind. It's hard to disobey Julian, even in this small thing, and that makes me determined to do so. "Let's layer up this mess."

As the hairstylist bustles around me, tugging and snipping at my hair, I watch the other people in the salon. After weeks of isolation on the estate, it feels odd to be among so many strangers. Nobody is paying me much attention, but I still feel uncomfortably exposed, as though everyone is staring at me. I'm also somewhat anxious. I know nobody here means me any harm, so the feeling is illogical, but some of Julian's paranoia is rubbing off on me.

Still, being here on my own is exciting. I know Julian's men are outside, so I don't truly have any freedom, but it feels like I do.

It feels like I'm a regular girl, out for a day of grooming and hanging out with her friends.

"All done," the stylist announces after a few minutes. "Now we just blow-dry, and you'll be all set."

I nod, trying to avoid looking at the long locks scattered all over the floor. It seems like a lot of hair, though the wet strands I see in the mirror don't appear particularly short.

"So, what do you think?" she asks after my hair is dry. She hands me a mirror. "How do you like it?"

I turn in the swiveling chair, studying my new hairstyle from all angles. It looks like a shampoo ad—long, dark, and sleek, with the shorter layers around my face adding some flattering volume.

"Perfect." I hand back the mirror with a smile. "Thank you so much."

Disobeying Julian seems to agree with me. Looks-wise, at least.

I still have some time to kill before meeting Leah and Jennie, so I go all out and get a mani-pedi at the same salon. In the middle of the pedi, my phone dings with an incoming message from Julian.

*You're still there?* he texts. *Thomas says it's been almost two hours.*

*Getting nails painted,* I respond. *How are things with you?*

*Probably not as colorful as with you.*

I grin and put my phone away. This all feels so wonderfully normal, even with the oversight from Thomas. It's like we're just a couple, with nothing dark and messed up in our lives.

Impulsively, I fish my phone out of my purse again.

*Love you,* I text, adding a smiley face at the end for emphasis.

There's no answer, but I didn't expect any. Julian would never acknowledge his feelings for me—whatever those may be—in a text. Still, my heart feels just a bit heavier as I put the phone away and pick up a gossip magazine instead.

Half an hour later, I'm as polished and shiny as the models in the magazine. My hair streams down my back in a smooth, glossy curtain, and my nails are prettier than they've been in months. Adding a generous tip, I pay and exit the salon, ready for the continuation of my day.

As expected, Thomas is waiting for me outside. I don't see any of the others from the security team, but I know they're there, guarding me from out of sight. Still, their lack of visible presence adds to the illusion of normality, and my spirits lift again as we drive to the seafood restaurant where Leah and Jennie agreed to meet me for lunch.

They're already there when I walk in, and the first few minutes are filled with hugs and excited exclamations over how long it's been since we've seen each other. I had been afraid that things might be tense with Leah after our last run-in at the mall, but my worries appear to have been unfounded. With the three of us together, it's like our high school days all over again.

"Oh gosh, Nora, I'd forgotten how beautiful you are," Jennie exclaims when we're all seated. "Either that, or living in the jungle is agreeing with you."

"Why, thank you," I say, laughing. "You look pretty great yourself. When did you decide to go red? I love that color on you."

Jennie grins, her green eyes sparkling. "When I started college. I decided it was time for a change, and it was either red or blue."

"I convinced her to go red," Leah says with a mischievous smile. "Blue wouldn't have matched her Irish complexion."

"Oh, I don't know," I say with a straight face. "I hear smurfs are all the rage lately."

Leah bursts into laughter, and Jennie and I join in. It feels so good to be back with the two of them. I've hung out with Leah a couple of times since my abduction, but I haven't seen Jennie in almost two years. She was studying abroad when I was home for those four months after the warehouse explosion, so we've never gotten a chance to reconnect beyond a few Facebook messages.

"Okay, Nora, spill," Jennie says after the waiter takes our orders. "What's it like being married to a modern-day Pablo Escobar? The rumors I hear are beyond bizarre."

Leah chokes on her water, and I burst out laughing again. I'd forgotten Jennie's propensity for shocking people.

"Well," I say when I calm down enough to speak, "Julian deals in weapons, not drugs, but otherwise, being married to him is quite nice."

"Oh, come on. Quite nice?" Jennie gives me an exaggerated frown. "I want all the gory details. Does he sleep with a machine gun under his pillow? Eat puppies for breakfast? I mean, the dude kidnapped you, for Pete's sake! Give us all the juicy—"

"Jennie," Leah cuts in sharply. She doesn't look the least bit amused. "I don't think this is a joking matter."

"It's okay," I reassure her. "Really, Leah, it's fine. Julian and I *are* married now, and we're happy together. We truly are."

"Happy?" Leah stares at me like I've grown horns.

"Nora, you know what he's capable of, what he's done. How can you be happy with a man like that?"

I look back at her, not knowing how to respond. I want to say that Julian is not that bad, but the words stick in my throat. My husband *is* that bad. In fact, he's probably worse than Leah thinks. She doesn't know about the mass eradication of Al-Quadar in recent months or the fact that Julian has been a killer since childhood.

Of course, she also doesn't know that *I'm* a killer. If she did, she'd probably think Julian and I deserve each other.

To my relief, Jennie comes to my rescue. "Stop being such a party pooper," she says, poking Leah in the ribs. "So she's happy with him. That's better than being miserable, right?"

Leah's fair complexion reddens. "Of course. Sorry, Nora." She attempts a weak smile. "I guess I just have a hard time understanding it all. I mean, here you are, finally back in the US, and you're planning to go back to Colombia with him."

"That's what happens when people marry," Jennie says before I can respond. "They live together. Like you and Jake. It's only natural that Nora would go back with her husband—"

"You and Jake are living together?" I interrupt, looking at Leah in shock. "Since when?"

"Since two weeks ago," Jennie says gleefully. "Leah didn't tell you?"

"I was going to tell you today," Leah says to me. She looks uncomfortable. "I wanted to tell you in person."

"Why? They just had one date," Jennie says reasonably. "It's not like they were boyfriend-girlfriend."

"Jennie's right," I say. "Really, Leah, I'm happy for the two of you. You don't have to be afraid to tell me stuff like that. I won't flip out, I promise." I give her a big smile before asking, "Are you renting an apartment off-campus?"

"We are," Leah says, looking relieved at my question. "We both had roommate issues, so we decided living together might be the best option."

"Makes sense to me," Jennie says, and for the next few minutes, we discuss the pros and cons of living with boyfriends versus roommates.

"What about you, Jennie?" I ask after the waiter brings our appetizers. "Any boyfriends on the horizon for you?"

"Ugh, no." Jennie makes a disgusted face. "There are barely a dozen okay-looking guys at Grinnell, and they're all taken. The two of you should've talked some sense into me when I decided to go to college in the middle of nowhere. Seriously, it's worse than being in high school."

"No!" I widen my eyes in mock horror. "Worse than being in high school?"

"Nothing's worse than being in high school," Leah says, and the two of them begin to argue about the comparative availability of guys in a suburban high school versus a tiny liberal arts college.

As the meal proceeds, we talk about anything and everything except my relationship with Julian. Leah tells us about an internship she got at a Chicago law firm, and Jennie shares amusing stories about her recent vacation in Curaçao. "They had an oil-processing plant right next to our hotel. Can you believe it?" she complains, and Leah and I agree that even a salt-water infinity pool—a cool feature of Jennie's hotel—can't make up for something as atrocious as an oil refinery in a vacation spot.

Eventually, the conversation turns to my life on the estate, and I tell them all about my online classes at Stanford, the art lessons I'm getting from Monsieur Bernard, and my growing friendship with Rosa. "I wanted her to join us today, but she couldn't," I explain, feeling slightly guilty about that. "My parents are coming over for dinner, and Julian asked Rosa to help with the meal." As I say that, I realize how spoiled I sound—and from the envious looks on Jennie and Leah's faces, they realize it too.

"Wow," Jennie says, shaking her head. "No wonder you're happy with this guy. He treats you like a freaking princess. If someone gave me Stanford, servants, and a huge estate, I wouldn't mind getting kidnapped either."

"Jennie!" Leah gives her an appalled look. "You don't mean that."

"No, I probably don't," Jennie agrees, grinning. "Still,

Nora, you have to admit, the whole thing is kind of cool."

I shrug, smiling. "Kind of cool" is one way to describe it. Messed up and complicated is another—but I'm happy to stick with Jennie's description for now.

"Wait, did you say your parents are coming over for dinner?" Leah asks, as if just now processing that part of my statement. "Like, to have dinner with you and him?"

"Yes," I say, enjoying the expressions on both of my friends' faces. "We had dinner at my parents' house last night, so today they're coming over to our place." And as Leah and Jennie continue to stare at me in shock, I explain that Julian purchased a house in Palos Park, so we'd have someplace secure to stay during our visits.

"Girl, I have to say, you live in a whole other world now," Jennie says, shaking her head. "Private island, an estate in Columbia, now this…"

"None of that makes up for the fact that he's a psychopath," Leah says, giving Jennie a sharp look before turning to me. "Nora, how are your parents dealing with him?"

"They're… dealing." I don't know how else to describe the wary acceptance on my parents' part. "It's obviously not easy for them."

"Yeah, I can imagine," Jennie says. "They're troopers, your parents. Mine would've gone nuts."

"I don't think 'going nuts' would've helped matters," Leah says astutely. "I'm sure Nora's parents are just happy to have her back."

I start to reply, but at that moment, both Jennie and Leah look up, gaping at something behind me. Instinctively, I turn, my heartbeat spiking—and look up straight into my former captor's blue gaze.

He's standing over me, his hand resting casually on the back of my chair and his lips curved in a dangerously sexy smile. "Mind if I join you, ladies?" he asks, looking amused.

"Julian." I jump in my seat, startled and more than a little flustered. "What are you doing here?"

"My meeting ended early, so I figured I'd swing by and see if you're ready to go home," he says. "But I see you're not done yet."

"Um, no. We were just about to get dessert." I cast an uncertain glance at Leah and Jennie, and see that they're both staring at Julian. Leah looks like she's ready to bolt, while Jennie's expression is a mixture of fascination and awe.

*Shit.* So much for a normal lunch with my friends. Turning my attention back to Julian, I say reluctantly, "I mean, I could be done if—"

"No, no, please join us if you have time," Jennie jumps in, apparently recovering from her shock. "They have great cheesecake here."

"Well, in that case, I must stay," Julian says smoothly, taking a seat next to me. "I wouldn't want to deprive Nora of such a delicacy." He smiles at me. "Your hair looks great, by the way, baby. You were right about the layers."

"Oh." Remembering my small act of rebellion, I touch my hair, feeling the shorter strands. His approval is both a disappointment and a relief. "Thanks."

"It does look nice on her," Leah says hoarsely, and I see that her eyes look less panicked now. Clearing her throat, she adds unnecessarily, "The new haircut, I mean."

Julian's smile broadens. "Yes. She looks gorgeous, doesn't she?"

"Yes, gorgeous," Jennie echoes, except she's looking at Julian instead of me. She seems mesmerized, and I can't blame her. With the scars on his face nearly gone and his eye implant indistinguishable from the real thing, Julian is as magnificent as ever, his masculine beauty dark and striking.

Finally gathering my scattered wits, I say, "Sorry, I've forgotten to introduce everyone. Julian—these are my friends Leah and Jennie. Leah, Jennie—this is Julian, my husband."

"It's nice to meet you both," Julian says with easy charm. "Nora's told me quite a bit about you."

"Oh?" Leah frowns. Unlike Jennie, she doesn't seem dazzled by his looks. "Like what?"

"Like the fact that the two of you have been friends since middle school," Julian says. "Or that you, Jennie, were Nora's date to the sophomore homecoming dance."

I blink, surprised. I had mentioned this to Julian at

some point, but I didn't expect him to remember such trivia.

"Oh, wow," Jennie breathes, her eyes still glued to Julian's face. "I can't believe she's told you all that."

Leah's mouth tightens, and she motions at the waiter. "A slice of cheesecake, please, and then the check," she requests when he comes over. "Their portions are huge," she explains, even though nobody objected to the size of her order. "We can all split it."

"That's fine with me," I say. I'm surprised Leah is willing to stay long enough to eat the cheesecake. I wouldn't have blamed her if she'd walked out right then and there. I know she's aware of what happened to Jake, and the fact that she's willing to be somewhat civil to Julian speaks volumes about her commitment to our friendship.

"So tell me," Julian says when the waiter departs, "how was your lunch so far? Did Nora already tell you the big news?"

I freeze, horrified that he's outing me like this. Telling my friends about the baby was something I'd planned to do much later, when it was inevitable. Not today, when I could still pretend to be a carefree college girl.

"What big news?" Jennie asks eagerly, leaning forward. Her eyes are wide with curiosity. "Nora didn't tell us anything."

"She didn't tell you about the gallery owner in Paris?"

Julian gives me a sidelong look. "The one who put in an offer to buy her paintings?"

"What?" Leah exclaims. "When did this happen, Nora?"

"Um, just yesterday," I mumble, a wave of relief sweeping away the sick feeling in my stomach. "Julian told me about it, but I haven't seen the offer yet."

"Wow, congratulations." Jennie beams at me. "So you're about to be a famous artist, huh?"

"I don't know about famous—" I begin, but Julian cuts me off.

"She is," he says firmly. "The gallery owner is offering ten thousand euros for each of the five paintings." And amidst my friends' exclamations of excitement, he explains that the gallery owner is a known art collector, and that my paintings are already gaining notoriety in Paris due to Monsieur Bernard's connections.

In the middle of all this, our cheesecake slice arrives. Leah had been right to order only one; the slice is nearly the size of my head. The waiter brings out four little plates, and we split the cake as Julian answers Jennie's questions about the Paris art scene and France in general.

"Wow, Nora, what an exciting life you're about to start," Jennie says, reaching for the check that the waiter brought. "You'll tell us when you have your first show, right?"

"I've got this," Julian says, picking up the check before Jennie can touch it. And before my friends can utter a word of protest, he hands two one-hundred-dollar bills to the waiter, saying, "Keep the change."

"Oh, thank you," Jennie says as the ecstatic-looking waiter hurries away. "You didn't have to do that. You just had a bite of the cheesecake, not any of the food."

"Please let us pay you for our portion," Leah says stiffly, reaching for her wallet, but Julian waves her off.

"Please, don't worry. It's the least I can do for Nora's friends." Rising to his feet, he extends his palm toward me. "Ready, baby?"

"Yes," I say, placing my hand in his. My few hours of freedom are over, but somehow I don't mind. As exciting as the day had been, it feels comforting to be claimed by Julian again.

To be back where I belong.

## 20

JULIAN

"Why did you come to meet me?" Nora asks as we get into the car after saying goodbye to her friends. "Were you afraid I might run away?"

"You wouldn't have gotten far if you tried." Turning to face her, I run my fingers through her hair. It's a bit shorter at the front, but still long and even silkier than usual.

"I wasn't going to run." Nora frowns up at me. "I don't want to run away from you. Not anymore."

"I know that, my pet." I force myself to stop touching her hair before I develop a fetish. "I wouldn't have brought you to America otherwise."

"So why did you come get me? I would've been home in an hour anyway."

I shrug, not wanting to admit how much I missed her. My addiction is completely out of control. No matter what I'm doing, I'm constantly thinking about her. Even a few hours apart are intolerable these days, as ridiculous as that may be.

"Okay, well, I'm glad Leah didn't freak out too much," Nora says when I remain silent. "I thought she'd run or call the police when you first showed up." She looks down, then glances up. "If you hadn't mentioned the big news, things would've been very awkward."

"Really?" I say silkily. "Maybe I should've told them the *really* big news." It was what I'd originally intended—to ask if Nora had already told them about the baby—but the horrified expression on her face gave away the truth before any of her friends could speak.

Nora reaches for my hand, her slender fingers curving around my palm. "I'm glad you didn't." She gives my hand a gentle squeeze. "Thank you for that."

"Why didn't you tell them?" I ask, placing my other palm over her small hand. "They're your friends—I would've expected you to share such things with them."

"I'm going to tell them." She looks uncomfortable. "Just not yet."

"Are you afraid they'll judge you?" I frown at her, trying to understand. "We're married. This is only natural. You know that, right?"

"They *will* judge me, Julian." Her soft lips twist. "I'll be a mother at twenty. Girls my age don't do marriage and babies. At least most that I know don't."

"I see." I study her thoughtfully. "What do they do? Parties? Clubs? Boyfriends?"

She lowers her gaze. "I'm sure you think it's silly."

It is, yet it isn't. It still catches me off-guard sometimes, how young she is. How limited her experience has been. I can't remember ever being that young. By the time I was twenty, I was already at the helm of my father's organization, having seen most of the world and done things that would make hardened mobsters shudder. Youth had skipped me by, and I keep forgetting that Nora still retains some of hers.

"Is that what you want?" I ask when she looks up at me again. "To go out? To have fun?"

"No—I mean, that would be nice, but I know it's not realistic." She draws in a deep breath, her hand twitching in my grasp. "It's fine, Julian. Really. I'm going to tell them soon. I just didn't want our lunch today to be all about that."

"Okay." Releasing her hand, I drape my arm over her shoulders and draw her closer. "Whatever you think best, my pet."

To my satisfaction, the second dinner with Nora's parents goes smoothly. Nora gives them a tour of the house while I catch up on some work, and by the time I join everyone for dinner, the Lestons seem much less tense than before.

"Wow, look at this table," Gabriela says when we all sit down. "Rosa, you prepared all this?"

Rosa nods, smiling proudly. "I did. I hope you all enjoy it."

"I'm sure we will," I say. The table is covered with dishes ranging from a white asparagus salad to the traditional Colombian recipe of *Arroz con Pollo*. "Thank you, Rosa."

"I'm still stuffed from that cheesecake," Nora says, grinning, "but I'll try to do this meal justice. Everything looks delicious."

As we dig into the food, the conversation revolves around Nora's day with her friends and the latest local gossip. Apparently, one of the Leston's divorced neighbors started dating a woman ten years his senior, while the man's miniature Chihuahua got into an altercation with another neighbor's Persian cat. "Can you believe it?" Tony Leston says, chuckling. "That cat outweighs the dog by a good ten pounds."

Nora and Rosa laugh while I observe the Lestons with bemusement. For the first time, I understand why Nora wanted to visit here so badly, what she meant when she said she needed a breather from the estate. The life Nora's parents lead—the life she used to lead before she met me—is so different I might as well be visiting another planet.

A planet populated by people blissfully ignorant of the realities of the world.

"What are you doing on Saturday, honey?" Gabriela asks, smiling warmly at her daughter. "Do you already have plans?"

Nora looks puzzled. "Saturday? No, not yet." And then her eyes widen. "Oh, Saturday. You mean my birthday?"

I suppress a flare of annoyance. I'd been hoping to surprise Nora again—preferably with a better outcome this time. Oh, well. Nothing to be done now. Leaning back in my chair, I say, "We do have something planned for the evening, but not during the day."

"Wonderful." Nora's mother beams at her. "Why don't you come over for lunch then? I'll make all of your favorite dishes."

Nora glances at me, and I give her a small nod. "We'd be happy to, Mom," she says.

Gabriela's smile dims slightly at the "we," so I lean forward and say to Nora, "I'm afraid I have some work to do, baby. Why don't you spend some time with your parents by yourself?"

"Oh, sure." Nora blinks. "Okay."

Tony and Gabriela look ecstatic, and I resume eating, tuning out the rest of their conversation. As much as I dislike the idea of being away from Nora, I want her to have some tension-free time with her parents—something that can only be achieved without my presence.

I want my pet to be happy on her birthday, no matter what it takes.

~

After the Lestons leave, Nora heads into the shower, and I pull out my phone to check my messages. To my surprise, there is an email from Lucas. It's just one line:

*Yulia Tzakova escaped.*

Sighing, I put the phone away. I know I should be furious, but for some reason, I'm only mildly annoyed. The Russian girl won't get far; Lucas will hunt her down and bring her back as soon as we return. For now, though, I picture his rage—the rage I can sense in the terse words of the email—and chuckle.

If the plane crash hadn't killed so many of my men, I'd almost feel sorry for the girl.

## 21

## NORA

"*An eye for an eye." Majid's eyes burn with hatred as he comes toward me, stepping over Beth's mangled body. The blood is ankle-deep as he walks, the dark liquid sloshing around his feet in a malevolent swirl. "A life for a life."*

*"No." I'm standing there shaking, the fear pulsing inside me in a sickening beat. "Not this. Please, not this."*

*It's too late, though. He's already there, pressing his knife against my stomach. Smiling cruelly, he looks behind me and says, "The head will make a nice little trophy—after I cut it up a bit, of course..."*

*"Julian!"*

My scream echoes through the room as I jump off the bed, trembling with icy terror.

"Baby, are you okay?" Strong arms close around me in the darkness, pulling me into a hard, warm embrace.

"Shh…" Julian soothes as I begin to sob, clinging to him with all my strength. "Did you have another dream?"

I manage a small nod.

"What kind of dream, my pet?" Sitting down on the bed, Julian pulls me into his lap and strokes my hair. "The old one about me and Beth?"

I bury my face against his neck. "Sort of," I whisper when I can speak. "Except Majid was threatening *me* this time." I swallow the bile rising in my throat. "Threatening the baby inside me."

I can feel Julian's muscles tensing. "He's dead, Nora. He can't hurt you anymore."

"I know." I can't stop crying. "Believe me, I know."

One of Julian's hands moves down to my belly, warming my chilled skin. "It'll be okay," he murmurs, gently rocking me back and forth. "Everything will be okay."

I hold onto him tightly, trying to quiet my sobs. I want to believe him so badly. I want the last few weeks to be the norm, not the exception, in our lives.

Shifting on Julian's lap, I feel a growing hardness pressing into my hip, and for some reason, it eases my fear. If there's anything I can be sure of, it's our bodies' desperate, burning need for one another. And suddenly, I know exactly what I need.

"Make me forget," I whisper, pressing a kiss to the side of his neck. "Please, just make me forget."

Julian's breathing alters, his body tensing in a

different way. "Gladly," he murmurs, turning to place me on the mattress.

And as he drives into me, I wrap my legs around his hips, letting the power of his thrusts push the nightmare out of my mind.

I wake up late on Friday morning, my eyes gritty from my middle-of-the-night crying bout. Dragging myself out of bed, I brush my teeth and take a long, hot shower. Then, feeling infinitely better, I go back into the bedroom to get dressed.

"How are you doing, my pet?" Julian steps into the room just as I zip up my shorts in front of the mirror. He's already dressed, his tall, muscular frame making the dark jeans and T-shirt he's wearing look like something out of GQ.

"I'm fine." Turning, I give him a sheepish smile. "I don't know why I had that dream last night. I haven't had one in weeks."

"Right." Leaning against the wall, Julian crosses his arms and gives me a penetrating look. "Did anything happen yesterday? Anything that could've triggered a relapse?"

"No," I say quickly. The last thing I want is for Julian to think I can't be on my own for a few hours. "Yesterday was an awesome day. I think it's just one of those things. Maybe I ate too much at dinner or something."

"Uh-huh." Julian stares at me. "Sure."

"I'm fine," I repeat, turning back toward the mirror to brush my hair. "It was just a stupid dream."

Julian doesn't say anything, but I know I haven't managed to allay his concerns. All through breakfast, he watches me like a hawk, undoubtedly looking for signs of an incipient panic attack. I do my best to act normal— a task greatly helped by Rosa's easy chatter—and when we're done eating, I suggest we go for a walk in the park.

"Which park?" Julian frowns.

"Any local park," I say. "Whichever one you think is most secure. I just want to get out of the house, get some fresh air."

Julian looks thoughtful for a second; then he types something on his phone. "All right," he says. "Give my men a half hour to prepare, and we'll head out."

"Will you come with us, Rosa?" I ask, not wanting to exclude my friend again, but to my surprise, she shakes her head.

"No. I'm going to the city," she explains. "Señor Esguerra"—she glances at Julian—"said he's fine with that as long as I take one of the guards with me. I don't need as much security as the two of you, so I figured I'd use the day to explore Chicago." She pauses and gives me a concerned look. "You don't mind, do you? Because I don't have to go—"

"No, no, you should definitely go. Chicago is a great city. You'll have fun." I give her a big smile, ignoring the sudden wash of envy. I want Rosa to have this kind of freedom; there's no reason for her to be stuck in the suburbs.

There's no reason for her to be confined like me.

The drive to the park takes less than thirty minutes. As we approach, I realize where we're going, and my stomach tightens.

I know this park.

It's the one where I was walking with Jake the night Julian kidnapped me.

The memories that come are sharp and vivid. In a dark flash, I relive the terror of seeing Jake unconscious on the ground and feeling the cruel prick of the needle on my skin.

"Are you okay?" Julian asks, and I realize I must've gone pale. His eyebrows come together. "Nora?"

"I'm fine." I attempt to smile as the car comes to a stop at the curb. "It's nothing."

"It's not nothing." His blue eyes narrow. "If you're not feeling well, we're going back to the house."

"No." I grab the door handle and tug at it frantically. The atmosphere in the car feels heavy all of a sudden, thick with memories. "Please, I just want some fresh air."

"All right." Apparently sensing my state, Julian motions to the driver, and the door locks click open. "Go ahead."

I scramble out of the car, the anxious feeling in my chest easing as soon as I step outside. Taking a deep breath, I turn to see Julian climb out of the car behind me, his face taut with worry.

"Why did you choose this park?" I ask, trying to keep my voice even. "There are others in the area."

He looks puzzled for a second; then understanding displaces worry on his face. "Because I had already scoped out this place," he says, stepping toward me. His hands close around my upper arms as he gazes down at me. "Is that what's bothering you, my pet? My choice of location?"

"Yes, somewhat." I take another deep breath. "It brings back certain… memories."

"Ah, of course." Julian's eyes gleam with sudden amusement. "I guess I should've been more cognizant of that. This just happened to be the easiest park to secure, since I had all the schematics from before."

"From when you stole me." I stare up at him. Sometimes his total lack of repentance still catches me off-guard. "You scoped out the park two years ago for my kidnapping."

"Yes." His beautiful lips curl in a smile as he releases my arms and steps back. "Now, are you feeling better, or should we go back?"

"No, let's take a walk," I say, determined to enjoy the day. "I'm fine now."

Julian takes my hand, lacing my fingers through his, and we enter the park. To my relief, in the daylight everything looks different than it did on that fateful evening, and it's not long before the dark memories recede, retreating back to that forbidden, closed corner of my brain.

I want to keep them there, so I focus on the bright sunlight and the warm spring breeze.

"I love this weather," I say to Julian as we pass by a playground. "I'm glad we came out."

He smiles and brings my hand up to brush a kiss across my knuckles. "Me too, baby. Me too."

As we walk, I see that the park is unusually busy for a Friday. There are older couples, moms and nannies with their charges, and a good number of people my age. I'm guessing they're college students, home for the long weekend. Here and there, I also spot a few military-looking types doing their best to blend in.

Julian's men. They're here to protect us, but their presence is also a stark reminder that I'm still a prisoner in a way.

"How were you able to find me?" I ask when we sit down on a bench. I know I should stop dwelling on the past, but for some reason, I can't stop thinking of those early days. "After our first meeting at the club, I mean?"

Julian turns to look at me, his expression unreadable. "I sent a guard to follow you home."

"Oh." So simple, yet so diabolical. "You already knew you wanted to steal me?"

"No." He clasps both of my hands between his palms. "I hadn't come to that decision yet. I told myself I just wanted to know who you were, to make sure you got home safely."

I stare at him, both fascinated and disturbed. "So when did you decide to abduct me?"

His eyes gleam a bright blue. "It was later, when I couldn't stop thinking about you. I went to your graduation because I told myself you couldn't possibly be the way I remembered you, the way you appeared in the pictures I had my guards take. I told myself that if I saw you in person again, this obsession would disappear... but of course it didn't." His lips curl with irony. "It got worse. It's still getting worse."

I swallow, unable to look away from the dark intensity in his gaze. "Do you ever regret it? Taking me the way you did?"

"Regret that you're mine?" He lifts his eyebrows. "No, my pet. Why would I?"

Why, indeed. I don't know what other answer I expected. That he fell in love with me and now regrets having caused me suffering? That I came to mean so much to him that he now sees his actions as wrong?

"No reason," I say quietly, pulling my hands out of his grasp. "I was just wondering, that's all."

His expression softens slightly. "Nora..."

I lean in, but before he can continue, we're

interrupted by a burst of childish laughter. A tiny girl with blond pigtails waddles toward us, a large green ball clutched tightly in her chubby hands.

"Catch!" she shrieks, launching the ball at Julian, and I watch in amazement as Julian extends his hand to the side and deftly catches the awkwardly thrown object.

The toddler laughs in joy and waddles toward us faster, her short legs pumping as she runs. Before I can say anything, she's already at our bench, grabbing Julian's legs as casually as if he were a tree.

"Hi," she drawls, giving Julian a dimpled smile. "Can I please have my ball back?" She pronounces each word with a clarity that would do an older child proud. "I want to play more."

"Here you go." Julian smiles as he hands it back to her. "You can definitely have it back."

"Lisette!" A harried-looking blond woman jogs up to us, her face flushed. "There you are. Don't bother these strangers." Grabbing the child by the arm, she gives us an apologetic look. "I'm so sorry. She ran off before I could—"

"No worries," I reassure her, grinning. "She's adorable. How old is she?"

"Two-and-a-half going on twenty," the woman says with visible pride. "I don't know where she gets it from; God knows her dad and I barely finished high school."

"I can read," Lisette announces, staring at Julian. "What about you?"

Julian moves off the bench and crouches down on

one knee in front of the girl. "I can too," he says gravely. "But not everybody can, so you're definitely ahead of the game."

The toddler beams at him. "I can also count to a hundred."

"Really?" Julian cocks his head to the side. "What else can you do?"

Seeing that we don't mind the child's presence, the blond woman visibly relaxes and lets go of her daughter's arm. "She knows all the words to that *Frozen* song," she says, smoothing the child's hair. "And can actually sing along."

"Can you really?" Julian asks the little girl with apparent seriousness, and she enthusiastically nods before belting out the song in a high-pitched, childish voice.

I grin, expecting Julian to stop her at any moment, but he doesn't. Instead, he listens attentively, his expression approving without being patronizing. When Lisette finishes with the song, he applauds and asks her about her favorite Disney movies, prompting the child to launch into excited chatter about *Cinderella* and *The Little Mermaid*.

"I'm sorry," her mother apologizes to me again when Lisette shows no signs of stopping. "I don't know what's come over her today. She's never this chatty with strangers."

"It's okay," Julian says, rising fluidly to his feet when

Lisette pauses to catch her breath. "We don't mind. You have a wonderful daughter."

"Do you have any children of your own?" Lisette's mother asks, smiling at him with the same adoring expression as her daughter. "You're so good with her."

"No"—Julian's gaze flicks down to my stomach—"not yet."

"Oh!" The woman gasps, giving us a huge, delighted smile. "Congratulations. The two of you will have beautiful babies, I just know it."

"Thank you," I say, feeling my face turn hot. "We're looking forward to it."

"Well, we must be off," Lisette's mother says, grabbing her daughter's arm again. "Come, Lisette, sweetie, say goodbye to the nice young couple. They have things to do, and we need to go eat lunch."

"Goodbye." The toddler giggles, waving at Julian with her free hand. "Have a nice day."

Smiling, Julian waves back at her, and then turns to face me. "That lunch doesn't sound like a bad idea. What do you think, my pet? Ready to go home?"

"Yes." I step closer to Julian and loop my hand through the crook of his elbow. My chest aches strangely. "Let's go home."

On our drive back, for the first time ever, I allow myself a small daydream. A fantasy in which Julian and I are a normal family. Closing my eyes, I picture my former captor as he was in the park today: a dangerous, darkly beautiful man kneeling next to a precocious little girl.

Kneeling next to *our* child.

A child that, for the duration of this fantasy, I crave with all my being.

## 22

### JULIAN

On Saturday morning, I get up early and make my way down to the kitchen. Rosa is already there, and after I verify that she has everything under control, I go back upstairs to Nora.

She's still sleeping when I enter the bedroom. Approaching the bed, I carefully pull the blanket off her, doing my best not to wake her up. She mumbles something, rolling over onto her back, but doesn't open her eyes. She looks unbelievably sexy, lying there naked like that, and I try to ignore the hard-on in my pants as I pick up the bottle of warm massage oil I brought from the kitchen and pour the liquid into my palm.

I begin with her feet, since I know how much my pet enjoys a foot rub. As soon as I touch her sole, her toes curl, and a sleepy moan escapes her lips. The sound makes me even harder, but I resist the urge to climb on the bed and bury myself in her tight, delicious body.

This morning, her pleasure is all that matters.

I rub one foot first, giving equal attention to each toe, then switch my focus to the other foot before working my way up to her slim calves and thighs. By then, Nora is all but purring, and I know she's awake even though her eyes are still closed.

"Happy birthday, baby," I murmur, leaning over her to massage the oil into her smooth, taut belly. "Did you sleep well?"

"Mmm." The inarticulate sound seems to be all she's capable of as I move my hands to her breasts. Her peaked nipples press into my palms, all but begging me to suck them. Unable to resist the temptation, I bend down and take one into my mouth, pulling on it with a strong sucking motion. Gasping, she arches up, her eyes flying open, and I turn my attention to her other breast, my oil-slick fingers slipping down her body to stimulate her clit.

"Julian," she moans, her breathing coming faster as I push two fingers into her tight, hot channel and curl them inside her. "Oh my God, Julian!" Her words end on a soft cry as her body goes taut, and then I feel her pulsing in release.

When her contractions ease, I withdraw my fingers from her swollen flesh and trail them up her ribcage. "Turn over, baby," I say softly. "I'm not done with you yet."

She obeys, and I reach for the massage oil again. Pouring a generous amount into my hand, I massage it

ANNA ZAIRES

into her neck, arms, and back, enjoying her continued moans of pleasure. By the time I get to the firm curves of her ass, I'm breathing heavily myself, my cock like an iron spike in my pants. Climbing onto the bed, I straddle her thighs and lean forward, covering her with my body.

"I want to fuck you," I whisper in her ear, knowing she can feel the hard pressure of my erection against her ass. "Do you want that, baby? Do you want me to take you and make you come again?"

She shudders underneath me. "Yes. Please, yes."

A dark smile forms on my lips. "Your wish is my command." Unzipping my pants, I pull out my cock and slide my left arm under her hips, elevating her ass for a better angle. On a different day, I'd pour the oil over her tiny asshole and take her there, reveling in her reluctance, but not today. Today, I'm going to give her only what she wants.

Pressing my cock to her small, slick entrance, I begin to push in.

Soft, wet heat engulfs me as I work my way deeper into her body. Despite the lust pounding through me, I move slowly, letting her adjust to my size. When I'm all the way in, she moans, clenching around me, and I nearly combust at the squeezing sensation, my balls tightening against my body.

"Julian…" She's panting again, squirming underneath me as I begin to thrust in slow, controlled movements. "Julian, please, let me come…"

Her begging pushes me over the edge, and with a low growl, I begin to fuck her harder, pounding into her tight, silky flesh. I can hear her cries, feel her body squeezing me even more, and when her contractions begin anew, I explode with a hoarse groan, my seed spurting into her spasming pussy.

Afterwards, I stretch out beside her and gather her into my arms.

"Happy twentieth birthday, baby," I murmur into her tangled hair, and she laughs softly, the sound full of delight.

"Oh, Julian, you really shouldn't have," Nora protests as I lock the delicate diamond pendant in place around her neck. "It's gorgeous, but—"

"But what?" I step back, admiring how the crescent-shaped stone looks against her golden skin in the mirror.

She turns away from the mirror to face me, her eyes dark and serious. "You already made the day so special for me, with the massage and the pancakes Rosa made for breakfast. You didn't need to get me such an expensive gift as well. Especially since I've never had a chance to get you anything for *your* birthday."

"My birthday is in November," I say, amused. "Last November you didn't even know that I survived the explosion, so there's no way you could've gotten anything for me. And the year before, well..." I smile, remembering how much she resented me her first few months on the island.

"Right." Nora's gaze is unblinking. "The year before, I had other things on my mind."

I laugh. "I'm sure. In any case, don't worry about it. I don't celebrate my birthday."

"Why not?" Her eyebrows pull together in a puzzled frown. "You don't like birthdays?"

"Not my own, no." My parents routinely forgot it when I was a child, and I'd learned to forget it as well. "In any case, that has nothing to do with this gift. If you don't like it, I can get you something else."

"No." Nora clutches the necklace possessively. "I love it."

"Then it's yours." Stepping toward her, I tilt her chin up with my fingers and press a brief kiss to her lips before stepping back. "Now you should get ready. Your parents are waiting to have lunch with you."

She blinks, staring at me. "What are we doing tonight? You told them we already have plans."

"We do. I'm taking you to a restaurant in the city." I pause, looking at her. "Unless you want to do something else? It's your choice."

"Really?" Her face lights up with excitement. "In that case, can we do something crazy?"

"Such as?"

"Can we go to a nightclub after dinner?"

My first inclination is to say no, but I bite back the words. "Why?" I ask instead.

She shrugs, looking slightly embarrassed. "I don't know. I just think it would be fun. I haven't been to a club since—" She falls silent, biting her lip.

"Since you met me."

She nods, and I recall the conversation we had after lunch with her friends. There had been a certain wistfulness in Nora's voice when she spoke of going out and having fun, a longing for things she thought she'd never experience.

"Which club do you want to go to?" I ask, unable to believe I'm even entertaining the idea.

Nora's eyes brighten. "Any club," she says quickly. "Whichever one you think is safest. I don't care where we go, just as long as there's music and dancing."

"How about the one where we met?" I suggest reluctantly. "My men are familiar with it from before, so it'll be easier—"

"Yes, perfect," she interrupts, beaming at me. "Can we take Rosa with us? I know she would love it too." My expression must reflect my thoughts because she swiftly clarifies, "Just to the club, not dinner. I also want the dinner to be just the two of us."

I sigh. "Sure. I'll have one of the guards drive her, so she can meet us at the club after dinner."

Nora squeals and throws her arms around my neck. "Thank you! Oh, I can't wait. This is going to be so great."

And as she heads out for lunch with her parents, I get together with Lucas to figure out how to secure a popular Chicago nightclub on a Saturday night.

～

"Wow, Julian, this is amazing," Nora exclaims as we walk into the high-end French restaurant I chose for our dinner. "How did you get a reservation? I heard people have to wait for months…" Then she stops and rolls her eyes. "Oh, never mind. What am I saying? Of course you of all people can get a reservation."

I smile at her obvious excitement. "I'm glad you like it. Let's hope the food is as good as the ambience."

The waiter leads us to our table, which is in a private nook at the back of the restaurant. Instead of wine, I order sparkling water for both of us, and also request the tasting menu after first explaining the restrictions associated with Nora's pregnancy.

"Very good, sir," the waiter says, bowing slightly, and before we know it, the first course is on our table.

As we nibble on asparagus risotto and langoustine ravioli, Nora tells me about her lunch and how happy her parents were to celebrate this birthday with her. "They got me a new set of paint brushes," she says, grinning. "I'm guessing that means my dad's no longer as skeptical about my hobby."

"That's good, baby. He shouldn't be. You have an amazing talent."

"Thank you." She gives me a glowing smile and reaches for her water glass.

As we talk, I find myself unable to look away from her. She's radiant tonight, more beautiful than I've ever seen her. Her strapless blue dress is sexy and elegant at the same time—though much too short for my peace of mind. When I saw her coming down the stairs tonight, in that dress and her silvery high-heeled shoes, it was all I could do not to drag her back upstairs and fuck her for three days straight. It doesn't help that she used some kind of make-up that makes her lips shiny and extra-lush. Every time she wraps those lips around a fork, I picture her sucking my cock and my pants get uncomfortably tight.

"You know, you never told me what you were doing in that club when we first met," she says when we're halfway through the third course. "Why were you in Chicago, in general? Most of your business is outside the US, isn't it?"

"Yes," I say, nodding. "I wasn't here for business in that sense. An acquaintance of mine recommended this hedge fund analyst to me, so I was interviewing him for the position of my personal portfolio manager."

"Oh." Nora's eyes widen. "Is that the guy you were meeting with the other day?"

"Yes. I liked what I saw two years ago, so I hired him. And then I decided to go out and see a bit of the city— which is how I ended up in that club."

"You weren't worried about security back then?"

"I had a few of my men with me, but no, Al-Quadar wasn't yet a major threat, and besides, I didn't have you to worry about." It wasn't until I acquired Nora that I became this paranoid about safety. My pet doesn't know how vulnerable she makes me, doesn't realize the lengths to which I would go to protect her. If I had been certain that Majid would let her go unharmed, I would've given him the explosive and whatever else Al-Quadar demanded.

I would've done anything to get her back.

"Were you planning to hook up with some woman that night?" Nora asks, taking a sip from her glass. Her tone is casual, but the look in her eyes is anything but.

I smile, pleased by her apparent jealousy. "Perhaps," I tease. "That's why most men go to clubs, you know. It's not for the dancing, I assure you."

"So did you?" She leans forward, her small hand tightening around her fork. "Did you pick up someone after I left?"

I'm tempted to tease her some more, but I can't bring myself to be that cruel. "No, my pet. I returned to my hotel room alone that night, unable to think of anything but this beautiful, petite girl I met." I also dreamed of her. Of her face that was so much like Maria's . . . of her silky skin and delicate curves.

Of the dark, twisted things I wanted to do to her.

"I see." Nora relaxes, a smile appearing on her face. "And the next day? Did you go out again?"

"No." I reach for a crab-stuffed fig. "I didn't see the point." Not when I was so obsessed I spent hours looking through the pictures my guards took of her.

Not when I already knew I'd never want any woman this much again.

## 23

### NORA

By the time we walk out of the restaurant, I feel like I'm in seventh heaven. Our dinner tonight was the closest thing we've had to a real date, and for the first time in months, I'm feeling hopeful about the future.

We may never be "normal," but that doesn't mean we can't be happy.

As we drive to the club, I allow myself that daydream again, the one where Julian and I are a family. It feels more real now, more substantial. For the first time, I can picture us raising our child together. It wouldn't be easy, and we'd constantly be surrounded by guards, but we could do it. We could make it work. We'd live on the estate most of the time, but we'd travel too. We'd visit my parents and friends, and we'd go to places in Europe and Asia. I would have a career as an artist, and Julian's business would be something that's in the background of our lives, instead of front and center.

It wouldn't be the kind of life I dreamed of when I was younger, but it would be a good life nonetheless.

It takes us half an hour to get to the club in downtown traffic. When we exit the car, Rosa is already standing there, waiting for us. Seeing me, she grins and runs up to the car.

"Nora, you look gorgeous," she exclaims before turning to Julian. "And you too, Señor." She gives us a huge, beaming smile. "Thank you so much for taking me with you tonight. I've been dying to go to a real American nightclub."

"I'm glad you were able to come," I tell her, smiling. "You look amazing." And she does. In sexy red heels and a short yellow dress that plays up her curves, Rosa looks hot enough to be a pinup girl.

"Do you really think so?" she says eagerly. "I got this dress in the city. I was worried it might be too much."

"There's no such thing," I say firmly. "You look absolutely phenomenal. Now, come, let's go dance." And grabbing her arm, I lead her to the club entrance, with an amused-looking Julian following on our heels.

Despite the club's location in an older, seedier part of downtown Chicago, there is a long line of people waiting by the door. The place must be even more popular now than it was two years ago. As we walk by, the men eye both me and Rosa, while the women gawk at Julian. I don't blame those women, even though some dark part of me wants to gouge their eyes out. My husband dressed up tonight, putting on a sharply tailored blazer and dark designer jeans, and he looks effortlessly hot, like a movie star coming out of a film premiere. Of course, movie stars don't usually conceal guns and knives under their stylish jackets, but I'm trying not to think about that.

One word from Julian to the bouncer, and we're inside, bypassing the waiting crowd. Nobody checks our IDs, not even at the bar where Julian buys Rosa a drink. I wonder if it's because Julian's men already warned the club management about us.

Either way, it's pretty neat.

It's only ten o'clock, but the club is already hopping, the latest pop and dance hits blaring from the speakers. Even though I've had no alcohol, I feel high, drunk with excitement. Laughing, I grab Rosa and Julian and drag them both to the dance floor, where tons of people are already grinding against one another.

When we get to the middle of the dance floor, Julian spins me around and pulls me against him, holding me from the back as we begin moving to the music. I instantly realize what he's doing. With the way he's holding me, I'm facing Rosa, and the three of us are sort of dancing together, but it's Julian's big body that surrounds me. Nobody can touch me, either on purpose or by accident, not without going through him first.

Even in the middle of a crowded dance floor, I belong to Julian and Julian alone.

Rosa grins, apparently also realizing Julian's agenda. She's even more excited than me, her eyes sparkling as she shakes her booty to the latest Lady Gaga song. Before long, a couple of good-looking young guys sidle up to her, and I watch, grinning, as she begins to flirt with them and gradually moves away from me and Julian.

As soon as she's occupied, Julian turns me around to face him. "How are you feeling, baby?" he asks, his deep voice cutting through the blasting music. The colored lights flicker over his face, making him look surreally handsome. "Any tiredness? Nausea?"

"No." Smiling, I vigorously shake my head. "I'm perfect. Better than perfect, in fact."

"Yes, you are," he murmurs, pulling me tighter against him, and I flush all over as I feel the hard bulge in his pants. He wants me, and my body responds immediately, the pulsing beat of the music echoing the sudden ache in my core. We're surrounded by people, but all of them seem to fade away as we stare at one another, our bodies beginning to move together in a primal, sexual rhythm. My breasts swell, my nipples pebbling as I press my chest against his, and even through the layers of clothing we're wearing, I can feel the heat coming off his large body... the same kind of heat that's building within myself.

"Fuck, baby," he breathes, staring down at me. His hips rock back and forth as we sway together, driven as much by our need for each other as the music's beat. "You can't wear this fucking dress ever again."

"The dress?" I stare up at him, my body burning. "You think it's the dress?"

He closes his eyes and takes a deep breath before opening them to meet my gaze. "No," he says hoarsely. "It's not the dress, Nora. It's you. It's always fucking you."

I half-expect him to drag me away then, but he doesn't. Instead, he loosens his grip on me, putting a couple of inches of space between us. I can still feel his body against mine, but the raw sexuality of the moment is reduced, enabling me to breathe again. We dance like that for a few more songs, and then I begin to feel thirsty.

"Can I please get some water?" I ask, raising my voice to be heard above the music, and Julian nods, leading me toward the bar. As we pass by Rosa, I see that she's still dancing with those two guys, seemingly content to be sandwiched between them. I give her a wink and a discreet thumbs-up, and then we're out of the dancing, writhing crowd.

Julian gets me a glass filled with ice water, and I gratefully chug it down, feeling parched. He smiles as he watches me drink, and I know he's remembering it too —our first meeting, right here by this bar.

As we turn to go back to the dance floor, I see Rosa walking toward the back, where the bathrooms are. She waves at me, grinning, and I wave back before turning to Julian.

"Let's dance some more," I say, grabbing his hand, and we dive back into the crowd just as a new song begins.

A few minutes later, I start to feel it—the familiar sensation of an overly full bladder.

"I have to pee," I tell Julian, and he grins, leading me off the dance floor again. We walk together to the back of the club, and I get in line to the girls' bathroom while Julian leans against the wall, watching as I wait my turn in the shadowed, circular hallway leading to the restrooms. I wonder if he's guarding me even here and almost snicker at the idea of him being worried enough to accompany me to the ladies' room.

Thankfully, he doesn't. Instead, he stays by the entrance to the narrow hallway, his arms crossed over his chest.

The line is long, and it takes almost fifteen minutes to get to my destination. When my turn finally comes, I step into the small three-stall room and do my business. It's only when I'm washing my hands that it occurs to me that Rosa disappeared in this direction, and I haven't seen her come out since.

Pulling out my phone from my tiny purse, I text Julian: *Did Rosa walk by you? Do you see her anywhere?*

There's no immediate answer, so I step out of the bathroom, about to head back, when a flash of something red a dozen feet away catches my attention. Frowning, I walk deeper into the circular hallway, past the restrooms, and then I see it.

A red, high-heeled shoe lying discarded on the floor.

My heart skips a beat.

Bending down, I pick it up, and a chill skitters down my spine.

There's no doubt now. It's Rosa's shoe.

My pulse speeding up, I straighten, looking around, but I don't see her anywhere. With the way the hallway curves, even the bathroom line is out of sight now.

Dropping the shoe, I pull out my phone again. There is a text from Julian in response to mine: *No, I don't see her.*

I begin to type out a reply, but at that moment, a door I hadn't noticed before swings open a few feet away.

A short, skinny guy steps out, closing the door behind him, and leans against the door frame.

A young guy, I realize, looking at him. More like a boy in his teens, his pale, freckled face unmarred by the slightest hint of stubble. His posture is casual, almost lazy, but something about the way he glances at me gives me pause.

"Excuse me." I approach him carefully, wrinkling my nose at the strong smell of alcohol and cigarettes coming off him. "Have you seen my friend? She's wearing a yellow dress—"

He spits on the floor in front of me. "Get the fuck outta here, bitch."

I'm so startled I step back. Then anger blasts through me, mixing with adrenaline. "Excuse me?" My hands curl into fists. "What did you just call me?"

The teenager's posture changes, becoming more combative. "I said—"

And at that moment, I hear it.

A woman's scream behind the door, followed by the sound of something falling.

My adrenaline levels surge. Without thinking, I step forward and swing upward with my right fist, just as Julian taught me. The momentum of my move adds to the force of the blow, and the guy gasps as my fist slams into his solar plexus. He starts to double over, and at that moment, my knee comes up, crushing his balls.

He bends over with a high-pitched scream, clutching his crotch, and I grab the back of his neck, using the momentum to pull him forward as I stick my right foot out.

It works even better than in training.

He pitches forward, arms flailing, and his head hits the wall on the opposite side of the hallway. Then he slides to the floor, his body limp and unmoving in front of me.

Shaking, I gape at it. I can't believe I just did that.

I can't believe I took down a guy in a fight—even if that guy was a drunk teenage boy.

Another scream behind the door snaps me out of my daze.

I recognize that voice now, and a fresh burst of adrenaline sends my heartbeat soaring. Operating solely on instinct, I jump over the young guy's fallen body and push open the door.

The room inside is long and narrow, with another door at the far end. A stained couch is by that door—and on that couch is my friend, struggling and sobbing under a man.

For a second, I'm too frozen to react, and then I notice streaks of red on the bright yellow of Rosa's torn dress.

A hot, dark rage explodes in my chest, sweeping away all remnants of caution.

"Let her go!" I yell, rushing into the room. Startled, the guy jumps off Rosa, and then, as if recalling his vile agenda, grabs her by the hair and drags her off the couch.

"Nora!" Rosa screams hysterically, pointing at something behind me.

Horrified, I spin around, but it's too late.

The other man is already on me, the back of his hand flying toward my face.

The blow knocks me into the wall, the impact of the hit jarring every bone in my back.

Dazed, I sink down to the floor, and through the

ringing in my ears, I hear a man's voice say, "You can fuck that one if you want. I'll take my turn with this one in the car."

And as rough hands start tearing at my clothes, I see Rosa's attacker dragging her toward the door on the far side of the room.

## 24

## JULIAN

*B*ored, I step away from the wall and peer into the hallway. Nora is already at the front of the line, so I lean back against the wall and prepare to wait some more. I also make a mental note never to return to this club. These lines must be a regular occurrence here, and I find it ridiculous that they haven't put in a bigger restroom for the women.

Taking out my phone, I check my email for the third time. As expected, nothing's happened since three minutes ago, so I put the phone away again and consider walking over to the bar to get myself a drink. I've been abstaining all night to keep my reflexes sharp in case of danger, but one beer shouldn't impact anything.

Still, I decide against it. Even though several of my guards are sprinkled throughout the club, I don't feel comfortable having Nora out of sight for more than a couple of minutes. I would've even waited in that line with her, but the curving hallway is so narrow that there's only room for the women and the occasional man pushing his way through.

So I wait, amusing myself by watching the dancers on the floor. With all the grinding bodies, the atmosphere is heavily sexual, but the flickering lights and pulsing beat do nothing for me. Without Nora in my arms to excite me, I might as well be standing on a street corner watching grass grow.

My phone vibrates in my pocket, distracting me from my thoughts. Pulling it out, I look at Nora's message and frown.

*Did Rosa walk by you? Do you see her anywhere?*

Stepping away from the wall again, I glance into the hallway. I don't see either Rosa or Nora there, but the girl who was behind Nora in line is still waiting her turn.

Satisfied that Nora must be inside the bathroom, I turn to survey the club, searching for a yellow dress in the crowd. It's hard to see, with all the people and the dim lighting, but Rosa's dress is bright enough that I should be able to spot her.

I don't see anything, though. Not by the bar and not on the dance floor.

Starting to feel uneasy, I push through the crowd to get to the other side of the bar and look again.

Nothing. No yellow dress anywhere.

My unease morphs into full-blown alarm. Grabbing the phone again, I check the location of Nora's trackers.

She's still in the bathroom or right next to it.

Feeling marginally calmer, I message Lucas to put the men on alert and text Nora my response before pushing my way back toward the restrooms. Maybe I'm being paranoid, but I need to have Nora with me. Right now. My instincts are screaming that something's wrong, and I won't relax until I have her securely by my side.

When I get to the hallway, I see that the line of women is even longer now, and there's even a line to the men's room. The narrow hallway is completely blocked, so I begin to shove people aside, ignoring their shouts of outrage.

Nora is not in this line, though the trackers indicate she's nearby. She's also not in the women's bathroom, I realize as I pass by it. According to my tracking app, she's about thirty feet ahead, a bit to the left of the curving hallway. The crowd clears out past this point, and I pick up the pace, my worry intensifying.

A second later, I see it.

A man's body on the floor, next to a closed door.

My blood turns to ice, the fear sharp and acrid on my tongue. If somebody took Nora, if she's been harmed in any way—

No. I can't allow myself to go there, not when she needs me.

An icy calm engulfs me, blocking out the fear. Crouching down, I grab the knife from my ankle holster and slide it into my belt buckle for easy access. Then, rising to my feet, I take out my gun and step over the body, ignoring the blood trickling from the man's forehead.

According to the app, Nora is only a few feet to the left of me—which means she's behind that door.

Taking a deep breath, I push open the door and step into the room.

Immediately, a muffled cry to my right catches my attention. Spinning, I see two figures struggling by the wall... and all traces of calm flee.

Nora—my Nora—is fighting with a man twice her size. He's on top of her, one of his hands muffling her screams and the other hand tearing at her clothes. Her eyes are wild and furious, her fingers curved into claws as she rakes at his face and neck, leaving bloody streaks across his skin.

A red fog descends on me, a rage more violent than anything I've known.

One leap, and I'm on top of them, dragging the man off Nora. I don't shoot—too risky with her near—but the knife is in my hand as I pin him to the floor, my left forearm crushing his throat. He's choking, his eyes bulging as I raise the knife and plunge it into his side, again and again. Hot blood spurts out, spraying all over me, and I smell his terror, his knowledge of impending death. His hands beat at me, but I don't feel the blows. Instead, I watch his eyes as I stab him again and again, reveling in his dying struggles.

"Julian!" Nora's cry snaps me out of my bloodlust,

and I spring to my feet, leaving her attacker's twitching body on the floor.

She's shaking, mascara and tears streaming down her face as she tries to stand up, holding the wall for support.

*Fuck.* Sickening fear fills my chest. I rush to her and gather her against me, frantically patting her down in search of injuries. Nothing feels broken, but her lower lip is split and puffy, and her dress has a small rip at the top. And the child— No, I can't think about that now.

"Baby, are you hurt?" My voice is barely recognizable as my own. "Did he hurt you?"

She shakes her head, her eyes still wild. "No!" She twists in my arms, pushing at me with surprising strength. "Let me go! We have to go after her!"

"What? Who?" Startled, I move back, holding her by one arm so she wouldn't fall.

"Rosa! He's got her, Julian! He grabbed her and dragged her out that way." Nora jabs her free hand in the direction of the door in the back. "We must go after her!" She sounds hysterical.

"Another man took her?"

"Yes! He said—" Nora's voice catches on a sob. "He said he was going to take his turn in the car. There were two of them here, and one took Rosa!"

I stare at her, a new fury building inside me. I may not be close to Rosa, but I like the girl and she's under my protection. The idea that someone dared to do this, to assault her and Nora this way—

"Hurry!" Nora implores, frantically tugging on the arm I'm holding to pull me toward the door. "Come on, Julian, we have to hurry! He *just* dragged her out that way, so we can still catch up!"

*Fuck.* I grit my teeth, every muscle in my body vibrating with tension. I've never been so torn in my life. Nora is hurt, and everything inside me screams that she's my first priority, that I should grab her and rush her to safety as quickly as possible. But if what she says is true, then the only way to save Rosa is to act immediately—and it'll take my men at least a few minutes to get to where we are.

"Please, Julian!" Nora begs, sobbing, and the panic in her eyes decides it for me.

"Stay here." My voice is cold and sharp as I release her arm and step back. "Do not move."

"I'm coming with you—"

"Like hell you are." Pulling out my gun, I thrust it into her hands. "Wait for me here, and shoot anyone you don't recognize."

And before she can argue with me, I stride swiftly toward the back door, messaging Lucas about the situation on the way.

## 25

### NORA

*A*s soon as Julian disappears through the door, I sink to the floor, clutching the gun he gave me. My legs are trembling and my head is spinning, waves of nausea rolling through me. I feel like I'm hanging on to my sanity by a thread. Only the knowledge that Julian is on his way to rescue Rosa keeps me from slipping into complete hysteria. Drawing in a shuddering breath, I wipe at the moisture on my face with the back of my hand, and as I lower my arm, a streak of red catches my attention.

Blood.

There's blood on me.

I stare at it, repulsed yet fascinated. It has to be from the man Julian killed. Julian was covered in blood when he touched me, and it's all over me now, the streaks of red on my arms and chest reminiscent of one of my paintings. Strangely, the analogy calms me a bit.

Drawing in another breath, I look up, turning my attention to the dead man lying a few feet away.

Now that he's not attacking me, I realize with shock that I recognize him. He's one of the two young men Rosa was dancing with. Does that mean that the second attacker is the other man? I frown, trying to remember the second man's features, but he's just a blur in my mind. I also don't recall ever seeing the teenage guy who was guarding the entrance to this room. Was he with Rosa's dancing companions? If so, why? None of this makes any sense. Even if the three of them are serial rapists, how could they have thought they'd get away with such a brutal assault in a club?

Of course, the motivations of the dead man don't matter anymore. I know he's dead because his body is no longer twitching. His eyes are open and his mouth is slack, a trickle of blood running down his cheek. He stinks of death too, I realize—of blood, feces, and fear. As the sickening smell registers, I scoot away, crawling a few feet to huddle closer to the couch.

Another man was killed in front of me. I wait for horror and disgust, but they don't come. Instead, all I feel is a kind of vicious joy. As if on a movie screen, I see Julian's knife rising and falling, sinking into the man's side again and again, and all I can think is that I'm glad the man is dead.

I'm glad Julian gutted him.

It's odd, but my lack of empathy doesn't bother me this time. I can still feel the man's hands on my body, his nails scraping my skin as he ripped at my clothes. He'd managed to pin me down while I was dazed from his blow, and even though I struggled as hard as I could, I knew I was losing. If Julian hadn't come when he did—

No. I shut that down mid-thought. Julian did come, so there's no need to dwell on the worst. All things considered, I've gotten off with minimal damage. My split lip throbs and my back feels like one giant bruise, but it's nothing irreparable. My body will heal. I've been hit before and survived.

The real question is: will Rosa?

The thought of her hurt, broken and violated, fills me with rage. I want Julian to slaughter the other man as savagely as he killed this one. In fact, I want to do it myself. I would've insisted on coming along, but arguing with Julian would've only slowed down Rosa's rescue.

For now, all I can do is wait and hope that Julian brings her back.

Spotting my little purse on the floor, I crawl over to pick it up. Every movement hurts, but I want that purse with me. It has my phone, which means I can reach Julian. And that's important—because it suddenly dawns on me that Rosa is not the only one in danger at the moment.

So is my husband.

No. I push that thought away too. I know what Julian is capable of. If anyone is equipped to handle this, it's the man who kidnapped me. Julian's life has been steeped in violence from childhood; killing a scumbag or two must be like cutting grass for him.

Unless said scumbag is armed or has buddies.

No. I squeeze my eyes shut, refusing to entertain such thoughts. Julian will return with Rosa, and all will be well. It has to be. We're going to be a family, build a life together...

*A family.*

My eyes pop open, my hand flying to my stomach as I gasp out loud. For the first time, it strikes me that without Julian's intervention, Rosa and I might not have been the rapists' only victims. If I had been brutalized, knocked around some more, there's no telling what might've happened to the baby.

The terrifying thought steals my breath away.

I begin to shake again, fresh tears forming in my eyes. I don't even know why I'm crying. Everything is fine. It has to be.

Clutching my purse, I focus on the door in the back. Any second now, Julian will walk through it with Rosa, and our lives will go back to normal.

Any second now.

The seconds tick by slowly. So slowly that it's all I can do not to scream. I stare at the door until the tears stop and my eyes begin to burn from dryness. No matter how much I try, I can't keep the dark imaginings away, and the fear inside me feels like it's going to swallow me from within, eat away at me until there's nothing left.

Finally, the door starts to creak open.

I jump to my feet, aches and pains forgotten, but then I recall Julian's parting words.

He's not the only one who might walk through that door.

Lifting the gun he gave me, I take aim with trembling hands and wait.

## 26

## JULIAN

*A*s soon as I send my message to Lucas, I open the door and step out into the alley behind the club. Immediately, the smell of garbage hits my nostrils, mixing with the pungent odor of urine. It must've rained while we were inside because the pothole-ridden asphalt is wet, the light from a distant street lamp reflecting in the oily-looking puddles.

Reining in my violent rage and worry, I methodically scan my surroundings. Later I will let myself think about Nora's tear-streaked face and how badly I fucked up, but for now I need to focus on saving Rosa.

I owe her and Nora that much.

I don't see anyone nearby, so I wind my way through the dumpsters, heading toward the street. A few rats scurry away at my approach. I wonder if they can sense the thrum of violence in my veins, the lust for blood that intensifies with every step I take.

One death was not enough. Not nearly enough.

My footsteps echo wetly as I round the corner, turning onto a narrow side street, and then I see it.

Two figures struggling by a white SUV some thirty yards away.

I can see the yellow of Rosa's dress as the man tries to drag her into the car, and black rage surges through me again.

Pulling out my knife, I sprint toward them.

I know the exact moment Rosa's attacker sees me. His eyes widen, his face twisting with fear, and before I can react, he shoves Rosa at me and scrambles into the car.

I put on a burst of speed, managing to catch Rosa before she falls, and she clutches at me, sobbing hysterically. I try to soothe her while extricating myself from her clinging grip, but it's too late.

The car starts up with a roar, and the tires squeal as Rosa's assailant slams on the gas, escaping like the coward that he is.

*Fuck.* I stare after the disappearing car, panting. I know my men are stationed at the intersection ahead, but a public shootout would draw too much attention. Holding Rosa with one arm, I pull out my phone and tell Lucas to follow the white car.

Then I turn my attention to the sobbing woman in my arms.

"Rosa." Ignoring the adrenaline pumping through me, I

gently pull her away from me to view the extent of her injuries. One side of her face is swollen and crusted with blood, and there are scratches and bruises all over her body, but to my relief, I don't see any broken bones. She looks so shaken, though, that I pitch my voice low, speaking to her as I would to a child. "How badly are you hurt, sweetheart?"

"He... they..." She seems to be incoherent as she stands there trembling, her dress ripped open, and I grit my teeth, fighting a fresh swell of fury. I can already see that whatever happened to her is not something she'll easily get over.

"Come, sweetheart, let me take you back to Nora." I keep my voice soft and soothing as I bend down to pick her up. Her shaking intensifies as I swing her up into my arms, and I clench my jaw tighter, walking back toward the alley as quickly as I can.

When we're in front of the door to the club, I lower Rosa to her feet. Then, holding her elbow for support, I carefully usher her through the doorway.

We're greeted by the sight of Nora pointing the gun in our direction. The second she spots us, however, her face lights up and she lowers the weapon.

"Rosa!" She drops the gun and runs across the room to us. "You got her, Julian! Oh, thank God, you got her!" Reaching us, she rises on her tiptoes and hugs me fiercely before wrapping her arms around Rosa and guiding her to the couch. I can hear her murmuring reassurances as Rosa clings to her, crying, and I use the opportunity to call for our car to come around to the alley.

A couple of minutes later, the car is ready.

"Come, baby. We have to go, get you both to the hospital," I say softly, approaching the couch, and Nora nods, her arms still wrapped around Rosa's shaking frame. My wife seems much calmer now, her earlier hysteria nowhere in sight. Still, I have to fight the urge to grab her and make sure she's as all right as she seems. The only thing that stops me is the knowledge that Rosa will fall apart without Nora's help.

Thankfully, my pet seems up to the task of dealing with her traumatized friend. That steel core I've always sensed within her has never been more evident than it is now. Even with the rage scorching my insides, I feel a flash of pride as I watch Nora get Rosa off the couch and lead her toward the exit into the alley.

Lucas is leaning against the car, waiting for us. As his gaze falls on Rosa, I can see his face changing, his impassive expression transforming into something dark and frightening.

"Those fuckers," he mutters thickly, walking around the car to open the door for us. "Those motherfucking fuckers." He can't seem to stop staring at Rosa. "They're going to fucking die."

"Yes, they will," I agree, watching with some surprise as he carefully separates Rosa from my wife and guides the crying girl into the car. His manner is so uncharacteristically caring that I can't help wondering if there's something between the two of them. That would be odd, given his fixation on the Russian interpreter, but weirder things have happened.

Shrugging mentally, I turn to Nora, who's standing by the open car door, her left hand gripping the top of the door frame. She seems lost in her own world, her gaze strangely distant as she lifts her right hand and places it on her belly.

"Nora?" I step toward her, a sudden fear gripping my chest, and at that moment, I see her face go chalk-white.

## 27

## NORA

The cramping sensation I began to feel a few seconds ago suddenly intensifies, turns into a sharp pain. It lances across my stomach, stealing my breath just as Julian steps toward me, his face tight with worry. Gasping, I double over, and instantly I feel his strong hands on me, lifting me off my feet.

"Hospital, now!" he barks at Lucas, and before I can blink, I find myself inside the car, cradled on Julian's lap as we screech out of the alley.

"Nora? Nora, are you all right?" Rosa's voice is filled with panic, but I can't reassure her at the moment, not with my insides cramping and twisting. All I can do is take short, gasping breaths, my hands digging convulsively into Julian's shoulders as he rocks me back and forth, his big body tense underneath me.

"Julian." I can't help crying out as a particularly vicious cramp rips through my belly. I can feel a hot, slippery wetness on my thighs, and I know if I look down, I'll see blood. "Julian, the child..."

"I know, baby." He presses his lips to my forehead, rocking me faster. "Hang on. Please, hang on."

We fly through the dark streets, the streetlights and traffic lights blurring in front of my eyes. I can hear Rosa talking to me, her soft hands smoothing over my hair, and I'm aware of a vague sense of guilt that she has to deal with this after everything she's been through.

Mostly, though, what I feel is fear.

A hideous fear that it's too late, that nothing will ever be all right again.

"I'm so sorry, Mrs. Esguerra." The young doctor stops next to my bed, her hazel eyes filled with sympathy. "As you might've guessed, you miscarried. The good news— if there can be any at a time like this—is that you were still in your first trimester, and the bleeding has already stopped. There might be some spotting and discharge for the next few days, but your body should return to normal fairly quickly. There's no reason why you wouldn't be able to try for another child soon... if you wish to do so, of course."

I stare at her, my eyes feeling like they've been scraped with sandpaper. I can't cry anymore. I've cried all the tears within me. I'm aware of Julian's hand holding mine as he sits on the edge of the bed, of the continued dull cramping in my belly, and all I can think is that I lost the baby.

I lost our baby, and it's all my fault.

"Where's Rosa?" My throat is so swollen I have to force the words out. "Is she all right?"

"She's in the room next to you," the doctor says softly. She's unusually pretty, with a pale, heart-shaped face framed by wavy chestnut hair. "Would you like to speak to her?"

"Are they done with her examination?" Julian's voice is as hard as I've ever heard it. His face and hands are clean now—he used bottled water to wipe most of the blood off us before we got out of the car—but his gray jacket is stained brown. I wonder what the doctors think of our appearance, whether they realize that not all of the blood on us is mine.

"Yes, they're done." The doctor hesitates for a second. "Mr. Esguerra, your friend said she doesn't want to press charges or speak to the police, but that's something we strongly recommend in cases like these. At the very least, she should let our sexual assault nurse examiner collect the evidence. Perhaps you can talk to Ms. Martinez, help us convince her—"

"Do any of her injuries require hospitalization?" Julian interrupts, his hand tightening around my fingers. "Or can she go home with us?"

The doctor frowns. "She can go home, but—"

"And my wife?" He gives the young woman a

piercing look. "You're certain there are no injuries beyond the bruises?"

"Yes, as I explained to you earlier, Mr. Esguerra, all the tests came back normal." The doctor meets his gaze without flinching. "There's no concussion or any kind of internal injuries, and there's no need for a D&C— dilation and curettage—procedure when the loss happens so early in the pregnancy. I recommend that Mrs. Esguerra take it easy for the next few days, but after that she can return to her normal activities."

Julian glances down at me. "Baby?" His tone softens a fraction. "Do you want to stay here until morning just in case, or would you rather go home?"

"Home." I swallow painfully. "I want to go home."

"Mrs. Esguerra..." The doctor places her hand on my forearm, her slender fingers warm on my skin. When I look up at her, she says gently, "I know it's little consolation for your loss, but I want you to know that the vast majority of miscarriages cannot be prevented. It's possible that the incident with you and your friend was a factor in this unfortunate event, but it's just as likely that there was some kind of chromosomal abnormality that would've caused this to happen regardless. Statistically speaking, some twenty percent of known pregnancies end in miscarriage, and up to seventy percent of first-trimester miscarriages occur because of those abnormalities—not something the mother did or didn't do."

I take in her words dully, my gaze slipping from her

face to the name tag pinned to her chest. *Dr. Cobakis.*
Something about that seems familiar, but I'm too tired
to figure out what.

Listlessly, I look up again. "Thank you," I murmur,
hoping she leaves the topic alone. I understand what
she's trying to do. The doctor's probably run into this
before—a woman's automatic tendency to blame herself
when something goes wrong with her pregnancy. What
she doesn't realize is that in my case, I *am* to blame.

I insisted on going to that club. What happened to
Rosa and the baby is my fault and no one else's.

The doctor gives my forearm a gentle squeeze and
steps back. "I'll get your friend ready for discharge while
you get dressed," she says, and walks out of the room,
leaving me alone with Julian for the first time since our
arrival at the hospital.

As soon as the doctor is gone, he releases my hand
and leans over me. "Nora…" In his gaze, I see the same
agony that's tearing me up inside. "Baby, are you still in
pain?"

I shake my head. The physical discomfort is nothing
to me now. "I want to go home," I say hoarsely. "Please,
Julian, just take me home."

"I will." He strokes the uninjured side of my face, his
touch warm and gentle. "I promise you, I will."

## 28

## JULIAN

*I*'ve never known an emptiness like this before, a burning void that pulses with raw pain. When I lost Maria and my parents, there had been rage and grief, but not this.

Not this awful emptiness mixed with the strongest bloodlust I've ever known.

Nora is still and silent as I carry her up the stairs to our bedroom. Her eyes are closed, her lashes forming dark crescents on her colorless cheeks. She's been like that—all but catatonic from blood loss and exhaustion—since we left the hospital.

As I lay her on the bed, I catch sight of her bruised cheekbone and split lip, and have to turn away to regain control. The violence seething within me feels so toxic, so corrosive, that I can't touch Nora right now—not without it marking her in some way.

After a few moments, I feel calm enough to face the

bed. Nora hasn't moved, still lying where I placed her, and I realize she's fallen asleep. Inhaling slowly, I bend over her and begin to undress her. I could let her sleep until morning, but there are traces of dried blood on her clothes, and I don't want her to wake up like that.

She'll have enough to deal with in the morning.

When she's naked, I take off my own clothes and scoop her up, cradling her small, limp body against my chest as I walk to the bathroom. Entering the shower stall, I turn on the water, still holding her tightly.

She wakes up when the warm spray hits her skin, her eyes flying open as she convulsively clutches at my biceps. "Julian?" She sounds alarmed.

"Shh," I soothe. "It's okay. We're home." She looks a bit calmer, so I place her on her feet and ask softly, "Can you stand on your own for a minute, baby?"

She nods, and I make quick work of washing her and then myself. By the time I'm done, she's swaying on her feet, and I see that it's taking all her strength to remain upright. Swiftly, I bundle her into a large towel and carry her back to bed.

She passes out before her head touches the pillow. I tuck a blanket around her and sit next to her for a few moments, watching her chest rise and fall with her breathing.

Then I get up and get dressed to go downstairs.

$\sim$

Entering the living room, I see that Lucas is already waiting for me.

"Where's Rosa?" I ask, keeping my voice level. Later I will think about our child, about Nora lying there so hurt and vulnerable, but for now I push it all out of my mind. I can't afford to give in to my grief and fury, not when there is so much to be done.

"She's asleep," Lucas responds, rising from the couch. "I gave her Ambien and made sure she took a shower."

"Good. Thank you." I cross the room to stand next to him. "Now tell me everything."

"The clean-up crew took care of the body and captured the kid Nora knocked out in the hallway. They're holding him in a warehouse I rented on the South Side."

"Good." My chest fills with savage anticipation. "What about the white car?"

"The men were able to follow it to one of the residential high-rises downtown. At that point, it disappeared into a parking garage, and they decided against pursuing it there. I've already run the license plate number."

He pauses at that point, prompting me to say impatiently, "And?"

"And it seems like we might have a problem," Lucas says grimly. "Does the name Patrick Sullivan mean anything to you?"

I frown, trying to think where I've heard it before. "It's familiar, but I can't place it."

"The Sullivans own half of this town. Prostitution, drugs, weapons—you name it, they have their fingers in it. Patrick Sullivan heads up the family, and he's got just about every local politician and police chief in his pocket."

"Ah." It makes sense now. I haven't had dealings with the Sullivan organization, but I'd made it my business to know potential clients in the US and elsewhere. Sullivan's name must've come up in my research— which means we might indeed have a problem. "What does Patrick Sullivan have to do with this?"

"He has two sons," Lucas says. "Or rather, he *had* two sons. Brian and Sean. Brian is currently marinating in lye at our rented warehouse, and Sean is the owner of the white SUV."

"I see." So the fuckers who attacked Rosa and my wife are connected. More than connected, in fact— which explains their idiotic arrogance in assaulting two women at a public club. With their daddy running this town, they must be used to being the biggest sharks in the pool.

"Also," Lucas continues, "the kid we've got strung up in that warehouse is their seventeen-year-old cousin, Sullivan's nephew. His name is Jimmy. Apparently, he and the two brothers are close. Or *were* close, I should say."

My eyes narrow in sudden suspicion. "Do they have any idea who we are? Could they have singled out Rosa to get at me?"

"No, I don't think so." Lucas's face tightens. "The Sullivan brothers have a nasty history with women. Date-rape drugs, sexual assault, gang bangs of sorority girls—the list goes on and on. If it weren't for their father, they'd be rotting in prison right now."

"I see." My mouth twists. "Well, by the time we're done with them, they'll wish they were."

Lucas nods grimly. "Should I organize a strike team?"

"No," I say. "Not yet." I turn and walk over to stand by the window, gazing out into the dark, tree-lined yard. It's four in the morning, and the only light visible through the trees comes from the half-moon hanging in the sky.

This community is a quiet, peaceful place, but it won't stay that way for long. Once Sullivan figures out who killed his sons and nephew, these neat, landscaped streets will run red with blood.

"I want Nora and her parents taken to the estate before we do anything," I say, turning back to face Lucas. "Sean Sullivan will have to wait. For now, we'll focus on the nephew."

"All right." Lucas inclines his head. "I'll begin making the arrangements."

He walks out of the room, and I turn to look out the window again.

Despite the half-moon, all I see out there is the darkness.

## 29

NORA

"Nora, honey…" A familiar gentle touch pulls me out of my restless slumber. Forcing my heavy eyelids open, I stare uncomprehendingly at my mom, who's sitting on the edge of the bed and stroking my hair. My head aches so much that it takes me a few moments to process her presence in our bedroom—and notice her red-rimmed, swollen eyes.

"Mom?" Holding the blanket, I sit up, suppressing a groan at the pain caused by the movement. My back feels stiff and sore, and my lower abdomen is cramping dully. "What are you doing here?"

"Julian called us this morning," she says, her voice shaking. "He said you and Rosa were attacked at a club last night."

"Oh." A flash of anger wakes me fully. How dare Julian worry my parents like this? I would've come up with something less frightening to tell them, some gentler way to explain the loss of the baby.

*The loss of the baby.*

The agony is so sharp and sudden that I can't hold it in. A raw, jagged sob bursts out of my throat, bringing with it a flood of burning tears. Shaking, I clamp my hand over my mouth, but it's too late. The pain wells up and spills out, the tears like acid on my skin. I can feel my mom's arms around me, hear her crying, and I know I have to stop, but I can't. It's too much, the grief, the knowledge that I did this.

Suddenly, it's no longer my mom who holds me. Instead, I'm bundled in the blanket on Julian's lap, his strong arms wrapped around me as he cradles me against him, rocking me like a child. I can hear my dad's voice, the timbre low and soothing, and I know Dad is consoling Mom, trying to calm her in *her* pain. At some point, he and Julian must've come into the room, but I don't know how or when it happened.

Eventually, Julian carries me to the shower. It's there, away from my parents' eyes, that I'm finally able to regain control. "I'm sorry," I whisper as Julian towels me off and dresses me in a thick, terrycloth robe. "I'm so sorry. Where's Rosa? How is she?"

"She's all right," he says quietly. His eyes are bloodshot, making me suspect he didn't sleep much last night. "Well, as all right as can be expected. She's still in her room, but Lucas spoke to her and said she's doing better. And you have nothing to be sorry for, baby. Nothing."

I shake my head, the awful guilt seizing me again. "I need to go see her—"

"Wait, Nora." He grabs my arm just as I'm about to rush back into the bedroom. "Before you do, there's something you and I need to discuss with your parents."

"My parents?"

He nods, looking down at me. "Yes. That's why I called them here. We all need to talk."

"The Sullivan crime family?" My dad's voice rises incredulously. "You're telling me that the men who attacked my daughter are part of the mob?"

"Yes," Julian says, his face hard and expressionless. He's sitting next to me on the couch, his left hand resting on my knee. "It's something I discovered last night, after we returned from the hospital."

"We need to go to the police right away." My mom leans forward, her hands clenched tightly in her lap. "Those monsters need to pay for this. If you know who they are—"

"They'll pay, Gabriela." Julian's gaze turns to steel. "You don't have to worry about that."

"It's because of you, isn't it?" my dad says savagely, getting up in a sharp motion. "They came after you—"

"No," I interrupt, shaking my head. I'm still reeling

from what I just learned, but if there's one thing I'm sure of, it's that for once, Julian's business is not at fault. "It was random, Dad. They had no idea who Rosa and I were. They were just"—I shudder, remembering—"just doing it for fun."

"Fun?" My dad stares at me, his features tense with anger as he sits down again. "Those assholes thought hurting two women would be fun?"

"Well, technically, they wanted only Rosa," I say dully. "I just happened to intervene."

Julian's hand tightens on my knee as he glances in my direction. For the first time this morning, I see a flash of fury behind his emotionless facade. I have no doubt that he blames me for this—for using my birthday to manipulate him into going to that club, for trying to rescue Rosa on my own.

For losing our child… the one I didn't even know I wanted until it was too late.

I have no idea what my punishment will be, but whatever it is, it'll be more than deserved.

"We have to go to the police," my mom says again. "We need to report—"

"No." This time, it's Julian who rises to his feet and begins to pace in front of the couch. "That wouldn't be wise."

"Why?" my dad asks sharply. "This is what civilized people do in this country. They go to the authorities—"

"The authorities are in Sullivan's pocket." Julian stops to give my dad a harsh look. "And even if they weren't, we might as well send Sullivan an email saying who we are."

"Right." I jump to my feet, ignoring the pain in my sore muscles. Finally, my sluggish brain connects all the dots, and I realize why Julian brought my parents here. If the man Julian gutted last night is indeed the head mobster's son, then my husband isn't the only dangerous criminal out for vengeance. "Mom, Dad, we can't do that."

My mom looks startled. "But, Nora—"

"It will be best if the two of you come visit us for a bit," Julian says, walking over to stand next to me. "Just until we get this situation sorted out."

"What?" My mom gapes at us. "What do you mean? Why? Oh." She abruptly falls silent. "You did something to one of those men last night, didn't you?" she says slowly, looking at Julian. "You don't want them to know who we are because... because—"

"Because one of Sullivan's sons is dead, yes." Julian might as well be corroborating the weather report. "They'll be looking for us, and when they figure out who we are, they'll come after you and Tony."

My mom visibly blanches, and my dad rises to his feet. "You're saying the mob is after us?" His voice is filled with angry disbelief. "That they might attack us because... because you—"

"Killed one of Sullivan's sons for trying to hurt Nora, yes." Julian's voice is the coldest I've ever heard it. "We can worry about casting blame later. For now, since I don't want Nora grieving for her parents, I suggest you notify your employers of your upcoming vacation and start packing."

"When are we leaving?" my mom asks, her face pale as she stands up as well. "And how long will this vacation be?"

"Gabs, you're not seriously thinking—" my dad begins, but my mom places her hand on his arm.

"I am." My mom's voice is steady now, her gaze filled with resolve. "I don't want this any more than you do, but you've heard about the Sullivans. They're bad news, and if Julian says we're in danger—"

"You trust this murderer?" My dad turns to glare at her. "You think we'll be safer with *him*?"

"Than here with the mob seeking vengeance? Yes, I think we will be," my mom retorts. "We don't exactly have many options, do we?"

"We can go to the police or the FBI—"

"No, Tony, we can't, not if what Julian says is true."

"Well, obviously *he* would be against going to the police—"

As they argue, I feel my headache intensifying. Finally, I can't take it anymore. "Mom, Dad, please." I step forward, ignoring the pounding in my temples. "Just come with us for a while. It doesn't have to be forever. Right, Julian?" I glance at my husband for confirmation.

Julian nods coolly. "Like I said, just until I get this

situation straightened out. Hopefully no more than a month or two."

"A month or two? How exactly will you straighten this out in just a month or two?" my mom asks while my dad stands there, vibrating with tense anger.

"Do you really want to know, Gabriela?" Julian asks softly, and my mom turns even paler.

"No, that's okay." She sounds slightly hoarse. Clearing her throat, she asks, "So what do we tell our work? How do we explain such a long vacation on short notice? I mean, it's really more of a leave of absence—"

"You can tell them the truth: that your daughter suffered a miscarriage and needs you for the next few weeks." Julian's harsh words make me flinch. Noticing my reaction, he reaches for me, his fingers curving around my palm as he says to my mom in a softer tone, "Or you can come up with some other story. It's really up to you."

"Okay, we'll do that," my mom says quietly, looking at us, and when I glance at my dad, I see that the anger has left his face. Instead, he seems to be holding back tears. Catching my gaze, he steps toward me.

"I'm sorry, honey," he says quietly, his deep voice filled with sorrow. "I didn't have a chance to say it yet, but I'm so, so sorry for your loss."

"Thank you, Dad," I whisper, and then I have to turn away so I don't start crying again.

Immediately, Julian's arms close around me, bringing me into his embrace. "Tony, Gabriela," I hear him say softly. His hand rubs soothing circles on my back as I stand there, fighting tears, my face pressed against his chest. "I think it's best if Nora rests for now. Why don't the two of you discuss this, and we can talk some more later today? Ideally, I want you and Nora to fly out tomorrow, before Sullivan figures out who we are."

"Of course," my mom says quietly. "Come, Tony, we have a lot to do." And before I can turn around, I hear their footsteps heading out of the room.

When they're gone, Julian loosens his hold and pulls back to gaze at me. "Nora, baby—"

"I'm okay," I interrupt, not wanting his pity. The guilt that I managed to push aside for the past hour is back, stronger than ever. "I'm going to go talk to Rosa now."

Julian studies me for a moment and then steps back, letting me go. "All right, my pet," he says softly. "Go ahead."

## 30

## JULIAN

*a*s I watch Nora exit the room, I'm cognizant of a thick, heavy pressure in my chest. She's trying to hide her pain, to be strong, but I can tell that what happened is ripping her apart. Her breakdown this morning was just the tip of the iceberg, and the knowledge that I'm to blame for this—that I'm to blame for everything—adds to the violent rage churning in my gut.

This is all my fault. If I hadn't been so fucking eager to please her, to make her happy by giving in to her every whim, none of this would've happened. I should've listened to my instincts and kept her on the estate, where nobody could've touched her. At the very least, I should've denied her request to go to that accursed club.

But I didn't. I let myself get soft. I let my obsession with her cloud my judgment, and now she's paying the price. If only I hadn't let her go alone to that restroom, if only I'd chosen a different club... The poisonous regrets swirl in my brain until I feel like my head will explode.

I need to find an outlet for my fury, and I need to do so now.

Turning, I head for the front door.

"I brought the cousin here," Lucas says as soon as I step out onto the driveway. "I figured you might not want to go all the way to Chicago today."

"Excellent." Lucas knows me too well. "Where is he?"

"In that van over there." He points at a black van parked strategically behind the trees farthest from the neighbors.

Filled with dark anticipation, I walk toward it, with Lucas accompanying me. "Has he given us any info yet?" I ask.

"He gave us access codes to his cousin's parking garage and building elevators," Lucas says. "It wasn't difficult to get him to talk. I figured I'd leave the rest of the interrogation to you, in case you wanted to speak to him in person."

"That's good thinking. I definitely do." Approaching the van, I open the back doors and peer into the dark interior.

A skinny young man is lying on the floor, gagged. His ankles are tied to his wrists behind his back, contorting him into an unnatural position, and his face is bloodied and swollen. A strong scent of piss, fear, and sweat wafts toward me. Lucas and my guards did a solid job of working him over.

Ignoring the stench, I climb into the van and turn around. "Are the walls soundproof?" I ask Lucas, who remains on the ground.

He nods. "About ninety percent."

"Good. That should suffice." I close the doors behind me, locking me in with the boy—who immediately begins to writhe on the floor, making frantic noises behind the gag.

Pulling out my knife, I crouch next to him. His struggles intensify, panicked noises growing in volume. Ignoring the terrified look in his eyes, I grab his neck to hold him still and wedge the knife between the gag and his cheek, slicing through the piece of cloth. A trickle of blood runs down his cheek where the knife cut him, and I watch it, relishing the sight. I want more of his blood. I want to see this van covered with it.

As if sensing my thoughts, the teenager begins to blubber. "Please don't do this, man," he begs, sobbing. "I didn't do nothing! I swear, I didn't do nothing—"

"Shut up." I stare at him, letting the anticipation build. "Do you know why you're here?"

He shakes his head. "No! No, I swear," he babbles. "I don't know nothing. I was in this club, and there was this girl, and I don't know what happened 'cause I just woke up in this warehouse, and I didn't do nothing—"

"You didn't touch the girl in the yellow dress?" I cock my head to the side, twirling the knife between my fingers. I know exactly how cats feel when they play with mice; this kind of thing is fun.

The young man's eyes widen. "What? No! Fuck, no! I swear, I didn't have nothing to do with that! I told Sean it was a bad idea—"

"So you knew they were going to do it?"

Instantly realizing what he's admitted to, the boy starts babbling again, tears and snot running down his battered face. "No! I mean, they don't ever tell me nothing until they do it, so I didn't know! I swear, I didn't know until we were there, and they said to watch the door, and I told them it's not fair, and they said I should just do it, and then this other girl came, and I told her to go away—"

"Shut up." I press the sharp edge of the knife against his mouth. He falls silent instantly, his eyes white with fear. "All right," I say softly, "now listen to me carefully. You're going to tell me where your cousin Sean eats, sleeps, shits, fucks, and whatever else he does. I want a list of every place he might ever visit. Got it?"

He gives a tiny nod, and I move the knife away. Immediately, the boy starts spewing out names of restaurants, clubs, underground fighting gyms, hotels, and bars. I use my phone to record all that, and when he's done, I smile at him. "Good job."

His cracked lips quiver in a weak attempt at an answering smile. "So now you're going to let me go, right? 'Cause I swear I didn't have nothing to do with that."

"Let you go?" I look down at the knife in my hand, as if considering his words. Then I look up and smile again. "Why? Because you betrayed your cousin?"

"But… but I told you everything!" His eyes are showing white again. "I don't know nothing else!"

"Yes, I know." I press the knife against his stomach. "And that means you're useless to me now."

"I'm not!" he begins yelling. "You can ransom me! I'm Jimmy Sullivan, Patrick Sullivan's nephew, and he'll pay to have me back! He will, I swear—"

"Oh, I'm sure he will." I let the knife's tip dig in, enjoying the sight of blood welling up around the blade. Tearing my eyes away from it, I meet the young man's petrified gaze. "It's too bad for you that his money is the last thing I need."

And as he lets out a terrified scream, I slice him open, watching the blood spill out in a dark, beautiful river of red.

After I wipe my hands on the towel someone thoughtfully left in the van, I open the door and jump out. Lucas is waiting for me, so I tell him to dispose of the body and head back into the house.

It's strange, but I don't feel much better. The kill should've relieved some of the pressure, eased the burning need for violence, but instead, it seems to have

HOLD ME

only added to it, the emptiness inside me growing and darkening with every moment.

I want Nora. I need her more than ever. But when I enter the house, the first thing I do is head into the shower. I'm covered in blood and gore, and I don't want her to see me like this.

Like the savage murderer her parents accused me of being.

When I emerge, the first thing I do is check the tracking app for Nora's location. To my intense disappointment, she's still in Rosa's room. I contemplate going there to retrieve her, but I decide to give her a few more minutes and catch up on some work in the meantime.

When I open my laptop, I see that my inbox is filled with the usual messages. Russians, Ukrainians, the Islamic State, supplier contract changes, a security leak at one of the Indonesian factories... I scan it all with disinterest until I come upon an email from Frank, my CIA contact.

Opening it, I read it swiftly—and my insides grow cold.

## 31

### NORA

"Hey there." Balancing a tray with tea and sandwiches in my hands, I push open the door to Rosa's bedroom and approach her bed.

She's lying on her side, facing away from the door, a blanket wrapped tightly around her. Setting the tray down on the nightstand, I sit down on the edge of her bed and gently touch her shoulder. "Rosa? Are you okay?"

She rolls over to face me, and I almost flinch at the bruising on her face.

"Pretty bad, huh?" she asks, noticing my reaction. Her voice sounds a little scratchy, but she looks remarkably calm, her eyes dry in her swollen face.

"Well, I wouldn't say it's good," I say carefully. "How are you feeling?"

"Possibly better than you," she says quietly, looking

at me. "I'm so sorry about the baby, Nora. I can't even imagine what you and Julian must be going through."

I nod, trying to ignore the stab of agony in my chest. "Thank you." I force a smile to my lips. "Now, are you hungry? I brought you something to eat."

Wincing, she sits up and glances dubiously at the tray. "You made this?"

"Of course. You know I'm capable of boiling water and putting cheese on bread, right? I used to do it all the time before Julian kidnapped me and made me live in luxury."

A ghost of a smile flits across Rosa's battered lips. "Ah, yes. Those dark times in the past when you had to fend for yourself."

"Exactly." I reach for a steaming cup of tea and carefully hand it to Rosa. "Here you go. Chamomile with honey. Should cure all ills, according to Ana."

Rosa takes a small sip and raises an eyebrow at me. "Impressive. Almost as good as Ana's."

"Hey now." I give her an exaggerated frown. "Almost? And here I thought I had this tea-making thing down."

Her smile is a shade brighter this time. "You're very close, I promise. Now let me try one of those sandwiches. I have to say, they look appetizing."

I give her a plate and watch as she eats her sandwich. "You're not joining me?" she asks halfway, and I shake my head.

"No, I grabbed a little something in the kitchen earlier," I explain.

"I shouldn't be hungry either," Rosa says after she polishes off most of her sandwich. "Lucas brought me an omelet earlier this morning."

"He did?" I blink at her in surprise. "I didn't know he can cook."

"I didn't know either." She takes the last few bites and hands the plate back to me. "That was really good, Nora, thank you."

"Of course." I stand up, ignoring the painful stiffness in my back. "Can I get anything else for you? Maybe a book to read?"

"No, that's okay." Wincing again, she pushes the blanket off, revealing a long T-shirt, and swings her feet to the floor. "I'm going to get up. I can't stay in bed all day."

I frown at her. "Of course you can. You should rest today, take it easy."

"Like you're resting?" She gives me a sardonic look and walks over to the dresser on the other side of the room. "I'm done lounging in bed. I want to talk to Lucas and find out what's being done about the fuckers who attacked us."

I look at her. "Rosa…" I hesitate, uncertain whether to proceed.

"You want to know what happened last night with those guys, right?" She pulls on a pair of jeans and stops to look at me, her eyes glittering. "You want to know what they did to me before you got there."

"Only if you want to tell me," I say quickly. "If you don't feel comfortable—"

She holds up her hand, silencing me mid-sentence. Then she takes a deep breath and says, "They followed me to the bathroom." There's only a hint of brittleness in her voice. "When I came out, they were there, both of them, and the older one, Sean, said there's a VIP room in the back that they want to show me. You know, like they sometimes have in the movies?"

I nod, feeling a growing lump in my throat.

"Well, idiot that I am, I believed them." She turns away, reaching into the dresser. I watch in silence as she pulls off her T-shirt and puts on a bra, followed by a black, long-sleeved shirt. There are scratches and bruises on her smooth skin, some in the shape of finger marks, and I have to hide my reaction as she turns back to face me and says, "I told them earlier that this was my first visit to this country, so I thought they wanted to show me a good time."

"Oh, Rosa..." I step toward her, my chest aching, but she holds up her hand.

"Don't." She swallows. "Just let me finish."

I stop a couple of feet from her, and she continues after a moment. "As soon as we got past the bathrooms, out of sight of the people standing in line, the younger one, Brian, jumped me and dragged me into that room. There was this teenage guy too, and he watched the whole thing before Sean told him to go stand out in the hallway and make sure no one came in. I think they were going to"—she stops to compose herself for a second —"going to give him a turn after they were both done."

As she speaks, the rage I felt in the club returns. It had gotten subsumed beneath the weight of grief, pushed aside by the agony of my own loss, but now I'm aware of it again. Sharp and burning hot, the anger fills me until I'm all but shaking with it, my hands clenching and unclenching by my sides.

"I think you know the rest of the story," Rosa continues, her voice growing more brittle by the second. "You came in just as I was trying to fight off Sean. If it hadn't been for you…" Her face crumples, and this time I can't hang back.

Closing the distance between us, I embrace her, holding her as she begins to shake. Underneath my anger, I feel helpless, utterly inadequate to the task at hand. What happened to Rosa is every woman's worst nightmare, and I have no idea how to console her. To an outsider, what Julian did to me on the island might seem the same, but even during that traumatic first time, he had given me some semblance of tenderness. I'd felt violated, but also cherished, as incongruous as that combination might be.

I've never felt the way Rosa must be feeling now.

"I'm sorry," I whisper, stroking her hair. "I'm so sorry. Those bastards will pay. We'll make them pay."

She sniffles and pulls away, her eyes shimmering

with tears. "Yes." Her voice is choked as she steps back. "I want them to, Nora. I want it more than anything."

"Me too," I whisper, staring at her. I want Rosa's attackers dead. I want them eliminated in the most brutal way possible. It's wrong, it's sick, but I don't care. Images of the man Julian killed last night float through my mind, bringing with them a peculiar sense of satisfaction. I want the other one—Sean—to pay the same way.

I want to unleash Julian on him and watch my husband work his savage magic.

A knock on the door startles us both.

"Come in," Rosa calls out, using her sleeve to wipe the tears from her face.

To my surprise, Julian enters the room, his expression tense and oddly worried. He's changed clothes since this morning, and his hair looks wet, as though he just took a shower.

"What's wrong?" I ask immediately, my heart rate spiking. "Did something happen?"

"No," Julian says, crossing the room. "Not yet. But we may need to expedite your departure." He stops in front of me. "I just learned that an artist's sketch of the three of us is being circulated in the local FBI's office. The brother who got away must have a good memory for faces. The Sullivans are looking for us, and if they're as well connected as we think, we don't have much time."

Fear wraps like barbed wire around my chest. "Do you think they already know about my parents?"

"I have no idea, but it's not entirely out of the question. Call them now, and tell them to pack what they can. We'll pick them up in an hour, and I'll bring all of you to the airport."

"Wait a minute." I stare at Julian. "All of *us*? What about you?"

"I need to deal with the Sullivan threat. Lucas and I will remain behind along with most of the guards."

"What?" I find it hard to breathe all of a sudden. "What do you mean, you'll remain behind?"

"I need to clean up this mess," Julian says impatiently. "Now, are we going to waste time talking about this, or are you calling your parents?"

I swallow the bitter objections rising in my throat. "I'm going to call them now," I say tightly, reaching for my phone.

Julian is right; now is not the time to argue about this. However, if he thinks I'm going to meekly go along with this, he's deeply mistaken.

I will do whatever it takes not to lose him again.

## JULIAN

*T*he drive to Nora's parents' house passes in tense silence. I'm busy coordinating the security logistics with my team, and Nora is furiously texting with her parents, who seem to be bombarding her with questions about the sudden change of plans. Rosa watches us both quietly, the black-and-blue swelling on her face hiding her expression.

As soon as we arrive, Nora hurries into the house, and I follow her in, not wanting to leave her alone for even a half hour. Rosa remains in the car with Lucas, explaining that she doesn't want to be in the way.

When I walk in, I see that Rosa was right to stay outside.

Inside, the Lestons' place is a madhouse. Gabriela is rushing around, trying to stuff as many items as possible into a huge suitcase, and her husband is speaking loudly on the phone, explaining to someone that yes, he has to leave the country now, and no, he's sorry he couldn't give more notice.

"They're going to fire me," he mutters darkly as he hangs up, and I resist the urge to say that no job is worth his life.

"If they fire you, I'll help you find another position, Tony," I say instead, sitting down at the kitchen table. Nora's father shoots me an angry glare in response, but I ignore him, focusing on the dozens of emails that managed to pile up in my inbox in the last few hours.

Forty minutes later, Nora finally gets the Lestons to stop packing.

"We have to go, Mom," she insists as her mother remembers yet another thing she forgot to take. "We have bug spray at the compound, I promise. And whatever else you need, we'll order and have it delivered for you. We don't live in a complete wilderness, you know."

Gabriela seems mollified by that, so I help her close the huge suitcase and haul it out to the car. The thing weighs at least two-hundred-and-fifty pounds, and I grunt with effort as I lift it into the trunk of the limo.

In the meantime, Nora's father brings out a second, smaller suitcase.

"I'll take it," I say, reaching for it, but he jerks it away.

"I've got it," he says sharply, so I step away to let him handle it on his own. If he wants to continue stewing, that's his business.

Once everything is loaded, Nora's parents climb into

the car, and Rosa goes to sit in the front next to Lucas. "To give the four of you more room," she explains, as though the back of the limo can't easily accommodate ten people.

"Do all these cars need to be here?" Nora's mother asks as I take a seat next to Nora. "I mean, is it really that unsafe?"

"Probably not, but I don't want to risk it," I say as we pull out of the driveway. In addition to the twenty-three guards split between seven SUVs—all of which are currently idling on this quiet block—I also have a stash of weapons under our seat. It's overkill for a peaceful trip to Chicago, but now that there's trouble, I'm worried that it's not enough. I should've brought more men, more weapons, but I didn't want Frank and company thinking I was here to do a deal.

"This is insane," Tony mutters, looking out the back window at the procession of cars following us. "I can't even imagine what our neighbors are thinking."

"They're thinking you're a VIP, Dad," Nora says with forced cheerfulness. "Haven't you ever wondered what it must be like for the President, always traveling with the Secret Service?"

"No, I can't say I have." Nora's father turns back to face us, his expression softening as he looks at his daughter. "How are you feeling, honey?" he asks her. "You should probably be resting instead of dealing with this craziness."

"I'm fine, Dad." Nora's face tightens. "And I'd rather not talk about it, if you don't mind."

"Of course, honey," her mother says, blinking rapidly —I presume to stop herself from crying. "Whatever you wish, my love."

Nora attempts to give her mother a smile, but fails miserably. Unable to resist, I reach out and drape my arm over her shoulders, pulling her against me. "Relax, baby," I murmur into her hair as she nestles against my side. "We'll be there soon, and you can sleep on the plane, okay?"

Nora lets out a sigh and mumbles into my shoulder, "Sounds good." She seems tired, so I stroke her hair, enjoying its silky softness. I could sit like this forever, feeling the warmth of her small body, smelling her sweet, delicate scent. For the first time since the miscarriage, some of the heaviness in my chest lifts, the dark, bitter grief easing slightly. The violence still pulses in my veins, but the awful emptiness is filled for the moment, the painful void no longer expanding within.

I don't know how long we sit like this, but when I glance across the limo aisle, I see Nora's parents watching us strangely. Gabriela, especially, seems fascinated. I frown at them and position Nora more comfortably at my side. I don't like that they're witnessing this. I don't want them to know how much I depend on my pet, how desperately I need her.

At my glare, they both look away, and I resume

stroking Nora's hair as we get off the interstate onto a two-lane highway.

"How much longer until we get there?" Nora's father asks a couple of minutes later. "We're going to a private airport, right?"

"Right," I confirm. "We're not too far now, I believe. There's no traffic, so we'll be there in about twenty minutes. One of my men has gone ahead to prepare the plane, so as soon as we get there, we'll be able to take off."

"And we can depart like this? Without going through customs?" Nora's mother asks. She still seems to be unusually interested in the way I'm embracing Nora. "Nobody will prevent us from re-entering the country or anything?"

"No," I say. "I have a special arrangement with—" Before I can finish explaining, the car picks up speed. The acceleration is so sharp and sudden that I barely manage to remain upright and hold on to Nora, who gasps and clutches at my waist. Her parents aren't so lucky; they fall onto their sides, nearly flying off the long limo seat.

The panel separating us from the driver rolls down, revealing Lucas's grim face in the rearview mirror.

"We have a tail," he says tersely. "They're onto us, and they're coming with everything they've got."

## 33

NORA

*M*y heart stops beating for a second; then adrenaline explodes in my veins.

Before I have a chance to react, Julian is already in motion. Unbuckling my seatbelt, he grabs my arm and drags me off the seat onto the limo floor.

"Stay there," he barks, and I watch in shock as he lifts the seat, revealing an enormous stash of weapons.

"What—" my mom gasps, but at that moment, the limo swerves, knocking me against the side of the stuffed leather seat. My parents cry out, clutching desperately at each other, and Julian grabs the edge of the raised seat to prevent himself from falling.

And then I hear it.

The *rat-tat-tat* of automatic gunfire.

Somebody is shooting at us.

"Gabriela!" My dad's face is stark white. "Hold on to me!"

The limo swerves again, causing my mom to let out a frightened scream. Somehow Julian remains upright, bending over the stash as the limo accelerates even more. From my position on the floor, all I can see through the windows are the tree tops flashing by. We must be flying down this highway at breakneck speed.

Another burst of gunfire, and the trees flash by faster, the greenery blurring in my vision. I can hear the drumming of my pulse; it almost drowns out the squeal of tires in the distance.

"Oh my God!" At my mom's panicked screech, I grab onto a seat and rise up on my knees to look out the back window.

The sight that greets me is like something out of a *Fast and Furious* movie.

Behind our guards' seven SUVs, there's a whole cavalcade of cars. About a dozen are SUVs and vans, but there are also three Hummers with giant guns mounted on their roofs. Men with assault rifles are hanging out of the cars' windows, exchanging fire with our guards— who are doing the same. As I watch in shock, I see one of the pursuers' cars gain on the last of our SUVs and smash into its side in an apparent effort to force it off the road. Both cars waver off course, sparks flying where their sides scrape together, and I hear another burst of gunfire, followed by the pursuers' car careening off the road and flipping over.

*One down, fifteen-plus to go.*

The math is crystal-clear in my mind. *Fifteen cars*

*versus eight, counting our limo.* The odds are not in our favor. My heart beats wildly as the high-speed battle continues, the cars smashing together amidst a hail of bullets.

*Boom!* The deafening sound vibrates through me, rattling every bone in my body. Stunned, I watch the guards' SUV in the back fly up, exploding in mid-air. Its gas tank must've been hit, I think dazedly, and then I hear Julian shouting my name.

My ears ringing, I turn and see him thrusting something bulky at me. "Put this on!" he roars before throwing two of the same items at my parents.

Bulletproof vests, I realize in disbelief.

He just handed us bulletproof vests.

The thing is heavy, but I manage to get it on, even with the limo swerving all over the place. I can hear my parents frantically instructing one another, and I turn to see Julian already wearing his own vest.

He's also holding an AK-47—which he thrusts into my hands before turning to lift a big, unusual-looking weapon out of the stash. I stare at it, puzzled, but then I recognize what it is.

A handheld grenade launcher. Julian had shown it to me once on the estate.

Shaking off my shock, I climb up on the seat, cradling the assault rifle with unsteady hands. I have to do my part, no matter how terrifying it may be. But before I can roll down the window and start shooting, Julian pulls me down to the floor again.

"Stay down," he roars at me. "Don't fucking move!"

I nod, trying to control my rapid breathing. The adrenaline sizzling through me both speeds everything up and slows it down, my perception foggy and sharp at the same time. I can hear my mom sobbing and Rosa and Lucas yelling something at the front, and then I see Julian's face change as he turns toward the front window.

"Fuck!" The expletive bursts out of his throat, terrifying me with its vehemence.

Unable to stay still, I rise up on my knees again . . . and my lungs cease working.

On the road ahead of us, just a few hundred feet away, is a police blockade—and we're barreling toward it at race-car speed.

## 34

### JULIAN

The cold, rational part of my mind instantly registers two things: there's nowhere for us to turn, and the four police cars blocking our way are surrounded by men wearing SWAT gear.

They were expecting us—which means they're in Sullivan's pocket and here to kill us all.

The thought fills me with terrified rage. I'm not afraid for myself, but the knowledge that Nora may die today, that I may never hold her again—

*No. Fuck, no.* Ruthlessly, I push the paralyzing thought aside and quickly assess the situation.

In less than twenty seconds, we'll reach the police barricade. I know what Lucas intends: to ram into the two cars that have the widest gap between them. The gap is only two feet wide, but we're going 120 miles an hour and the car is heavily armored, which means momentum is on our side.

All we need to do is survive the collision.

Gripping the grenade launcher in my right hand, I yell at Nora's parents, "Brace yourselves!" and drop to the floor, surrounding Nora with my body.

A few seconds later, our limo slams into the police cars with bone-jarring force. I can hear Nora's parents screaming, feel the inertia of the impact dragging me forward, and I tense every muscle in my body in an effort to stop the slide.

It works, barely. My left shoulder slams into the side of the seat, but I keep Nora safe underneath me. I have no doubt I'm crushing her with my weight, but it's better than the alternative. I can hear the metallic ding of bullets hitting the side and windows of the car, and I know they're firing at us.

If we were in a regular car, we'd already be riddled with holes.

As soon as I feel the limo speeding up again, I jump to my feet, noting out of the corner of my eye that Nora's parents seem to have survived the impact. Tony is cradling his arm with a pained grimace, but Gabriela seems merely dazed.

I don't have time to look closer, though. If we're to have any chance of surviving this, we need to take care of Sullivan's men, and we need to do it now.

The grenade launcher is still in my hand, so I press a button on the side of the door to activate the hidden opening in the roof. Then I stand up in the middle of the aisle, my head and shoulders sticking out of the car.

Lifting the weapon, I point it at the cars pursuing us—which now include one police cruiser on top of the fifteen Sullivan vehicles.

No, *thirteen* Sullivan vehicles, I correct myself after doing a quick count. My men managed to take out two more of them in the last couple of minutes.

It's time to even out the odds some more.

Bullets whizz by my head, but I ignore them as I aim carefully. I only have six shots in this launcher, so I have to make each one count.

*Boom!* The first shot goes off with a hard kick. The recoil hits my shoulder, but the grenade finds its target —the police cruiser that's right on our tail. The car flies up, exploding in the air, and lands on its side, burning. One of the Hummers slams into it, and I watch in grim satisfaction as both cars blow up, causing one of Sullivan's vans to career off the road.

Eleven enemy vehicles left.

I aim again. This time my target is more ambitious: one of the remaining Hummers farther back. It has a single-shot grenade launcher mounted on its roof; that's what took out one of our SUVs earlier, and I know they'll use the weapon again as soon as they reload.

*Boom!* Another hard recoil—and to my disgust, I miss. At the last second, the Hummer swerves sharply, ramming into one of our SUVs with brutal force. I watch in helpless rage as my men's car flips over, rolling off the road.

We're now down to five guard SUVs and our limo.

Pushing aside all traces of emotions, I aim the next shot at a closer van. *Boom!* This time, I'm spot-on. The vehicle flips, exploding in the process, and the two Sullivan SUVs directly behind it smash into it at full speed.

Eight enemy vehicles left.

I point the launcher again, doing my best to compensate for the constant zig-zagging of the limo. I know that Lucas is weaving all over the road in an effort to make us a more difficult target, but that also makes *them* more difficult targets for me.

*Boom!* I take the shot, and another Sullivan SUV explodes, taking out the one behind it in the process.

Six enemy vehicles left, and I have two more grenades to launch.

Taking a deep breath, I aim again—and at that moment, both Hummers spit fire. Two of our SUVs fly into the air, rolling off the side of the road.

Three guard SUVs left.

Suppressing my fury, I hold the weapon steady and aim at the Hummer that's gaining on us. One, two... *boom!* The grenade hits its target, and the massive car careens off the road, smoke rising from its hood.

One Hummer and four enemy SUVs left.

I have one last grenade.

Taking a deep breath, I aim, but before I can squeeze the trigger, one of the enemy cars swerves and crashes into another. My men must've shot the driver, improving our chances some more. The Sullivan forces are now down to one Hummer and two SUVs.

Relieved, I take aim again… and then I hear it.

The unmistakable roar of helicopter blades in the distance.

Looking up, I see a police chopper coming from the west.

*Fuck.*

It's either more dirty cops, or the US authorities caught wind of this skirmish.

Either way, it doesn't bode well for us.

## 35

NORA

*A*s the new sound reaches my ears, my adrenaline levels spike. I didn't know it was possible to feel like this—numb and acutely alive at the same time. My heart is racing a million miles a minute, and my skin is tingling with prickles of icy fear. However, the panic that gripped me earlier is gone; it disappeared at some point between the second and third explosion.

Apparently one can get used to anything, even cars blowing up.

Gripping the weapon Julian gave me, I hold on to the seat with my free hand, unable to look away from the battle taking place outside the car window. The road behind us is like something out of a war zone, with crashed and burning cars littering the empty stretch of narrow highway.

It's as if we're in a video game, except the casualties are real.

*Boom!* One press of a controller button, and a car goes flying. *Boom!* Another car. *Boom! Boom!* I catch myself mentally directing each grenade, as though I can guide Julian's aim with my thoughts.

A game. Just a realistic shooting game with stunning sound effects. If I frame it like that, I can cope. I can pretend there aren't dozens of burning corpses behind us, both on our side and on theirs. I can tell myself the man I love isn't standing in the middle of the limo holding a grenade launcher, his head and upper body exposed to the hail of gunfire outside.

Yes, a game—in which there's now a helicopter. I can hear it, and when I climb up on the seat and lean closer to the window, I can see it too.

It's a police chopper, heading directly for us.

It should be a relief that the authorities are trying to intercede—except the blockade we just went through didn't seem like an attempt to restore law and order. I saw the police cruiser pursuing us right alongside Sullivan's forces; they weren't trying to arrest all the criminals involved in this deadly chase.

They were trying to take us out.

A new wave of terror washes over me, puncturing my false calm. This is *not* a game. There are people dying all around us, and if it weren't for the armor on this limo and Lucas's driving skills, we'd already be dead too. If it were just me, it wouldn't matter as much. But everyone I love is in this car. If something happens to them—

*No, stop.* I feel myself starting to hyperventilate, and I force the thought away. I can't afford to panic now. Glancing toward the front, I see my parents huddling together on the seat, gripping their seatbelts. They're so pale, they look almost green. I think they're both in shock now, since my mom is no longer screaming.

The limo takes a sharp right turn, nearly throwing me off the seat.

"I'm going for the hangar!" Lucas yells from the front, and I realize we just turned off the highway onto an even narrower road. The small airport looms directly ahead, beckoning with the promise of salvation. The roar of the helicopter is directly above us now, but if we can get to our plane and take off—

*Boom!* My vision goes dark, all sounds fading for a second. Gasping, I clutch at the edge of the seat, desperately trying to hang on as the limo swerves and speeds up even more. As my senses return, I realize that the guards' SUV directly behind us was hit. There's now a gaping, smoking hole in its roof. I watch in horrified shock as it careens into another one of our cars, colliding with it with shattering force. Tires squeal, and then both cars are rolling off the road in a tangle of crushed metal.

The police chopper shot at us, I realize with a jolt of

panic. It shot at us and took out two of our cars, leaving only one guard vehicle to protect us.

Turning, I cast a frantic glance at the front window again. The hangar where our plane is parked is close, so close. Just a few hundred yards, and we'll be there. Surely we can survive that long—

*Boom!* My ears ringing, I twist to see the Hummer behind us go up in flames. Julian must've hit it, I realize with relief. There's just the helicopter and two SUVs pursuing us now, and we still have guards in that last SUV. Another couple of shots like that, and we'll be safe—

"Nora!" Powerful arms wrap around my waist, dragging me down to the floor. A furious Julian is kneeling over me, his face like thunder. "I fucking told you to stay down!"

In a split second, I register two things: he's uninjured, and his hands are empty.

The grenade launcher must be out of ammunition.

*Boom!* A blast rocks the limo, sending us both flying. I'm vaguely aware that Julian twists around me, protecting me with his body, but I still feel the brutal impact as we slam into the partition. All air leaves my lungs, and the interior of the car spins around me, my vision blurring as something sharp bites at my skin. My head is pounding from the inside, as though my brain is struggling to get out.

"Nora!" Julian's voice reaches through the ringing whine in my ears. Dazed, I try to focus in on him. As some of the blurriness clears, I realize we're on the floor again, with him lying on top of me. His face is covered with blood; it's trickling down, dripping on me. He's also saying something, but his words don't register in my mind.

All I see is the vicious, deadly red of his blood.

"You're hurt." The terrified croak bears little resemblance to my voice. "Julian, you're hurt—"

He grips my jaw, hard, stunning me into silence. "Listen to me," he grits out. "In exactly a minute, I'm going to need you to run. Do you understand me? Run straight for the fucking plane and don't stop, no matter what."

I stare at him, uncomprehending. *Drip. Drip. Drip.* The red drops keep coming down. I can feel the wetness on my face, taste the metallic warmth on my lips. His eyes are bright blue amidst all that red, blue and incredibly beautiful...

"Nora!" he roars, shaking me. "Do you understand me?"

Some of the ringing in my skull abates, and the meaning of his words finally reaches me.

*Run. He wants me to run.*

"What about—" *you*, I want to say, but he cuts me off.

"You'll take your parents, and you will *all* fucking run." His voice is sharp enough to cut through steel, his gaze burning into me. "You'll have the gun with you, but I don't want you playing hero. Do you understand, Nora?"

I manage a small nod. "Yes." Through the pounding in my temples, I realize the car is still going, still driving despite whatever it was that hit us. I can hear the helicopter hovering over us, but we're alive for now. "Yes, I understand."

"Good." He holds my gaze for a couple of moments longer, and then, as if unable to resist, he lowers his head and takes my mouth in a hard, searing kiss. I taste the salt and metal of his blood, and the unique flavor that is Julian, and I want him to keep kissing me, to make me forget the nightmare we're in. All too soon, though, his lips move over to my neck, and I feel the warmth of his breath as he whispers in my ear, "Please get yourself and your parents to the plane, baby. Thomas is already there, and he can pilot the plane if need be. Lucas will take care of Rosa. This is our only chance to get out of this alive, so when I tell you to run, you run. I'll be right behind you, okay?"

And before I can say anything, he jumps up and pulls me to my knees, handing me the AK-47 that I'd dropped. My head spins from the sudden movement, but I shake off the dizziness, gripping the weapon with all my strength. Everything feels off, my body strangely uncooperative, but I'm able to focus enough to see that the rear window is gone and there's smoke rising from the back of the car. To my relief, my parents are still strapped into their seats, bleeding and dazed-looking but alive.

The back window must've shattered, sending

fragments of glass flying into the car—which explains the blood on them and Julian.

The limo begins slowing down, and Julian grips my jaw again, bringing my attention back to him. "In ten seconds," he says harshly, "I'm going to open this door and come out. In that moment, you escape through the other door. Understand, Nora? You jump out and run like hell."

I nod, and when he releases me, I turn to my parents. "Take off your seatbelts," I say hoarsely. "We're going to make a run for the plane as soon as the car stops."

My mom doesn't react, her face blank with shock, but my dad begins fumbling with the seatbelt buckles. Out of the corner of my eye, I see the hangar coming up, and I frantically begin helping my parents, determined to free them before the car stops.

I succeed in unbuckling my mom's seatbelt, but my dad's seems stuck, and we both desperately tug at it, our hands in each other's way as the limo barrels through a tall, open gate into a warehouse-like building.

"Hurry!" Julian shouts as the limo screeches to a halt. I'm nearly thrown again, but I manage to hang on to the seatbelt strap.

"Now, Nora!" Julian yells, throwing open his door. "Go now!"

The seatbelt buckle finally pops loose, and I grab my dad's hand as he grabs my mom's. Pushing open the opposite door, we scramble out of the car, falling onto our hands and knees. My heart pounding, I swivel my head, looking for our plane, and then I see it.

It's standing near the exit on the opposite side of the hangar, with a dozen other planes between us and it.

"This way!" I jump to my feet, tugging at my dad. "Come on, we have to go!"

We start running. Behind us, there is another screech of brakes, followed by a furious burst of gunfire. Twisting my head, I see Julian and Lucas shooting at an SUV that just barreled into the building behind us. Rosa is running too; she's right on our heels. My heart hammering, I slow down, everything inside me screaming to turn back, to help Lucas and Julian, but then I recall his words.

Our best chance of survival lies in getting everyone to that plane. Even with my help, my parents are barely functioning as is.

So I suppress the urge to rush back toward the limo and instead yell, "Hurry!" to Rosa, who's nearly caught up with us. Then the four of us are running again, my dad towing my mom along. He's deathly pale and his eyes look wild, but he's putting one foot in front of another, and that's all I need him to do at the moment. If we get through this, I'll worry about the impact on my parents' psyche and agonize about my role in all this.

For now, our only task is survival.

Still, even knowing this, I can't stop myself from casting frantic glances behind us as we run. Fear for

Julian is a giant knot in my stomach. I can't imagine losing him again. I don't think I'd survive it.

The first time I glance back, I see that Julian and Lucas took shelter behind the limo and are exchanging fire with men hiding behind the SUV. There are already two corpses on the ground, and a bloody hole in the SUV's windshield.

Even in my panic, I feel a flash of pride. My husband and his right-hand man know what they're doing when it comes to taking lives.

The second glance I steal reveals an even better situation. Four enemy corpses and Lucas making his way around the limo to get at the remaining shooter while Julian provides cover fire.

By the third glance, the final shooter is eliminated, and the gunfire stops, the hangar oddly silent after all the racket. I see Lucas and Julian on their feet, apparently uninjured, and tears of joy start rolling down my cheeks.

We did it. We survived.

We're already by the plane, and I see Thomas, the driver from my hair appointment, standing by the open door. "Please get them inside," I tell him in a shaking voice, and he nods, shepherding my parents and Rosa up the stairs. "I'll be with you in a second," I tell my dad when he tries to get me to join them. "I just need a moment." Liberating myself from his grip, I turn back toward the limo.

"Julian!" Raising the AK-47 above my head, I wave at him with the weapon. "Over here! Come, let's go!"

He looks at me, and I see a huge smile light up his face.

Half-laughing, half-crying, I begin to run toward him, cognizant of nothing but my joy—and then the wall next to the limo explodes, sending him and Lucas flying.

## JULIAN

*P*ain. Darkness.

For a second, I'm back in that windowless room, with Majid's knife slicing through my face. My stomach heaves, vomit rising in my throat. Then my mind clears, and I become cognizant of a dull ringing in my ears.

That didn't happen in Tajikistan.

I didn't feel this hot there, either.

Too hot. So hot I'm burning.

*Fuck!* A spurt of adrenaline chases away all traces of mental fog. Moving with lightning speed, I roll several times, putting out the flames eating at my vest. Nausea grips at my insides, my head throbbing with agony, but when I stop, the fire is gone.

Panting furiously, I lie still and try to regain my senses. What the fuck just happened?

The ringing in my head eases slightly, and I pry open

my eyelids to see burning pieces of rubble all around me.

An explosion. It must've been an explosion.

As soon as the realization comes to me, I hear it.

A burst of gunfire, followed by answering shots.

My heart stops beating. *Nora!*

The jolt of panic is so intense, it supersedes everything. No longer cognizant of pain, I surge to my feet, stumbling as my knees buckle for a second before stiffening to support my weight.

Whipping my head from side to side, I look for the source of gunshots, and then I see it.

A small figure darting behind a large plane after letting loose another volley of shots. Behind her is a group of four armed men, all dressed in SWAT gear.

In a split second, I take in the rest of the scene. The hangar wall near the limo is gone, blown into pieces, and through the opening, I see the police chopper sitting on the grass, its blades now still and silent.

My men in that last SUV must've lost the fight, leaving us exposed to Sullivan's remaining forces.

Before that thought is fully formed in my mind, I'm already on the move. The limo is burning next to me, but the fire is in the front, not the back, so I still have a few seconds. Leaping toward the car, I wrench open one of the doors and climb inside. The weapons are still in the stash, so I grab two machine guns and jump out, knowing the car could blow up at any moment. As I do so, I notice Lucas struggling to get to his feet a dozen yards away. He's alive; I register that with a distant sense of relief.

I don't have time to dwell on it more. A hundred yards away, Nora is weaving around the planes, exchanging shots with her pursuers. My tiny pet against four armed men—the thought fills me with sickening terror and rage.

Gripping both weapons, one in each hand, I begin running. The second I have a clear line of sight at Sullivan's men, I open fire.

*Rat-tat-tat!* One man's head explodes. *Rat-tat-tat!* Another man goes down.

Realizing what's happening, the two surviving men turn around and begin firing at me. Ignoring the bullets whizzing around me, I continue running and shooting, doing my best to zig-zag around the planes. Even with the vest protecting my chest, I'm far from immune to gunfire.

*Rat-tat-tat!* Something slices across my left shoulder, leaving a burning trail in its wake. Cursing, I grip the guns tighter and return fire, causing one of the men to jump behind a small service truck. The second one continues shooting at me, and as I run, I see Nora step out from behind one of the planes and take aim, her eyes dark and enormous in her pale face.

*Pop!* The shooter's head explodes with a bang. Her bullet hit its target. Twisting, she turns and fires at the one hiding behind the truck.

Using the distraction she's providing, I change my

course, snaking around the truck where the remaining man is taking shelter. As I come up behind him, I see him aiming at Nora—and with a bellow of rage, I squeeze the trigger, peppering him with bullets.

He slides down the side of the truck, a bloody mass of lifeless meat.

There are no more shots, the resulting silence almost startling.

Panting, I lower my guns and step out from behind the truck.

NORA

*a*s Julian emerges from behind the truck, bloodied but alive, I drop the AK-47, my fingers no longer able to hold on to the heavy weapon. The emotion filling my chest goes beyond happiness, beyond relief.

It's elation. Stunning, savage elation that we killed our enemies and survived.

When the wall exploded and armed men ran into the hangar, I thought that Julian had been killed. Gripped by blinding fury, I opened fire on them, and when they began shooting at me, I ran mindlessly, operating on pure instinct.

I knew I wouldn't last more than a couple of minutes, and I didn't care. All I wanted was to live long enough to kill as many as I could.

But now Julian is here, in front of me, as alive and vital as ever.

I don't know if I run toward him, or if he runs toward me, but somehow I end up in his embrace, held so tightly that I can barely breathe. He's raining hot, burning kisses all over my face and neck, his hands roaming over my body in search of injuries, and all the horror of the past hour disappears, pushed away by wild joy.

We survived, we're together, and nothing will ever tear us apart again.

"These two were near the chopper," Lucas says when we come out of the hangar in search of him. Like Julian, he's bloodied and unsteady on his feet, but no less deadly for that—as evidenced by the state of the two men lying on the grass. They're both groaning and crying, one clutching his bleeding arm and the other attempting to contain blood spurting out of his leg.

"Is that who I think it is?" Julian asks hoarsely, nodding toward the older man, and Lucas smiles savagely.

"Yes. Patrick Sullivan himself, along with his favorite—and last remaining—son Sean."

I gaze at the younger man, now recognizing his contorted features. It's Rosa's assailant, the one who got away.

"I'm guessing they came in the chopper to observe the action and swoop in at the right time," Lucas continues, grimacing as he holds his ribs. "Except the right time never came. They must've learned who you were and called in all the cops who owed them favors."

"The men we killed were cops?" I ask, beginning to shake as my adrenaline-fueled high starts to fade. "The ones in the Hummers and the SUVs, too?"

"Judging by their gear, many of them were," Julian replies, wrapping his right arm around my waist. I'm grateful for his support, as my legs are beginning to feel like cooked noodles. "Some were probably dirty, but others just blindly following orders from their higher-ups. I have no doubt they were told we were highly dangerous criminals. Maybe even terrorists."

"Oh." My head starts hurting at the thought, and I suddenly become aware of all my aches and bruises. The pain hits me like a tidal wave, followed by an exhaustion so intense that I lean against Julian, my vision going gray.

"Fuck." With that muttered expletive, my world tilts, turning horizontal, and I realize that Julian picked me up, lifting me against his chest. "I'm going to take her to the plane," I hear him saying, and I use all of my remaining strength to shake my head.

"No, I'm fine. Please let me down," I request, pushing at his shoulders, and to my surprise, Julian complies, carefully setting me on my feet. He keeps one arm around my back, but lets me stand on my own.

"What is it, baby?" he asks, looking down at me.

I gesture toward the two bleeding men. "What are you going to do with them? Are you going to kill them?"

"Yes," Julian says. His blue eyes gleam coldly. "I will."

I take a slow breath and release it. The girl Julian brought to the island would've objected, offered him some reason to spare them, but I'm not that girl anymore. These men's suffering doesn't touch me. I've felt more sympathy for a beetle turned onto its back than for these people, and I'm glad Julian is about to take care of the threat they present.

"I think Rosa should be here for this," Lucas says. "She'll want to see justice served."

Julian glances at me, and I nod in agreement. It may be wrong, but in this moment, it seems right for her to be here, to see the one who hurt her come to this end.

"Bring her here," Julian orders, and Lucas heads back into the hangar, leaving Julian and me alone with the Sullivans.

We watch our captives in grim silence, neither one of us feeling like speaking. The older man is already unconscious, having passed out from heavy bleeding, but Rosa's attacker is quite vocal in his pleas for mercy. Sobbing and writhing on the ground, he promises us money, political favors, introduction to all the US cartels... whatever we want if only we would let him go. He swears he won't touch any woman again, says it was a mistake—he didn't know, didn't realize who Rosa was... When neither Julian nor I react, his bargaining attempts turn into threats, and I tune him out, knowing nothing he says will change either of our minds. The anger within me is ice-cold, leaving no room for pity.

For what he's done to Rosa and for the child we lost, Sean Sullivan deserves nothing less than death.

A minute later, Lucas comes back, leading a shaky-looking Rosa out of the hangar. The second she lays eyes on the two men, however, her face regains color and her gaze hardens. Approaching her attacker, she stares down at him for a couple of seconds before raising her eyes to us.

"May I?" she asks, holding out her hand, and Lucas smiles coldly, handing her his rifle. Her hands steady, she aims at her assailant.

"Do it," Julian says, and I watch yet another man die as his face is blown apart. Before the echo from Rosa's shot fades, Julian steps toward unconscious Patrick Sullivan and releases a round of bullets into his chest.

"We're done here," he says, turning away from the corpse, and the four of us walk back to the plane.

On the way home, Thomas pilots the plane while Lucas rests in the main cabin with Julian, myself, and Rosa. Upon seeing all of us alive, my mom breaks down in hysterical sobs, so Julian leads my parents into the plane's bedroom, telling them to take a shower and relax there. I want to go see how they are, but the combination of exhaustion and post-adrenaline slump finally catches up to me.

As soon as we're in the air, I pass out in my seat, my hand held tightly in Julian's grip.

I don't remember landing or getting to the house. The next time I open my eyes, we're already in our bedroom at home, and Dr. Goldberg is cleaning and bandaging my scrapes. I vaguely recall Julian washing the blood off me on the plane, but the rest of the trip is a blur in my mind.

"Where are my parents?" I ask as the doctor uses tweezers to get a small piece of glass out of my arm. "How are they feeling? And what about Rosa and Lucas?"

"They're all sleeping," Julian says, watching the procedure. His face is gray with exhaustion, his voice as weary as I've ever heard it. "Don't worry. They're fine."

"I examined them upon arrival," Dr. Goldberg says, bandaging the sullenly bleeding wound on my arm. "Your father bruised his elbow pretty badly, but he didn't break anything. Your mother was in shock, but other than a few scratches from the broken glass and a bit of whiplash, she's fine, as is Ms. Martinez. Lucas Kent has a couple of cracked ribs and a few burns, but he'll recover."

"And Julian?" I ask, glancing at my husband. He's already clean and bandaged, so I know the doctor must've seen to him while I was sleeping.

"A mild concussion, same as you, along with first-degree burns on his back, a few stitches in the arm where a bullet grazed him, and some bruising. And, of course, these little wounds from the flying glass." Taking another piece of glass out of my arm, the doctor pauses, looking at us both as if trying to decide how to proceed. Finally, he says quietly, "I heard about the miscarriage. I'm so sorry."

I nod, fighting to contain a sudden swell of tears. The pity in Dr. Goldberg's gaze hurts more than any shard of glass, reminding me of what we lost. The agonizing grief I'd buried during our fight for survival is back, sharper and stronger than ever.

We might've survived, but we didn't emerge unscathed.

"Thank you," Julian says thickly, getting up and walking over to stand by the window. His movements are stiff and jerky, his posture radiating tension. Apparently realizing his blunder, the doctor finishes treating me in silence and departs with a murmured "good night," leaving us alone with our pain.

As soon as Dr. Goldberg is gone, Julian returns to the bed. I've never seen him this tired. He's all but swaying as he walks.

"Did you sleep at all on the plane?" I ask, watching as Julian pulls off the T-shirt and sweatpants he must've changed into when we got home. My chest aches at the sight of his injuries. "Some bruising" is a serious understatement. He's black and blue all over, with much of his muscular back and torso wrapped in white gauze.

"No, I wanted to keep an eye on you," he replies wearily, climbing onto the bed next to me. Lying down facing me, he drapes one arm over my side and draws me closer. "I guessed you might be concussed from that tumble you took in the car," he murmurs, his face mere inches from mine.

"Oh, I see." I can't look away from the intense blue of his gaze. "But you also have a concussion, from the explosion."

He nods. "Yes, I figured as much. Another reason for me to stay awake earlier."

I stare at him, my ribcage tightening around my lungs. I feel like I'm drowning in his eyes, getting sucked deeper into those hypnotic blue pools. Unbidden, recollections of the explosion slither into my mind, bringing with them the full horror of these recent events. Julian flying from the blast, Rosa's rape, the miscarriage, my parents' terrified faces as we speed down the highway amidst a hail of bullets... The horrible scenes jumble together in my brain, filling me with suffocating grief and guilt.

Because I dragged us to that club, in a span of two short days I lost my baby and nearly lost everyone else who matters to me.

The tears that come feel like blood squeezed out of my soul. Each drop burns through my tear ducts, the sounds bursting out of my throat hoarse and ugly. My new world isn't just dark; it's black, utterly without hope.

Squeezing my eyes shut, I attempt to curl into a ball, to make myself as small as possible to keep the pain from exploding outward, but Julian doesn't let me. Wrapping his arms around me, he holds me as I break apart, his big body warming me as he strokes my back and whispers into my hair that we survived, that everything will be all right and we'll soon go back to normal... The low, deep sound of his voice surrounds me, filling my ears until I can't help but listen, the words providing comfort despite my awareness of their falseness.

I don't know how long I cry like this, but eventually the worst of the pain ebbs, and I become cognizant of Julian's touch, of his enormous strength. His embrace, once my prison, is now my salvation, keeping me from drowning in despair.

As my tears ease, I become aware that I'm holding him just as tightly as he's gripping me, and that he also seems to derive comfort from my touch. He's consoling me, but I'm consoling him in return—and somehow that fact lessens my agony, lifting some of the dark fog pressing down on me.

He's held me while I cried before, but never like this. Directly or indirectly, he's always been the cause of my tears. We haven't been united in our pain before, have never gone through joint agony. The closest we've come to experiencing loss together was Beth's gruesome death, but even then, we didn't have a chance to mourn together. After the warehouse explosion, I mourned

Beth and Julian on my own, and by the time he came back for me, there was more anger than grief within me.

This time, it's different. My loss is his loss. More *his* loss, in fact, since he wanted this child from the very beginning. The tiny life that was growing within me— the one he guarded so fiercely—is gone, and I can't even imagine how Julian must feel.

How much he must hate me for what I've done.

The thought shatters me again, but this time, I manage to hold the agony in. I don't know what's going to happen tomorrow, but for now, he's comforting me, and I'm selfish enough to accept it, to rely on his strength to get me through this.

Letting out a shuddering sigh, I burrow closer to my husband, listening to the strong, steady beating of his heart.

Even if Julian hates me now, I need him.

I need him too much to ever let him go.

## 38

## JULIAN

*A*s Nora's breathing slows and evens out, her body relaxes against mine. An occasional shudder still ripples through her, but even that stops as she sinks deeper into sleep.

I should sleep too. I haven't closed my eyes since the night before Nora's birthday—which means I've been awake for over forty-eight hours.

Forty-eight hours that count among the worst of my life.

*We survived. Everything will be all right. We'll soon go back to normal.* My reassurances to Nora ring hollow in my ears. I want to believe my own words, but the loss is too fresh, the agony too sharp.

A child. A baby that was part me and part Nora. It should've been nothing, just a bundle of cells with potential, but even at ten weeks, the tiny creature had

341

made my chest overflow with emotion, twisting me around its minuscule, barely formed finger.

I would've done anything for it, and it hadn't even been born.

It died before it had a chance to live.

Dark, bitter fury chokes me again, this time directed solely at myself. There are so many things I could've—should've—done to prevent this outcome. I know it's pointless to dwell on it, but my exhausted brain refuses to let it go. The useless what-ifs keep spinning round and round, until I feel like a hamster in a wheel, running in place and getting nowhere. What if I'd kept Nora on the estate? What if I'd gotten to the bathroom faster? What if, what if... My mind spins faster, the void looming underneath me once more, and I know if I didn't have Nora with me, I'd tumble into madness, the emptiness swallowing me whole.

Tightening my grip on her small, warm body, I stare into the darkness, desperately wishing for something unattainable, for an absolution I don't deserve and will never find.

Nora sighs in her sleep and rubs her cheek on my chest, her soft lips pressing against my skin. On a different night, the unconscious gesture would've turned me on, awakening the lust that always torments me in her presence. Tonight, however, the tender touch only intensifies the pressure building in my chest.

*My child is dead.*

The stark finality of it hits me, smashing through the

shields numbing me since childhood. There's nothing I can do, nothing anyone can do. I could annihilate all of Chicago, and it wouldn't change a thing.

*My child is dead.*

The pain rushes up uncontrollably, like a river cresting over a dam. I try to fight it, to hold it back, but it just makes it worse. The memories come at me in a tidal wave, the faces of everyone I've lost swimming through my mind. *The baby, Maria, Beth, my mother, my father as he had been during those rare moments when I loved him...* The surge of grief is overwhelming, crowding out everything but awareness of this new loss.

*My child is dead.*

The anguish sears through me, excruciating but somehow purifying too.

*My child is dead.*

Shaking, I hold on to Nora as I stop fighting and let the pain in.

# IV

## THE AFTERMATH

## 39

NORA

Two weeks after our arrival home, Julian deems it safe for my parents to return to Oak Lawn.

"I'll have extra security around them for a few months," he explains as we walk toward the training area. "They'll need to put up with some restrictions when it comes to malls and other crowded places, but they should be able to return to work and resume most of their usual activities."

I nod, not particularly surprised to hear that. Julian has been keeping me informed of his efforts in this area, and I know the Sullivans are no longer a threat. Utilizing the same ruthless tactics he employed with Al-Quadar, my husband accomplished what the authorities have been unsuccessfully trying to do for decades: he rid Chicago of its most prominent crime family.

"What about Frank?" I ask as we pass two guards

wrestling on the grass. "I thought the CIA didn't want any of us coming back to the country."

"They relented yesterday. It took some convincing, but your parents should be able to return without anyone standing in their way."

"Ah." I can only imagine what kind of "convincing" Julian had to do in light of the devastation we left behind. Even the cover-up crew dispatched by the CIA hadn't been able to keep the story of our high-speed battle under wraps. The area around the private airport might not have been densely populated, but the explosions and gunfire hadn't gone unnoticed. For the past couple of weeks, the clandestine Chicago operation to "apprehend the deadly arms dealer" has been all anyone's talked about on the news.

As Julian speculated in the car, the Sullivans had indeed called in some serious favors to organize that attack. The police chief—formerly a Sullivan mole and currently bloody goo swimming in lye—took the information the Sullivans dug up about us and used the "arms dealer smuggling explosives into the city" pretext to hurriedly assemble a team of SWAT operatives. The Sullivan men joining them were explained away as "reinforcements from another area," and the entire rushed operation was kept secret from the other law enforcement agencies—which is how they were able to catch us off-guard.

"Don't worry," Julian says, misreading my tense expression. "Besides Frank and a few other high-level officials, nobody knows your parents were involved in what happened. The extra security is just a precaution, nothing more."

"I know that." I look up at him. "You wouldn't let them return if it weren't safe."

"No," Julian says softly, stopping at the entrance to the fighting gym. "I wouldn't." His forehead gleams with sweat from the humid heat, his sleeveless shirt clinging to his well-defined muscles. There are still a few half-healed scars from the shards of glass on his face and neck, but they do little to detract from his potent appeal.

Standing less than two feet away and watching me with his piercing blue gaze, my husband is the very picture of vibrant, healthy masculinity.

Swallowing, I look away, my skin crawling with heat at the memory of how I woke up this morning. We might not have had intercourse since the miscarriage, but that doesn't mean Julian has been abstaining from sex with me. *On my knees with his cock in my mouth, tied down with his tongue on my clit...* The images in my mind make me burn even as the ever-present guilt presses down on me.

Why does Julian keep being so nice to me? Ever since our return, I've been waiting for him to punish me, to do something to express the anger he must feel, but so far, he's done nothing. If anything, he's been unusually tender with me, even more caring in some ways than during my pregnancy. It's subtle, this shift in his behavior—a few extra kisses and touches during the day, full-body massages every evening, asking Ana to make more of my favorite foods... It's nothing he hasn't done before; it's just that the frequency of these little gestures has gone up since we came back from America.

Since we lost our child.

My eyes prickle with sudden tears, and I duck my head to hide them as I slip past Julian into the gym. I don't want him to see me crying again. He's had plenty of that in the past couple of weeks. That's probably why he's holding off on punishing me: he thinks I'm not strong enough to take it, afraid I'll turn back into the panic-attack-stricken wreck I was after Tajikistan.

Except I won't. I know that now. Something about this time is different.

Something within *me* is different.

Walking over to the mats, I bend over and stretch, using the time to compose myself. When I turn back to face Julian, my face shows nothing of the grief that ambushes me at random moments.

"I'm ready," I say, positioning myself on the mat. "Let's do this."

And for the next hour, as Julian trains me how to take down a two-hundred-pound man in seven seconds, I succeed in pushing all thoughts of loss and guilt out of my mind.

After the training session, I return to the house to

shower and then go down to the pool to tell my parents the news. My muscles are tired, but I'm humming with endorphins from the hard workout.

"So we can return?" My dad sits up in his lounge chair, distrust warring with relief on his face. "What about all those cops? And those gangsters' connections?"

"I'm sure it's fine, Tony," my mom says before I can answer. "Julian wouldn't send us back if it weren't all taken care of."

Dressed in a yellow one-piece swimsuit, she looks tan and rested, as though she's spent the past couple of weeks on a resort—which, in a way, is not that far from the truth. Julian has gone out of his way to ensure my parents' comfort and make them feel like they're truly on vacation. Books, movies, delicious food, even fruity drinks by the pool—it's all been provided for them, causing my dad to admit reluctantly that my life at an arms dealer's compound is not as horrible as he'd imagined.

"That's right, he wouldn't," I confirm, sitting down on a lounge chair next to my mom's. "Julian says you're free to leave whenever you want. He can have the plane ready for you tomorrow—though, obviously, we'd love it if you stayed longer."

As expected, my mom shakes her head in refusal. "Thank you, honey, but I think we should head home. Your dad's been anxious about his job, and my bosses have been asking daily when I'll be able to return..." Her voice trailing off, she gives me an apologetic smile.

"Of course." I smile back at her, ignoring the slight squeezing in my chest. I know what's behind their desire to leave, and it's not their jobs or their friends. Despite all the comforts here, my parents feel confined, hemmed in by the watch towers and the drones circling over the jungle. I can see it in the way they eye the armed guards, in the fear that crosses their faces when they pass by the training area and hear gunshots. To them, living here is like being in a luxurious jail, complete with dangerous criminals all over the place.

One of those criminals being their own daughter.

"We should go inside and pack," my dad says, rising to his feet. "I think it's best if we fly out first thing tomorrow morning."

"All right." I try not to let his words sting me. It's silly to feel rejected because my parents want to return home. They don't belong here, and I know it as well as they do. Their bodies might've healed from the bruises and scratches they sustained during the car chase, but their minds are a different matter.

It will take more than a few hours of therapy with Dr. Wessex for my suburban parents to get over seeing cars blow up and people die.

"Do you want me to help you pack?" I ask as my dad drapes a towel around my mom's shoulders. "Julian's talking to his accountant, and I don't have anything to do before dinner."

"It's okay, honey," my mom says gently. "We'll

manage. Why don't you take a swim before dinner? The water's nice and cool."

And leaving me standing by the pool, they hurry into the air-conditioned comfort of the house.

"They're leaving tomorrow morning?" Rosa looks surprised when I inform her of my parents' upcoming departure. "Oh, that's too bad. I didn't even have a chance to show your mom that lake you were telling them about."

"That's okay," I say, picking up a laundry basket to help her load the washer. "Hopefully, they'll come visit us again."

"Yes, hopefully," Rosa echoes, then frowns as she sees what I'm doing. "Nora, put that down. You shouldn't—" She abruptly stops.

"Shouldn't lift heavy things?" I finish, giving her an ironic smile. "You and Ana keep forgetting that I'm no longer an invalid. I can lift weights again, and fight and shoot and eat whatever I want."

"Of course." Rosa looks contrite. "I'm sorry"—she reaches for my basket—"but you still shouldn't do my job."

Sighing, I relinquish it to her, knowing she'll only get upset if I insist on helping. She's been particularly touchy about that since our return, determined not to have anyone treat her any differently than before.

"I was raped; I didn't have my arms amputated," she snapped at Ana when the housekeeper tried to assign her lighter cleaning tasks. "Nothing will happen to me if I vacuum and use a mop."

Of course that made Ana burst into tears, and Rosa and I had to spend the next twenty minutes trying to calm her down. The older woman has been very emotional since our return, openly grieving my miscarriage and Rosa's assault.

"She's taking it worse than my own mother," Rosa told me last week, and I nodded, not surprised. Though I'd only met Mrs. Martinez a couple of times, the plump, stern woman had struck me as an older version of Beth, with the same tough shell and cynical outlook on life. How Rosa managed to remain so cheerful with a mother like that is something that will always be a mystery to me. Even now, after everything she's been through, my friend's smile is only a bit more brittle, the sparkle in her eyes just a shade less bright. With her bruises nearly healed, one would never know that Rosa survived something so traumatic—especially given her fierce insistence on being treated as normal.

Sighing again, I watch as she loads the washer with brisk efficiency, separating out the darker clothes and placing them into a neat pile on the floor. When she's done, she turns to face me. "So did you hear?" she says. "Lucas located the interpreter girl. I think he'll go after her after he flies your parents home."

"He told you that?"

She nods. "I ran into him this morning and asked how that's going. So yeah, he told me."

"Oh, I see." I don't see, not in the least, but I decide against prying. Rosa's been increasingly closemouthed about her strange non-relationship with Lucas, and I don't want to press the issue. I figure she'll tell me when she's ready—if there's anything to tell, that is.

She turns back to start the washer, and I debate whether I should share with her what I learned yesterday... what I still haven't shared with Julian. Finally, I decide to go for it, since she already knows part of the story.

"Do you remember the pretty young doctor who treated me at the hospital?" I ask, leaning against the dryer.

Rosa turns back toward me, looking puzzled at the change of topic. "Yes, I think so. Why?"

"Her last name is Cobakis. I remember reading it on her name tag and thinking that it seemed familiar, like I'd come across it before."

Now Rosa looks intrigued. "And did you? Come across it, that is?"

I nod. "Yes. I just couldn't remember where—and then yesterday, it came to me. There was a man by the name of George Cobakis on the list I gave to Peter."

Rosa's eyes widen. "The list of people responsible for what happened to his family?"

"Yes." I take a deep breath. "I wasn't sure, so I checked my email last night, and sure enough, there it was. George Cobakis from Homer Glen, Illinois. I noticed that name originally because of the location."

"Oh, wow." Rosa stares at me, mouth open. "You think that nice doctor is somehow connected to this George?"

"I know she is. I looked up George Cobakis last night, and she came up in search results. She's his wife. A local newspaper wrote about a fundraiser for veterans and their families, and they had their picture in there as a couple who's done a lot for that organization. He's apparently a journalist, a foreign correspondent. I can't imagine how his name ended up on that list."

"Shit." Rosa looks both horrified and fascinated. "So what are you going to do?"

"What can I do?" The question has been tormenting me ever since I learned of the connection. Before, the names on that list were just that: names. But now one of those names has a face attached to it. A photo of a smiling dark-haired man standing next to his smart, pretty wife.

A wife whom I'd met.

A woman who'll be a widow if Julian's former security consultant gets his revenge.

"Have you spoken to your husband about this?" Rosa asks. "Does he know?"

"No, not yet." Nor am I sure that I want Julian to know. A few weeks ago, I told Rosa about the list I sent to Peter, but I didn't tell her that I did it against Julian's wishes. That part—and what happened after we learned of my pregnancy—is too private to share. "I'm guessing Julian will say there's nothing to be done now that the list is in Peter's hands," I say, trying to imagine my husband's reaction.

"And he'll probably be right." Rosa gives me a steady look. "It's unfortunate that we met the woman and all, but if her husband was somehow involved in what happened to Peter's family, I don't see how we can interfere."

"Right." I take another deep breath, trying to let go of the anxiety I've been feeling since yesterday. "We can't. We shouldn't."

Even though I gave Peter that list.

Even though whatever's going to happen will be my fault once again.

"This is not your problem, Nora," Rosa says, intuiting my concern. "Peter would've learned about those names one way or another. He was too determined for it not to happen. You're not responsible for what he's going to do to those people—Peter is."

"Of course," I murmur, attempting a smile. "Of course, I know that."

And as Rosa resumes sorting through the laundry, I change the topic to our newest guard recruits.

## 40

### JULIAN

*A*fter wrapping up the conversation with my accountant, I get up and stretch, feeling the loosening of tension in my muscles. Immediately, my thoughts turn to Nora, and I pull up her location on my phone. I do that at least five times a day now, the habit as deeply ingrained as brushing my teeth in the morning.

She's in the house, which is exactly where I expected her to be. Satisfied, I put the phone away and close my laptop, determined to be done for the evening. Between all the paperwork for a new shell corporation and the interviews I've been conducting with potential guard replacements, I've been working upward of twelve hours a day. Once, that wouldn't have mattered—business was all I had to live for—but now work is an unwelcome distraction.

It prevents me from spending time with my beautiful, strangely distant wife.

I'm not sure when I first noticed it, the way Nora's eyes constantly slide away from mine. The way she withholds something of herself even during sex. At first, I ascribed her withdrawn manner to grief and the aftermath of trauma, but as the days wore on, I realized there's something more.

It's subtle, barely discernible, this distance between us, but it's there. She talks and acts as if things are normal, but I can tell they're not. Whatever secret she's keeping from me, it's weighing on her, causing her to erect barriers between us. I could sense them during our training today, and it solidified my determination to get to the bottom of the matter.

According to the doctors, she's finally fully healed from the miscarriage—and one way or another, tonight she's going to tell me everything.

At dinner, I watch Nora as she interacts with her parents, hungrily taking in every minute movement of her hands, every flicker of her long eyelashes. I would've thought it impossible, but my obsession with her has reached a new peak since our return. It's as if all the grief, rage, and pain inside me coalesced into one heart-ripping sensation, a feeling so intense it tears me from within.

A longing that's entirely focused on her.

As we finish the main course, I realize I've hardly said a word, spending most of the meal absorbed in the sight of her and the sound of her voice. It's probably just as well, given that it's Nora's parents' last evening here. Although her father is no longer openly hostile toward me, I know both Lestons still wish they could free their daughter from my clutches. I would never let them take her from me, of course, but I don't have a problem with the three of them spending some time on their own.

To that end, as soon as Ana brings out the dessert, I excuse myself by saying I'm full and go to the library, letting them finish the meal without me.

When I get there, I take a seat on a chaise by the window and spend a few minutes answering emails on my phone. Then the puzzle of Nora's uncharacteristic distance creeps into my mind again. The way she's been these past couple of weeks reminds me of when I first forced the trackers on her. It's as if she's upset with me —except this time, I have no idea why.

Glancing at the clock on the wall, I realize that it's already been a half hour since I left the table. Hopefully, Nora's already gone upstairs. When I check her location, however, I see she's still in the dining room.

Mildly annoyed, I contemplate getting a book to read while I wait, but then I get a better idea.

Pulling up a different app on my phone, I activate the hidden audio feed from the dining room, put on my Bluetooth headset, and lean back in the chaise to listen.

A second later, Gabriela's frustrated voice fills my ears.

"—people died," she argues. "How can that not bother you? There were police officers among those criminals, good men who were just following orders—"

"And they would've killed us by following those orders." Nora's tone is unusually sharp, causing me to sit up and listen more intently. "Is it better to die by the bullet of a good man than to defend yourself and live? I'm sorry that I'm not showing the remorse you expect, Mom, but I'm *not* sorry that all of us are alive and well. It's not Julian's fault that any of that happened. If anything—"

"He's the one who killed that gangster's son," Tony interrupts. "If he'd done the civilized thing, called nine-one-one instead of resorting to murder—"

"If he'd done the civilized thing, I would've been raped and Rosa would've suffered even more before the police got there." There is a hard, brittle note in Nora's voice. "You weren't there, Dad. You don't understand."

"Your dad understands perfectly well, honey." Gabriela's voice is calmer now, edged with weariness. "And yes, maybe your husband couldn't stand by and wait for the cops to arrive, but you know as well as I do that he could've abstained from killing that man."

Abstained from killing the man who hurt and nearly raped Nora? My blood boils with sudden fury. The fucking bastard's lucky I didn't castrate him and stuff his balls into his bowels. The only reason he died so easily was because Nora was there, and my worry for her was greater than my rage.

"Maybe he could've." Nora's tone matches her mother's. "But there's every reason to believe the Sullivans would've walked free, given their connections. Is that what you want, Mom, for men like that to continue doing this to other women?"

"No, of course not," Tony says. "But that doesn't give Julian the right to set himself up as judge, jury, and executioner. When he killed that man, he didn't know who he was, so you can't use that excuse. Your husband killed because he wanted to and for no other reason."

For a few tense seconds, there's silence in my headset. The fury inside me grows, the anger coiling and tightening as I wait to hear what Nora has to say. I don't give a fuck what Nora's parents think about me, but I very much care that they're trying to turn their daughter against me.

Finally, Nora speaks. "Yes, Dad, you're right, he did." Her voice is calm and steady. "He killed that man for hurting me without giving it a second thought. Do you want me to condemn him for that? Well, I can't. I won't. Because if I could've, I would've done the same thing."

Another prolonged silence. Then: "Honey, when you left the plane and there were all those gunshots, was that you?" Gabriela asks quietly. "Did you shoot anyone?" A short pause, then an even softer, "Did you kill anyone?"

"Yes." Nora's tone doesn't change. I can picture her

sitting there, facing her parents without flinching. "Yes, Mom, I did."

A sharply indrawn breath, then another few beats of silence.

"I told you, Gabs." It's Tony who speaks now, his voice weighed down by sadness. "I told you she must've. Our daughter's changed—he's changed her."

There's a scraping noise, like that of a chair moving across the floor, and then a shaky, "Oh, honey." It's followed by a choked sob and Nora's voice murmuring, "Don't cry, Mom. Please, don't cry. I'm sorry I've disappointed you. I'm so sorry…"

I can't bear to listen anymore. Jumping off the chaise, I stride out of the library, determined to collect Nora and bring her upstairs. This guilt-tripping is the last thing she needs, and if I have to protect her from her own parents, so be it.

As I walk, I hear them speak again, and I slow down in the hallway, listening despite myself.

"You didn't disappoint us, honey," Nora's father says thickly. "It's not that, not at all. It's just that we see now that you're no longer the same girl… that even if you came back to us, it wouldn't be the same."

"No, Dad," Nora replies quietly. "It wouldn't be."

A couple more seconds pass, and then her mother speaks again. "We love you, honey," she says in a low, strained voice. "Please, don't ever doubt that we love you."

"I know, Mom. And I love you, both of you." Nora's

ANNA ZAIRES

voice cracks for the first time. "I'm sorry that things have worked out this way, but I belong here now."

"With *him*." Curiously, Gabriela doesn't sound bitter, just resigned. "Yes, we see that now. He loves you. I never would've thought I'd say that, but he does. The way the two of you are together, the way he looks at you…" She lets out a shaky laugh. "Oh, honey, we'd give an arm and a leg for it to be someone else for you. A good man, a kind man, someone who'd hold down a normal job and buy you a house near us—"

"Julian did buy me a house near you," Nora says, and her mother laughs again, sounding a little hysterical.

"That's true," she says when she calms down. "He did, didn't he?"

Now the two women laugh together, and I let out a relieved breath. Maybe Nora doesn't need my interference after all.

Another sound of a chair scraping across the floor, and then Tony says gruffly, "We're here for you, honey. No matter what, we're always here for you. If anything ever changes, if you ever want to leave him and come home—"

"I won't, Dad." The quiet confidence in Nora's voice warms me, chasing away the remnants of my anger. I'm so pleased that I nearly miss it when she adds softly, "Not unless he wants me to."

"Oh, he won't," Nora's father says, and he does sound bitter. "That much is obvious. If that man had his way, you'd never be more than ten feet away from him."

I only half-listen to his words, mulling over Nora's strange statement instead. *Not unless he wants me to.* She sounded almost as if she's afraid that's the case. Or is it that she *wants* it to be the case? An ugly suspicion snakes through me. Is that why she's been so distant in recent days—because she wants me to let her go? Because she no longer wants to be with me and hopes that I'll let her leave as a way to atone for what happened?

My chest tightens with sudden pain even as a new kind of anger kindles within me. Is that what my pet expects? Some sort of grand gesture where I give her freedom? Where I beg her for forgiveness and feign regret for having taken her in the first place?

*Fuck that.*

I tear the headset out of my ear, dark fury rolling through me as I turn and take the stairs two steps at a time.

If Nora thinks I'm that far gone, she couldn't be more mistaken.

She's mine, and she'll stay that way for the rest of our lives.

## NORA

*T*ired yet hyper after talking to my parents, I walk up the stairs toward our bedroom. Though a part of me still wishes I could've shielded my family from my new life, I'm relieved that they now know the truth.

That they know the woman I've become and still love me.

Reaching the bedroom, I open the door and step inside. No lights are on in the room, and as I close the door behind me, I wonder where Julian might be. While I'm glad I got the chance to clear the air with my parents, the fact that he left dinner without a good explanation worries me. Did something happen, or did he simply get tired of us?

Did he get tired of *me*?

Just as the devastating thought crosses my mind, I notice a dark shadow standing by the window.

My pulse jumps, my skin prickling with primitive terror as I fumble for the light switch.

"Leave it." Julian's voice comes out of the darkness, and my knees almost buckle with relief.

"Oh, thank God. For a second, I didn't realize it was —" I begin, and then his harsh tone registers. "You," I finish uncertainly.

"Who else would it be?" My husband turns and crosses the room, approaching me with the silent gait of a predator. "It's our bedroom. Or have you forgotten that?" He places his hands on both sides of the wall behind me, caging me in.

I draw in a startled breath, pressing my palms against the cold wall. Julian is clearly in a mood, and I have no idea what set him off. "No, of course not," I say slowly, staring at his shadowed features. There's so little light that all I can make out is the faint glitter of his eyes. "What do you—"

He steps closer, molding his lower body to mine, and I gasp as I feel his hard cock against my belly. He's naked and already aroused, his hot male scent surrounding me as he holds me trapped in place. Even through the separating layer of my dress, I can feel the lust pulsing within him—lust and something much, much darker.

My body awakens with a jolt, my pulse quickening on a surge of fear. This must be it: the punishment I've been expecting. With the doctors having deemed me healed earlier today, my reprieve is over.

"Julian?" His name comes out on a choked breath as

he grips the nape of my neck, his long fingers nearly encircling my throat. His huge body is all muscle, hard and uncompromising around me. One squeeze of those steely fingers, and he'd crush my throat. The thought chills me, yet a hollow ache coils in my core, my nipples peaking with harsh arousal. The anger coming off him is palpable, and it calls to something savage inside me, fueling the dark fire simmering within.

If he's decided to finally punish me, I'm going to make damn sure I get what I deserve.

He leans into me, his breath warm on my face, and at that moment, I make my move. My right hand forms a fist at my side, and I swing upward with all my strength, striking the underside of his chin. At the same time, I twist to the right, breaking his grip on my neck, and duck under his extended arm, whirling around to hit him in the back.

Except he's no longer there.

In the half-second it took me to turn, Julian moved, as quick and deadly as any assassin. Instead of connecting with his back, the sharp edge of my palm slams into his elbow, and I cry out as the impact sends a shock of pain through my arm.

"Fuck!" His furious hiss is accompanied by a blurringly fast movement. Before I can react, he's got me encircled in his arms, my wrists crossed in front of my chest and his left leg wrapped around my knees to prevent me from kicking. With him holding me from behind, I can't bite him, and my attempts to head-butt his chin fall woefully short as he keeps his face out of my reach.

All that training, and he subdued me in three seconds flat.

Frustration mingles with adrenaline, adding to the fury brewing inside me. Fury at him for taunting me with tenderness these two weeks, and most of all, fury at myself.

*My fault, my fault, it's all my fault.* The words are a vicious drumbeat in my mind. Guilt, bitter and thick, rises in my throat, choking me as it mixes with the aching grief.

*Rosa. Our baby. Dozens of men dead.*

The sound that bursts out of my throat is something between a growl and a sob. Despite the futility of it, I begin to fight, bucking and twisting in Julian's iron hold. I don't have much leverage, but with one of his legs restraining mine, my frantic, jerky movements are enough to push him off-balance.

With a loud curse, he falls backward, still gripping me tightly. His back takes the brunt of the fall. I hardly feel the impact as he grunts and immediately rolls over, pinning me to the hard wooden floor. Disregarding his heavy weight on top of me, I continue fighting, struggling with all my strength. The cold wood presses into my face, but the discomfort barely registers.

*My fault, my fault, all my fault.*

Half-panting, half-sobbing, I try to kick back, to scratch him, to make him feel even a tiny fraction of the pain consuming me inside. My muscles scream with strain, but I don't stop—not when Julian wrenches my wrists back and ties them at the small of my back with his belt, and not even when he drags me up by my elbow and hauls me to the bed.

I fight as he tears off my dress and underwear, as he fists his hand in my hair and forces me up on my knees. I fight as though I'm fighting for my life, as though the man holding me is my worst enemy instead of my greatest love. I fight because he's strong enough to take the fury inside me.

Because he's strong enough to take it away from me.

As I writhe in his brutal hold, his knee forces apart my legs, and his cock presses against my entrance. In one savage thrust, he penetrates me from behind, and I cry out at the pain, at the unutterable relief of his possession. I'm wet, but not enough, not nearly enough, and each punishing thrust scrapes me raw, hurting me, healing me. My thoughts scatter, the chant inside my mind disappearing, and all that's left is the feel of his body inside mine, the pain and the agonizing pleasure of our need.

I'm rushing toward orgasm when Julian begins talking to me, growling that he'll always keep me, that I'll never belong to anyone but him. There is a dark threat implicit in his words, a promise that he'll stop at nothing. His ruthlessness should terrify me, yet as my body explodes in release, fear is the last thing on my mind.

All I'm cognizant of is sheer and utter bliss.

He flips me onto my back then, releasing my wrists, and I realize that at some point, I did stop fighting. The fury's gone, and in its place is deep exhaustion and relief.

Relief that Julian still wants me. That he'll punish me, but won't send me away.

So when he grips my ankles and props them on his shoulders, I don't resist. I don't fight when he leans forward, nearly folding me in half, and I don't struggle when he scoops the abundant moisture from my sex and smears it between my ass cheeks. It's only when I feel his thickness poised at that other opening that I utter a wordless sound of protest, my sphincter tightening as my hands move to push against his hard chest. It's a weak, mostly symbolic gesture—I can't possibly move Julian off me that way—but even that slight hint of resistance seems to enrage him.

"Oh, no, you don't," he growls, and in the faint light from the window, I see the dark glitter of his eyes. "You don't get to deny me this, to deny me anything. I own you... every inch of you." He presses forward, his massive cock forcing me open as he whispers harshly, "If you don't relax that ass, my pet, you'll regret it."

I shudder with perverse arousal, my nails digging into his chest as the tight ring of muscle gives in to the merciless pressure. The burning invasion is agonizing, my insides roiling as he pushes in deeper and deeper. It's been months since he's taken me like this, and my body's forgotten how to handle this, how to relax into the overly full sensation. Squeezing my eyelids shut, I attempt to breathe through it, to remain strong, but tears, stupid, betraying tears, come anyway, trickling out from the corners of my eyes.

It's not the pain that makes me cry, though, or my body's twisted response to it.

It's the knowledge that my punishment isn't over, that Julian still hasn't forgiven me.

That he may never forgive me.

"Do you hate me?" The question escapes before I can hold it back. I don't want to know, but at the same time, I can't bear to keep silent. Opening my eyes, I stare at the dark figure above me. "Julian, do you hate me?"

He stills, his cock lodged deep within me. "Hate you?" His big body tenses, his lust-roughened voice filling with disbelief. "What the fuck, Nora? Why would I hate you?"

"Because I miscarried." My voice quavers. "Because our child died because of me."

For a second, he doesn't respond, and then, with a low curse, he pulls out, making me gasp in pain.

"Fuck!" He releases me, moving back on the bed. The sudden absence of his heat and his heavy weight over me is startling, as is the light from the bedside lamp he turns on. It takes a moment before my eyes adjust to the brightness and I make out the expression on his face.

"You think I blame you for what happened?" he asks hoarsely, sitting back on his haunches. His eyes burn with intensity as he stares at me, his cock still fully erect. "You think it was somehow your fault?"

"Of course it was." I sit up, feeling the stinging soreness deep inside, where he was just buried. "I'm the one who wanted to go to Chicago, to go to that club. If not for me, none of this would've—"

"Stop." His harsh command vibrates through me even as his features contort with something resembling pain. "Just stop, baby, please."

I fall silent, staring at him in confusion. Wasn't that what this whole scene was about? My punishment for disappointing him? For endangering myself and our child?

Still holding my gaze, he takes a deep breath and moves toward me. "Nora, my pet..." He takes my face in his large palms. "How could you possibly think that I hate you?"

I swallow. "I'm hoping you don't, but I know you're angry—"

"You think I'm angry because you wanted to see your parents? To go out dancing and have fun?" His nostrils flare. "Fuck, Nora, if the miscarriage is anyone's fault, it's mine. I shouldn't have let you go to that bathroom on your own—"

"But you couldn't have known—"

"And neither could you." He takes a deep breath and lowers his hands to my lap, clasping my palms in his warm grasp. "It wasn't your fault," he says roughly. "None of it was your fault."

I dampen my dry lips. "So then why—"

"Why was I angry?" His beautiful mouth twists. "Because I thought you wanted to leave me. Because I misinterpreted something you said to your parents tonight."

"What?" My eyebrows pull together in a frown. "What did I— Oh." I recall my offhand comment, born of fear and insecurity. "No, Julian, that's not what I meant," I begin, but he squeezes my hands before I can explain further.

"I know," he says softly. "Believe me, baby, now I know."

We stare at each other in silence, the air thick with echoes of violent sex and dark emotions, with the aftermath of lust and pain and loss. It's strange, but in this moment, I understand him better than ever. I see the man behind the monster, the man who needs me so much he'll do anything to keep me with him.

The man I need so much I'll do anything to stay with him.

"Do you love me, Julian?" I don't know what gives me the courage to pose the question now, but I have to know, once and for all. "Do you love me?" I repeat, holding his gaze.

For a few moments, he doesn't move, doesn't say anything. His grip on my hands is tight enough to hurt. I can feel the struggle within him, the longing warring with the fear. I wait, holding my breath, knowing he may never open himself up like this, may never admit the truth even to himself. So when he speaks, I'm almost caught off-guard.

"Yes, Nora," he says hoarsely. "Yes, I love you. I love you so fucking much it hurts. I didn't know it, or maybe I just didn't want to know it, but it's always been there. I spent most of my life trying not to feel, trying not to let people get close to me, but I fell for you from the very beginning. It just took me two years to realize it."

"What made you realize it?" I whisper, my heart aching with relieved joy. *He loves me.* Up until this moment, I didn't know how desperately I needed the words, how much their lack weighed on me. "When did you know?"

"It was the night we came back home." His muscular throat moves as he swallows. "It was when I lay here next to you. I let myself truly feel it then—the pain of losing our baby, the pain of losing all those other people in my life—and I realized I'd been trying to protect myself from the agony of losing *you.* Trying to keep myself from loving you so it wouldn't destroy me. Except it was too late. I was already in love with you. I had been for a long time. Obsession, addiction, love—it's all the same thing. I can't live without you, Nora. Losing you *would* destroy me. I can survive anything but that."

"Oh, Julian…" I can't imagine what it took for this strong, ruthless man to admit this. "You won't lose me. I'm here. I'm not going anywhere."

"I know you're not." His eyes narrow, all traces of

vulnerability fading from his features. "Just because I love you doesn't mean I'll ever let you go."

A shaky laugh escapes my throat. "Of course. I know that."

"Ever." He seems to feel the need to emphasize that.

"I know that too."

He stares at me then, his hands holding mine, and I feel the pull of his wordless command. He wants me to admit my feelings too, to bare my soul to him as he's just bared his to me. And so I give him what he demands.

"I love you, Julian," I say, letting him see the truth of that in my gaze. "I'll always love you—and I don't want you to ever let me go."

I don't know if he moves toward me then, or if I make the move first, but somehow his mouth is on mine, his lips and tongue devouring me as he holds me in his inescapable embrace. We come together in pain and pleasure, in violence and passion.

We come together in our kind of love.

The next morning, I stand next to the runway and watch as the plane carrying my parents home takes off. When it's nothing more than a small dot in the sky, I turn to Julian, who's standing beside me holding my hand.

"Tell me again," I say softly, looking up at him.

"I love you." His eyes gleam as he meets my gaze. "I love you, Nora, more than life itself."

I smile, my heart lighter than it's been in weeks. The shadow of grief is still with me, as is the lingering feeling of guilt, but the darkness no longer clouds everything. I can picture a day when the pain will fade, when all I'll feel is contentment and joy.

Our troubles aren't over—they can't be, with us being who we are—but the future no longer frightens me. Soon, I'll need to bring up the pretty doctor and Peter's plan for revenge, and at some point later, we'll have to discuss the possibility of another child and how to deal with the ever-present danger of our lives.

For now, though, we don't need to do anything but enjoy each other.

Enjoy being alive and in love.

## EPILOGUE – THREE YEARS LATER

### JULIAN

"*N*ora Esguerra!"

As the president of Stanford University calls out her name, I watch my wife walk across the stage, garbed in the same black cap and gown as the rest of the graduates. The robe billows around her petite frame, hiding the small, but already visible bump of her stomach—the child we both eagerly await this time.

Stopping in front of the university official, Nora shakes his hand to the sound of applause and then turns to smile for the camera, her delicate face glowing in the bright morning sun.

The flash goes off, startling me even though I knew it was coming.

Catching myself clutching the gun at my waist, I force my hand to uncurl and move away from the weapon. With a hundred of our best guards securing the field, my gun isn't necessary. Still, I feel better having it on me—and I know Nora is glad her semi-automatic is tucked inside her purse. Though the opening of her second art show in Paris went off without a hitch last year, we're both more than a little paranoid today, determined to do whatever it takes to ensure the safety of our unborn daughter.

Another flash goes off beside me. Glancing at the seats to my right, I see Nora's parents taking pictures with their new camera. They look as proud as I feel. Sensing my gaze on them, Nora's mother looks in my direction, and I give her a warm smile before turning my attention back to the stage.

The next graduate is already up, but I don't notice who it is. All I see is my pet, carefully making her way down the left side of the stage. The leather folder with the diploma is in her hands, and the tassel on her cap is hanging on the other side of her face, signifying her new diploma-recipient status.

She's beautiful, even more beautiful than at her high school graduation five years earlier.

As she makes her way through the rows of graduates and their families, our eyes meet, and I feel my heart expanding, filling with the mixture of dark possessiveness and tender love she always evokes in me.

My captive. My wife. My entire world.

I will love her to the end of time, and I will never, ever let her go.

**THE END**

SNEAK PEEKS

Thank you for reading! If you would consider leaving a review, it would be greatly appreciated.

While *Hold Me* concludes Nora & Julian's story, there is a spin-off series with Lucas & Yulia. Their series is called *Capture Me*.

If you'd like to be notified when the next book is out, please sign up for my new release email list at http://annazaires.com/.

If you enjoyed *Hold Me,* you might enjoy these other books by Anna Zaires featuring characters from Julian and Nora's story:

- ***The Capture Me Trilogy*** – Lucas & Yulia's story

- *The Tormentor Mine Series* – Peter and Sara's story

Craving something different? Check out some of my other steamy stories:

- *Wall Street Titan* – an opposites-attract romance with an irresistible alpha billionaire
- *The Mia & Korum Trilogy* – an epic sci-fi romance with the ultimate alpha male
- *The Krinar Captive* – Emily & Zaron's captive romance, set just before the Krinar Invasion
- *The Krinar Exposé* – my scorching hot collaboration with Hettie Ivers, featuring Amy & Vair—and their sex club games
- *The Krinar World stories* – Sci-fi romance stories by other authors, set in the Krinar world

Collaborations with my husband, Dima Zales:

- *The Girl Who Sees* – the thrilling tale of Sasha Urban, a stage illusionist who discovers unexpected secret powers
- *Mind Dimensions* – the action-packed urban fantasy adventures of Darren, who can stop time and read minds
- *Transcendence* – the mind-blowing technothriller featuring venture capitalist

Mike Cohen, whose Braincyte technology will forever change the world

- ***The Last Humans*** – the futuristic sci-fi/dystopian story of Theo, who lives in a world where nothing is as it seems
- ***The Sorcery Code*** – the epic fantasy adventures of sorcerer Blaise and his creation, the beautiful and powerful Gala

Additionally, if you like audiobooks, please visit my website to check out this series and our other books.

And now please turn the page for a little taste of *Wall Street Titan, Capture Me, Tormentor Mine,* and *The Girl Who Sees*.

# EXCERPT FROM WALL STREET TITAN

**A billionaire who wants a perfect wife...**

At thirty-five, Marcus Carelli has it all: wealth, power, and the kind of looks that leave women breathless. A self-made billionaire, he heads one of the largest hedge funds on Wall Street and can take down major corporations with a single word. The only thing he's missing? A wife who'd be as big of an achievement as the billions in his bank account.

**A cat lady who needs a date...**

Twenty-six-year-old bookstore clerk Emma Walsh has it on good authority that she's a cat lady. She doesn't necessarily agree with that assessment, but it's hard to argue with the facts. Raggedy clothes covered with cat hair? Check. Last professional haircut? Over a year ago.

Oh, and three cats in a tiny Brooklyn studio? Yep, she's got those.

And yes, fine, she hasn't had a date since... well, she can't recall. But that part is fixable. Isn't that what the dating sites are for?

**A case of mistaken identity...**

One high-end matchmaker, one dating app, one mix-up that changes everything... Opposites may attract, but can this last?

I'm all but bouncing with excitement as I approach Sweet Rush Café, where I'm supposed to meet Mark for dinner. This is the craziest thing I've done in a while. Between my evening shift at the bookstore and his class schedule, we haven't had a chance to do more than exchange a few text messages, so all I have to go on are those couple of blurry pictures. Still, I have a good feeling about this.

I feel like Mark and I might really connect.

I'm a few minutes early, so I stop by the door and take a moment to brush cat hair off my woolen coat. The coat is beige, which is better than black, but white hair is visible on anything that's not pure white. I figure Mark won't mind too much—he knows how much

Persians shed—but I still want to look presentable for our first date. It took me about an hour, but I got my curls to semi-behave, and I'm even wearing a little makeup—something that happens with the frequency of a tsunami in a lake.

Taking a deep breath, I enter the café and look around to see if Mark might already be there.

The place is small and cozy, with booth-style seats arranged in a semicircle around a coffee bar. The smell of roasted coffee beans and baked goods is mouthwatering, making my stomach rumble with hunger. I was planning to stick to coffee only, but I decide to get a croissant too; my budget should stretch to that.

Only a few of the booths are occupied, likely because it's a Tuesday. I scan them, looking for anyone who could be Mark, and notice a man sitting by himself at the farthest table. He's facing away from me, so all I can see is the back of his head, but his hair is short and dark brown.

It could be him.

Gathering my courage, I approach the booth. "Excuse me," I say. "Are you Mark?"

The man turns to face me, and my pulse shoots into the stratosphere.

The person in front of me is nothing like the pictures on the app. His hair is brown, and his eyes are blue, but that's the only similarity. There's nothing rounded and shy about the man's hard features. From the steely jaw to the hawk-like nose, his face is boldly masculine, stamped with a self-assurance that borders on arrogance. A hint of five o'clock shadow darkens his lean cheeks, making his high cheekbones stand out even more, and his eyebrows are thick dark slashes above his piercingly pale eyes. Even sitting behind the table, he looks tall and powerfully built. His shoulders are a mile wide in his sharply tailored suit, and his hands are twice the size of my own.

There's no way this is Mark from the app, unless he's put in some serious gym time since those pictures were taken. Is it possible? Could a person change so much? He didn't indicate his height in the profile, but I'd assumed the omission meant he was vertically challenged, like me.

The man I'm looking at is not challenged in any way, and he's certainly not wearing glasses.

"I'm... I'm Emma," I stutter as the man continues staring at me, his face hard and inscrutable. I'm almost certain I have the wrong guy, but I still force myself to ask, "Are you Mark, by any chance?"

"I prefer to be called Marcus," he shocks me by answering. His voice is a deep masculine rumble that tugs at something primitively female inside me. My heart beats even faster, and my palms begin to sweat as he rises to his feet and says bluntly, "You're not what I expected."

"Me?" *What the hell?* A surge of anger crowds out all other emotions as I gape at the rude giant in front of me.

The asshole is so tall I have to crane my neck to look up at him. "What about you? You look nothing like your pictures!"

"I guess we've both been misled," he says, his jaw tight. Before I can respond, he gestures toward the booth. "You might as well sit down and have a meal with me, Emmeline. I didn't come all the way here for nothing."

"It's *Emma*," I correct, fuming. "And no, thank you. I'll just be on my way."

His nostrils flare, and he steps to the right to block my path. "Sit down, *Emma*." He makes my name sound like an insult. "I'll have a talk with Victoria, but for now, I don't see why we can't share a meal like two civilized adults."

The tips of my ears burn with fury, but I slide into the booth rather than make a scene. My grandmother instilled politeness in me from an early age, and even as an adult living on my own, I find it hard to go against her teachings.

She wouldn't approve of me kneeing this jerk in the balls and telling him to fuck off.

"Thank you," he says, sliding into the seat across from me. His eyes glint icy blue as he picks up the menu. "That wasn't so hard, was it?"

"I don't know, *Marcus*," I say, putting special emphasis on the formal name. "I've only been around you for two minutes, and I'm already feeling homicidal." I deliver the insult with a ladylike, Grandma-approved smile, and dumping my purse in the corner of my booth seat, I pick up the menu without bothering to take off my coat.

The sooner we eat, the sooner I can get out of here.

A deep chuckle startles me into looking up. To my shock, the jerk is grinning, his teeth flashing white in his lightly bronzed face. No freckles for him, I note with jealousy; his skin is perfectly even-toned, without so much as an extra mole on his cheek. He's not classically handsome—his features are too bold to be described that way—but he's shockingly good-looking, in a potent, purely masculine way.

To my dismay, a curl of heat licks at my core, making my inner muscles clench.

*No.* No way. This asshole is *not* turning me on. I can barely stand to sit across the table from him.

Gritting my teeth, I look down at my menu, noting with relief that the prices in this place are actually reasonable. I always insist on paying for my own food on dates, and now that I've met Mark—excuse me, *Marcus*—I wouldn't put it past him to drag me to some ritzy place where a glass of tap water costs more than a shot of Patrón. How could I have been so wrong about the guy? Clearly, he'd lied about working in a bookstore and being a student. To what end, I don't know, but everything about the man in front of me screams wealth and power. His pinstriped suit hugs his broad-shouldered frame like it was tailor-made for him, his blue shirt is crisply starched, and I'm pretty sure his subtly checkered tie is some designer brand that makes Chanel seem like a Walmart label.

As all of these details register, a new suspicion occurs to me. Could someone be playing a joke on me? Kendall, perhaps? Or Janie? They both know my taste in guys. Maybe one of them decided to lure me on a date this way—though why they'd set me up with *him,* and he'd agree to it, is a huge mystery.

Frowning, I look up from the menu and study the man in front of me. He's stopped grinning and is perusing the menu, his forehead creased in a frown that makes him look older than the twenty-seven years listed on his profile.

That part must've also been a lie.

My anger intensifies. "So, *Marcus*, why did you write to me?" Dropping the menu on the table, I glare at him. "Do you even own cats?"

He looks up, his frown deepening. "Cats? No, of course not."

The derision in his tone makes me want to forget all about Grandma's disapproval and slap him straight across his lean, hard face. "Is this some kind of a prank for you? Who put you up to this?"

"Excuse me?" His thick eyebrows rise in an arrogant arch.

"Oh, stop playing innocent. You lied in your message to me, and you have the gall to say *I'm* not what you expected?" I can practically feel the steam coming out of my ears. "*You* messaged *me*, and I was entirely truthful on my profile. How old are you? Thirty-two? Thirty-three?"

"I'm thirty-five," he says slowly, his frown returning. "Emma, what are you talking—"

"That's it." Grabbing my purse by one strap, I slide out of the booth and jump to my feet. Grandma's teachings or not, I'm not going to have a meal with a jerk who's admitted to deceiving me. I have no idea what would make a guy like that want to toy with me, but I'm not going to be the butt of some joke.

"Enjoy your meal," I snarl, spinning around, and stride to the exit before he can block my way again.

I'm in such a rush to leave I almost knock over a tall, slender brunette approaching the café and the short, pudgy guy following her.

Go to www.annazaires.com to order your copy of *Wall Street Titan* today!

EXCERPT FROM CAPTURE ME

**Author's Note**: *Capture Me* is the first book in Lucas & Yulia's dark romance series. The following excerpt is from Yulia's POV. This scene takes place in Moscow, when Lucas & Julian were there to meet with the Russian officials.

*She fears him from the first moment she sees him.*

Yulia Tzakova is no stranger to dangerous men. She grew up with them. She survived them. But when she meets Lucas Kent, she knows the hard ex-soldier may be the most dangerous of them all.

One night—that's all it should be. A chance to make up

for a failed assignment and get information on Kent's arms dealer boss. When his plane goes down, it should be the end.

Instead, it's just the beginning.

**He wants her from the first moment he sees her.**

Lucas Kent has always liked leggy blondes, and Yulia Tzakova is as beautiful as they come. The Russian interpreter might've tried to seduce his boss, but she ends up in Lucas's bed—and he has every intention of seeing her there again.

Then his plane goes down, and he learns the truth.

She betrayed him.

Now she will pay.

He steps into my apartment as soon as the door swings open. No hesitation, no greeting—he just comes in.

Startled, I step back, the short, narrow hallway suddenly stiflingly small. I'd somehow forgotten how big he is, how broad his shoulders are. I'm tall for a woman—tall enough to fake being a model if an assignment calls for it—but he towers a full head above

394

me. With the heavy down jacket he's wearing, he takes up almost the entire hallway.

Still not saying a word, he closes the door behind him and advances toward me. Instinctively, I back away, feeling like cornered prey.

"Hello, Yulia," he murmurs, stopping when we're out of the hallway. His pale gaze is locked on my face. "I wasn't expecting to see you like this."

I swallow, my pulse racing. "I just took a bath." I want to seem calm and confident, but he's got me completely off-balance. "I wasn't expecting visitors."

"No, I can see that." A faint smile appears on his lips, softening the hard line of his mouth. "Yet you let me in. Why?"

"Because I didn't want to continue talking through the door." I take a steadying breath. "Can I offer you some tea?" It's a stupid thing to say, given what he's here for, but I need a few moments to compose myself.

He raises his eyebrows. "Tea? No, thanks."

"Then can I take your jacket?" I can't seem to stop playing the hostess, using politeness to cover my anxiety. "It looks quite warm."

Amusement flickers in his wintry gaze. "Sure." He takes off his down jacket and hands it to me. He's left wearing a black sweater and dark jeans tucked into black winter boots. The jeans hug his legs, revealing muscular thighs and powerful calves, and on his belt, I see a gun sitting in a holster.

Irrationally, my breathing quickens at the sight, and

it takes a concerted effort to keep my hands from shaking as I take the jacket and walk over to hang it in my tiny closet. It's not a surprise that he's armed—it would be a shock if he wasn't—but the gun is a stark reminder of who Lucas Kent is.

*What* he is.

It's no big deal, I tell myself, trying to calm my frayed nerves. I'm used to dangerous men. I was raised among them. This man is not that different. I'll sleep with him, get whatever information I can, and then he'll be out of my life.

Yes, that's it. The sooner I can get it done, the sooner all of this will be over.

Closing the closet door, I paste a practiced smile on my face and turn back to face him, finally ready to resume the role of confident seductress.

Except he's already next to me, having crossed the room without making a sound.

My pulse jumps again, my newfound composure fleeing. He's close enough that I can see the gray striations in his pale blue eyes, close enough that he can touch me.

And a second later, he does touch me.

Lifting his hand, he runs the back of his knuckles over my jaw.

I stare up at him, confused by my body's instant response. My skin warms and my nipples tighten, my breath coming faster. It doesn't make sense for this hard, ruthless stranger to turn me on. His boss is more handsome, more striking, yet it's Kent my body's reacting to. All he's touched thus far is my face. It should be nothing, yet it's intimate somehow.

Intimate and disturbing.

I swallow again. "Mr. Kent—Lucas—are you sure I can't offer you something to drink? Maybe some coffee or—" My words end in a breathless gasp as he reaches for the tie of my robe and tugs on it, as casually as one would unwrap a package.

"No." He watches as the robe falls open, revealing my naked body underneath. "No coffee."

And then he touches me for real, his big, hard palm cupping my breast. His fingers are callused, rough. Cold from being outside. His thumb flicks over my hardened nipple, and I feel a pull deep within my core, a coiling of need that feels as foreign as his touch.

Fighting the urge to flinch away, I dampen my dry lips. "You're very direct, aren't you?"

"I don't have time for games." His eyes gleam as his thumb flicks over my nipple again. "We both know why I'm here."

"To have sex with me."

"Yes." He doesn't bother to soften it, to give me anything but the brutal truth. He's still holding my breast, touching my naked flesh as though it's his right. "To have sex with you."

"And if I say no?" I don't know why I'm asking this.

This is not how it's supposed to go. I should be seducing him, not trying to put him off. Yet something within me rebels at his casual assumption that I'm his for the taking. Other men have assumed this before, and it didn't bother me nearly as much. I don't know what's different this time, but I want him to step away from me, to stop touching me. I want it so badly that my hands curl into fists at my sides, my muscles tensing with the urge to fight.

"Are you saying no?" He asks the question calmly, his thumb now circling over my areola. As I search for a response, he slides his other hand into my hair, possessively cupping the back of my skull.

I stare at him, my breath catching. "And if I were?" To my disgust, my voice comes out thin and scared. It's as if I'm a virgin again, cornered by my trainer in the locker room. "Would you leave?"

One corner of his mouth lifts in a half-smile. "What do you think?" His fingers tighten in my hair, the grip just hard enough to hint at pain. His other hand, the one on my breast, is still gentle, but it doesn't matter.

I have my answer.

So when his hand leaves my breast and slides down my belly, I don't resist. Instead, I part my legs, letting him touch my smooth, freshly waxed pussy. And when his hard, blunt finger pushes into me, I don't try to move away. I just stand there, trying to control my frantic breathing, trying to convince myself that this is no different from any other assignment.

Except it is.

I don't want it to be, but it is.

"You're wet," he murmurs, staring at me as he pushes his finger deeper. "Very wet. Do you always get so wet for men you don't want?"

"What makes you think I don't want you?" To my relief, my voice is steadier this time. The question comes out soft, almost amused as I hold his gaze. "I let you in here, didn't I?"

"You came on to *him*." Kent's jaw tightens, and his hand on the back of my head shifts, gripping a fistful of my hair. "You wanted *him* earlier today."

"So I did." The typically masculine display of jealousy reassures me, putting me on more familiar ground. I manage to soften my tone, make it more seductive. "And now I want you. Does that bother you?"

Kent's eyes narrow. "No." He forces a second finger into me and simultaneous presses his thumb against my clit. "Not at all."

I want to say something clever, come up with some snappy retort, but I can't. The jolt of pleasure is sharp and startling. My inner muscles tighten, clutching at his rough, invading fingers, and it's all I can do not to moan out loud at the resulting sensations. Involuntarily, my hands come up, grabbing at his forearm. I don't know if I'm trying to push him away or get him to continue, but it doesn't matter. Under the soft wool of his sweater, his arm is thick with steely muscle. I can't control its movements—all I can do is hold onto it as he pushes deeper into me with those hard, merciless fingers.

"You like that, don't you?" he murmurs, holding my gaze, and I gasp as he begins flicking his thumb over my clit, side to side, then up and down. His fingers curl inside me, and I suppress a moan as he hits a spot that sends an even sharper pang of sensation to my nerve endings. A tension begins to coil inside me, the pleasure gathering and intensifying, and with shock I realize I'm on the verge of orgasm.

My body, usually so slow to respond, is throbbing with aching need at the touch of a man who scares me—a development that both astonishes and unnerves me.

I don't know if he sees it on my face, or if he feels the tightening in my body, but his pupils dilate, his pale eyes darkening. "Yes, that's it." His voice is a low, deep rumble. "Come for me, beautiful"—his thumb presses hard on my clit—"just like that."

And I do. With a strangled moan, I climax around his fingers, the hard edges of his short, blunt nails digging into my rippling flesh. My visions blurs, my skin prickling with heated needles as I ride the wave of sensations, and then I sag in his grasp, held upright only by his hand in my hair and his fingers inside my body.

"There you go," he says thickly, and as the world comes back into focus, I see that he's watching me intently. "That was nice, wasn't it?"

I can't even manage a nod, but he doesn't seem to

need my confirmation. And why would he? I can feel the slickness inside me, the wetness that coats those rough male fingers—fingers that he withdraws from me slowly, watching my face the whole time. I want to close my eyes, or at least look away from that penetrating gaze, but I can't.

Not without letting him know how much he frightens me.

So instead of backing down, I study him in return, seeing the signs of arousal on his strong features. His jaw is clenched tight as he stares at me, a tiny muscle pulsing near his right ear. And even through the sun-bronzed hue of his skin, I can see heightened color on his blade-like cheekbones.

He wants me badly—and that knowledge emboldens me to act.

Reaching down, I cup the hard bulge at the crotch of his jeans. "It *was* nice," I whisper, looking up at him. "And now it's your turn."

His pupils dilate even more, his chest inflating with a deep breath. "Yes." His voice is thick with lust as he uses his grip on my hair to drag me closer. "Yes, I think it is." And before I can reconsider the wisdom of my blatant provocation, he lowers his head and captures my mouth with his.

I gasp, my lips parting from surprise, and he immediately takes advantage, deepening the kiss. His hard-looking mouth is surprisingly soft on mine, his lips warm and smooth as his tongue hungrily explores the interior of my mouth. There's skill and confidence in that kiss; it's the kiss of a man who knows how to please a woman, how to seduce her with nothing more than the touch of his lips.

The heat simmering within me intensifies, the tension rising inside me once more. He's holding me so close that my bare breasts are pressing against his sweater, the wool rubbing against my peaked nipples. I can feel his erection through the rough material of his jeans; it pushes into my lower belly, revealing how much he wants me, how thin his pretense of control really is. Dimly, I realize the robe fell off my shoulders, leaving me completely naked, and then I forget all about it as he makes a low growling sound deep in his throat and pushes me against the wall.

The shock of the cold surface at my back clears my mind for a second, but he's already unzipping his jeans, his knees wedging between my legs and spreading them open as he raises his head to look at me. I hear the ripping sound of a foil packet being opened, and then he cups my ass and lifts me off the ground. Instinctively, I grab at his shoulders, my heartbeat quickening as he orders hoarsely, "Wrap your legs around me"—and lowers me onto his stiff cock, all the while holding my gaze.

His thrust is hard and deep, penetrating me all the way. My breathing stutters at the force of it, at the uncompromising brutality of the invasion. My inner muscles clench around him, futilely trying to keep him out. His cock is as big as the rest of him, so long and thick it stretches me to the point of pain. If I hadn't been so wet, he would've torn me. But I *am* wet, and after a couple of moments, my body begins to soften, adjusting to his thickness. Unconsciously, my legs come up, clasping his hips as he instructed, and the new position lets him slide even deeper into me, making me cry out at the sharp sensation.

He begins to move then, his eyes glittering as he stares at me. Each thrust is as hard as the one that joined us together, yet my body no longer tries to fight it. Instead, it brings forth more moisture, easing his way. Each time he slams into me, his groin presses against my sex, putting pressure on my clit, and the tension in my core returns, growing with every second. Stunned, I realize I'm about to have my second orgasm... and then I do, the tension peaking and exploding, scattering my thoughts and electrifying my nerve endings.

I can feel my own pulsations, the way my muscles squeeze and release his cock, and then I see his eyes go unfocused as he stops thrusting. A hoarse, deep groan escapes his throat as he grinds into me, and I know he's found his release as well, my orgasm driving him over the edge.

My chest heaving, I stare up at him, watching as his pale blue eyes refocus on me. He's still inside me, and all of a sudden, the intimacy of that is unbearable. He's nobody to me, a stranger, yet he fucked me.

He fucked me, and I let him because it's my job.

Swallowing, I push at his chest, my legs unwrapping from around his waist. "Please, let me down." I know I should be cooing at him and stroking his ego. I should be telling him how amazing it was, how he gave me more pleasure than anyone I've known. It wouldn't even be a lie—I've never come twice with a man before. But I can't bring myself to do that. I feel too raw, too invaded.

With this man, I'm not in control, and that knowledge scares me.

I don't know if he senses that, or if he just wants to toy with me, but a sardonic smile appears on his lips.

"It's too late for regrets, beautiful," he murmurs, and before I can respond, he lets me down and releases his grip on my ass. His softening cock slips out of my body as he steps back, and I watch, my breathing still uneven, as he casually takes the condom off and drops it on the floor.

For some reason, his action makes me flush. There's something so wrong, so dirty about that condom lying there. Perhaps it's because I feel like that condom: used and discarded. Spotting my robe on the floor, I move to pick it up, but Lucas's hand on my arm stops me.

"What are you doing?" he asks, gazing at me. He doesn't seem the least bit concerned that his jeans are still unzipped and his cock is hanging out. "We're not done yet."

My heart skips a beat. "We're not?"

"No," he says, stepping closer. To my shock, I feel

him hardening against my stomach. "We're far from done."

And using his grip on my arm, he steers me toward the bed.

*Capture Me* is now available. If you'd like to find out more, please visit my website at www.annazaires.com/.

# EXCERPT FROM TORMENTOR MINE

**Author's Note**: *Tormentor Mine* is the first book in Peter's dark romance series. The following excerpt is from Peter's POV.

~

*He came to me in the night, a cruel, darkly handsome stranger from the most dangerous corners of Russia. He tormented me and destroyed me, ripping apart my world in his quest for vengeance.*

*Now he's back, but he's no longer after my secrets.*

*The man who stars in my nightmares wants me.*

~

"Are you going to kill me?"

She's trying—and failing—to keep her voice steady. Still, I admire her attempt at composure. I approached her in public to make her feel safer, but she's too smart to fall for that. If they've told her anything about my background, she must realize I can snap her neck faster than she can scream for help.

"No," I answer, leaning closer as a louder song comes on. "I'm not going to kill you."

"Then what do you want from me?"

She's shaking in my hold, and something about that both intrigues and disturbs me. I don't want her to be afraid of me, but at the same time, I like having her at my mercy. Her fear calls to the predator within me, turning my desire for her into something darker.

She's captured prey, soft and sweet and mine to devour.

Bending my head, I bury my nose in her fragrant hair and murmur into her ear, "Meet me at the Starbucks near your house at noon tomorrow, and we'll talk there. I'll tell you whatever you want to know."

I pull back, and she stares at me, her eyes huge in her pale face. I know what she's thinking, so I lean in again, dipping my head so my mouth is next to her ear.

"If you contact the FBI, they'll try to hide you from me. Just like they tried to hide your husband and the others on my list. They'll uproot you, take you away from your parents and your career, and it will all be for nothing. I'll find you, no matter where you go, Sara... no matter what they do to keep you from me." My lips brush against the rim of her ear, and I feel her breath hitch. "Alternatively, they might want to use you as bait. If that's the case—if they set a trap for me—I'll know, and our next meeting won't be over coffee."

She shudders, and I drag in a deep breath, inhaling her delicate scent one last time before releasing her.

Stepping back, I melt into the crowd and message Anton to get the crew into positions.

I have to make sure she gets home safe and sound, unmolested by anyone but me.

*Tormentor Mine* is available everywhere. If you'd like to find out more, please visit my website at http://annazaires.com/.

## EXCERPT FROM THE GIRL WHO SEES
## BY DIMA ZALES

I'm an illusionist, not a psychic.

Going on TV is supposed to advance my career, but things go wrong.

Like vampires and zombies kind of wrong.

My name is Sasha Urban, and this is how I learned what I am.

~

"I'm not a psychic," I say to the makeup girl. "What I'm about to do is mentalism."

"Like that dreamy guy on the TV show?" The makeup girl adds another dash of foundation to my cheekbones. "I always wanted to do his makeup. Can you also hypnotize and read people?"

I take a deep, calming breath. It doesn't help much. The tiny dressing room smells like hairspray went to war with nail polish remover, won, and took some fumes prisoner.

"Not exactly," I say when I have my anxiety and subsequent irritation under control. Even with Valium in my blood, the knowledge of what's about to come keeps me on the edge of sanity. "A mentalist is a type of stage magician whose illusions deal with the mind. If it were up to me, I'd just go by 'mental illusionist.'"

"That's not a very good name." She blinds me with her lamp and carefully examines my eyebrows.

I mentally cringe; the last time she looked at me this way, I ended up getting tortured with tweezers.

She must like what she sees now, though, because she turns the light away from my face. "'Mental illusionist' sounds like a psychotic magician," she continues.

"That's why I simply call myself an illusionist." I smile and prepare for the makeup to fall off, like a mask, but it stays put. "Are you almost done?"

"Let's see," she says, waving over a camera guy.

The guy makes me stand up, and the lights on his camera come on.

"This is it." The makeup girl points at the nearby LCD screen, where I have avoided looking until now because it's playing the ongoing show—the source of my panic.

The camera guy does whatever he needs to do, and the anxiety-inducing show is gone from the screen, replaced by an image of our tiny room.

The girl on the screen vaguely resembles me. The heels make my usual five feet, six inches seem much taller, as does the dark leather outfit I'm wearing. Without heavy makeup, my face is symmetric enough, but my sharp cheekbones put me closer to handsome than pretty—an effect my strong chin enhances. The makeup, however, softens my features, bringing out the blue color of my eyes and highlighting the contrast with my black hair.

The makeup girl went overboard with it—you'd think I'm about to step into a shampoo commercial. I'm not a big fan of long hair, but I keep it that way because when I had it short, people used to mistake me for a teenage boy.

That's a mistake no one would make tonight.

"I like it," I say. "Let's be done. Please."

The TV guy switches the screen back to the live feed of the show. I can't help but glance there, and my already high blood pressure spikes.

The makeup girl looks me up and down and wrinkles her nose minutely. "You insist on that outfit, right?"

The really cool (in my opinion) borderline-dominatrix

getup I've donned today is a means to add mystique to my onstage persona. Jean Eugène Robert-Houdin, the famous nineteenth-century French conjuror who inspired Houdini's stage name, once said, "A magician is an actor playing the part of a magician." When I saw Criss Angel on TV, back in elementary school, my opinion of what a magician should look like was formed, and I'm not too proud to admit that I see influences of his goth rock star look in my own outfit, especially the leather jacket.

"How marvelous," says a familiar voice with a sexy British accent. "You didn't look like this at the restaurant."

Pivoting on my high heels, I come face to face with Darian, the man I met two weeks ago at the restaurant where I do table-to-table magic—and where I'd impressed him enough to make this unimaginable opportunity a reality.

A senior producer on the popular *Evening with Kacie* show, Darian Rutledge is a lean, sharply dressed man who reminds me of a hybrid between a butler and James Bond. Despite his senior role at the studio and the frown lines that crisscross his forehead, I'd estimate his age to be late twenties—though that could be wishful thinking, given that I'm only twenty-four. Not that he's traditionally handsome or anything, but he does have a certain appeal. For one thing, with his strong nose, he's the rare guy who can pull off a goatee.

"I wear Doc Martens at the restaurant," I tell him. The extra inches of my footwear lift me to his eye level, and I can't help but get lost in those green depths. "The makeup was forced on me," I finish awkwardly.

He smiles and hands me a glass he's been holding. "And the result is lovely. Cheers." He then looks at the makeup girl and the camera guy. "I'd like to speak with Sasha in private." His tone is polite, yet it carries an unmistakable air of imperiousness.

The staff bolt out of the room. Darian must be an even bigger shot than I thought.

On autopilot, I take a gulp of the drink he handed to me and wince at the bitterness.

"That's a Sea Breeze." He gives me a megaton smile. "The barman must've gone heavy on the grapefruit juice."

I take a polite second sip and put the drink on the vanity behind me, worried that the combination of vodka and Valium might make me woozier than I already am. I have no idea why Darian wants to speak to me alone; anxiety has already turned my brain to mush.

Darian regards me in silence for a moment, then pulls out a phone from his tight jeans' pocket. "There's a bit of unpleasantness we must discuss," he says, swiping across the screen of the phone before handing it to me.

I take the phone from him, gripping it tight so it doesn't slip out of my sweaty palms.

On the phone is a video.

I watch it in stunned silence, a wave of dread washing over me despite the medication.

The video reveals my secret—the hidden method

behind the impossible feat I'm about to perform on *Evening with Kacie.*

I'm so screwed.

"Why are you showing me this?" I manage to say after I regain control of my paralyzed vocal cords.

Darian gently takes the phone back from my shaking hands. "You know that thing you went on about at the restaurant? How you're just pretending to be a psychic and that it's all tricks?"

"Right." I frown in confusion. "I never said I do anything for real. If this is about exposing me as a fraud—"

"You misunderstand." Darian grabs my discarded drink and takes a long, yet somehow elegant sip. "I have no intention of showing that video to anyone. Quite the contrary."

I blink at him, my brain clearly overheated from the adrenaline and lack of sleep.

"I know that as a magician, you don't like your methods known." His smile turns oddly predatory.

"Right," I say, wondering if he's about to make a blackmail-style indecent proposal. If he did, I would reject it, of course—but on principle, not because doing something indecent with a guy like Darian is unthinkable.

When you haven't gotten any for as long as I haven't, all sorts of crazy scenarios swirl through your head on a regular basis.

Darian's green gaze turns distant, as though he's

trying to look through the nearby wall all the way into the horizon. "I know what you're planning on saying after the big reveal," he says, focusing back on me. In an eerie parody of my voice, he enunciates, "'I'm not a prophet. I use my five senses, principles of deception, and showmanship to create the illusion of being one.'"

My eyebrows rise so high my heavy makeup is in danger of chipping. He didn't approximate what I was about to say—he nailed it word for word, even copying the intonation I've practiced.

"Oh, don't look so surprised." He places the now-empty glass back on the vanity dresser. "You said that exact thing at the restaurant."

I nod, still in shock. Did I actually tell him this before? I don't remember, but I must have. Otherwise, how would he know?

"I paraphrased something another mentalist says," I blurt out. "Is this about giving him credit?"

"Not at all," Darian says. "I simply want you to omit that nonsense."

"Oh." I stare at him. "Why?"

Darian leans against the vanity and crosses his legs at the ankles. "What fun is it to have a fake psychic on the show? Nobody wants to see a fake."

"So you want me to act like a fraud? Pretend to be for real?" Between the stage fright, the video, and now this unreasonable demand, I'm just about ready to turn tail and run, even if I end up regretting it for the rest of my life.

He must sense that I'm about to lose it, because the predatory edge leaves his smile. "No, Sasha." His tone is exaggeratedly patient, as though he's talking to a small child. "I just want you to not say anything. Don't claim to be a psychic, but don't deny it either. Just avoid that topic altogether. Surely you can be comfortable with that."

"And if I'm not, you would show people the video? Reveal my method?"

The very idea outrages me. I might not want people to think I'm a psychic, but like most magicians, I work hard on the secret methods for my illusions, and I intend to take them to my grave—or write a book for magicians only, to be published posthumously.

"I'm sure it wouldn't come to that." Darian takes a step toward me, and the bergamot scent of his cologne teases my flaring nostrils. "We want the same thing, you and I. We want people to be enthralled by you. Just don't make any claims one way or another—that's all I ask."

I take a step back, his proximity too much for my already shaky state of mind. "Fine. You have a deal." I swallow thickly. "You never show the video, and I don't make any claims."

"There's one more thing, actually," he says, and I wonder if the indecent proposal is about to drop.

"What?" I dampen my lips nervously, then notice him looking and realize I'm just making an inappropriate pass at me that much more likely.

"How did you know what card my escort was thinking of?" he asks.

I smile, finally back in my element. He must be talking about my signature Queen of Hearts effect—the one that blew away everyone at his table. "That will cost you something extra."

He arches an eyebrow in silent query.

"I want the video," I say. "Email it to me, and I'll give you a hint."

Darian nods and swipes a few times on his phone.

"Done," he says. "Do you have it?"

I take out my own phone and wince. It's Sunday night, right before the biggest opportunity of my life, yet I have four messages from my boss.

Deciding to find out what the manipulative bastard wants later, I go into my personal email and verify that I have the video from Darian.

"Got it," I say. "Now about the Queen of Hearts thing... If you're as observant and clever as I think you are, you'll be able to guess my method tonight. Before the main event, I'm going to perform that same effect for Kacie."

"You sneaky minx." His green eyes fill with mirth. "So you're not going to tell me?"

"A magician must always be at least one step ahead of her audience." I give him the aloof smile I've perfected over the years. "Do we have a deal or not?"

"Fine. You win." He gracefully sits on the swivel chair

where I went through my eyebrow torture. "Now, tell me, why did you look so spooked when I first came in?"

I hesitate, then decide it will do no harm to admit the truth. "It's because of that." I point at the screen where the live feed from the show is still rolling. At that precise moment, the camera pans to the large studio audience, all clapping at some nonsense the hostess said.

Darian looks amused. "Kacie? I didn't think that Muppet could frighten anyone."

"Not her." I wipe my damp palms on my leather jacket and learn that it's not the most absorbent of surfaces. "I'm afraid of speaking in front of people."

"You are? But you said you want to be a TV magician, and you perform at the restaurant all the time."

"The biggest audience at the restaurant is three or four people at a dinner table," I say. "In that studio over there, it's about a hundred. The fear kicks in after the numbers get into the teens."

Darian's amusement seems to deepen. "What about the millions of people who'll be watching you at home? Are you not worried about them?"

"I'm more worried about the studio audience, and yes, I understand the irony." I do my best not to get defensive. "For my own TV show, I'd do street magic with a small camera crew—that wouldn't trigger my fear too much."

Fear is actually an understatement. My attitude toward public speaking confirms the many studies showing that this particular phobia tends to be more pervasive than the fear of death. Certainly, I'd rather be eaten by a shark than have to appear in front of a big crowd.

After Darian called me about this opportunity, I learned how big the show's studio audience is, and I couldn't sleep for three days straight—which is why I feel like a Guantanamo Bay detainee on her way to enhanced interrogation. It's even worse than when I pulled a string of all-nighters for my stupid day job, and at the time, I thought it was the most stressful event of my life.

My roommate Ariel didn't give me her Valium lightly; it took a ton of persuasion on my part, and she only gave in when she could no longer bear to look at my miserable face.

Darian distracts me from my thoughts by fiddling with his phone again.

"This should inspire you," he says as soothing piano chords ring out of the tinny phone speaker. "It's a song about a man in a similar situation to yours."

It takes me a few moments to recognize the tune. Given that I last heard it when I was little, I up my estimate of Darian's age by an extra few years. The song is "Lose Yourself," from the *8 Mile* movie, where Eminem's character gets a chance to be a rapper. I guess my situation is similar enough, this being my big shot at what I want the most.

Unexpectedly, Darian begins to rap along with

Eminem, and I fight an undignified giggle as some of the tension leaves my body. Do all British rappers sound as proper as the Queen?

"Now there's that smile," Darian says, unaware or uncaring that my grin is at his expense. "Keep it up."

He grabs the remote and turns up the volume on the TV in time for me to hear Kacie say, "Our hearts go out to the victims of the earthquake in Mexico. To donate to the Red Cross, please call the number at the bottom of the screen. And now, a quick commercial—"

"Sasha?" A man pops his head into the dressing room. "We need you on stage."

"Break a leg," Darian says and blows me an air kiss.

"In these shoes, I just might." I mime catching the kiss, throwing it on the floor, and stabbing it with my stiletto.

Darian's laugh grows distant as my guide and I leave the room, heading down a dark corridor. As we approach our destination, our steps seem to get louder, echoing in tune with my accelerating heartbeat. Finally, I see a light and hear the roar of the crowd.

This is how people going to face a firing squad must feel. If I weren't medicated, I'd probably bolt, my dreams be damned. As is, the guide has to grab my arm and drag me toward the light.

Apparently, the commercial break will soon be over.

"Go take a seat on the couch next to Kacie," someone whispers loudly into my ear. "And breathe."

My legs seem to grow heavier, each step a

monumental effort of will. Hyperventilating, I step onto the platform where the couch is located and take tiny steps, trying to ignore the studio audience.

My dread is so extreme that time flows strangely; one moment I'm still walking, the next I'm standing by the couch.

I'm glad Kacie has her nose in a tablet. I'm not ready to exchange pleasantries when I have to do something as difficult as sitting down.

Knees shaking, I lower myself onto the couch like a fakir onto a bed of nails (which is not a feat of supernatural pain resistance, by the way, but the application of scientific principles of pressure).

Time distortion must've happened again, because the music signifying the commercial break comes to an abrupt close, and Kacie looks up from her tablet, her overly full lips stretching into a smile.

The pounding of my pulse is so loud in my ears I can't hear her greeting.

This is it.

I'm about to have a panic attack on national TV.

Go to www.dimazales.com to order your copy of *The Girl Who Sees* today!

# ABOUT THE AUTHOR

Anna Zaires is a *New York Times, USA Today,* and #1 international bestselling author of sci-fi romance and contemporary dark erotic romance. She fell in love with books at the age of five, when her grandmother taught her to read. Since then, she has always lived partially in a fantasy world where the only limits were those of her imagination. Currently residing in Florida, Anna is happily married to Dima Zales (a science fiction and fantasy author) and closely collaborates with him on all their works.

To learn more, please visit http://annazaires.com/.

Printed in Great Britain
by Amazon

22531822R00238